AMASKAN'S WAR

THE BOAHIM TRILOGY: BOOK II

RAVEN OAK

GREY SUN
— PRESS —

AMASKAN'S WAR
The Boahim Trilogy: Book II

Raven Oak

Grey Sun Press
PO Box 1635
Bothell, WA 98041

Cover art by Jamie Noble
Map by Raven Oak

ISBN: 978-0-9908157-1-6

Library of Congress Control Number: 2018950751

His feet carried him out of the building and down to the paths. Like a well-trained pup, Bredych fled to the coast where he'd walked with his daughter.

She had cursed him for sending her away, for sending her into the hands of her birth father. She had thrown questions at him, and he had answered by removing the tattoo that had marked her Amaskan.

Tears mixed in the dirt below, which he allowed in the moment before rage bubbled up and burst from his mouth with a shriek. The blade slid easily from its hiding place at his waist. Practiced hands swept it across his chin before the brain could register the sting. When it arrived, it was both less and worse than the ache in his heart.

The tattoo he had worn for fifty-four years landed in a bloody heap of skin in the soil below.

In the morning, he would ride for Alexander.

He would ride for answers...and for vengeance.

OTHER TITLES BY RAVEN OAK

The Boahim Trilogy

Amaskan's Blood (Book I)

Amaskan's War (Book II)

Amaskan's Honor (Book III)*

The Xersian Struggle

The Eldest Silence (Book I)*

Class-M Exile

Joy to the Worlds: Mysterious Speculative Fiction for the Holidays

Untethered: A Magic iPhone Anthology

Magic Unveiled: An Anthology

* forthcoming from Grey Sun Press

This book is dedicated to Erik as always.
May you ever be my sounding board, cheerleader, and when plot-tangles drive me mad, my laughter machine.

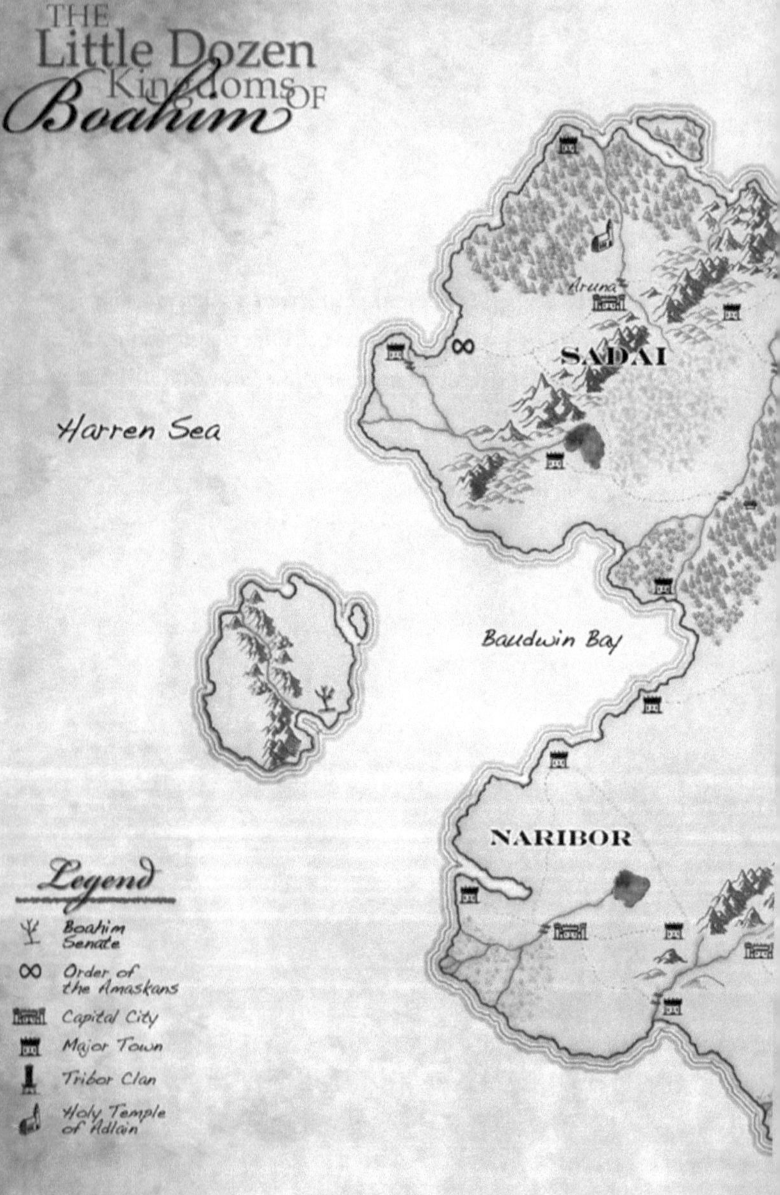

THE Little Dozen Kingdoms OF Boahim
Harren Sea
Aruna
SADAI
Baudwin Bay
NARIBOR
Legend
Boahim Senate
Order of the Amaskans
Capital City
Major Town
Tribor Clan
Holy Temple of Adlain

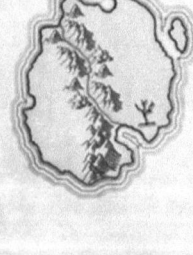

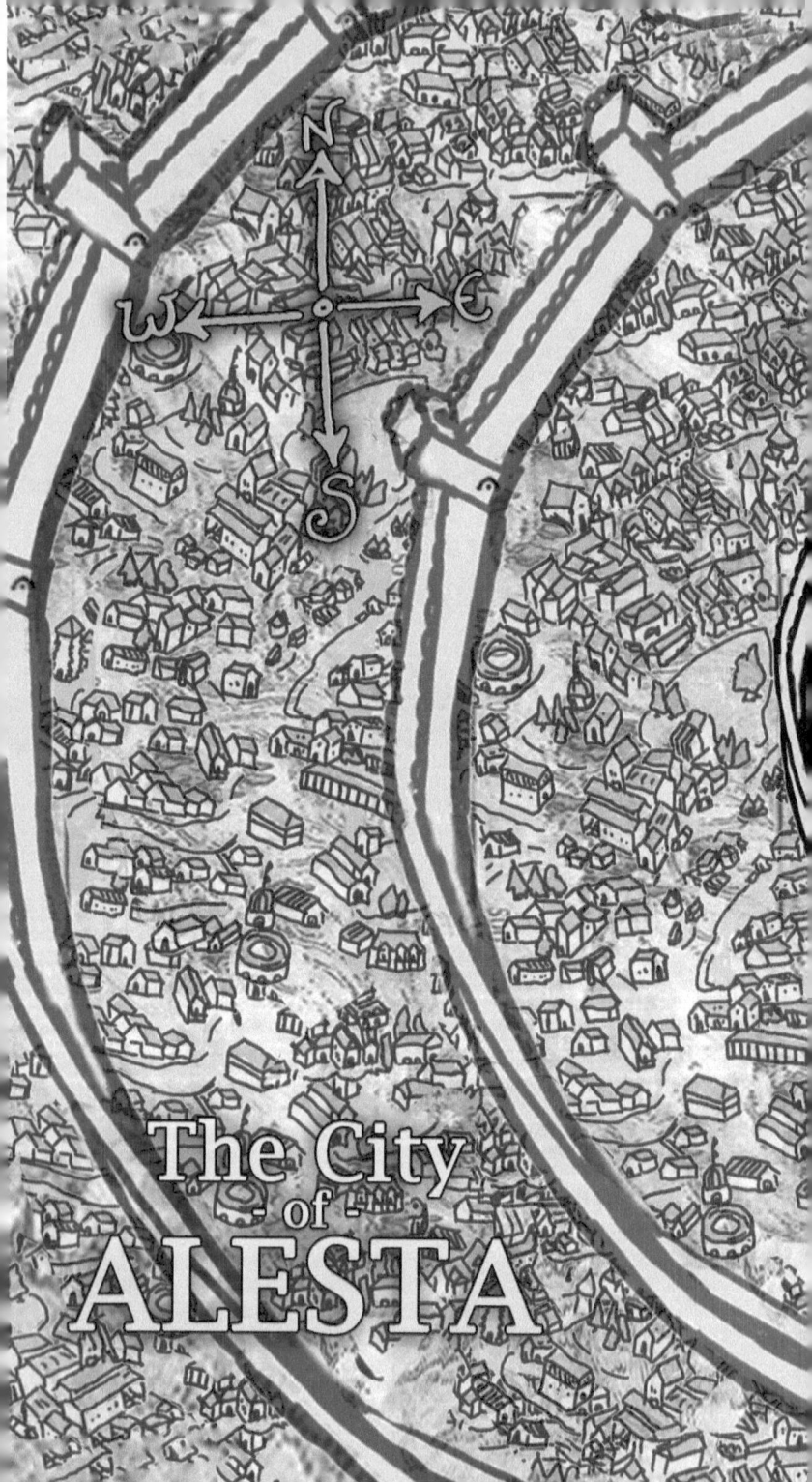

The City
- of -
ALESTA

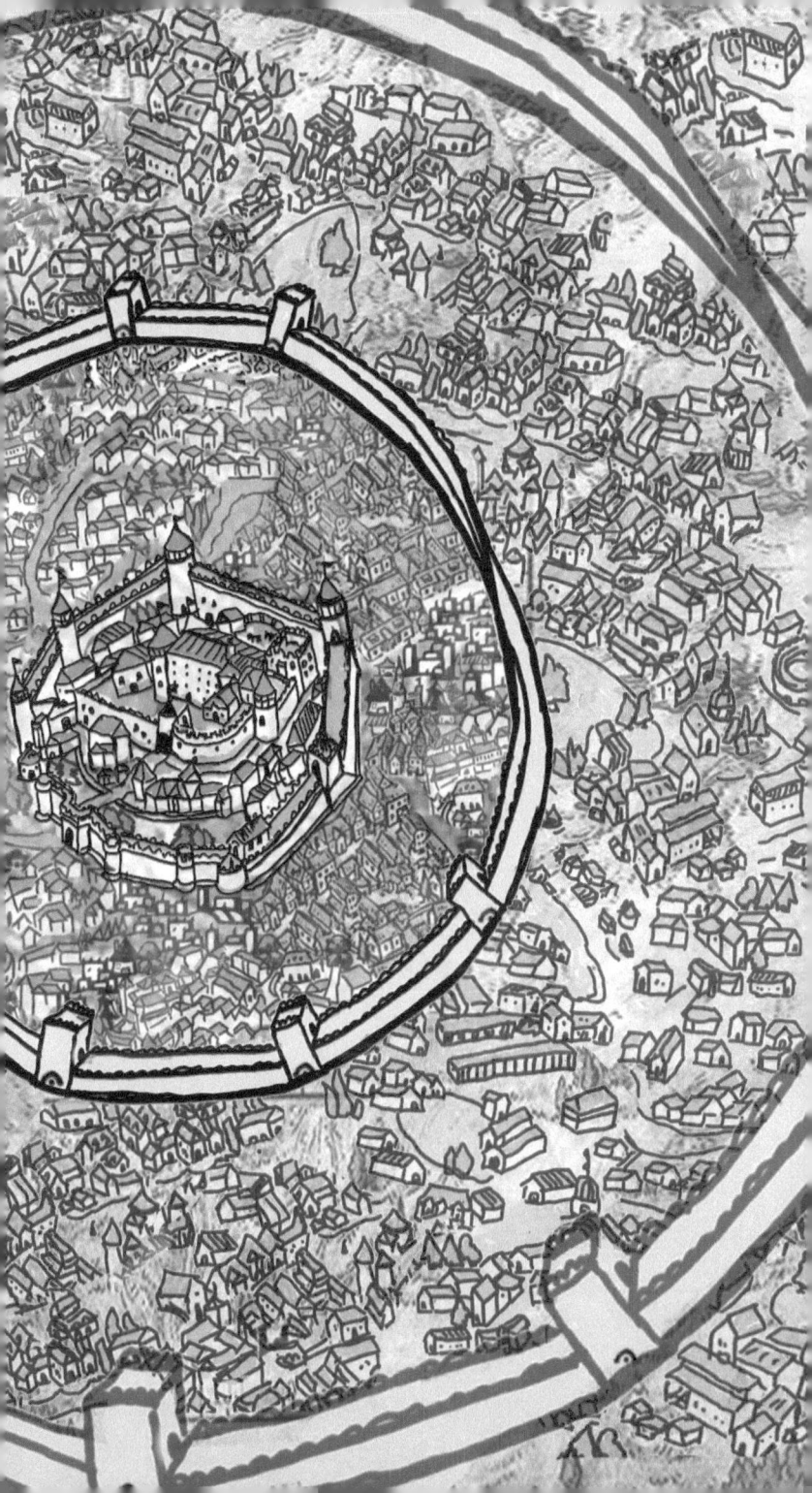

PROLOGUE

257 DELORCIN 19TH

The rumors crept their way across Sadai's border the way a water droplet rolls across a stone—it finds a crevice, a weakness if one will, then trickles inside without warning, forever changing more than the stone's surface.

Chatter had reached the Order of Amaska, but Bredych had paid it no mind. What did he care of King Leon's struggles? But the whispers had created chasms that echoed and bounced inside his mind. He had tried lying to himself, but news traveled fast these days.

When a trader had mentioned travelers fleeing the Kingdom of Alexander, fear had forced his fingers into fists. The next caravan to pass the Order had painted a grimmer picture—some poor soul had been hanged in the square at high noon for assassinating a prince. The word *assassin* had leapt from their tongues like cinders, and his fists had turned into knives. When a single Amaskan approached the Alexandrian border on Bredych's orders, the rumors painted the council room black, and Bredych seethed.

An Amaskan had seduced the prince. No, she had

seduced the King. Never mind that, she had tried to kill her own sister! No matter, the King had strung her up for treason and eaten her entrails in celebration.

A dozen different tales, each one darker than the one before.

Yet Bredych had refused to believe. His daughter was stronger than that. She was the best he had ever trained.

He had sent a dozen Amaskans to the border for answers, and as their horses disappeared from sight, his knees had trembled like a first-year trainee rather than the Amaskan Grand Master.

Walls painted blue and green left him somber as the sun set on another day his daughter would not see. The powdered gold mixed into the paint glittered, mocking him as the Thirteen stared with knowing looks from their frozen frames.

Alone in the council room, Bredych traced the carved figures of the Thirteen with his fingers before depressing the eye of Anur, God of Justice. At first, the wall merely trembled in response. After three breaths, a click sounded in the wall to his right.

He pushed against the wall, and it slid open to expose a room covered in several lifetimes of dust. At its center, a single orb glowed. Bredych pulled his hood closer about his face. Could the Boahim Senate see him through the sleeping orb?

No other Amaskans knew of the room's existence. The orb was an artifact surviving from a different time—something his dear *sister* had discovered shortly after he'd been named Grand Master. But the words needed to bring it to life had been *his* discovery.

"*Ta'asor Ley*," he whispered, and the orb's glow dimmed.

While many seasons had played across his body, the woman in the orb appeared unchanged from the last time he'd seen her. "You dare call upon us! I should curse you where you stand!" she said as she glared.

"You could, but then we would be forced to build boats to reach you."

"What do you want, assassin?"

"Knowledge."

"About?"

He paused for a moment, then answered. "The Kingdom of Alexander."

The sudden paleness of her face washed out any beauty she'd held. "War trembles at their border. Beyond that, I won't disclose."

"War with whom?"

"An old enemy with poison in its veins."

She spoke in nothingness as well as Bredych, but the twitch of her eye muscles gave her away. "There's more to this warning of war, Senator. We've heard rumors of death—"

The woman in the orb nodded. "Indeed. But then, you already knew this." The foggy shroud cleared as she leaned forward and whispered, "*Itovestah.*" The crystalline pendant around her neck twinkled once, then the image faded until only darkness remained.

Bredych touched the orb, but it was as cold as her stare had been. He repeated, "*Ta'asor Ley.*"

Nothing. The orb was dead.

Loud footfalls warned of someone's quick approach. He left the orb room and rolled the wall back into place. Someone knocked upon the council room door, and when he opened it, a trainee stood outside, face down and waiting.

Like his daughter once had been.

Bredych blinked back the moisture that threatened to ruin his composure. "You have a message for me?"

The blond haired boy nodded. "Delmon's returned—with news—should I summon the council?" The words tumbled out of his mouth, and at Bredych's nod he was off down the corridor again.

Instead of the bed his exhausted body craved, Bredych remained in the room and claimed a seat at the long table's end. Fifteen minutes of silence until the Amaskan council members shuffled into the room, followed by Delmon himself.

Dark circles made a raccoon of Delmon, and a jagged wound stretched across his forehead—a twin to match the one across his left cheek. The Amaskan fell into the offered chair, and after a moment's rest, he bowed his head before the thirteen council members. One poured a glass of water, which Delmon accepted with a grateful nod. When offered a glass, Bredych shook his head. His stomach churned enough on its own.

"Master Bredych—" Delmon swallowed a large gulp of water before continuing. "There are troops moving within Alexander, and word has it that to the south, the Shadian army approaches."

"War between Shad and Alexander? Would they dare with the Senate watching?" Bredych asked, but Delmon ignored the question.

"I wish that was the worst of the news, Grand Master. No matter where I traveled, people spoke of Amaskans. None of it was new information. That is, until I gained passage into Alexander."

No wonder he bore a scar. He had been lucky that was the worst of it. Bredych said, "You were ordered not to cross the border."

"I—I had no choice, Grand-Master."

"Explain."

The man ran a trembling hand across his bald head. "When I reached the border, word came that...that one of our own had been killed. I sent messages to the others, and we met in a barn. It was a trap, Grand Master. The man who'd given me this information reported us to the border guards. We were hooded, tied up, and tossed into the back of a wagon. We crossed the border unwillingly, where a man interrogated us. He thought we came to kill Queen Margaret."

One council member asked, "Queen? So the rumors of Leon's death are true?"

Bredych dismissed her question with a hand wave. "How did you escape?" Like water over stone, the cold wrapped itself around his shoulders as Delmon spoke.

"I didn't escape. They released me, Grand-Master, so that I could pass along a message from the Queen herself." Delmon took another sip of his water. "Any Amaskan caught inside their borders will be killed without question."

"And my daughter?"

Delmon stared at his glass. "When the wagon reached the capital city, the others were killed. Queen Margaret herself witnessed it from her balcony. They took me to where they would dispose of the bodies, and...and that's when I saw her."

The man's hands trembled, and water sloshed over the side of his glass. Bredych's muscles quivered with inaction.

"Master Bredych, I'm sorry. Her—her body still hung for all to see. Queen Margaret said nothing of it, but the rumors are that your daughter was hanged for treason. The Prince of Shad is dead—"

5

Ah. So that was why Shad's troops moved to the Alexander border.

"—The Senate encased her body with some spell or another. They meant to use her as an example, Grand Master."

The old woman in the orb had known all along. She had frozen his daughter in place. What magics did one require to stop time?

Bredych's jaw ached from clenching his teeth too long, and he stood. "Thank you, Delmon. You may leave." To the others, he said, "Arrange a memorial for our missing brothers and sisters. And someone fetch a physician to treat Delmon's wounds."

His feet carried him out of the building and down to the paths. Like a well-trained pup, Bredych fled to the coast where he'd walked with his daughter.

She had cursed him for sending her away, for sending her into the hands of her birth father. She had thrown questions at him, and he had answered by removing the tattoo that had marked her Amaskan.

Bredych's fingers buried themselves in the rocky soil as the waves crashed in the distance like footfalls too loud in his ears. Something about the scenario didn't make sense. *If Leon loved her even half as much as I do, Leon wouldn't...he couldn't have allowed this to happen. He couldn't put his own daughter to death.*

But then, Margaret stood as queen. Perhaps Leon had nothing to do with his daughter's death at all.

Tears mixed in the dirt below, which he allowed in the moment before rage bubbled up and burst from his mouth with a shriek.

Whether it was Leon, Margaret, or the Senate that had hung the noose around his daughter's neck mattered little.

Bredych wiped the remnants of tears on his sleeve and straightened his shoulders.

The blade slid easily from its hiding place at his waist. Practiced hands swept it across his chin before the brain could register the sting. When it arrived, it was both less and worse than the ache in his heart.

The tattoo he had worn for fifty-four years landed in a bloody heap of skin in the soil below.

In the morning, he would ride for Alexander.

He would ride for answers...and for vengeance.

PART I

1

Gone was the twinkle and warmth in his brown eyes. The mass of bed sheets dwarfed his once tall frame as he curled in on himself, more remnant of a toddler than king. In what the physicians warned would be his final days, Margaret's father begged for death as he fought the poison in his veins.

He cried like a child. He shouted and writhed. And when he was done with that, he wet himself.

In a rare moment of clarity, he whispered to his daughter, "Call the Senate."

After a sip of some smelly concoction the physicians had whipped up, he spoke of a hidden room with an orb and the words needed to call upon the Boahim Senate.

There was no time to question his words as King Leon slipped into a drug-induced sleep. Under her hand, the veins of his neck pulsed with a weak current.

"Is there anything you need, Your Highness?"

Margaret buried her slim hands in the ruffles of her dress lest she forget herself and wring them. She shook her head rather than lash out at the physician. It was not his fault King Leon lay dying any more than it was the physician's fault Adelei's corpse still hung from a magical noose outside the city walls.

She half expected the guards to escort her from her father's chambers, but they maintained their downcast glances. Her orders not to be disturbed held meaning— maybe even...authority? Margaret stifled a laugh as she closed the door behind her.

The hallways were empty as Margaret sought her father's council room. Any visitors to the castle had long since been sent away. Between the threat of war and her father's failing health, it served no purpose to hold court. Inside the council room, a thin layer of dust coated the table and chairs, and the bookcase along the rear wall. "*The Histories of Thirteen Kings,*" she mumbled as she trailed her fingers along the book's spines. It took the better part of thirty minutes to track down all thirteen books, which she then pulled out of place.

When she stepped back, no decipherable pattern appeared and she sighed. If there had been one, it would have made future ventures easier and less time consuming. Margaret pushed the books forward until an audible click sounded. She tugged on the bookcase, but it didn't budge. With a grunt, Margaret leaned her hip against the wood and shoved, only to tumble backwards into a chair when the bookcase slid sideways to expose a small chamber. Self-defense practice left bigger bruises than the tumble would, though she still winced when she stood.

She *should* close the bookcase behind her, but...no. There was no light and besides, no one else knew where she was. As she approached the orb, its blue glow pulsed once, and she flinched. When nothing else happened, she whispered, "*Ta'asor Ley.*"

At the command, the mist inside the orb cleared, and a man's face appeared. Margaret released a startled squeak. "You—you're not her," she said.

His wrinkles multiplied when he smiled. "Senator Whitlen? No, my name is Senator Montero."

"You're Alexander's Senator."

"And you must be Queen Margaret," he said.

She blinked furiously at the sudden tears. "P-Princess Margaret still, though the physicians say my father won't last the week."

"My apologies, Princess Margaret. Usually the first time someone new calls upon us is after the passing of a ruler. Have you need of the Senate?"

"I do, Senator. My father—the King—he ails from a poison no physician can stop. It's a vile concoction out of Shad. The physicians tell me my father's been poisoned for nearly two decades, and I wish..." His kind smile faltered as she spoke. "I ask...I require that the Senate heal him."

"I know this must be difficult for you, but we can't heal your father. I'm truly sorry."

From behind him came the shuffling of fabric and a flash of light. Then an old woman's face appeared over the senator's shoulder. He stepped aside for her, and when she glared into the orb, Margaret's fingers trembled at her sides. "Senator Whitlen—"

"Princess Margaret, this Senate is not at your beck and call—"

"Senator Whitlen," Margaret repeated as she straightened her shoulders. "I understand that you're the enforcers of the Thirteen, but does not the *Book of Shlosheser* say that the body...the temple is a gift? If life is a gift, should you not uphold such things? The Shadians would rob Alexander of its ruler far too soon because of a personal vendetta."

The Senator's jaw throbbed. "Do not disturb us again for such frivolous matters, Princess Margaret."

If Margaret could have struck something, she would have. Instead, she jabbed a finger at the orb. "My father is not—" Her finger passed through the glowing mist and touched the Senator's wrinkled cheek. Margaret yanked her finger back as Senator Whitlen pursed her lips. "—Not frivolous! You healed Adelei's shoulder when last you were here. Why heal an assassin and not a king?"

"Adelei's wounds were magically created, while your father's...well, Leon's wounds are of the natural world. There is little we can do to fix such maladies. Even if we could, would you have us at the beck and call of every dying citizen?"

"He's not merely a dying citizen! He is a king!"

"Exactly why we shouldn't intervene—a lesson you would do well to learn if you wish to be a wise ruler. We are not physicians, Your Highness. Besides, 'Those who submit to the way of the world, find unity in both life and death.'"

"Don't speak to me of death. What good *are* you if you can't heal him?" They were the words of a child, but Margaret did not care. "You're little more than thieves who ride in and steal away family members—"

"Who are murderers? Yes, yes." The Senator waved her hand at the orb. "If you wish for help—" The old woman retrieved a sheet of parchment from somewhere out of view. "The Shadian army approaches your border. Do not engage them."

The orb darkened with a pop, leaving Margaret alone.

It was then she allowed herself the solace of a good cry.

IN HIS YOUNGER DAYS, CROSSING SADAI'S DESERT HAD been an adventure, but as Bredych crossed it now, his age weighed him down as much as the dreaded sand itself. Rather than the week-and-a-half it should have taken, the journey to the Alexander border stretched to three weeks.

Instead of a mass of soldiers stationed in the garrisoned border town, Breighton had appeared relatively empty, the exception being the junipers and sage brush that peppered the landscape. A few soldiers had patrolled the stone walls that spread between two lookout towers, soldiers who had waved through his "hired sword" façade. Bredych's features were too lean and angular these days to be anything else, though the soldiers had laughed at the "old man" who thought he could help with the upcoming war.

Their naivety was a pity. Once the Shadians and their pet *Tribor* crossed the border, many of these men and women would kiss Itova, the Death Goddess, before bloodying their blade. Once across the border, the pathway to Alesta was relatively quick, though crowded with large caravans of people who had fled their small towns for the safety of Alesta. Horses pulled wagons of people and belongings, while a few livestock trailed behind.

Bredych reached the capital city before the throngs of people, though the city's outer walls were thick with troops. Empty or not, he held his breath as he spied several nooses swinging in the light breeze. If his daughter's body had once swung from the noose, her body was gone now. While he supposed he should be grateful for such an action, he couldn't help clenching his teeth as he rode past the ropes. Nearer the gate, he dismounted from his horse and winced when his hip popped. Stiffness held him in place long enough to count the number of guards. Sneaking in was not an option with so many eyes and ears on him.

Ten feet from the gate, a burly guard stopped him with a crossbow. "What's yer business here?" he yelled.

Several others turned toward him, suspicion in their gazes. He'd be a fool to think the others unarmed, though they probably bore the same ill-made crossbows. Bredych slowly raised both hands in the air. He shifted his Alexandrian dialect to one befitting a hired sword. "I'm armed. Wish t'lend a hand in the coming battle."

The burly guard jabbed his crossbow in Bredych's direction. "You? Yer too old. Best to flee with the rest of 'em."

Before the guardsman had done more than blink, Bredych's throwing knife wobbled from the guard's crossbow limb. The guardsman's brows inched upward. "I guess yer good with that short sword, too?"

Bredych nodded as the guardsman returned his throwing knife. "Aye. Fair shot with a bow and could teach your kingdom a few tricks in making better crossbows. It's all 'bout the glue of the river sturgeon."

The guardsman frowned and tightened his grip on his crossbow. "Ya said 'yer kingdom.' You be from out Kingdom?"

"Aye."

"Which kingdom?"

The crossbow hovered near Bredych's head. "Sadai. That a problem?"

"Not if yer speaking truthful-like."

Bredych reached into the coin purse tied to his belt. Most of his money was well hidden, but the coin purse added to the role he played. He fetched two coins and held them out to the guardsman who glanced at image carved on their fronts. Three ships sailed against the setting sun, and the guardsman's frown deepened.

"You coulda swiped them from some poor fellow. If yer from Sadai, say something in Sadain. Like who yer king be."

"King Adir. Means strong and mighty." Bredych smiled at the guardsman. *Damned fool. So believing.* If only getting into the castle would be as easy. The guardsman lowered his crossbow for a second time and stepped aside. "Who'd I talk to 'bout joining up? I heard you have a lady captain or some-such."

The guardsman shook his head. "Guess the news ain't spread out there in Sadai, but Captain Warhammer's been dead a while now. You'll wanna talk with the new guy. Captain Fenton. Should be in the...."

Bredych's heart raced, but he forced his face into a neutral wall. He had not understood the joy upon discovering Shendra, or Ida as they knew her, was alive any more than he currently understood the sudden grief that swept over him as the guardsman talked. Over the years, rumors had reached him about a woman leading the royal army of Alexander, though he never thought the woman his sister. Before all that, she had left him little choice but to slit her throat. It had been his first assassination as Grand Master of the Order of Amaska. And his last.

He found his voice about the time the guardsman finished speaking and asked, "How'd she die?"

"Eh? Whadoya care?"

"Been lookin' forward to meetin' such a captain. My apologies. Was idol curiosity."

As Bredych passed through the gate, the guardsman who followed behind dropped his hand on Bredych's shoulder. "I don't rightly know the details, but rumor says it were the Shadians. Seems they're ta blame for a lot of untimely deaths these days. Good luck to ya."

The city itself was ringed with multiple sets of walls, the first of which he had passed through without incident. Dirt covered the roadway Bredych followed, and the shadows bore shadows as the sun dipped below the buildings. As with many cities, busy people packed away their wares as they closed down cobbled together booths that lined the streets. The poor of Alesta brushed past him as they sought their homes for the evening. Somewhere in the shadows, eyes watched him—of that much he was certain—and he ignored the guards he suspected trailed him. When he passed through a second set of city walls, there was another conversation with the guardsmen and a brief example of his talent. The road toward the castle transitioned to packed dirt, and when he reached the third gate, a guardsman waved him through with a stifled yawn.

No one stopped him as he passed by a strip of brick homes abandoned by the wealthier citizens. Alesta was a thieves' paradise, and were he a mere thief, he would be tempted to avail himself of some wine and maybe a set of more comfortable shoes. Instead, Bredych led his tired horse through a phantom section of the city with a frown.

When war comes calling, only the wealthy manage to escape its blade.

The six-hundred-year-old castle loomed ahead, its walls bearing pocks and nicks from battles past. From Bredych's hiding spot fifty feet back, he counted six men standing guard at the arched gate serving as the main entry. He tied his horse's reins to a wooden post that held up one side of an abandoned home before emptying his saddlebags. Food, water, and other necessities he carried to the rear, where he stowed them beneath the porch's wooden floorboards. The home's rear door was open a crack, though whether it was left that way by the fleeing owner or someone else was difficult to say.

Bredych carried nothing that would mark him as Amaskan, only a few weapons and his torch. The door whined when he nudged it open with his boot, though nothing inside moved. Wadded up across a finely woven couch, a ratty blanket spoke of hunger and abject poverty.

Someone else was here.

No one who lived in a home this fine would subject themselves to a blanket not fit for use in the stables. Bredych's gaze traveled across several stools near a long, cleared table and a stone fireplace bearing an oak mantel. A cedar chest carved with horses sat in the room's corner and beside it, a well-loved writing bureau lay littered with scraps torn from a rich collection of books. Somewhere deeper into the house, something clattered as it landed on the stone floor, and a muffled curse followed. He snuffed out the torch with his heel before crouching closer to the stone floor.

Bredych moved heel to toe, testing out each step before transferring full weight to it as he approached the hallway. No flickering light indicated the intruder, but another curse to Bredych's left betrayed their location. With one hand, he gripped the hilt of a throwing knife while the other slid carefully along the wall. When his fingers met air, he paused at the doorway a second before peering around its edge.

To the right, an open window spilled what sunlight lingered into a small kitchen. A beggar rifled through a wooden pantry, his back to Bredych. Sweat mixed with the pungent stench of excrement. A third scent, one of moldy bread, reached Bredych's nose as the beggar thrust a round object into his mouth.

"Where you planning to pay for that?" asked Bredych.

With a yelp, the rest of the beggar's meal tumbled to the ground. He didn't have much, but the man held out a blunt, wooden object that was less knife and more stick as he yelled at Bredych. "Ge'out! 'Smine!"

"I believe you're the trespasser here."

"Whatcher meanin'?"

Bredych slowed his gaze as he looked the man up one side and down the other. "Only that a man such as yourself would never be in possession of finery such as this." He thumbed in the direction of the fireplace behind him. "Take, for example, that fine hearth of polished stone and marble. Have you ever seen such marvels?"

The beggar shifted his weight to his left, toward the open window, and Bredych shook his head. "I don't think so, friend. Empty your pockets before you leave."

A gold trinket, three pennies, and a hunk of moldy cheese later, the beggar said, "They empty, sor."

"The knife, too."

The makeshift weapon clattered on the table, and Bredych patted the beggar down. When he was convinced that the man was no harm, he tucked the cheese into a coat pocket and handed back the knife. "Take your blanket and go. I don't wish to see your face in this home again, understand?"

"Yes, sor. Thankee, sor."

The beggar crawled through the open window and fell into the shadows as night rose. Bredych retreated to the hallway where he proceeded up the wooden stairwell to another hallway bearing five open doors. Sunset had been on his right when he had entered, meaning he faced south.

He took the last doorway on the right, the one closest to the castle. Farimun was with him tonight as the room not only bore a window, but it opened away from the castle gate and the guards' prying eyes. Bredych unbuckled his belt and removed his sheathed short sword, which he laid on the floor. If Farimun blessed his luck further, he would be back for it shortly.

Bredych crawled through the window and onto the first floor roof. He hugged the second story wall as he approached the wall surrounding the castle courtyard, which spanned four, maybe five men tall. No trellis to climb, though the nicks in the old wall would provide decent footholds for climbing.

After retreating to inside the abandoned house, Bredych spread his legs shoulder-width apart and stretched his hands far above his head. His arms transitioned into a slow arc down to his booted feet and moved on to wrap him in a hug. He closed his eyes, his body flowing like the water within until the stillness of his mind left his body limber.

On his way to the back porch, he stowed his short sword under the planks. Saddlebag before him, he traded his hired-hand disguise for the gear of his trade. He tucked the ends of his breeches into toe-fitted shoes and tied their laces around his ankles. Long swathes of black silk were wrapped around his waist, wrists, and ankles to bind the tunic and breeches in place for easier movement. Bredych walked several houses away from the castle's gate until the wall curved out of the guardsmen's view. He leaned against the wall with his hands tucked behind his head for a full ten minutes. When no one approached or noticed him, he turned to get a better look at the holes that peppered the wall. A few pockmarks would force a stretch he would pay for in the morning, but all held enough depth for his purpose.

The first ten feet of the climb was like any other he had made in his career—deceptively easy—and his muscles settled into the rhythm of stretch, hold, and stretch again. He was halfway up when someone muttered nearby. Bredych froze in place as he searched the area around him.

No one hid in the shadows. *They must be on the other side.*

Old bones ached when he asked them to reach for a handhold near the top. His fingers touched stone for a moment before the powdery substance crumbled, leaving him hanging by one arm. Heart pounding in his ears, he reached for a second, closer notch, which he gripped by his fingertips while his feet found their footholds. For one lengthy minute he rested in the x-position.

He gripped the embrasure and pulled himself upright enough to peer out across the wall. A guardsman stood ten feet away, his back to Bredych. No one else manned the wall—not in visible range—and Bredych pulled the rest of his body up and over. The drop to stone rattled his teeth and set his hip to screaming, but he forced his muscles to relax as he settled into a crouch. Someone called to the guardsman, who walked away, and Bredych used the opportunity to creep along the shadows cast by the hip-high wall.

He waddled along for a good stretch before stopping before a group of guards huddled near a torch. The cry of war approached and here they stood with a joke on their tongues and a slouch in their stance. *The enemy could break through their gates, and they would be none the wiser.* As they bandied jokes about, Bredych inched his way forward to the flanking tower. As he reached it, one guardsman turned in his direction, and Bredych ducked through the open doorway. Once his eyes adjusted to the dimness, he maneuvered down the nearby stairs.

Rather than head toward the inner keep, Bredych kept to the inner bailey's shadows until the smell of roast pig assaulted his nose, which he followed to a water well and yet another door where a dozen servants scurried about as they prepared for supper. He skipped past this one and checked two more before he found the outer door to the laundry.

The washroom lay empty, as did its closet. Piles of bedsheets were bundled in the corner, along with some pants and tunics in varying colors of blue. Something soaked in a half-filled basin, which he ignored in favor of a set of baskets and shelves along the back wall. *The guardsmen outside were wearing dark blue, weren't they?* Bredych riffled through one pile of clothes and then another until he spotted a tunic in the offending color. He removed his belt, tossed the tunic over his clothes, and fastened the belt above his hips. He could pass as one of them...as long as no one studied his appearance too closely.

When he entered the castle proper, he avoided the shadows and strode with purpose until he reached a set of stairs. King Leon's rooms would not be on the first floor, nor were they likely to be on the second floor in a castle of this size. There were too few guards on the third floor for the royal chambers, but when he poked his head around the corner on the fourth, a long row of guardsmen lined the hallway.

Despite the confirmation, he followed the stairs up another floor to an open room full of stools, pillows, and books—all in shades of perfumed mauve that made his nose itch. While an offense on the eyes, the room held several windows and no guards, and Bredych pushed open a window with a rooftop view.

Perfect. He could enter Leon's bedroom through a window and avoid the guards altogether.

Then they would have a little chat.

2

———

By the time Bredych had found the correct window, the moon had long since risen, although it had ducked behind a wall of clouds by the time the old king's physician retreated. It had been too long since Bredych had been on a job. Even with the fresh air from outside, the pungent odor of waste burned Bredych's nose and watered his eyes—a reaction to which any other Amaskan would be long since accustomed.

Bredych crossed the room with long strides, locked and barred the door, and then settled himself on the bed beside King Leon. For a moment, he studied the man before him—a man who had aged well beyond his fifty-seven years. His baggy flesh near melted off his large frame, and the sky blue of his bedding drowned out what little color remained in his pallid skin. His thick knuckles still bore his family's sapphire signet ring, though it dangled near the knuckle, evidence of his significant weight loss. Leon muttered in his sleep, but otherwise did not move. Bowls of some paste or another sat on the bedside table and a quick sniff labeled them as medicinal in nature.

He could do it. Bredych could reach out and cover Leon's mouth and nose with his hands and snuff the life from him. The same way Leon had—

The king's eyelids snapped open, and his gaze wandered around as he stared at the ceiling without meaning. He blinked once, then again, before his eyes focused on Bredych's hand as it hovered above Leon's face. His brown eyes followed the hand up the arm and finally to Bredych's face.

Leon's gaze curved around Bredych's jaw to the scab below the ear, and the whites of his eyes almost swallowed his pupils. "Y-you!" he stuttered, and Bredych nodded.

"You seem surprised to see me," said Bredych. Phlegm gathered at the corner of Leon's mouth as he coughed. Bredych fetched a corner of the king's bedsheet and dabbed at the saliva. "There, there. No need to trouble yourself with greeting me. A man as ill as yourself should rest up. One never knows when Itova will come to court."

"H-He...Hel...." His call for help was weak and broken by coughs. White knuckled, King Leon glanced between the door and Bredych.

"No one's coming. The good king has had his medicine for the evening, and now it's time for him to rest, yes? I am curious though. How did you know who I was?"

The corners of King Leon's mouth tilted up a hint. "I'd recognize her features anywhere."

Bredych frowned. The man was more addled than he had originally thought. "Adelei—"

"N-no. Ida. Or Sh-Shendra as you knew her."

A panther-sized cough leapt from the king's chest, and the next few minutes were spent in a battle to breathe. If the fool died now, Bredych wouldn't have the honor. He offered the King a glass of some foul-smelling liquid, but Leon brushed it aside. "I wasn't aware you knew my sister," said Bredych.

King Leon attempted a laugh, which dissolved into another coughing fit. This time he accepted the liquid which his shaking hands sloshed onto his bed-robe. "I would th-thank you, but the action seems absurd. Your spies tell you plenty, I'm sure, so no need to throw about twaddle. Why are you here?"

"Adelei," said Bredych as he leaned closer to King Leon. "I have to know. Did you take ill before or after you murdered my daughter? Was this illness her doing? Punishment for her forced return to your side perhaps?"

Leon's face flushed a bright purple. "N-Not me. Never me. Could never...."

"Really? Because there was a time when you sent her away. You claimed it was for her own protection, but it was abandonment nonetheless."

Bredych leaned closer to the sick king's lips as Leon whispered, "And you sent her to me. First Ida, then Adelei. You n-never could keep those you love."

A thin, red line welled where Bredych's knife leaned against the king's wrinkled neck. His muscles had reacted to the taunt, and the king's wheezing laughter exploded in Bredych's ears. His heart raced too fast as King Leon reached up and gripped his wrist.

"G-go ahead. I'm already dying," said Leon.

Bredych brushed aside the king's weak grip and tucked the knife into his shirt sleeve. "Not yet. Not until you tell me how she died."

"Which *she*?"

Bredych opened his mouth to say his daughter's name, but the word on his tongue twisted with his gut. "Ad-Shendra. Both."

King Leon's face fell at her name. He would have to investigate the last decade of his sister's life. It seemed she had been closer to the king than Bredych originally had suspected. King Leon grabbed for a nearby bag and missed.

When Bredych pulled the drawstrings loose, the bag held a mix of dark green herbs that burned his nose when he sniffed them.

"Don't sniff too hard. It's dangerous, or so my physician says," said King Leon.

"How much?"

"A good handful."

"So much?"

Leon nodded. "It's the only thing that can help me now."

Bredych tossed a handful into the mug and filled it with water. Leon did not stir the medicine but gulped it down in several long draws. "Ida was the Captain of the Royal Guard for a time. Worked her way up after the Little War of Three. But I made her my *sepier*."

"*Sepier*? From *Sep* in old tongue?" When Leon nodded, Bredych asked, "*Sep* means hidden, so *sepier* means what? She was your spy?"

"Yes." King Leon's gaze drifted off to the open window as he spoke. "But she was more. I only say this so you'll know...I had n-nothing to do with her death. Damn Shadians and their pet *Tribor*. She died in service to the crown."

"She died with honor then," said Bredych.

Leon slammed the mug on the bedside table. "She needn't have died at all!"

"You loved her."

Leon glanced at Bredych. "And you didn't. You slit her

throat because she wouldn't follow along with your twisted plans."

"She embarrassed me before the Order with her disloyalty. I was still a newly named Grand Master when the plan to wipe out your family line presented itself. What could I have done? She ignored orders, killed her fellow brothers, and brought your daughter into the Order. We now had a witness to our plans. My sister named us butchers of children. Had I not stopped her, the Order would have dissolved into chaos."

"Were I stronger, I'd kill you, you monster. I promised her—" Another coughing fit swept over King Leon, and this time when he leaned back against his pillow, his body shrank in on itself.

He *really had* loved her.

Leon's words did not say it, but his body betrayed it as both anger and sorrow warred for control. Bredych's sister's survival had been a surprise, as had her entrance into Sadai. Word reached the Order that someone had inquired after Adelei, but before Bredych could reach Ida, his sister had disappeared across the Alexandrian border. Surprisingly, his heart ached at her death—more than it should after so many decades—but the thought of her serving Leon poked holes in his resolve.

Bredych said, "If you would have me believe you loved her, I would have you believe me when I say I loved Adelei more than the children of my flesh."

"I know."

Bredych's heart caught in his throat. How could Leon understand?

"She and I spoke near the...end. She loved both of her fathers."

He turned away from Leon's words and away from that

knowing gaze. Bredych blinked back the moisture that blurred his vision.

"You took her from me and twisted her into a killer, but in the end she was mine, Bredych. She was my Iliana again. She died to keep her kingdom safe, a concept you could n- never understand."

"The Order of Amaska exists to protect *all* of the Little Dozen Kingdoms' people. The Book of Ja'ahr speaks of a holy being, a *kenturi*. It's a creature with the face and hooves of the Gods and a glowing light to lead those lost. It's believed that those who are truly without the self—" Leon frowned, and Bredych paused. "Those who are...I think the word in Alexandrian is *selfless?* Those who follow this path are reborn at the feet of the Thirteen as the *kenturi*. If my daughter died as you say, surely she looks down on me now. Amaskans live for justice and honor, to keep people safe from merciless kings and senators who live without rules. It's a calling *you* will never understand."

Leon cleared his throat, and Bredych faced the dying king. "You came here to kill me, Bredych. You heard she'd died, and you came here seeking vengeance. If *our* daughter is one of those...*kenturi*...what would she think of you now? A vengeful Amaskan. You're a walking contradiction." Weak though he was, his voice had strengthened, and someone moved in the antechamber outside. Bredych folded his legs up on the bed and drew the bedcurtain closer about himself. To Leon he whispered, "There are many ways to kill a king. Fein sleep, or yours will be of long suffering."

King Leon closed his eyes as the door opened, and Bredych withdrew his knife. Someone drew close to the bed and refilled the mug with a minty liquid before retreating.

Bredych counted to a slow ten before he released his breath and nudged the king.

"Tell me how Adelei died. The details if you will."

"Adelei's twin, Margaret, was to marry Prince Gamun of Shad. It was a marriage to heal our two kingdoms, but the Shadians laid a trap to seize control of the throne. Adelei found evidence of Prince Gamun's involvement in many crimes against the Thirteen."

Bredych hissed. "You called the Senate."

"*She* called the Senate. It was her choice, Bredych."

So *that* was why her body hung at the city gates—an untouchable example for all to remember. Bredych clenched his teeth. That fool senator thought herself clever to hint at such, knowing Bredych would seek out answers. Damn the Dozen, she was cunning.

"There was a fight, and Adelei saved Senator Whitlen's life. Our daughter's reward for her selflessness was her death. The Boahim Senate unraveled all the information they could from her, and then they killed her."

The fight had drained out of Leon as he lay back against his pillows. As much as he hated the man, Bredych couldn't kill him. Not now. The man had candlemarks, maybe a day or two at most, and killing him would be a blessing. He said as much, and Leon shrugged.

"I'll find myself at my daughter's side before the sun rises again."

The finality with which he said it unnerved Bredych, and he snatched the mug from the bedside table. He dabbed at a small glob near the cup's lip and rubbed it between his fingers before touching a bit to his tongue. "Tastes bitter. Dries out the tongue. But minty...*perin?*"

Leon smiled.

"You fool," said Bredych. "Too much is lethal."

"That was the purpose. I ordered my physician to bring me enough three days ago. It's only a matter of time before I drown in my own spit, and I'll not have Margaret watch longer than necessary. Your arrival gave me the courage I needed, and for that I thank you."

Bredych set the mug down. "It's a pity we had not met in person before now. I suspect you and I would have many topics to ponder."

The king's eyes closed as he mumbled an affirmation, and a few minutes' silence passed before gentle snores whistled through Leon's nose.

He should kill Leon—have his vengeance upon the dying king—but there would be no honor in the action. If anyone deserved his blade, it was the Boahim Senate. So smugly they sat on their island as they spied on the world from afar. Bredych stood slowly from the bed and returned to the window.

The Senate would pay for Adelei's death.

And for her fathers' grief.

Margaret stared at her fingers—in particular, at the hangnail she had worried until it had bled and scabbed over. It was better than staring at the bookcase lining the rear wall of her father's council room. Better than thinking of that spiteful senator. Roland cleared his throat, and she glanced up from her trembling index finger.

"I apologize for the late hour, Your Highness, but the council still awaits your decision," said Master Roland Havis, the royal physician.

The only member of her father's council who dared meet with her, even if it were under false pretenses.

Margaret frowned for the third time in five minutes. "If we are to speak on kingdom matters, should not the rest of my father's council be present?"

"We felt it better if such decisions were discussed with a friend."

"What kind of decisions?" she asked, her gaze drifting to her fingers. When was the last time her lady-in-waiting had soaked her hands or rubbed chamomile into her skin? Instead of the fine manicured hands of a princess, she wore defensive calluses from working with daggers and short swords.

"Your attendance to kingdom matters has...lacked the attention needed, though rightfully so!" The words tumbled out of his mouth at her glare. "The council would prefer to act in your father's absence. He—We believe Your Highness has more pressing matters to attend with His Majesty ill."

"There's nothing more that can be done for my father, though I am certain he appreciates the council's concern. After all, you have our Kingdom's best interests in mind." Margaret near whispered the sentence to disguise the anger in her voice.

Lord Cornish, highborn warthog that he was, cared little for what decisions were made as long as he were the one to make them. *Not that he's present. That would require more courage than he possesses.* Every meeting with her father's council left her tearing lace from her dress hems. They took her for a simpleton. A fool. Her questions frustrated them, and now they had sent poor Roland to wrest control away from her. *A little puppet is what they would make of me. Even worse, I'm exhausted enough that I'm tempted to allow them to do so.*

Roland patted her hand, and she bit her tongue to keep from flinching. "My apologies, Your Highness. I realize how difficult this must be for you, but your father isn't able to make such decisions. With Shadian troops on the move, we must act swiftly—"

"What proof is there that the Shadian army is on the move?" she asked, and Roland gave her a flat look she could not decipher. "You say they would soon cross our border, but what proof do you have of such an action? Where does this information come from?"

If Adelei were here—she dismissed the thought. There was no use in following that path.

"No pigeons have arrived from the Meridi Pass. No runners. Certainly not from inside the Kingdom of Shad. In fact...." Margaret rifled through a stack of papers an inch thick until she found the sought report. "The Grand Marshal sent this report last week stating that our spies noted increased border patrols but little else. The Shadians have played mind games with us these past two years, but they are nothing more than that—mind games. So I reiterate, how do you know that the Shadian army is on its way here?"

Roland glanced at his own stack of papers before meeting her gaze. The folded letter he passed her way bore a wax insignia she had seen in dusty old tomes, most of which lived on the bookshelf across from the council room table. The simple tree with four equal branches set her fingers trembling as she stared at the Boahim Senate insignia. Inside, long, firm script detailed the information Roland had shared, direct from Senator Whitlen herself.

Margaret asked, "You received a message from the Boahim Senate? Why wasn't I notified?"

"Your father took to his bed the day this arrived. We thought it best if you focused your attention on his remaining time in this world rather than bother yourself with the mundane."

"I'd hardly describe an approaching army as 'mundane,' but we'll discuss that momentarily. Since when has the Senate involved themselves in kingdom...."

"Quabbles? Frivolity?" he suggested.

The word ignited her tongue like a branding iron as Senator Whitlen's words circled her mind. Rather than spill the tears held back by pure stubbornness, she ground her teeth. "My father lives still, and as long as he lives, he is King. But if my father is unable to rule this kingdom, that duty falls to me and me alone. You are his council and by extension, mine, but that is all you are—the supplier of council. The decisions of this kingdom are mine to make, and I'll thank you to remember that as reports and letters are received."

Only the barest warmth creeped across her cheeks. The pride she felt at such a speech shriveled beneath his gaze. She was but a child to him. To all of them. The same spoiled child who played at being princess while her sister hung outside the city walls. Margaret took a slow and steady breath. "It appears the Shadians have ceased their hinting and now move against us. Presumably in retribution for my former husband's death, correct?"

Roland nodded.

"What response does the Grand Marshal recommend?"

He flipped through several more papers until he found the one he was looking for and pulled it closer where he could read it. "Increased border patrols, especially at the Meridi Pass, though that was done the moment Prince Gamun died. The Grand Marshal believes they will set forth for Alesta."

"For me."

"For you. Grand Marshal Doublis wishes to send your father and you into hiding, away from the capital city."

Margaret shook her head. "According to you, moving my father would result in his death, and as for me, I've done enough hiding in my lifetime, thank you. Someone must remain to give the people hope." The corners of his eyes twitched, and she asked, "What is it, Roland?"

"Doublis believes the people should flee, those that haven't already."

"He believes the city indefensible."

"Your Highness, Alesta has stood through the rise and fall of Boahim, the Little War of Three, and countless other battles. But it has paid for every battle." Roland unrolled a map that bore the Grand Marshal's scribbles. "The last war, several portions of the outer walls fell to the Shadian army. Those walls were repaired, but your father has grown too used to peace. Once compromised, a patched, old wall will remain a weak point. We can't defend the people here from an army of this size."

Margaret poured herself a glass of water and sipped it to coat her parched throat. After a moment's passing, she said, "I won't leave Alesta or my father. We will bring all of our armies back to Alesta. Those previously stationed along the Shadian border will remain."

"Your Highness, I am no strategist, but it would leave our borders mostly undefended. If that were the better option, I'm sure Grand Marshal Doublis would have suggested it."

"Pass my command along to Doublis."

Roland gathered up his papers before bowing once. "By your leave, Your Highness?"

This time her voice quivered when she spoke, and she cursed the sound. "One more thing, Roland. There is the matter of my sister's body." The spell holding her sister's body in place had dissolved this morning, leaving the city unsettled as no rot or insect had plagued Adelei's body. The power of such a spell—Margaret shivered. "There are arrangements to be made."

"Yes, Your Highness. The council suggests a quiet burning."

By the way he frowned sympathetically, he had expected her to cry. Instead, Margaret gave what she hoped was a level look. "My sister was a member of the royal family and will be attributed such honors."

"Yes, Your Highness." Roland bowed once again before fleeing the council chambers.

Margaret had no idea what she was doing. None at all. She tugged at a hangnail once, then settled her hands in her lap. The only skill she wielded was her love for her father. How could someone like her possibly understand war? Margaret made it three steps toward the bookshelf before halting her steps.

They wouldn't answer. They didn't involve themselves in the *mundane*.

With a sigh, she fled from the orb, the council room, and all the useless people who refused to save her father. As she passed through hallways empty of the nobles who should be gossiping on their way to dinner, she rubbed her sleeved arms where the hair suddenly prickled and chafed. Margaret paused outside her father's chambers, but the only eyes on her were those of the guards.

She cast one last glance into the shadows at the corridor's end, but no one returned her stare. The door behind her burst open, and she let loose a startled squeak.

"Your Highness, come quickly!" The servant beckoned from the doorway, and she followed into her father's prison.

Margaret retched at the smell, a foul stench of sickness and herbs at war with one another. His bedsheets had been tossed aside and several healers held him down as he rocked and twitched violently. His pallor was a sickly yellow, and his tongue, which stuck out at an odd angle, bore foam and pustules.

"What in the Thirteen have you done to my father?" she shouted, and the healers loosened their grip. King Leon lurched from the bed and caught his foot in the bedsheets. Margaret rushed forward and caught him before he tumbled to the floor. Whatever poison leeched its way across his body had robbed him of his once strong frame and she bore his weight easily.

"Margaret!"

His shout startled her, but when she met his gaze, his eyes focused on something far away. The tremors stopped and she whispered, "I'm here, Papa." He sagged in her arms as she helped him settle against his pillows. To the healers she said, "Go fetch Roland."

When they hesitated, she spun and shouted, "Fetch my father's physician! Now!"

Two healers fled while the third stirred a mix of crushed herbs into a glass of water, which he then pressed against her father's lips. Her father jerked his head away from the pungent brew.

"Give me that." Margaret seized the offered glass and set it on the bedside table. "This useless mix will not help him now. Only the Thirteen can save him."

Her father moaned and kicked at her. "Shhhh...." she said as she pressed her hand into one of his. Those hands used to carry her. They used to hold her. "Things were much simpler before Adelei returned. I miss those days, Father."

"D-don't...." The word was less a word and more a croak as her father struggled to speak. He freed his hand from hers and lurched toward the glass.

Margaret reached behind his frail shoulders to pull him toward her where she pressed the glass against his lips. He took two meager swallows before falling back against the deep blue pillows. "Do you want any more?" she asked.

Her father shook his head as his eyes closed. "Don't blame...your sister."

"Anything you wish." She blinked back the moisture in her eyes. He could ask anything of her, and she would do it. Anything if it meant he would live.

He gave her hand a child-like squeeze, and when he opened his dark brown eyes, the pain had faded from them. They twinkled with humor and love in the moments before his seizures resumed and his body cried for relief.

"Itova, pass over him!" she cried as the healers behind her chanted the rituals of passing. Margaret seized a nearby cup and threw it. The cup bounced once before rolling across the rug. "Stop that!" she shouted at them. "He can't die! If you're going to pray, at least ask for him to live!"

The healer flinched but continued his litany. The bed ceased shaking, and her father grabbed her by the wrist. It hurt where his fingers dug in, but she ignored it as her father's eyes opened too wide. "Be a good girl and mind your sister, Margaret," he mumbled.

As suddenly as the shakes had come upon him, his body slumped into the bedding. His brown eyes, now almost black, gazed unblinking at the ceiling, and his chest rose no more. "Papa?" Margaret shook his shoulders. "Papa? Can you hear me?"

The door opened behind her, and Roland shuffled to the bedside. When his hands touched her shoulders,

Margaret shrugged them off. Her father's physician, for all he had training, knelt helplessly beside her father's body. Roland's hands hovered above her father's mouth and nose, then the physician moved his hands beneath her father's shirt where they rested against her father's chest.

"What are you doing? How dare you violate him so!" Margaret cried.

Roland glanced at her, but his hands remained in place until he gave a brief shake of his head. Behind them, the healer's chanting increased in volume.

"Stop!" Margaret yelled as she glanced over her shoulder. When her attention returned to her father, his eyes were closed. Margaret's breath caught in her mouth. *He's so still. Like a child almost.* Her vision swam, but she remained upright. She refused to faint. An army marched for her, and fainting would not save her.

I have to be strong now. There's no one else to be strong for me.

Margaret held her father's hand until the sun rose.

3

S ergeant!"

"What is it?" Leolin asked without taking his eyes from a patch of scraggly shrubs in the distance. Two years at the Sadai-Alexander border had left Leolin with a deep tan and a short temper. No one wanted into Alexander these days—not with the rumors of war on every tongue.

"Lieutenant wants to see you, sir!"

Leolin turned to face the young soldier. Pale face and a need to do the lieutenant's bidding marked the soldier a new recruit. Leolin had barely muttered his thank you before the soldier was off across the wall and down the stairs into the tower's cool interior.

What did the lieutenant want now? Yet another practice drill?

He followed the young soldier's path at a much slower pace, every now and again wiping sweat from his brow. When Leolin dipped into the shade he sighed openly, and several nearby soldiers chuckled in knowing response. The soldier outside the lieutenant's office saluted once before opening the door.

Sweat beads gathered on his balding head as Lieutenant Thomas paced behind his desk, an action he continued as Leolin approached and saluted. "Have a seat," the lieutenant said.

"You wished to see me, sir?"

Lieutenant Thomas's pacing halted a foot from Leolin's chair, where he handed Leolin a piece of folded parchment. "This letter came for you last week from Alesta. Go ahead and read it. I'm sure you'll plague me with a mound of questions until you do."

Last week? And I'm only now receiving it? Leolin ground his teeth. Leave it to the lieutenant to make him wait. When he flipped the parchment over, it bore the Alexandrian royal seal, two circles overlapping to create a sideways eight. The paper trembled in his hands. With his mother dead, there was but a single reason for him to receive a letter from the royal family. His mother's ashes.

Two years had passed since his mother, Former Captain and King's *Sepier* Ida Warhammer, had died. Two long years while he waited to entrust his mother's ashes to the Thirteen. When he opened the seal, the handwriting confirmed the rumors circling Breighton.

To Sergeant Leolin of the Alexandrian Royal Army

from the desk of Her Majesty Queen Margaret I,

It is with regret that We inform you that Our Father, King Leon Poncett III, has fled his mortal prison. News of his death has not been confirmed as the Shadian army gnaws at our border, but news will spread readily enough with the burning of Our Father.

Her Holiness of the Holy Few has held your mother's ashes until such a time that they can be mixed with Our Father's and carried by the Thirteen into the afterlife. It is an honor your mother deserved after many years' service to the crown. I know Our Father would have wanted this.

Our Father will burn on the eve of the twenty-fourth day of Cercian, and his ashes, along with your mother's, will be sung into the afterlife with the rising sun. Your presence is requested.

May your travels be swift and sturdy,

Her Majesty Queen Margaret Poncett I

His fingers brushed over her signature. *So formal.* Eight years since his mother had sent him away from, and eight years since he'd seen his childhood friend. Was time the reason for the formality, or was it something else? Leolin glanced at the letter again.

Two days until his mother's ashes would be at peace, but even if he left this minute, he wouldn't arrive until two days after. This was the lieutenant's doing. It had to be. Leolin closed the letter, then leaned forward to place it upon the good lieutenant's desk. Maybe he could use it to prop up the corner. "Sir, may I speak frankly?"

Lieutenant Thomas paused in his pacing and nodded.

"The royal family will honor my mother in three days and requests my immediate presence."

"I'm aware. They do *know* a battle approaches, do they not?"

"Yes—" Leolin froze as he followed the lieutenant's gaze to the royal signet. In his rush, he hadn't noticed the hint of red atop the deep blue. *Damn the Dozen! The bastard read my letter!* To Lieutenant Thomas he said, "Since you're aware of the situation, *sir*, you must know that with the delay in receiving this, arriving on time would be nigh impossible." *Not without killing my horse anyway.* "But with your permission, I'll be on a horse within a candlemark."

A curt nod of his pointy chin was all the good lieutenant gave as he returned to pacing, his back to Leolin.

He didn't wait for the lieutenant to change his mind as he flew from the room and packed with the speed of a messenger pigeon. One change in clothing and something more formal for the ceremony were all he allowed besides some dried meats and a water pouch. He tied the lone saddlebag to a horse and set off for Alesta at a gallop. Leolin's heart raced with his horse. No matter the ill occasion, he was going home. At some point he'd have to stop to allow his horse rest, but perhaps he could change mounts at Tarmsworth. *I could keep going with a new horse. Maybe even make it by the ceremony's end. Wouldn't be the first time I've eaten and slept in the saddle. Sharmus be with me and my horse.*

We'll need all the luck we can get.

BELOW MARGARET, CROWDS TRICKLED INTO THE castle bailey. Some walked singularly, but more often they were clumped into groups of twos and threes, each forehead marked with a thumbprint of ash to protect them from evil.

Her balcony remained empty for the moment as Margaret stood behind a thin veil of curtains. She was nothing more than shadow, assuming anyone below thought to look up the tower wall. As the sun had risen on the thirteenth day of Cercian, Her Holiness of the Holy Few had crowned Margaret, Queen of Alexander, before a full audience.

Where the people had come from, she didn't know. Against her wishes, the people living in Alesta had been ordered to flee, to head for the safety of another city, yet many returned to see her crowned. Many more to see their king burn.

The silver circlet had been polished until it shined like a spring day, but when it had touched her head, Margaret was five again. Her mother's dead weight pinned her to the horse as it wandered along, lost in the forest. Only when Her Holiness had sung of her crowning, did the sun touch Margaret's face and her mind return to the present.

Leon's council—now Margaret's—had pledged their allegiance in the span of a candlemark. Their faces had blurred in the dizzying mass of people. Similar to now as she gazed outside from the balcony. Finery gone, she waited for sunset in a simple gown of blue. Silver threads created the hint of circles at the gown's hem, a finery wasted on the day's darkness.

Somewhere beyond the sea of heads, Her Holiness and the other priestesses serving the Kingdom of Alexander marked each entrant with a mixture of ashes kept and prepared in the temple. *It's the spirit of our ancestors giving us strength*, her father used to say, though his words in her head gave her little comfort. Soon the sun would set, and her father's body would burn.

Behind her, someone knocked lightly on the door.

"Come," she said, and her voice cracked.

"Your Highness called for me?"

Margaret stepped away from the door as Dumont shuffled into the room. Red-rimmed and pale, his gaze paused at the crown on her head, then drifted to the floor.

"This day wears on us both, Dumont. I would ask your favor, if you would give it." When he nodded, she seated herself on a nearby couch and gestured for him to join her. The lines around his eyes tightened as he lowered himself to the cushion below, and Margaret frowned. "Dumont, before you were my father's Grand Advisor, you were his best friend. He told stories of you as boys running through these halls." She glanced at the painting of her father on the wall. "I would have you serve me, as you did him, but—"

"You worry how many races this old horse has left in him."

Her cheeks warmed, but she nodded. "I'll be Queen but a week when the Shadians arrive at our border. I'd be a fool to think otherwise, so I've no time for courtesies or niceties. Tonight, my father will burn, and tomorrow...tomorrow I must prepare to lead a kingdom into war. I need your help and your advice."

"It's yours for the asking, but I doubt that was the favor you had in mind."

A shout went up outside, and for a moment, Margaret froze. Whatever caused the outcry died down as quickly as it had sprung up. She pointed at the light that streamed through the door and unwound her fingers from her skirts. "The sun moves with the Senate's speed these days," she said, and Dumont said nothing, for which she was grateful. When she found her voice again, she whispered, "My council thinks me a fool, Dumont, and I fear they are correct. I have no head for ruling."

Margaret laughed, though the sound wilted on her tongue. "My instructors have taught me to read, to write, to understand maths and even the histories of our kingdom, but what do I know of war? My father taught me only of peace. My father, the Thirteen be with him, lies out there and all his knowledge with him. I was to marry someone who would rule, I think. He never intended me to rule alone, did he, Dumont?"

Dumont took her hand in his. Both shook—his from the ailments of age and hers from fear. Or was it exhaustion? When was the last time she had eaten? Or slept?

"Your father spoiled you, as he could not your sister, but you have more brains than naught since your prince turned traitor. You're not alone, Your Majesty. Your council exists to help guide you."

To rule for me, you mean.

She opened her mouth to speak the words but couldn't. Not even to her father's must trusted friend. Instead she said, "I'm glad for their council. All I ask is that you remain as honest with me as you were with my father." Another knock at the door made her flinch. "Come."

"Her Holiness is ready for you," a servant said before withdrawing.

Dumont's joints popped as he rose, and she touched his hand to stop him. "Will you stand with me tonight? I think my father would have wished it."

Tears gathered in the old man's eyes. "You do me great honor in asking, Your Majesty."

Despite the effort, she flinched at the title.

He didn't suspect her intentions, but just in case, she said, "I intended for Captain Warhammer's son, Leolin, to stand beside me, but it seems my message did not reach him in time. Since you were family to my father, I would be honored to have you with me. I think my father would want it."

The remnants of sun slivered across the floor as she took Dumont's offered arm. *I need to have someone fetch him a chair or stool. His old joints will not make it through the thirteen candlemark vigil.* Margaret held her head high as they descended the stairs to the first floor and kept it high as they exited upon the dais where her father's body lay waiting upon a stone and wooden cairn. Beyond her father lay another body, that of her sister.

Silk the shade of a deep lake wrapped her father's body from head to toe. Not an inch of him lay exposed to the elements. Her sister, too, was wrapped in blue, though this one of the skies. As Margaret approached, her nose burned straight down to the back of her throat, and her eyes watered. For a moment, she held her breath as she scanned the people gathered, hoping to find Leolin at the crowd's front, but his face was absent from the ceremony.

Her Holiness stood near King Leon's head, though wrapped as he was, his head and feet could be either end. Margaret took her place at the foot with Dumont a step behind her. While Her Holiness raised an eyebrow at the change in ceremony, she said nothing as silence spread across the bailey.

"This temple hovers between this world and the next. Only the flames can carry the vessel to the afterlife," said Her Holiness as she used a silver dagger to cut away a fingernail sized piece of the King Leon's shroud. She handed it to Margaret, who rested it on her tongue.

At Margaret's brief nod, Her Holiness cut a second piece—this one from Adelei's wrappings—and handed it to Dumont. Had she living family, they would have taken the piece of *meshoi*. Tonight, Dumont would serve as surrogate.

Not unheard of—not according to the histories Margaret had found in her father's personal library—but it would raise a few eyebrows for sure.

When Dumont stuck the piece of silk in his mouth, whispers wrapped themselves around Margaret's bare shoulders. She refused to tremble as Her Holiness continued.

"The temple is sacred. The temple creates life."

King Leon's city—now *her* city—echoed Her Holiness's words as the herb-treated *meshoi* burned Margaret's tongue.

Her Holiness exchanged the dagger for a small box. "Queen Catherine Poncett will accompany her husband into the afterlife," she said as she sprinkled a handful of ashes at the cairn's head.

Margaret's advisors watched with approval from their row of seats below the dais, and she blinked hard to keep from swallowing. *I'll know soon enough if they knew of Father's indiscretions.*

Tribute paid to the former queen, Her Holiness retrieved an unlit torch and held it high in the air. "The temple is a gift—a gift of life everlasting." As the attendees echoed the words, another priestess stepped forward with a flint stone and the dagger. The young priestess struck the two together thirteen times. Sparks landed on the torch, and Her Holiness blew on the tiny flame until it birthed fire. "Life should be loved and in the end, honored."

Margaret spit the *meshoi* into Her Holiness's waiting hand, as did Dumont. They both took the offered cups of brown liquid. Margaret swallowed it without hesitation, though her nostrils flared at the medicinal taste, which was almost as sharp as the *meshoi* had been. To pause or hesitate would tarnish her father's memory. *I look weak enough to my people as it is.*

In the time it had taken her to swallow, the torch's fire leapt across her father's body. Whatever alchemies the Holy Few had applied caused the flames to erupt in a wave of oranges and reds that released a sour smell.

"His Majesty King Leon Poncett III has been anointed and blessed by the Holy Few," said Her Holiness. She handed Margaret a blackened bowl of herbs. "May the God of Journeys, Farimun, grant him luck as his spirit travels to Itova's darkened halls."

Margaret passed the bowl to Dumont and a murmur spread across the crowd.

The old man's hands trembled as he whispered, "Your Majesty?"

He would forgive her or he wouldn't, but if she was to be in control of her council, she needed his unwavering loyalty. "I confirm Dumont Darras as my Grand Advisor and name him a member of the Poncett family. May he be known as Dumont Darras-Poncett, brother in more than spirit to my late father, King Leon Poncett III."

Mumbles and hushed whispers reached her, but she ignored them as she held her hands out for the urn Her Holiness held. Its polished stone was heavier than Margaret had expected, and she staggered dangerously close to the flames. Dumont seized her elbow and tugged her back, but not before she saw the burning silk molding itself to her father's familiar features. Bile sought to escape, and she clamped her teeth down to keep it firmly in her mouth.

"Former Captain of the King's Royal Army and King's *Sepier* Ida Warhammer, formerly named Shendra Abner of the Order of Amaska—" The crowd hummed as Her Holiness spoke, and below the dais someone cried out angrily. As Margaret located the voice's owner, several others took up the call.

"Traitor! Assassin!" they cried.

Her Holiness raised her arms above her head, and the sun's remaining light flickered as though no cloud crossed the sky. People held their tongues once more, and Margaret broke from tradition to speak. "My father's *sepier* and confidant, Ida Warhammer, shared a portion of my father's life that my late mother could not. She was more than a king's mistress! She gave her life to protect the two things that mattered most to her: my father and this kingdom."

She cast another glance at the crowd, but Leolin remained absent. *Forgive me, Leolin.* Margaret tipped the heavy urn until the ashes poured from it to the cairn. At her nod, Dumont scattered herbs across the flames to keep them burning. It was a risk to use the herbs this early—they might be needed as morning approached—but if the flames died from the ashes.... She couldn't risk it.

"Her ashes will lie with my father's and my mother's. May her spirit accompany them into Itova's Hall."

Someone nearby hissed, and further back someone booed. She had not expected people to actually object. Certainly not openly. "My father would have wanted both women he loved to be beside him," she called out. "To shame this is to cast a shadow on our kingdom. Let us remember the deeds of my father and his *sepier*."

The change in tradition done, Her Holiness touched the lit torch to the second body. While the flames spread, the priestesses of the Holy Few chanted in silence. Like cresting waves, the fire's tips burned blue as Dumont sprinkled a few herbs over the flames as they licked at the second shroud. Sweat sprinkled across his brow as the temperature around them rose.

"Iliana Poncett, formerly Adelei of the Order of Amaska, has been anointed and blessed by the Holy Few.

May the God of Journeys, Farimun, grant her luck as her spirit travels to Itova's darkened halls," said Her Holiness.

Another change and one Margaret had resisted. She might have been born a princess, but in the end her sister had died an Amaskan. To strip her of her past...but her advisors had insisted. *Forgive me, my sister. I fight one too many wars this day.*

The attendees' facial features ranged from shock and anger to sadness at the proclamation, but this time, no one spoke. If anything, they seethed. Her portion of the ceremony complete, Her Holiness stepped down from the dais to take her place with the other members of the Holy Few, who huddled nearby in their red robes. Their silent chanting continued as Margaret stepped back from the flame's heat.

"My father was a generous man and a fair king. He ruled over Alexander like his father before him and kept it safe when our enemies sought to tear it down. My sister lived to protect, to serve justice when others could or would not," Margaret said as night cloaked them all in melancholy. "Tonight we honor our king. We honor his *sepier* and partner, his Queen, and lastly, we honor my sister. Tonight we stand vigilant in their wakes. May they pass through and be welcome, as they welcomed you into this kingdom."

Would the Shadians wait until sunrise to breech the border, or had they already slunk their way across the Meridi Pass in the dark? As she continued the prepared litany of her father's deeds, the flames reached out for the stars. Surely her father's spirit would find peace with his daughter and his mistress. Surely they could forgive her for whatever came next.

As the half-moon continued its ascent across the sky, an acolyte of the Holy Few placed a chair nearby for Dumont, though Margaret remained standing as people approached the dais to pay their respects. Each one bowed before her father's cairn, though none bowed before her sister. Not that she blamed them.

A hundred faces and more passed before her, yet she could not tell if any meant her ill will. Not a single one.

What kind of Queen did that make her?

Margaret turned her face up to the stars and prayed.

4

At first, the empty homes had provided plenty of places for Bredych to hide and sleep, but with the king's death, people trickled through the gates, then poured through as they returned to their homes to await the burning. The longer he remained in Alesta, the greater chance he would be caught. Most of the Order's contacts remained, though many avoided him. One paused long enough in the streets to pass him a message, which set a fire in Bredych's heart. He had not approached the castle proper since the day Leon died. Maybe it was fear or old age that kept him from taking the risk, but on the thirteenth day of Cercian, he mingled in the crowds that gathered in the castle bailey.

Along with everyone else crowding through the gates, Bredych had received the ash blessing, though the priestess had hesitated a moment too long when she'd touched her thumb to his forehead. Maybe it had been his imagination, but her contact had momentarily burned his skin.

Rather than angle for a nearby view, he had tucked

himself near the left wall and claimed a seat with a family of five on some farmer's cart. The children pried dried chunks of mud from their sandals, which they tossed at each other in boredom. Though the wound at his jaw had scabbed over cleanly, the adults gave him disapproving glares until their youngest boy cried at the mud stuck up his nose.

Had he chosen a spot close to the dais, his hand-for-hire clothing would have been a dead giveaway in the mix of upper and middle-class citizens. The farmers beside him were all peasants and beggars come to pay their respects.

The King's body, that he'd expected, but who was the second? On a whim, he asked the couple, "'Cuse me, but who else they be burnin' with His Majesty?"

The woman's lips pursed silently as the man answered. "Don't rightly know. 'Spose we fin'out soon 'nough."

Bredych followed the man's glance. Queen Margaret stepped out onto the dais, and Bredych resisted the urge to stare. She held herself with a different kind of grace and her body was more curved, but there was no doubt she was Adelei's twin. Black hair and dark eyes, she moved forward with a sorrow Bredych understood too well. He didn't recognize the man near her, not even when she named him family. Bredych feigned mumbling when the crowd spoke and waited for the second body to be identified.

When Queen Margaret named Bredych's sister and mixed her ashes with King Leon's, Bredych's muscles tensed in unison. His sister was little more than a traitor, and certainly not royalty. No wonder people booed. His brain still processed his late sister's newfound honor when the crowd silenced. Her Holiness set fire to the second body and spoke a name.

His daughter's name.

Bredych leapt off the cart. People muttered as he pushed past them, until a hand clamped down on his shoulder.

"What's the hurry?" The guardsman did not release his grip, though a side-glance showed his gaze remained firmly on the dais.

When they stripped her of her Amaskan honor, Bredych opened his mouth, then shut it as he glanced sideways at the guardsman. Something about the man's demeanor…. Or was it the circular blue weave along his tunic's collar that marked him as something more than a mere guard? Rather than pull away, Bredych dropped his shoulder and fell to a crouch. The man had no choice but to release his weak hold and once free, Bredych faced him. "I only wish'd for a closer looksee. Never did see a famed Amaskan b'for," he said.

"Sure you haven't."

The crowd shifted as one-by-one, people moved forward to pay their respects to those dead and those left behind. Bredych used the jostling crowd to duck his way between a heavily perfumed woman in green silk and her escort. He was five elbows through the crowd when he spotted a certain mud-nosed boy a few feet ahead. Bredych scanned the faces around him—at least those he could see in the spotty torchlight. The rest of the boy's family was nowhere to be seen. Rather than give the guardsman another chance to find him, Bredych weaved his way through the masses in the boy's direction. "Where's yer da?" he asked when he reached him.

The boy pointed toward the dais where two fire-lit faces watched the flames as they flicked and whipped their way across the dead. At first, Bredych had missed it—for the man was one shadow among many as he kept to those without torches—but the glimmer when something metallic reflected the fires' lights gave the "farmer" away.

Bredych would never make it in time.

The man was too close to the dais, and half the crowd lay between him and Bredych, who pushed his way forward nonetheless. Whoever the man was, he moved like a farmer the same way that Bredych did. The length of his stride, the dip of his shoulder, even the way he lowered his face against the torch light, spoke of someone with fighting experience.

"You'll need to get in line, sir."

Bredych ignored the voice at his elbow as his fingers sought and found his throwing knives. His short sword had been checked at the gate, but they hadn't searched the thickly wrapped fabric at his wrists.

Someone ahead cried out as the man jostled into them, but by the time they voiced their displeasure, he had already faded into the shadows. Like Bredych, several guards searched the crowd, and finding nothing beyond a bruised lord, they moved on. Gaze trained on the spot below the dais, Bredych waited two breaths before the he spotted the glint of metal.

There.

Silver flickered in the fire a scant thirty feet away. Whatever weapon the man held moved toward his cheek as he mimed itching his ear. It would give away Bredych's purpose, but it was this or allow this man to mar his daughter's passing into the afterlife.

With only a breath of hesitation, Bredych vaulted off the shoulders of the man in front of him and let loose the throwing knife before falling to the ground in a roll. The farmer's arm fell away as the screams began. Bredych continued his forward momentum and reached the dais a breath before the guards. Blood splatters led away from the crowds and back toward the cart.

Beyond the flames, Queen Margaret stared down at Bredych with wide eyes. For a moment, he could almost believe they were *her* eyes—especially with the chill they held. He wrested himself away from their strange familiarity to follow the trail of blood. The farmer must have used the cart to blend in and better look the part of a traveler. But the kids? What had been their role? He could think of only one such group that would use their own children as shields.

The *Tribor*.

He doubled his pace, though it was difficult in the crowd's scattering chaos. The Holy Few chanted as he passed them, and he caught a glimpse of red-tinged brown a few steps ahead.

Bredych grabbed the man's shoulders as a guard cried out. "Halt!"

The throwing knife had left a river of blood down the man's throat. The guard caught the man as he wavered and fell, and Bredych lifted his hands in front of him. "I be meanin' you no harm. This man here was sent t'kill Her Majesty," he said with a glance at the empty cart. Whoever the woman and children had been, whether they had played a role in this or not, they had long since fled.

Bredych recognized one of the approaching guards—the one with that fancy collar who held his sword at the ready as he asked, "Sent by whom?"

"Iffen I may?" asked Bredych, and when the man nodded, Bredych pulled off the attacker's boots and hitched the legs of his breeches up to bare his ankles. The left one bore a single triangle tattooed in black ink. He gestured at the mark and said, "That there's the markin's of the *Tribor*." Bredych spit on the ground. "Looks like you gots a mess about. If you'll beg me pardon, I'll see meself out."

The guardsman's shoulders tensed as he stepped near nose-to-nose with Bredych. "My guards reported someone matching your description entering the city to...what was it? 'Help in the war,' I believe? I have yet to make your acquaintance as you've not reported to my lieutenant, so what's your real reason for being in Alesta?"

"Yo'r lieutenant?"

One guard punched him in the arm. "Doncha know who yer talkin' to? This here's Captain Fenton!"

Damn. Fancy collar definitely had meant something. It was poor luck being stopped by the guards, but now he'd been stopped by the good captain himself.

"How do we know *you're* not *Tribor*?" asked Captain Fenton, and he shrugged.

Bredych did not fight them as they removed his boots to check his ankles, not even when the torch moved dangerously close and burned him a smidge above his anklebone.

Evidently the captain wasn't satisfied as he seized the torch from one of his men and held it up to Bredych's face. "I saw you earlier this evening."

"Aye."

Strong hands—hands whose calluses spoke of many years of sword work—gripped his jaw and turned it this way and that. When Captain Fenton's gaze finally settled on Bredych's scar, the captain nodded to his men, who bound Bredych's hands behind his back. He could have escaped such an attempt, but with the way the captain stared at him, Bredych would be dead before he reached the gates. No

Amaskan could outrun the number of guards pacing the bailey.

"You're the third person to cross this border with such a scar. You may not be *Tribor*, but I can't trust that you're the friendly type of assassin either," said Captain Fenton.

Someone's elbow in his back nudged Bredych forward and away from the funeral pyre. When they passed the cart, a clump of dried mud hit him in the cheek. No one stared back, nor did any other dirt chunks find their way out of the cart. He should have said something to the guards. It might have earned him sway with the good captain, but something laid still his tongue. Maybe it was a risk to allow the *Tribor*-spawn to escape, child or no. A younger grand master would have shown no mercy, but surely the boy was innocent in this.

Bredych clenched his teeth as the guards corralled him through a door and down a torch lit hallway. Maybe it was this kingdom—here a month and already he had gone soft. Maybe he should have left when Leon died. Then he would not have felt the need to spare the child.

With a glance toward the captain, Bredych thought, *Hopefully I'll live long enough to regret the decision.*

WHERE THEY HAD TAKEN THE *TRIBOR* WAS A MYSTERY, but the guards had tossed Bredych into a room with a great heaping man whose wrists were like books and his chest as broad as the desk he sat behind. He had to be a man of some importance as the circles on his collar lay in overlapping rows, and his uniform was clean, though it stank from the burning. The man may not have seen a battle recently, but when he did, he would crush skulls in an impressive manner, of that Bredych was certain.

Captain Fenton cut the ties on Bredych's wrists, while the man behind the desk gestured for Bredych to be seated. "I'll stand if ya please," he said, and the man shrugged before flipping through a few pieces of parchment. Fenton approached the man and whispered something in his ear. Whatever it had been, the parchment fell into a messy stack on the desk as the man studied Bredych.

Rather than portray the nervous sword for hire, Bredych was himself: relaxed yet aware of the room and its occupants. Other than the man's wooden chair, two additional chairs awaited occupants in an otherwise plain room. A map hung on the wall behind the desk, and a simple wool rug blended in with the gray stone floor. Important or not, this was not the man's normal workroom, leaving Bredych to assume it an impromptu meeting.

"I am Levon Doublis, Grand Marshal of the Queen's Army." When the man spoke, his voice was the perfect picture of a military leader—all bark with the promise of bite. "I would have your name, sir."

"Maurus."

"And your family name?"

Bredych frowned. "Never did know who my da was."

"Your accent's almost perfect, I'll give you that. But you can drop it along with the rest of the falsities." Doublis pointed at Bredych. "You have an opportunity before you... Maurus. See, I find myself with a small problem. I've got a *Tribor* who's tried to kill the Queen on a day of mourning and an Amaskan who tried to stop him. The *Tribor* won't see the rising sun, but you, however, might if you're honest with me."

Saving the Queen to prevent the *Tribor* from

dishonoring Adelei's burning had been one thing, but to be honest with the Alexandrians? Bredych glanced at Captain Fenton, whose hand rested on the hilt of his sheathed sword. Doublis caught the glance and waved one hand in the captain's direction. The captain's jaw pulsed a moment before he took his leave.

When Bredych opened his mouth to speak, Doublis interrupted him. "Another of your kind was here before. A woman called Adelei, though she was known to us by another name as well. Oddly enough, she bore an almost identical scar on her jaw. I can't recall having ever seen an Amaskan before her, but if you're anything like the *Tribor*, I'm betting you have your own tattoos and marks. Possibly around the jaw?"

We are nothing like the Tribor. Pity you had to make that comparison. The metallic taste of blood spread across Bredych's mouth. "Very few could compare the Amaskans to the *Tribor* and live to talk about it," Bredych said, dropping his adopted accent. Long practice kept his muscles relaxed though they fought to move. "To do so after sending your captain away...some would call that a fool's decision."

Doublis's laughter never reached his eyes. "If you wanted me dead, I would be lying on the floor bleeding out like the *Tribor*. While Captain Fenton was convinced of this Adelei's goodness, I believe one killer is like another, no matter what markings they wear."

"Have you ever killed someone, Marshal Doublis?" asked Bredych, and the Grand Marshal's eyes narrowed. "Ah, I thought you had. One does not get to be Grand Marshal without taking a few lives. One could say that you and I are alike...if 'one killer is like another,' as you say. I came here seeking answers, nothing more. The funeral's timing was happenstance, and when the opportunity to rid this world of vermin presented itself, I took it. Nothing more."

"What answers were you looking for? Our Queen has made it very clear that Amaskans caught in Alexander would be killed on sight."

Bredych inclined his head a brief amount. "Rumor of death reached us—the Amaskan you speak of. Then news of others' deaths from our Order. I was sent to discover why."

"The why is easy. They crossed into this kingdom."

"Those people you killed without hesitation were her friends. They were her family. They were sent to find out why she was killed. If I recall correctly, she was summoned here." *By her own father. Did you know that? Or did Leon keep that information to himself until the end?*

It was Doublis's turn to nod, but when he remained silent, Bredych added, "I saved Her Majesty's life tonight."

"I suppose you did at that. How did you know the man was *Tribor?*"

"I didn't—not at first—but when the fires glinted off his weapons, I followed him to the dais. When someone raises a weapon, they only have two motives: to protect themselves or to harm another. Since there was nothing to protect himself from, I surmised the latter."

Doublis stood, his frame towering over the desk as he then leaned across it. "You will remain in this room until the sun rises. Since it was her life you saved, I will leave it to Her Majesty to decide your future."

"How do you know I'll not escape?" Bredych asked, and Doublis crossed the room in a few strides.

When Doublis opened the door, Captain Fenton entered carrying heavy iron chains. Doublis gestured again at the chairs and said, "I think it's time you had that seat...Maurus."

There were too many men between Bredych and the gate. Too many swords and too many innocents to get in the way. Maybe Queen Margaret could be reasoned with. After all, "Maurus" had saved her life.

Bredych took a seat and waited.

5

The barest hint of herbs remained in the bowl by the time the sun peeked over the horizon. The fire had long since reduced the bones of her father to ash, though its blue and red flames continued to devour the remaining herbs. While the ever-rotating Holy Few chanted silently, soon enough Her Holiness would iterate how the Thirteen had blessed her family, that it was the Gods' air that continued the flames, but watching the hints of blue dance across ash and bone, Margaret pursed chapped lips together. Not that she would know the practices of the Holy Few, but watching them, something more than simple prayers helped burn her family's remains. Besides, the Thirteen had allowed her father to succumb to poison. In the end, they certainly hadn't spared her sister. Their presence felt far away as the touches of plums and pinks filled the sky.

Her Grand Advisor, Dumont, had made it three candlemarks standing before he succumbed and settled into the proffered chair, leaving Margaret standing alone beside the cairns. By the last candlemark, her feet were partially numb, though not so much that they didn't ache with the spring chill.

As midnight had approached, the residents of Alesta left as they had arrived, a trickling few at a time, until only the Holy Few, Dumont, and Margaret had remained. Whatever guards walked the castle walls had done so silently, though it had unnerved her to see Captain Fenton and Grand Marshal Doublis pass by the dais every candlemark. Now that the sun blessed the sky, her people returned to see if the flames had survived the thirteen candlemark vigil. How many returned to see if *she* had survived probably surpassed the former.

She stood a perfect mask of grief and strength, though her cheeks were chapped and her feet asleep as she waited for Her Holiness to pronounce the dead had passed into the afterlife in Itova's Hall.

"It's almost time," whispered Dumont.

Margaret glanced to her right where he sat upon a wooden chair. "One would think the sun slowed, if only to delay our rest."

As her toes tingled with cold and ache, Her Holiness sprinkled a white powder across the embers, then used the ashes to tamp out any remaining flames. "While those dead have passed to Itova's grasp, the living remain. May we find peace in the knowledge they have found everlasting life. Every chill winter brings is but their breath reminding us that they live again." She gestured and the other priestesses scooped half the ashes into a silver urn engraved with sigils known only to the Holy Few. The rest were placed into a bowl which was handed to Margaret.

When she stepped forward, her legs trembled and pitched her forward into the cairn's stone remnants.

Dumont offered his arm to steady her, but she ignored it. *I must show no pain.*

Each step resulted in sharp needles as blood flow returned feeling to exhausted muscles. While guards stood between her and the crowd, every cough and random whisper as she passed left her flinching. When Margaret reached the outer gardens, she raised the bowl of ashes toward the sun and said, "May your spirits protect us, now and forever."

Margaret lowered the bowl to the ground and upended it. She lowered her fingers into the slew of ashes and spread it across the soil, where she mixed the two until the earth was an ashy-brown. When she rose, she resisted the urge to wipe the gray from her hands as she followed the path that would circle the garden thirteen times. Like fine silt, the ashes would bless the roses that grew there for many seasons. Seeing the earth covered in sunless gray tugged at her heart but she refused to dab her eyes when her vision swam. *I may know nothing of war, but Itova, you have given me too much knowledge of death. Father, please, tell me what to do. And give me the strength to do it.*

Some distance behind her, Dumont cleared his throat.

Margaret sniffed as she blinked back the tears. She exhaled with a slight shudder and closed her eyes. When she opened them, the crowd still waited.

One step after another. One breath after the next.

The empty bowl returned to Her Holiness, Margaret approached the castle. When the heavy doors slammed shut behind her, Margaret's knees buckled, and she landed on knees and knuckles on the stone floor.

"Fetch a physician!" Dumont shouted, but Margaret shook her head.

"I am fine, Dumont. Just tired."

Dumont—ancient before her birth and almost gray with exhaustion—offered his hand, but even in the privacy of the castle entryway, she ignored it. Before, she had been the background on an expansive canvas. Like a castle tucked into the corner and out of the way. But now.... Every guard was watchful. Every servant cast glances her way when they thought she wasn't looking. Even Her Holiness waited to take her cues from Margaret.

Small, careful steps carried her down the hallway. A trail of people—from the shuffling Dumont to her new lady-in-waiting—followed her toward the stairs at the hall's end. A set of footfalls fell out of sync with the entourage—a pounding slap to their minced taps—and Margaret tensed.

"Your Majesty!" Captain Fenton called.

Without turning her head, Margaret held her hand up and tapped two fingers together.

Her lady-in-waiting, a tiny slip of a girl, tiptoed forward. "Yes, Your Majesty?" she whispered, and Margaret winced.

At least her previous lady-in-waiting had come from an unusual background, one that left reason for her soft-spoken and diminutive demeanor. Margaret's council had been correct to recommend she dismiss the woman—of that she had no doubt. Her loyalties to Shad had left too many questions—but at thirteen, Lady Claretta de Gant was in some ways a mirror to Margaret's former self. Too quiet but naive enough to find trouble. *She reminds me too much that I'd rather sequester myself away in my bower than make ready for war.*

Margaret shook her head and said, "Tell Captain Fenton I will meet with him later this evening."

Lady de Gant closed her eyes a moment before she left Margaret's side. Something about the captain bothered the girl, though Margaret could not get Claretta to confide in her. At least not yet.

Halfway down the hallway, the footfalls picked up again, and Margaret stopped when Captain Fenton bowed beside her.

"Did Claretta not give you my message?" asked Margaret.

"She did, Your Majesty." Captain Fenton rose at her nod. "My apologies, but I have a matter of some urgency. Grand Marshal Doublis wishes to see you immediately."

Margaret refrained from sighing audibly by biting her inner cheek. Her body ached from a long night in the cold, and her heart panged from grief. She stifled a yawn, but when the captain remained by her side, she said, "I will receive you both in my fa—my sitting room in a candlemark. Whatever it is can wait until I have cleaned the ash from me."

The way his brows burrowed, creating a mass of wrinkles above his nose, a candlemark was too long a wait. But as his gaze drifted to the gray at her gown's hem and the ash that coated her hands, whatever words played on the tip of his tongue were swallowed back as he retreated. She managed to reach the stairs without further accosting, though her muscles quivered in exhaustion as she climbed to the fourth floor.

Dumont cleared his throat when she passed her father's rooms.

Of course. They are my rooms now.

"Thank you," she whispered before opening the door to the sitting room. It remained as it had been: rich, mahogany chairs with blue velvet cushions scattered throughout the small room, including the chair that had been her mother's; a rug that was a rainbow of blues and golds covering the space between chairs and fireplace; and books scattered across tables, along with parchment bearing her father's scrawl. Memories whispered promises that could not be kept. Her father would never again receive close friends from the comfort of his chair, he would never chat with her about the future, or hold her hand as she admitted her fears about marriage.

Like the sitting room, his study remained untouched, though a fine layer of dust coated both books and parchment. A reminder of his lengthy sojourn in his bed. Assuming the Shadians didn't invade immediately, the untouched letters would need dealing with, and she closed her eyes against the tears that threatened to overwhelm her. Most of the procession had left her at the door to her suite, but Her Holiness trailed behind her as she patiently waited. Entering the bedchamber left Margaret's legs unsteady as her father's prison stared at her from behind navy blue bed curtains.

If she opened them, would he still remain tucked into his covers like a child?

Servants had removed her father's personal clothing and replaced it with her own. Books and trinkets from her room had found homes in this new space, though her reading chair faced the window rather than the fireplace and the braided silk strand lay across the mantel rather than tucked inside her book where she had left it. The room was a mix of two people—a mix of the past and the now. As much as Margaret's body craved sleep, the idea of sleeping where her father had died left bile burning her throat.

Her Holiness touched Margaret's shoulder to guide her toward the bathing chamber. "If you're to meet with the Grand Marshal, we cannot dally."

Inside, a trail of red hibiscus petals led from the

doorway to the steaming bath tub. Margaret took a step forward, and Her Holiness tightened her grip. "Undress here," she said.

The only jewelry allowed to Margaret for the funeral had been her crown, which she removed with trembling hands and set aside on a table. She pulled the simple gown over her head, then allowed it to drop to the floor beside her. Her Holiness offered her a hand as she guided Margaret to the tub. After thirteen candlemarks standing, Margaret sighed with relief when tense muscles relaxed in the hot water. Rather than the typical soap she normally used, Her Holiness handed Margaret a white bulb. Dirt still clung to the soap and when Margaret created a lather, the scent released burned her nostrils straight back to her tonsils.

"This will wash away any lingering essence of death. Be sure to wash thoroughly," said Her Holiness.

The substance, which tingled her scalp, brightened her skin to a healthy pink. Behind the bathing tub, Her Holiness lit a stick of incense to cover the smell and chanted in the old tongue, *Ja'aran*. While Margaret could decipher a word or two, Her Holiness rattled off a slew of words too quickly for Margaret to follow. When Her Holiness finished, Margaret asked, "Do the dead really cling to us?"

Sometimes when Her Holiness smiled, she could have been Margaret's age, but when imparting knowledge as she did now, her features shifted to that of someone ancient enough to have served Margaret's father's father. The momentary glimpse of the woman beneath the title startled Margaret, and she swallowed hard. Saliva tickled the back of her throat and the mix of it, incense, and the soap sent her into a cough that near rattled her teeth.

"Itova is jealous of our time in Agaia's light. If She could, She'd take the world with her into the After."

Margaret renewed scrubbing her skin and when it shifted from a mild flush to a deep pink, she returned the soap to Her Holiness. Her legs trembled as she stood, and Margaret stifled a yawn as she stepped out of the warm water. She dried herself with the proffered cloth as Her Holiness extinguished the incense in silence. "Is—" The holy woman held up a hand for silence, and Margaret followed her into the outer dressing chamber where her handmaidens waited.

"Nothing more is required for the burial, but you should bath again this evening and again in the morning with the soap," Her Holiness said as she gestured to the servants who began to dress Margaret with an efficiency she had missed. "While your handmaidens may dress you, you should bathe alone these next two days in silence. For their safety and yours."

Her Holiness left Margaret before she could ask, though the question lay unanswered on her tongue. Had Dumont suffered the same cleanse? Did it even matter with war on her doorstep? More death would come soon enough.

Her servants pushed and pulled her along as they dressed her and brushed her hair until the melted candle wax hovered above the notch. Margaret arrived in her sitting room a few seconds before Captain Fenton and Grand Marshal Doublis entered, a bound man with stubbled hair in their wake.

The puffy round scar at his jaw bore an eerie familiarity, and when she caught the Grand Marshal's gaze, his slight nod confirmed her suspicions. They pushed the man to his knees before both men bowed to her. Captain Fenton excused himself to a position outside her door while Doublis sat in the proffered chair.

A second look at the Amaskan left her shaken. This

man wasn't an average Amaskan, he was an *old* Amaskan, something Adelei had implied never happened. The man was easily in his fifties—the age of her late father—if not older, and his body bore the scars to prove it. Old lines crossed his face and his hands. A jagged white line peeked out from the sleeve at his wrist. If he were stripped down, there would be more, of that she was certain.

"It must be of dire importance to bring an Amaskan before me during the mourning period," Margaret said, and was disappointed when Doublis didn't have even the good manners to react to her reprimand. "I assume it had something to do with the scuffle during the burial?"

Doublis nodded. "He says his name's Maurus, though I believe that about as much as I believe the sun to be green—"

"What is your name? Answer truthfully," said Margaret.

"My name is Maurus."

Margaret waved a hand at Doublis, who continued, "There was a man—*Tribor*, Your Majesty—at the ceremony. Maurus claims he was passing through to gather information when he spotted the *Tribor*. When Maurus saw the man pull his blade, he dealt with the assassin. I've interrogated this Maurus, but he's told me very little."

"Begging your pardon, Your Majesty, but I explained my purpose at length to your Grand Marshal. I suspect he didn't hear the tale of betrayal he wished and hoped you would order me silenced instead of...."

"Instead of what?" Margaret asked.

"Hiring me to deal with your problem."

Margaret flinched. "The Kingdom of Alexander? Hire an Amaskan?"

"And why not?" Bredych shifted his weight on his

knees. "You've done so before, an opportunity that saved your life in fact."

And what would you know of my sister, Adelei? Margaret frowned but said nothing in response. If there was one lesson her sister had taught her, it was to let the fools hang themselves.

"It was not by chance, Your Majesty, that I was there this morning to stop the *Tribor*. Where there is one, there are more, and they will keep coming for you until the job is done. I've stopped this one. I can stop another."

"How do I know that I can trust you?" She had expected a frown, but he gave her nothing. No twitch of the lip, no narrowing of the eyes. His wrinkled, gaunt face remained expressionless.

"You don't. But know this—had I wanted you dead, you'd be dead already."

Margaret glanced over the man's shoulder at Doublis, who inclined his head a fraction of an inch. "Why did you come to Alexander?"

"Rumors reached the Order of the death of an Amaskan. Others were sent to investigate and when they were killed, more were sent to find out why."

"And you are one of those 'others'?" When he nodded, she continued, "And what would you do if I told you that I ordered their deaths?"

His gaze met hers—two cold, gray stones amidst a calm lake—but he remained silent. Doublis slapped Maurus across the back of the head. "Answer Her Majesty, or I'll personally remove your tongue."

"Nothing."

"Nothing?" Margaret resisted the urge to smooth the wrinkles that furrowed her forehead. "You wouldn't kill me?"

"Murder is the role of the *Tribor*. I am Amaskan. Unless decreed by the Thirteen or my Order to take your life, I will not seek revenge." Doublis cleared his throat, but Maurus ignored the Grand Marshal. "Unlike *Tribor*, *we* follow the Thirteen."

Margaret nodded, then flushed. Body movements gave away information. Wasn't that what Adelei always said? When she met Maurus's gaze again, the corners of his mouth lifted slightly. *He's laughing at me!* Her cheeks burned at the thought.

"I will allow you to stay for the time being," she said and ignored the Doublis' glare. "If you can prove your trustworthiness to me and protect me, perhaps we might come to a more permanent arrangement." *And while you are here, I can find out more about your Amaskans. Not to mention why you are so keen on Adelei's death.*

She gestured for him to rise and then rang a bell on the side table. Her lady-in-waiting entered and bowed. Margaret said, "Please show Master Maurus to a guest room. See that some...proper attire is provided to him."

He bowed before he left and once gone, Grand Marshal Doublis sighed. "Your father would have discussed such an action with me before proceeding. To allow an Amaskan—"

"I am not my father."

"As you will, Your Majesty."

The days pressed against her bones like too-thick blankets in the summer, smothering her until she thought she might break. Only thirteen days since his death, yet the passage of time could have been an eternity. "My father would have done as he wanted, you and the council be damned, and you know it. Besides, this is an opportunity for us. A chance to learn more about our long-time enemy."

"And the enemy of my enemy is my friend, perhaps?"

He smiled a slow and cunning smile. The kind that made goose pimples dance across her skin and chilled her despite the room's heat. "We'll play along with this idea for now. Who knows? Perhaps we'll gain what we need to take down the Shadian army. Or better yet, the Amaskans themselves. By your leave, Your Majesty?"

She nodded, and he withdrew to leave her in a sitting room not wholly her own. Alone.

Maybe it was better this way.

Maybe it was better to be alone.

6

It would have been simpler could the man write more than his name. Then perhaps the audience chamber of King Havin Bajit of Shad wouldn't reek of manure and sweat. Not even the sweet-smelling incense burning beside him could mask the stench as the *Tribor* knelt before King Havin. "Whatever news you have, make it quick. I require time to air out this room before my son arrives home," said Havin as he gestured for the man to rise.

"Your Majesty, I gots news from Alexander."

While the man was smart enough to keep his gaze mostly on the stone floor, he glanced once in the direction of the woman sitting beneath Havin. She massaged Havin's bare feet, but it wasn't her deft fingers that caught the man's notice. Havin snapped his fingers, and the man's head snapped up to the stone throne. "You've not been in my castle before, have you?" When the man shook his head, King Havin continued, "I know. Do you know how I know?"

"No, Your Majesty."

"Because you've failed me, and you've only just arrived."

The man's gaze returned to the floor as sweat broke out across his brow. "Sorry, Your Majesty."

Havin shook off the woman's attentions, and she scurried behind his throne and out of view. When he stood, his tall frame cast a long shadow across the *Tribor*. The man balled his trembling fists on his thighs as he awaited punishment. When Havin tilted the man's face up to look at him, the *Tribor*'s eyes widened. "I assume you are newly *Tribor*, but surely when Rajami sent you, he warned you against looking upon your master."

"Y-Yes, Your Majesty."

"Tell me your news. If it's good, perhaps I'll allow you to live."

"King Leon Poncett III of Alexander—'e's dead, Your Majesty. Likely they be burnin' his body right now."

The small blade tucked into Havin's palm dropped within the *Tribor*'s view, and Havin grinned when the man tried to wrest his way out of Havin's grip. The King allowed it, his laughter splitting the silence like thunder. "This is good news indeed! *Tribor* man, tell me your name that I might remember who brought me such good tidings."

"Name's Mailei, Your Majesty."

When the King slapped Mailei on the shoulder, the *Tribor* man gave him a hesitant smile which faded as the blade pierced his heart. His mouth opened, but no sound escaped. "Thank you, Mailei, for bringing me such good news. Pity you had to ruin it by forgetting the rules, not to mention ruining my new carpet. I promise to remember your name...at least for a moment."

Mailei glanced down at the thick, green rug as his body collapsed, and behind Havin, the woman shrieked as blood soaked into the emerald fabric, creating a muddy brown the color of her eyes. When Havin turned toward her, she buried her face in trembling hands as he laughed. "Get me my son," he snapped to a waiting servant. "We have much to plan."

He laid a gentle hand on the woman's bare shoulder, and when she flinched, he knelt beside where she cowered. "I'm sorry, my love. I know how you hate the sight of blood."

She burrowed her face in his silk shirt while a scurry of activity occurred behind them. Once both body and rug were gone from the room, she released her hold on Havin. "If the evil King's dead, does that mean I'm safe?" she asked.

"Not yet." He brushed a tear from her cheek with a well-calloused thumb. "No one's safe until the Poncetts are but a moment in history. But soon, my love. Soon."

When she smiled, it warmed the chilly room.

There was *so* much to plan.

7

The idea of rest had left her knees trembling, though she had found it impossible to crawl into the bed that was once her father's. Instead, Margaret had sought refuge in rooms formerly hers, where she had slept until late in the evening. Only then had she returned to the rooms that had been his, and only then because she felt useless and helpless all at once. While the city mourned, her mind sought to escape.

Despite her belongings occupying the space, the room was very much his. The chip in the stone floor from something he dropped, the way the opened window hung slightly crooked from the way he had pulled on the knob too hard for too long. It was Margaret's rugs and bedding that decorated the room, but it mattered little. It was his frame that she pictured in her chair, and his footprints she imagined marred her rug's weave.

When she slipped through the door to his office, the smell of pine cones and crushed eucalyptus leaves threatened to set loose a waterfall from her eyes. Very little of her appeared in this room. Very little of her *belonged* in this room.

A brief stack of papers from her previous office—one she rarely used—sat on the corner of King Leon's wooden desk. Carvings of small dogs at play punctuated the gaps between treaties and books and inkwells. An unused quill sat beside a blank document and a well-used book she recognized by its untitled spine and rounded corners.

Her father's journal. Or the most recent of them.

Margaret flipped to the most recent entry, dated a month before her father's illness had left him bedridden. Mostly news from various towns in the kingdom, financial reports, and the odd note about his council. Partially through the entry, the handwriting shifted to a more relaxed hand. *He must have returned to it after an interruption.* Her name began the sentence on the next page, and she paused in her skimming to pay attention.

Word from the border is that the Shadian army moves closer to our border with each passing day. The Boahim Senate, for all that they hold the power, seems powerless to prevent the coming war. No matter how much I plead with them, they refuse to do anything more than wave their hands and entreat me to be patient. If my people die, patience will not be my friend nor theirs.

When I am gone from this world, Margaret will rule, a fact that scared me less upon Adelei's return and more upon her death. Adelei would have been the strength Margaret needed, and now that she's gone, Margaret will be alone. Knowing my council, they will attempt to rule over her rather than advise her, and she won't have the strength to assert her position. I fear I've done her a great disservice in my raising of her. She has her mother's gentle disposition, something that won't serve her well as Queen. I thought perhaps her marriage to Gamun would give her spirit, but I fear his abuse only served to drive her further within herself. If she doesn't find her own strength, she won't know how to fight the battle that's coming.

Agaia, Goddess of Life, grant me the strength to survive this ailment. I can't yet leave this world. She's not ready!

The letters of her father's signature blurred, and Margaret blinked rapidly to keep the tears in check. Not even her father had had confidence in her ability to rule, yet he had gone and died anyway, leaving her alone. He was right—his advisors ignored her opinions the way one tries to ignore a small child underfoot—and it stung.

The next page bore a partial entry written in a hand that trembled, leaving the letters jagged and blotchy.

These orbs...I speak some words and can speak with the Boahim Senate miles and miles away, but to what end? They neither help, nor can I think they wish to. I can't help but cringe when I meet with my advisors knowing that the orb lay in such close proximity. What's to keep them from listening to everything we say and every decision we make? Is this how they enforce the Thirteen? Do they lie and listen, waiting for some sin to be committed? Then strike out in the name of Justice?

How very Amaskan of them. I must warn Margaret.

Margaret flipped through the following pages which remained blank. *Must warn me of what? Using the orb, using the council room, or something else entirely?* When she tucked the journal into a desk drawer, a worn corner poking out of a stack of otherwise neat papers caught her attention. She tugged at it until the parchment was free, then set it on the desk in front of her.

Scraggly letters in a hand she didn't recognize begged forgiveness of her father. Margaret flipped the parchment over until her gaze rested on the signature. Sepier Ida Warhammer, the late King's spy and confidant. Formerly Captain of the Royal Guard and King Leon's mistress, and before her time in Alexander, an Amaskan. She shivered to recall the puffy scar that had run from ear to ear across Ida's throat.

The date on the letter placed it a day before her father had ordered Ida to the Shadian border in pursuit of *Tribor* assassins. Her face grew warm as her gaze crossed over a rather intimate paragraph, but it was further down the page that sent her skin prickling.

Leon, if I don't come back from this, if the Tribor or the Shadians or hell, the weather kills me before you're ready to talk, I hope you'll forgive me in time for my role in Iliana's abduction. I'm not big on lookin' back at what can't be changed, but there're things in my past that would be best kept there, and others still that Leolin will need to know. Things about his father and how he died. Give him the attached letter. It'll explain everything. He'll be hurt, Leon—a lot like you actually—but maybe one day he'll understand why I kept the truth from him. Promise me you'll tell him about the woman I became, not the woman I was.

The letter continued another paragraph or two, these expressly about and for Margaret's father, and she put the letter aside to dig for the aforementioned attachment. Empty parchment, a used ink jar, and a few scraps of random notes were all the desk drawer comprised. Whatever letter Leon was to have passed along, he had either hidden elsewhere or sent along already to Ida's son.

Margaret would have to ask Leolin when he arrived. Whenever that would be. He had already missed his mother's funeral.... She stretched her fingers out across the desk's wooden top and stared at the map tacked to its surface. Most of it lay under the mound of parchment, but the *Harren Sea* peeked out from beneath a stack and with it, the unnamed island where the Boahim Senate resided.

It would be so easy to ask for help.

The Shadian army's promise to cross their border served as a direct violation of the Thirteen Laws. Or so she had been told.

Damn the Thirteen.

Everything was *told* to her. Everything was handed to her in reports and given to her in whispers. Everything but what she needed. Margaret swore again, and her face grew warm. If her father didn't have the answers, perhaps her sister would.

If the guards were surprised by her return to her former rooms, they gave no indication other than to open the locked door leading to the former royal nursery. While her sister's residency in the temporary guest room had been brief, the only change since her death was a thick layer of dust that coated every surface. *I guess Papa couldn't bear to have it touched. Not that I blame him.*

Margaret set her candle on the lone desk. While rather dark in the windowless room, enough light streamed in from the sitting room to give a clear view of Adelei's room. The chest at the bed's foot opened easily to expose Adelei's clothing. Margaret picked up an article at random, a head scarf, and held it to her nose. When she inhaled, the mild hint of sandalwood made her smile, and a quick riffle through the chest identified the smell's source. A small, incense bundle lay wrapped inside a cloak, along with two bound books.

The first, a slim, green book, bore only a circle on the cover, while the second carried no decoration or embellishment, only a simple binding. Margaret set aside the plain book in favor of the first. When she glanced at the spine, she gasped. *The Book of Ja-ahr! I didn't realize she had brought this with her!*

Holding the holy book of Adelei's Order was almost like having her here again, or at least a piece of her. Margaret curled up on the dusty bed where her sister had once slept and flipped through the first section. Mostly histories of the Order, the book's ebb and flow held a poetic style, which shifted once the book delved into the beliefs of the Amaskans.

During the darkest moments of our days, only then will we be made to see the light. But only if one is a vessel worthy of receiving. Prepare the vessel to be worthy. Come before the Gods as an empty being. Come vulnerable and willing, and you shall receive balance, clarity, and neutrality, the three tenets necessary to serve Justice.

Margaret frowned. There was nothing light about her father's death. There was no justice in his passing, nor in her grief's darkness. She skimmed a few more pages and stopped when she spotted her sister's handwriting in the margin.

Remember, be like stone.

Had that been her secret? The way her sister maintained her strength despite the Thirteen Hells that threatened to swallow her whole? The note had been penned to the right of something called the *hagahi*, a "meditation to calm the mind." Margaret glanced at the chest where the incense lay. Perhaps she could find peace in something that brought it to her sister....

The old incense's tip crumbled at the touch, though it lit readily enough, and she set it on the desk beside her candle. Weaponless, though dressed, was what *The Book of Ja'ahr* had instructed, and with a glance at the empty sitting room, she complied. Both throwing knives and the dagger at her waist she laid on the bed. After lowering herself into a cross-legged position on the floor, she set the holy text in front of her, its pages dancing in the candle light.

"Empty the vessel," she read from the book. "Like water, I flow to the sea. Nothing between it and me."

She repeated the phrase twice more and when nothing happened, she frowned. "What does that mean? Am I supposed to be stone or water?"

The incense burned while wax dripped from her candle, yet no sudden wisdom filled her mind, nor was there peace from the grief that gnawed at her heart. *I thought this would have answers for me as it had for you. But I must be missing something. Or maybe I'm too weak to be worthy.* Margaret snapped the book shut, stood, and tossed the book on the dusty bed beside her weapons.

Though plain, the untitled book caught her attention.

When she opened it to its first page, small and smooth handwriting gave ownership to the personal journal, and Adelei's voice filled her mind. Margaret's cheeks grew warm at her sister's initial thoughts about the assignment that had sent her home. *She hated me, at least at first. Though one could hardly blame her. My naivety alone was enough to test the most patient of wills.*

Margaret flipped to the last entry, and tears blurred the words on the page. The candle wouldn't make it through the reading of it. With trembling hands, she returned her weapons to her person before gathering up both books. The incense would burn itself out, though she carried the candle with her to her rooms, where she settled into her mother's blue chair. If *The Book of Ja'ahr* couldn't answer her questions, perhaps her sister could....

I find myself in the oddest of moods as my time in Alexander grows short. It's not so much that I can't handle someone as dangerous as Prince Gamun or the Tribor who beg his favor, but it's the Senate that worries me. Sooner or later, our father will have to call on them. He doesn't see the power they hold over him, but it's all I see.

Once I gain the needed evidence against Gamun, our father will summon the Senate to get Margaret out of this horrific sham of a marriage. Then their gaze will fall to me —the once-a-princess-now-a-killer who's been brainwashed by her Master and other father. The Amaskan who's a danger to everyone around her. Maybe even herself.

They'll call for me to confess my sins or betray my family, possibly both families if I'm honest, and I can do neither. Something in the way Margaret looks at me these days... I know she feels it, too.

Despite this, I worry about this sister of mine. I can almost believe her capable, but sometimes the words that spill out her mouth make me wish for Itova! Typical of a sister, I suppose, but how could someone be so selfless and yet so selfish? How can one be so brave and yet so afraid?

And a queen can't be afraid. If being here has taught me anything, it's that a ruler must be strong. In some ways, stronger than an Amaskan. Master Bredych would wince to hear my thoughts, but it's true. I've watched our father split himself into two men in order to do what's best for his people. Even with Ida's death, he brushed his grief aside like water when asked.

It's a duality we Amaskans appreciate, though not one I'd expected to see outside the Order. It's certainly a duality I don't see in Margaret. Or I hadn't until recently. She knows her father's dying and begged me to help her be a just and good queen, but that's not knowledge I can give her. Only experience can teach her how to do right by her people.

"Like water over stone" she must embrace that which would hurt her. Separate the emotions that would weaken her. Only then will she be capable of making tough decisions.

Decisions our father has made from the very beginning. Gods! Why am I only now seeing this! Now when I have so little time?

Gods be with her and with me as well.

Adelei had known the Senate would use her, yet she had gone willingly into their reach! Margaret rubbed her eyes as she stared at the journal. There was wisdom in her sister's words. A queen couldn't be afraid. *Like Papa, I must brush aside my grief. Like water over stone, was it?* Deep inhalations steadied her mind, though they did little to calm the way her heart trembled.

Maybe not today, not when her father's ashes lay as new soil in the gardens, but soon she would find the strength she needed to protect her people.

At least I hope so.

8

Four guards trailed behind Margaret as she left her rooms the next morning, but it was not until she reached the castle's second floor that she noticed the fair number of servants in the halls. They shuffled this way and that as they carried all manner of bags and belongings. She paused outside the ambassadorial suites to watch a wiry man with equally wiry hair struggle with a leather handbag. He flinched when he spotted her, then bowed deeply. "Your Majesty."

"Ambassador Ruisso," she said, her gaze dropping to the bag tucked beneath his arm. "Has Monpoli recalled you?"

The top of his almost bald head flushed as scarlet as his cheeks. "I'm sorry, Your Majesty. Y-yes, Your Majesty."

Margaret frowned. "I received no notice of your replacement. Does something ail your father again?"

"N-no, Your Majesty." The bag shook in his clutches as he bowed a second time. "I've been t-told to return to Monpoli at once."

"So I gathered by your rush to escape your rooms."

"If I may?" he asked, and when she nodded, he rushed down the hall as fast as his shortened stature allowed.

Margaret leaned back against the wall to watch the scurry of activity. The grass green and silver of Lorecliff and the sky blue of Halelind, followed a few moments later by the rose red of Nicen; servants carried royal colors from their guest suites and down stairs, presumably to the stables. Monpoli wasn't the only kingdom recalling their ambassador.

By the time she had reached her council chambers, Margaret had counted half a dozen ambassadors leaving in addition to the visiting lords and ladies who had arrived in time for her father's burning. Six members of her father's—now her—advisory council stood when she entered and claimed the seat at the foot of the ovular stone table. Its wooden inlay held a carving of a tree, its branches and roots reaching out to each seat at the table. When she rested her hand on its oak surface, it whispered from far away in a language long dead, and she sighed. Two chairs remained empty, Dumont's, and the one her sepier would take. The latter was a position she had not filled, not since Adelei's death, but the former should be there.

Where is my Grand Advisor?

As if summoned by the thought, Dumont hobbled in, his wooden cane leaving behind indentations in the rug that had been her father's favorite—something her mother had woven during the long candlemarks while pregnant with Margaret and her sister, Adelei. A servant placed a platter of cheeses and fruits on the table before pouring mulled wine into several cups. Margaret dismissed her with a hand before asking her council members, "Have you noticed the unusual...traffic in the castle today?"

Several nodded their heads, including Dumont, who

said, "There is quite the foot traffic on the second floor in particular."

"The ambassadors are being recalled, as the council suspected they would be." Margaret glanced around the table. Roland, the royal physician, studied his wine as if it contained either poison or an antidote—which, Margaret couldn't be sure—while Grand Marshal Doublis glared at her with a fury she did not understand. She took a sip of her wine, then asked, "Do you wish to add something, Grand Marshal?"

"No, Your Majesty."

Margaret frowned, but Captain Fenton gave a slight shake of his head. Whatever bothered her Grand Marshal, now was not the time. Lord Cornish and Lady Mara Britus sat next to each other, both stifling yawns. Six advisors and not a one of them a true friend. *How often had my father found himself alone in this crowded room?*

"I fear it's worse than that, Your Majesty. We expected the ambassadors from kingdoms sympathetic to Shad to leave Alexander," said Dumont. Deep circles under his eyes matched Margaret's own, and the old man tugged at his tunic as if suddenly noticing its crookedness. "This morning, the ambassador for Liallan left."

"Last we spoke, he made no indication to such an action," Margaret said.

"We weren't expecting our supporters to leave at all. Much concerning." Dumont glanced at Lady Mara. "You've family in Liallan who hold favor with Queen Lorellyn. Perhaps you could inquire as to the reason?"

"I'll inquire at once," said Lady Mara as she clutched the chipped ruby that hung around her neck. Its former brilliance waned the longer the woman wore it.

Replacing the woman would be a priority...if the

upcoming battle gave Margaret a moment to do so. "If even our allies are abandoning us, what does this mean in terms of the possible war with Shad? Are we to lose the battle before it has begun?"

Grand Marshal Doublis frowned. "More kingdoms will join. The battle won't stop with Shad."

"Civil war? But there hasn't been the hint of one since Boahim fell and the Boahim Senate formed." Margaret gripped her cup with both hands to hide their trembling.

"The Boahim Senate are fools if they refuse to intervene," said the Grand Marshal.

While the faces of the Thirteen carved into the tree were meant to comfort, Margaret could not escape their gazes. Whether she turned her head this way or that, their eyes appeared to follow her, and she shivered. Were they like the orb? If her father suspected the Senate used the device as a means to spy on the royal family, could they do the same with stone?

"Maybe that's the point. Perhaps the Senate wishes for war," said Dumont.

Margaret gasped. "But to what end? What do the dead gain them?"

Dumont shrugged. "If I knew that, I suspect we'd all sleep easier, Your Majesty. I don't know what they aim to get from such a coup, but they're planning something. In the past, if there was even the hint of armies gathering at a border, the Boahim Senate stepped in. You're right to be concerned, Your Majesty, and you must know, your father didn't trust the Senate any more than he trusted the Shadians."

But what reason is that? I wish I had paid more attention in my father's meetings with the council. If I ask, my council will know me for the fool I am. Margaret took a long drink from her cup, then a second. *I wish this wasn't watered down.*

"The Senate follows a law of their own making. Who are we to question it?" asked Lady Mara.

Margaret's third drink of the mulled wine was soured by Lady Mara's inaneness, and she resisted the urge to kick the woman beneath the table. Reading through her father's notes had revealed his distrust of a senate that increasingly refused to follow its own laws, but the notes lacked any real substance. But if she told Dumont about the notes, it would reveal the orb's existence. *Father was adamant about keeping it secret. Another mystery I'm left to solve.* Rather than break her vow, Margaret pressed her lips together.

"Perhaps you could send word to our senator?" Dumont suggested and returned his empty glass to the table. "Maybe he will be more understanding of our plight."

Her gaze settled on her now empty glass. They all waited for her to make a decision or come up with a grandiose plan to save them all. As if she possessed the answers to all the Little Dozen Kingdoms' problems. When she shook away her thoughts, their gazes rested on her, and Margaret bit her lip. "Leave me. I must think on this further. Let the frightened ambassadors leave. For all we know, they return home to fortify their defenses in case the Shadian army decides to issue official declarations of war." Margaret spoke the words, but they rang hollow.

The Shadian army did not march to practice weapons any more than Prince Gamun had married Margaret for her beauty. But why his father, King Havin, blamed Alexander for his son's death escaped her. *The Boahim Senate ordered his death. If anything, he should blame them.* The closer their army drew to the Meridi Pass, the more Margaret's stomach tried to twist itself into one of those knot puzzles her father had loved.

She knew as little about war as she knew about love. She needed someone she could trust. Or perhaps someone who could be bought.

"Dumont?" she called out and her Grand Advisor paused on his way out the door.

"Yes, Your Majesty?"

"Have the Amaskan invited to dinner."

THE INVITATION TO A ROYAL DINNER CAME AS NO surprise—after all, Bredych *had* saved the Queen's life—but receiving such a formal invitation had startled Bredych. He'd traveled light across the border, with little more than his persona's mercenary garb in his packs and certainly not the finery required for King Leon's final banquet. As such, Bredych had required the Lord Steward's assistance to ensure he didn't disgrace himself before using this potentially new resource.

The Kingdom of Alexander might have been making ready for war, but it didn't show in ways Bredych expected. There was a thinning of ambassadors and certain lords and ladies, but at the final banquet, the wine flowed and delicacies were lofted through the great hall on servant shoulders. It spoke of a calm that shouldn't exist on the twilight of war. A servant seated Bredych at the high table across from the Queen, who had yet to arrive.

To Bredych's left sat the Grand Marshal, whose jaw throbbed with every glance in Bredych's direction, and beside him, the good captain. To the right was a haggard lady drowning in enough emeralds to clash rather than complement the particular violet shade of her corset. Nestled in the green, a lone, chipped ruby on a dirty chain. She took offerings from each offered food platter but made no motion to ingest any. When she spotted Bredych watching her, she pursed her lips together and said, "I take it you're the sword-for-hire who saved Her Majesty."

"I am. And who might you be, my lady?"

Her brow furrowed. "Lady Mara Britus, member of the Queen's Council. I suppose you have a name?"

"Maurus."

"Just Maurus?" Bredych nodded and she said, "Typical mercenary bastard then."

Queen Margaret chose that moment to make her entrance, her figure a mere shadow along the back wall. Whether she had chosen to observe a minute or two before being announced or it was a product of her demeanor, he knew not, though he kept the smile from his face by glancing instead at Lady Mara, whose frown deepened. Margaret's gaze lingered on Lady Mara before it flitted to him. A herald announced the Queen's arrival, and wood scratched across the stone floor as those eating paused to stand.

Once seated, Bredych returned to his stool where he clenched his hands in his lap as those brown eyes remained on him. Eyes so like his Adelei's. The fire in them—he hadn't expected that—and the sorrow. The loss. For a moment, he almost forgot his purpose as he lost himself in past memories. So much so that he didn't hear her speak until she repeated herself.

"How are you enjoying your visit to Alexander?" she asked.

"Quite well, Your Majesty. Thank you."

Her facial muscles twitched. She wished to ask him

something further but held her tongue, leaving him to the inane complaints of Lady Mara. Bredych kept his commentary to a minimum, choosing instead to observe, like the Queen had upon entrance to the Great Hall.

Short fingernails spoke of the Queen's worry as did her lack of appetite. The food might have been plentiful that evening, but like Lady Mara, she touched little of it. She smiled when spoken to, but the expression never lit her eyes as it should, nor did she utter more than an occasional pleasantry. Not even colored powders could hide the dark circles under her eyes or the gauntness of her cheeks. Queen Margaret avoided speaking to him directly, but when he answered Lady Mara, the Queen leaned forward an inch or two as if to listen. Servants arrived to usher away left over food and dishes, and a harpist entertained them while the high court nibbled on a dessert of fresh fruit.

Those seated at benched tables stretching the room's length took their leave first, and still she said not a word to him. It wasn't until Lady Mara and others seated at the high table trickled out that she turned her attention his way. "Master Maurus, how did you know that man was *Tribor*?"

He smiled gently at her worry. "Who else would attempt to kill someone during a burning ceremony? Only the *Tribor* lack such ethics."

"He bore the mark. On his ankle, though I suppose you would not have been able to see that with his boots on. Grand Marshal Doublis said you spoke to the man. Tell me about him."

"I asked him who was being burned alongside the late king, and the man admitted he didn't know. After that, we spoke no more."

"The *Tribor* gave you no indication to his identity or his purpose?"

Bredych shrugged and said, "No, Your Majesty."

Her hands curled into fists on the table as she stared off at something unknown in the distance. He allowed her a moment to calm herself, though her fists remained clenched when she next spoke. "You speak as one with morals, yet you're Amaskan. Had I not met one such as you, one rare enough to be bound by a moral code, I would think Amaskans no better than *Tribor*. Are all Amaskans like you?"

"Amaskans live by the words of Anur, God of Justice."

"He's also the God of War. Not exactly the most... peaceful of deities for a group sworn to uphold the Thirteen. I would think Asti's blessing a better choice, if the Amaskans truly wish Justice."

Bredych flinched. Her words came nigh close to the test given in secret greeting between Amaskans. Had it been coincidence or had Adelei told her sister more about the Amaskans than she should have? That should have been impossible—not with the conditioning in place.

"Would you like more wine?" she asked, interrupting his thoughts. Her gaze didn't waver from him, not even to blink.

He nodded to cover his mistake, then swallowed a large mouthful of newly poured wine. Rumors had painted Margaret as a simpleton, a delicate flower who sat upon a thorny crown and cried at the unjust scenery, but this woman before him was hardened, less naive than he'd been led to believe. For a moment, if he closed his eyes, he could almost allow himself to believe it was *her*.

But she wasn't—a fact proven when he opened his eyes.

Strength and fear warred for dominance in her. He would have to tread carefully.

Fear won out, and she asked, "Have I offended you by

asking this question? I know there are some things held sacred to the Amaskans, information being one of them, but I fear civil war is at my door. If I'm to keep my people safe, information is something of a critical commodity."

"You've given no offense, Your Majesty. You spoke of meeting another Amaskan. May I ask who, if you knew their name?"

Queen Margaret glanced around at the few who remained in the Great Hall: mostly servants, though some lord lingered nearby as he chatted with a guardsman. Whoever it was resembled no threat, and she answered, "My sister."

He set his face to one of puzzlement at her confirmation. "I thought Princess Iliana died during the Little War of Three."

"My sister was kidnapped by your leader in an attempt to destroy my father. When she returned to us, she was no longer a princess but an Amaskan. Before her death, she served her Kingdom well in providing information about your Order to my father."

She's lying. She has to be. Adelei's conditioning would never have allowed her to share Amaskan secrets. Bredych swallowed another gulp of wine, not tasting a drop. "Amaskans are sent all over the Little Dozen Kingdoms on a variety of jobs, and while I admit I'm not told of every job accepted by my Order, I'm not aware of anyone being sent into Alexander. There's a saying among my people—once an Amaskan—"

"Always an Amaskan. That was a phrase she used too."

"I'm not sure I follow." His own lie lay like poison on his tongue. If she was implying what he thought she was, if the Alexandrians had found a way to break the conditioning—

"My sister returned to us broken. Her mind and body

used for a purpose that serves no one, especially not *justice*." The words spit from her mouth sparked a deep anger that singed her brown eyes with hints of red. "In the end, she was more than an Amaskan. She was my sister. Do you have siblings, Master Maurus?"

He shook his head. Another lie, and he wished his glass held more wine.

"I thought not. Siblings don't keep secrets from one another. In the end, my sister had little else to do but talk. Even in her last moments, she spoke of the Amaskans. 'If justice is to prevail,' she said, 'then there's no room in this world for *Tribor* and Amaskans.'"

She might as well have punched him. What had they done to his daughter, to Adelei? Who was this woman to speak so casually of Adelei betraying her people and her way? What powers did this Queen Margaret possess to have bewitched Adelei?

Unshed tears gathered at the edges of Margaret's eyes as she spoke. "Before they hung the noose around her neck, she whispered something. I have never been one who believed the Thirteen watch our every breath and action, but someone or something stood beside me as my sister died, Master Maurus. Though it was impossible, I heard her words as if she whispered directly in my ear."

"And what was it she said?" he asked.

"Home is where I die. Delorcini has blessed me twice."

Every year of his life weighed upon him as she spoke. The one person who meant the most to him was not only dead, but she had died an oath-breaker. "I'm glad your sister found her peace with both worlds in the end. I wish I could have met such a person. The way of an Amaskan is never an easy path and many forgo family for that reason. But you spoke of civil war. Is that why I'm a guest in this castle? Do you wish to use me in your war with the Shadians?"

Queen Margaret's gaze softened as she leaned across the table and whispered, "I could use you, yes, but what I wish is your help. While my council would advise against it, I know what it means to be Amaskan...or I believe I do. I find myself in short supply of allies these days and could use someone...to advise me in matters well beyond my experience. Though it pains me to admit it, war is not something I understand."

"And you think it's something I know?" he asked, and she flushed as she nodded. "How would such an agreement benefit me?"

When she answered, the heat rose to her eyes again as they sparked in the candlelight. "Justice."

She played a dangerous game. Had she any idea *how* dangerous? Justice against the Shadians? Or against the Senate?

Margaret was more alike Adelei than she realized. The corner of his mouth perked up as he nodded. The laughter stayed with him until he retreated to his room, where he shed his clothing and knelt his knees to the hard, stone floor. Whether the daughter of his heart was an oath-breaker or not, her soul traveled on to the halls of Anur to further serve in the afterlife. Or perhaps it dwelled here, closer to the home of her birth, where it guided her sister toward Justice.

Once an Amaskan, *always* an Amaskan.

9

Your Majesty, while I appreciate your...difficult situation, those fleeing the border bring stories of armies marching toward Alesta. What will you do to protect your people?"

The vassal before her spoke with a trembling voice that mimicked Margaret's hands as she listened. Older than her by many seasons, he was the fifth in the past candlemark to speak on the "Grand Army of Shad." Men stationed at the pass spoke of Shadians and Alexandrians alike fleeing mounted troops who killed indiscriminately. Whether it was true or not mattered little when the frightened homeless arrived in a flood at her gates.

"Our royal army will protect the people of Alexander," she said, her hands buried in her skirt layers to hide their shaking. "Grand Marshal Doublis watches the border, and We have called upon the Boahim Senate."

While he nodded at her words, the worry lines never left the man's face. A long line of citizens snaked through her formal audience chamber, and as the man stepped away, a woman trudged forward, a small child in her arms. "Speak your peace," said a herald, and the woman held the child out before her.

Dark bruises stretched across the child's arms and legs, a crusty scab sat atop a knot on his forehead, and his eyes stared up at her with an emptiness that cut deeply. "M'boy, Yer Majesty. This's what them Shadians did t'him. Ya sit up there worryin' 'bout 'em, but they're already here, hidin' where ya least 'spect 'em. Ya best do somethin' more than talkin'."

As the woman carried her son away, Margaret dabbed at the corner of her eyes with her sleeve. The more they filtered through her audience chamber, the more she clenched her teeth to keep from screaming. Her father had burned two days before, yet everyone's expectations and pain left her ragged. By the time her Grand Advisor had sent the remaining vassals away for the evening, Margaret required a hot bath and the silence of her room. Dumont's expression told her she would get neither, not for a while, and she gestured for him to approach.

The past few days had left their mark on him as the bags beneath his eyes carried bags of their own, though his brief smile brought light to an otherwise dim audience chamber. "Dumont, I-I would know something of you," she said as she dismissed the guards from the room with a gesture.

"You have but to ask, Your Majesty."

"How did my father listen to their worries day after day without losing his sanity?"

Dumont sighed as he nodded. "Their worries may seem trivial, but—"

"Were their concerns about where one keeps the sheep or whether to breed this horse with another, I would grant them trivial. If only they were, Dumont, but these people have lost their homes. They've lost their families and have no answers as to *why*. I sit on this throne and tell them that we make plans to protect them, but what plans have been made? I find myself struggling to awake each morning with the thought of my father gone, let alone make decisions that have such grave consequences."

"No one expects you to solve this issue immediately. This is what your council's for, dear. To *counsel* you in difficult times and provide needed information. Not even your father had all the answers," he said.

"But what if I...." Margaret shook her head. If she mentioned her distrust of them now, Dumont might mention it to the rest of her council, family friend or not. "That woman whose son was injured fleeing the Shadians. Isn't there something we can do to help her? Perhaps one of the abandoned homes in the city could be given to her as a temporary place to stay, or my physician could see to her boy's injuries."

The smile he wore failed to reach his eyes as his shoulders rounded. "Your Majesty, the woman's a beggar out of Menoir. Before his illness, she came before your father on a monthly basis."

"To what end?"

Dumont shrugged. "Perhaps she hoped he would give her some pennies or a notch. I'll not pretend to know the ways of a beggar."

"And the boy?"

He stared at the floor rather than meet Margaret's gaze. "Her son, and the bruises are from her, not the Shadians," he said. What had begun the morning as a comfortable chair, now dug into Margaret at odd points as she sat on her throne. Tears welled in her eyes, and when she said nothing, Dumont cleared his throat before glancing up at her. "What your father loved most about you was how easily you wear your heart for all to see, though I fear it'll do you harm, Your Majesty. I don't say this to upset you, but you must show no weakness before these people, or the vipers will come for you. They will use you until there is nothing more to use."

"I must be like stone," she whispered.

"I'm sorry?"

Margaret shook her head. "Perhaps the Amaskan can teach me how better to distance my emotions from the job I must do."

His weight shifted as he watched her, but whatever he searched for in her face, he didn't find as he frowned. "Make no decisions today, Your Majesty. You're grieving. 'Twould be easy to lean on the Amaskan the way you did your father, and a murderer such as that would encourage it, to take advantage of a young woman early in her rule."

"Or perhaps I would use him."

"Please, Your Majesty. Do nothing until Leolin arrives. If help is what you need and you don't wish to worry your council, speak with a friend who means you well," Dumont said and bowed.

And where is Leolin? Margaret dismissed Dumont but remained on the throne until the room was empty. While Dumont meant well, he had been her father's friend, not hers. What did he understand of her situation? The man lectured her about the dangers of the Amaskan as if she were a babe at the teat.

She closed her eyes and took a deep breath through her nose. When she exhaled, she envisioned a stone wall wrapped around her, from her shoulders down to her toes. The stone was cool to the touch, and Margaret shivered as it enveloped her completely. No light reached her, nor sound.

No woman with a battered child.

No council to maneuver her where they wished.

No armies marching toward her home.

When she opened her eyes, she pretended the wall remained as the world came rushing back. Maybe the wall would allow her to be the queen Alexander needed. It wasn't perfect, but it helped as she returned to her bedchamber.

The woman in the mirror looked like a queen. A crown graced her head, while powders decorated high cheek bones and eyelids. She even held herself with an air of regality that came from good breeding and a lifetime of good posture. But her fingers trembled as she removed the crown from her brow, marring the image of a queen, and her stone wall crumbled.

As her lady-in-waiting helped her undress, glimpses in the mirror did more than hint at the stress Margaret carried with her. Bruises from her own attempts at self-defense work left marks here and there across a too-thin frame. "You need to eat more, Your Majesty," Lady Claretta said as she helped Margaret step out of her dress, leaving only her chemise behind. "Perhaps a grand dinner among friends will help."

Margaret dismissed both comments with a wave. "Now hardly seems the time."

"There's always a reason to celebrate, cousin. Besides, it would take your mind off of...recent events."

And give you a reason to talk to the squire who arrived yesterday. Margaret glanced sidelong at the thirteen-year-old who smoothed out the dress's wrinkles before tucking it into a chest. Perhaps the idea held some merit. *Besides, if Leolin arrives soon, it would be nice to welcome him home.*

Once Claretta excused herself, Margaret found herself alone in her bedchamber. Hints of her father spilled across the desk, and her shoulders slumped as she stood before the mirror.

She had played her part with the Amaskan well, if his reactions had been any indication, but the effort left her weary and heartsick. Who was she to pretend she was anything other than a weak puppet for her council? When she closed her eyes, her father's face mocked her, laughed at her inability to wrestle anything critical out of the Amaskan.

Something about the way he had looked at her when she spoke...he was more than he said. Certainly not as trustworthy as she needed him to be, but perhaps with time he could be shaped into the tool she needed. Assuming she could hold this façade together long enough to shape him.

Margaret crawled into the bed that was her father's, an action that made her a child again.

If only he were here to chase the monsters away.

Her gaze landed on the mirror again. An imposter stared back at her, and she seized the bedside candle from the table and hurled it at the mirror. This time it landed squarely on the fragile glass, which splintered into a spider-web and split her face into a mess of wrong angles and jagged lines. When she frowned, a terrible monster stared back.

When the sun rose, Margaret remained buried under the blanket, wide awake and afraid.

10

When Leolin arrived in Alesta, he hadn't expected a huge welcoming party. Bad weather and a lame horse had delayed him, forcing him to arrive after the burning, a fact which set him cursing the lieutenant and his purposefully dreadful timing. But he certainly hadn't expected to arrive in the middle of a celebratory dinner as if an army wasn't marching toward Alexander with every intent to destroy it.

People danced and the wine flowed as he entered the Great Hall. Queen Margaret sat upon the dais with a strange man beside her. He whispered something to her, and she turned toward the double doorway where Leolin stood. This time when she smiled, it felt more genuine than the one a moment before, and she waved in his direction. Leolin brushed past the dancers to stop before the dais, where he bowed deeply.

"Leolin! Come—have you eaten yet? You arrive at a fortuitous time," said Margaret.

A servant rushed forward to place a glass of wine and a platter of meats and breads before the table's empty seat.

Warmth spread to his cheeks. He'd never been invited to the high table before, and the thought sent a panic through him. Perhaps the army was already in Alexander, and this was one last celebration before a battle on the morrow. "I apologize for my late arrival, Your Majesty," he said as stood before the empty seat.

"Please, sit!" she said, gesturing toward the chair.

He claimed the seat but did so with the gnashing of teeth. Battle or not, what reason was there to celebrate?

She must have caught his frown, as her smile faltered a moment before she forced it back into place. "What news is there from Breighton? You look like you've ridden with Itova at your back."

"I might well have, as death was my impetus." *As it should be yours.* He didn't bother saying it aloud, though he bit his tongue to prevent the words from tumbling out. "I've ridden almost nonstop in hope I would make it here to see my mother released to the afterlife, and I arrive to find a celebration. If I may be so bold...Your Majesty, your own father was burned but a few days ago."

Despite their friendship, the way her face flushed crimson set worry in his belly that he'd pushed her too far. The old man beside her stared down at Leolin with a gaze that could wilt a desert-born Prickly Saibra. The arch of the old man's brow reminded Leolin all too well of his late mother, and his heart tensed in response.

"Everyone grieves in their own way. Would it not be prudent to allow Her Majesty an equal opportunity to do so?" the old man said.

"My apologies—" Leolin glanced at the old man's attire. While the clothing lacked the worn-in look of shirt well-loved, it draped across the old man's wiry frame all wrong, and his breeches ballooned out at the ankles a touch too much. The clothes did not belong to the old man, and Leolin reassessed the man's status. "—Master...?"

"Maurus of Sadai."

"I don't believe we've had the acquaintance, Master Maurus. Sergeant Leolin Nicholl, Queen's Royal Army. Her Majesty and I grew up together in this castle."

When the old man faced him, Leolin spotted a lightened scar on Maurus's jaw below the ear. The scar reminded him of a former Amaskan his mother had known, and Leolin frowned.

"I'm sure Her Majesty grew up with many people, as royalty does," said Maurus.

Leolin flinched. "My mother was King Leon's *sepier*. Are you familiar with the word?"

"We have something of the sort in Sadai. A spy or confidant, yes? Is that what encouraged you to join the Royal Army?"

Leolin stabbed a chunk of meat with a knife and chewed on it for a moment. The hairs on Leolin's arms tingled as they stood on end. Whatever this man's game, it wouldn't end well for Margaret. Not with a scar like that. "My duty to the Crown encouraged me. How did you make the acquaintance of Her Majesty?" *And when? Did the King know you, or are you another opportunist seeking a vulnerable queen?*

"He saved my life," said Margaret.

"Then I owe you my profound thanks for the life of my Queen and friend." Leolin inclined his head in the old man's direction before helping himself to some wine. Even if the old man had saved Margaret's life, he must have done so for his own gain. "We live in dangerous times, and with so many assassins running about, a newly crowned queen would be quite the coup, would it not?"

Margaret tapped her knuckles on the wooden table. "Enough talk of death. This evening is a celebration of life."

However short it may be, Maggie?

The rest of the meal proved a dampened affair as Margaret spent it in her wine. Leolin and Maurus studied each other with subtle glances and furrowed brows, and it wasn't until Margaret excused herself that Leolin had the opportunity to follow her into the hallway. "A moment if you will, Your Majesty."

She halted, then swayed a moment before grabbing Leolin's arm for stability. "Why so formal, old friend?" she asked, her voice slightly slurred.

He wished to ask, *You began the formality with your letter, did you not?* Rather than give into his irritation, he took a deep breath. "Your Majesty should know something about the man she keeps company with."

"What secrets do I not know 'bout you, Leo?" He glanced at her honor guard, and she followed his gaze. "Never mind them, what do you wish to say?"

He motioned for her to continue walking and took up stride beside her. "This Maurus, he's not who you think he is."

"And who do *you* think he is?"

"He's an Amaskan. I've seen that manner of scar before—"

Margaret laughed as she traversed the stairs like a toddler, wobbling and tilting her way to the fourth floor. "Maurus admitted as much to the Grand Marshal and I when he saved my life."

"And yet you asked him to remain?"

She stopped outside her chambers, but rather than opening the door, she tumbled in its general direction. Her guards stared at their shoes, while she fumbled with the knob. What had been King Leon's sitting room still resembled his sitting room, right down to the mahogany wood chairs, but hints of Margaret had creeped their way inside by way of books and needlework. Not the books her father had read—mostly fantastical tales rather than histories and accountings—but books all the same. Now a few more overflowed from a shelf and one found itself tucked into an overstuffed chair.

Margaret fell into the chair, displacing both a deep blue pillow and the book. She dismissed her guards with a wave and with more sobriety than he thought her capable of, she asked, "Did it ever occur to you that I'm using him?"

Now it was Leolin who laughed.

"What? Is that so unusual a possibility? He has information I need and abilities that could be helpful in this war," she said. When Leolin continued to laugh, she seized the blue pillow and tossed at it at him. Even drunk, it hit him square in the face, and he stopped laughing.

"Since when could you throw straight?"

Her grin slid away like sand. "Since Father fell ill, and the Shadian army threatened my borders."

"He never meant you to rule alone."

"He never meant me to rule at all," she whispered and retrieved the book from the floor where it had fallen open.

Leolin caught a glimpse of King Leon's handwriting before Margaret closed the book and tucked it away behind another pillow. "I'm sure your father meant to rule for many more years before you would take the crown." While he said the words, his tongue tasted bitter with the lie. The entire purpose of the diplomatic marriage with the Kingdom of Shad had been to provide a co-ruler for Margaret. She wasn't wrong in her assumptions, and with both her husband and father dead, she stood in a place no one had foreseen.

Margaret's eyes drooped as she stared at the opposing wall where a portrait of her mother hung. "I'm too much like her and not enough like them."

"Them?"

"My father. My sister. Adelei received all of his spirit, while I'm left with fear and confusion. And distrust."

He frowned at the name. Another Amaskan. Another person whose own agenda had cost others their lives.

"If you're going to bring up Amaskans, don't," she said, and he flinched. "Leolin, I-I need all the allies I can manage."

"You have allies. Your council—" More bitterness than he'd expected erupted from her laugh. "Fine. If you don't trust your council, release them. Appoint new people to help guide you."

"Who?" she asked. "If you haven't noticed, the ambassadors have fled. Most of the lords and ladies have as well. Only those who wish to seize power for themselves have remained, or those too afraid to be elsewhere. My own council makes decisions without my leave, and when I make a choice on my own, they treat me like a simpleton."

She rubbed her forehead with her fingers and groaned. "I may not have my father's knowledge, but I spent most of my childhood with tutors whose job it was to impart the knowledge needed to rule. I know little of war, but I am *still* queen...a queen who can't trust anyone outside of an Amaskan and a childhood friend."

"Order me stationed here, and I'll do what I can to help. Better yet, if you're going to keep the Amaskan around, make me your *sepier*," Leolin said, and her eyes snapped open.

"I...."

His cheeks flushed at her hesitation. "My apologies for being presumptuous. I should not have assumed your intent." The familiarity between them was gone as the Queen stood. He mentally kicked himself.

He was no better than her own council.

"We'll talk about it another time. For now, I'll order you stationed in Alesta as a member of my honor guard."

When she inclined her head, he bowed before withdrawing from her sitting room.

It was a demotion of sorts but it would have to do. This way he would have the time and proximity to see what the Amaskan's intentions were.

And perhaps it would give him time to figure out his own.

LONG AFTER THE BOY HAD FOLLOWED THE QUEEN OUT of the Great Hall like a lovesick fool, Bredych had remained in the Great Hall. Observation often brought more answers than an inquisition, so he tucked himself onto a stool wedged into a corner to watch and wait. Fragments of information trickled toward him as people passed, though none of it of any use. Certainly none of it related to Adelei or her death. Only one person spoke her name, and that was to admonish the Queen for burning her alongside King Leon. As more people retired for the night, Bredych climbed the stairs to the second floor and his room.

A simple guest room, it bore a lone window that led nowhere but down, though the room's location near the stairwell made it useful should Bredych need to flee in a hurry. The bed's stuffed mattress was certainly more comfortable than the bed he used at the Order, but the chair beside it left Bredych's hip aching if he remained in it too long.

Rather than retire, he stripped off the borrowed clothes in favor of a black tunic and breeches. Neither were Amaskan in appearance, but they would blend in the shadows of a dark castle enough to do what was required. He left the room as he had entered and took the stairs to the Queen's bower. The window remained cracked open a hair from when he'd last used it, and without hesitation, Bredych climbed through it onto the roof. His grappling hook remained lodged on the parapet's coping stone, and the rope snaked its way across the rooftop.

After a quick check of the knot used to attach the rope and hook, he lowered himself down to the royal bedchamber's window ledge. Having oiled the hinges the last time he'd crawled through it, the window opened silently at his touch, and he paused to listen. Silence greeted him, and Bredych slid one leg and then the other over the sill. His boots touched the floor with a louder thud than he liked, but no one occupied the bedchamber to hear it. Throughout the evening's dinner, he had encouraged the Queen to drink her wine until her words had slurred, expecting her to fall into a drunken slumber, but her bedchamber was as empty as her conversation had been. One ear toward the door, he gave her room a thorough look before settling on the small study tucked off to the side.

If the Queen held detailed evidence of Adelei's death, surely it would be among her personal papers. The desktop held an array of reports, mostly details of the Shadian army's comings and goings, though a few personal letters were tucked beside a stack of empty parchment. A few castle accountings, an ink bottle, and a silk scarf were all the top drawer held, though the bottom one held the Queen's personal journal.

Dated three years prior, the first entry was a simple note on her new lady-in-waiting and a gift from her then-to-be future husband, Prince Gamun. Bredych leafed through the pages until the year 255 appeared. Most of the short paragraphs spoke of the upcoming wedding and later, Adelei's arrival, though none went into any detail. Halfway through the volume, an entry mentioned the Boahim Senate, and he glanced at the door leading out. The Queen could return at any moment.... When only the wind outside the window answered him, he settled himself on a stool to read.

The Boahim Senate's arrival was everything my sister feared, though she would never speak of such an emotion. I thought them come to rid me of the monster I married, but as with everyone these days, their motives were complex and hidden and their own.

My husband is dead, though I feel little beyond relief at this fact, and my sister sits in our dungeon having confessed her sins before the senators. She tells me that they will likely punish her for her actions as an Amaskan, a fact I fail to understand. My sister is a just woman! The people she's killed have been criminals of the highest echelon: murderers, rapists, and sick people who felt no remorse for their crimes. How can she be punished for seeking justice when the Senate would not?

There is an unfairness to the Senate's methods that makes me question everything I've been told about them. Father's sick, though he will not admit it to me, and soon, he, too, will be gone from this world. I need Adelei by my side. They cannot take her from me as we've only just found each other! She and Papa are the only family I have left.

I'll not let them take her. Somehow, I have to find a way to stop this.

The next entry bore tear blotches, and Bredych closed his eyes a moment to brace himself. He made it two sentences in before his own tears added to the spots that marred the otherwise delicate penmanship.

Never before have I hated my own people. These simpletons whom we are supposed to protect...what they said to my sister as she passed them in the city streets, the way they tore at her clothing and kicked her. They cared nothing for how many people she's saved, myself included, nor how they live under the banner of Alexander rather than Shad because of her actions. All they could see was an assassin. A murderer.

I thought perhaps the Senate would see reason and take pity upon her, but she is an example for them to parade about to demonstrate their power. They hanged my sister at high noon, and she went willingly, brave and fierce until the end. We pled for them to release her body for burning, but the Senate would hear nothing of it. "She must remain a symbol of the Senate's justice," they said.

What justice is there in killing a protector of the people? Adelei was no monster. She was no Gamun.

This night, my father wore a fragility I've not seen as he sneaked about in the dark. I met him where she hanged, and when he touched her body, something dark shimmered between his fingers and her skin. To know my husband a user of magic, something forbidden since the Fall of Boahim, is one thing, but to see the Senate use such means to keep my sister's remains in place is an evilness I don't understand. My father nearly fainted from the shock he received. He could not hold Adelei nor say goodbye.

How long will she hang in the city? Will the sun rot her flesh from her bones, or will this magic keep her preserved, her spirit unable to move on?

My stomach churns with the thought and while I swear I will see her body burned, I know not how or when. Oh Gods! How can we heal when she's to be a constant reminder of our loss?

The Thirteen be with us as the Senate surely is not!

Bredych flipped through the few remaining entries, which focused on Leon's ailing health. No surprise that her journal echoed what she had told him about Adelei's death, and he ground his teeth. Who had called the Senate in the first place and why? He placed the journal back in the drawer before moving on to a chest, which held naught but clothes. When he pressed his ear to the door leading to the Queen's informal sitting room, no sound reached him, and he tested the doorknob a fraction before turning it all the way.

The door opened a crack, and he stared out into a room he recognized. Wherever the Queen was, she wasn't here. Perhaps she was with the boy giving him a proper welcome. *That* would certainly give Bredych more time to search. He slid through the door and into the room where the Queen had first questioned his motives. Histories and fantastical tales comprised most of the room's books, though the corner of one stuck up from behind a blue cushion. Bredych tilted the pillow down to remember the book's location before retrieving it, and when he opened it, he found himself face-to-face with the King's journal from the year 255.

Why has the Queen been reading this? Why this particular year?

The door that led to the fourth floor hallway was rather silent as Bredych listened. Several guards shuffled their feet and yawned, but with the late hour, no one else was about this floor of the castle. Two doors led to unused rooms while a third led to a storage closet. Should the Queen return unexpectedly, the closet would serve as a hiding spot until he could return to the window and escape. King Leon's journal bore cramped handwriting that more closely resembled Adelei's than Queen Margaret's, and Bredych's heart lurched as he flipped through it.

Notes about Shendra's visit to Sadai and her meeting with an Amaskan confirmed how Leon had known the location of the Order when he had demanded Adelei's return home. A note tucked between the pages told of Shendra's discovery of Adelei and her betrayal of Leon. *Once an oath breaker, always an oath breaker, eh?* The candle beside him flickered as it grew low, but he continued reading about how Leon schemed false attacks on Margaret to bolster his "need" to have Adelei sent to Alexander.

To think Adelei had called Bredych ruthless. At least he hadn't orchestrated false attacks on his family in order to bring about his desires. Leon's heartbreak at having his daughter return "a killer" made Bredych smile. The man had deserved the pain of watching his daughter turn her back on him. But the more Bredych read, the more the narrative changed. The more Leon's pain gave way to closure. Even if it was intended to be Margaret's, Leon's joy at seeing Adelei in a wedding dress brought tears to Bredych's eyes. To have seen such a sight! Reading about how Gamun toyed with Adelei, he shared Leon's anger and rage. In the end, it was Leon's grief and guilt that left Bredych's heart sorest.

> *For fourteen years I mourned the loss of Adelei, and now I mourn her once again.*
>
> *My heart sang when Iliana returned to me. Even if it was not the Iliana I knew, the woman she became, this Adelei was someone I trusted and loved in the end. Someone I was proud to call Daughter. Would they have allowed it, I would've taken her place in that noose. My days are limited, and Margaret needs someone strong beside her. It's a role Adelei should have filled.*
>
> *Damn the Senate. Damn them for this.*
>
> *What use is it to call upon them to defend the Thirteen if they turn it against you? And she knew, damn it all, she knew! Adelei knew they would sentence her to death, and yet she demanded that I call them. Why did I listen? It's my fault my little girl is dead.*
>
> *Again.*

The final word blurred into a black blob as tears welled in Bredych's eyes. He'd thought it surely Leon's stupidity that brought the Senate to Alesta, but no, it had been *hers*. Amaskan to the end.

A female voice outside caught his attention, and he tucked the book behind the pillow before retreating to Margaret's bedchamber. Bredych was up the rope before the door opened.

Whatever answers he sought would have to wait for another time.

11

———

Despite the pounding head and the fuzzy feeling behind her eyes, the idea of sleep made Margaret's head spin more than the wine had. Rather than sleep, she threw on a heavy robe and set out for her father's private library.

The hallways were empty with the exception of the guards stationed at the hallways' ends, and the only footsteps besides her own were those of her honor guard, the latter of which followed her down the stairs and past the main library. Her father's private library lay behind a door she had not yet brought herself to enter. Not since before he had fallen ill.

She retrieved the key from her pocket and turned to a guardsman. "Hold this please," she said, handing him her candle. Margaret opened the door with trembling hands and sneezed. Invisible though they were in the candlelight, dust motes stirred the air. Woody scents mixed with the sharp tang of *perin,* her father's medicine, brought tears to her eyes. She reclaimed her lit candle through a wet blur and said, "Remain outside."

Yawning, the two men took up position outside the door, which she closed softly. She laughed at the old habit—always move quietly. Never let someone know you are present until you wish them to know. At first, the lesson had been one instilled by tutors who wished to instill a sense of docility in their future ruler, especially after the whirlwind she had become when her mother died and her sister had gone missing.

But now, it was a lesson of survival.

Moonlight streamed in from the lone window, casting light in the corner where her father had spent many an evening reading. When she stepped forward, her shin barked against a table leg, and she bit her lip as it throbbed. Maybe daylight would have been a better time to venture into his library.

It took her a span of ten minutes to reach his chair, and when she lowered herself into it, the sharpness of *perin* burned her nose while the hint of lilies enveloped her small frame.

Her father would never fill this chair again.

He would never again be lost in the pages of some vellum bound book or be late for supper after researching some treatise or another.

He would never regret sending Ida Warhammer to her death, and he would never break under the loss of Margaret's sister, Adelei.

While glad that her father would never scowl at the burn of his medicine or lose his breath to another coughing fit, she would rather have him suffer both if it meant one more day with him still here.

She pictured herself acting as her father would have—throwing the candle to the floor in a fit of anger—but her imagination followed the action to its inevitable conclusion.

The books would erupt in flames until her father's library lay as her father, ashes to coat the garden soil.

Instead, she set the candle on the table beside her and drew her knees into the chair to tuck them under her chin. Great sobs erupted from her then. Her teeth chattered as she squeezed her legs to her chest. Despite her sorrow, the moon continued to move, and the people in Alesta continued to sleep and breathe. And live.

The moon had moved far past her view from the window when she fell from grief into a sleep troubled by visions of flames and swords and death. Rather than ivy, her castle was covered in ash and blood, and bodies lined the city streets five deep. Margaret woke when sunlight creeping over the horizon lightened the room through the frost-covered window.

Dried wax covered the table corner where the candle had long since melted, but the rising sun gave light enough for her to see the reason for her stuffy nose as a thick layer of dust covered the long table at the room's center as well as the bookshelves built into the walls. The one nearest her held the most recent bound records from her father's rule, but if she followed the cases toward the door, books from her great-great-great grandsire's time and a few before lined the shelves. Among the history of Alesta, she padded barefoot across the chilled stone floor to stop before the bound records from the War of Three.

Her fingers drifted past records during the war. *Too early.* What she needed were records from a few months after, when the commoners returned to their homes. *Assuming there were homes to return to.* One binding caught her attention, and she set it on the table before her.

The temperature in the room warmed considerably before she found anything remotely helpful, but six months into the records, she found a document granting land rights to Alexander for a property along the northern border. Her father's seal marked the contract, and she frowned. Five pages later, another contract granted similar rights, though to a smaller portion of land. When Adelei had mentioned the rumors of Alexander's ever-changing border, she had thought it surely a jest. The Little Dozen Kingdoms' borders had stayed the same, with the exception of natural land shifts, for as long as her family had ruled. Since the Boahim Senate's forming.

To change the border would be to invite civil war.

Someone wrapped on the door, and she jumped up with a swift inhale. "Come," she called, and one of her honor guards stepped inside.

"My apologies, Your Majesty, but Master Maurus seeks a meeting with you."

"I will meet with him later this—" She glanced at the window where the sun no longer kissed the horizon but beamed solidly through it. "Later this afternoon."

He nodded and withdrew, leaving Margaret to shelve the book and fetch another.

The further back she went, the more evidence she found of Alexander's border changes. All of them were minute shifts, none of them as large as a town and none of them all at once. Some lord needed access to land for a well, or a farmer wished protection from his neighbor, and the King wiggled the border in their favor. The reasons given seemed perfectly acceptable...if someone wasn't looking particularly hard at the contract's outcome, but there it was, hidden where even Margaret could see it.

The truth left her stomach hollow. *This is why the ambassadors fled. This civil war may be justified. Are they leaving all the kingdoms or just Alexander?*

Whatever the crime, at least it had not begun with her father. At least his sins were inherited. Perhaps the Boahim Senate already knew of this.

Margaret closed her eyes and prayed they would not hold it against her.

ONE SLIP OF PARCHMENT.

That was all it took to send Margaret to the orb and the Senate on the other side.

She sighed in relief when it was her own Senator Montero and not Senator Whitlen whose face appeared in the orb. Not that the woman scared her, but Senator Whitlen's nature left Margaret's skin raw.

"What may I—"

"Did you know?" she asked, interrupting Senator Montero.

"I'm sorry?"

"Did you know? About the Shadian army?"

The old man blinked slowly as people moved in the background. Whatever room he stood in was dark enough that she couldn't see their faces, only hear their feet shuffle across the stone floor. Senator Montero waited until the motions stopped and a door closed before responding. "We are aware of Shad's movements, yes."

"But they've done it! They've crossed my border! I was told the Senate would prevent this action from occurring, but now I find they've gone from threatening an action to taking one." When he sighed, Margaret clenched her fists at her sides. Damned fool would watch her people...*his* people die before taking action, wouldn't he? She bit her tongue against the words.

"We have told King Havin that a war with your kingdom is a violation of the Thirteen, and he has assured us that he means no harm to the people of your kingdom—"

"And you believe him? His army marches across my border! What reason could he have for such an action?"

Another look, another sigh. "Technically, it's not your border. Alexander does not control the Meridi Pass."

The anger in Margaret's belly emptied itself as bile rose to burn the back of her throat. The Senate *did* know. To Senator Montero, she said, "I don't understand."

"Come now, Margaret. Your family has been renegotiating your borders for generations. Surely your father's library revealed such facts."

Bile turned to ice as her insides quivered.

He tilted his head, his eyes peering at her across the miles. "Where the Shadian army stands hasn't been your land since your great-grandsire's time, a fact known to you as of this morning. Am I wrong?"

"No, Senator," she whispered. How could he know that? She slid one hand and then the other behind her back to hide their trembling.

The wrinkles surrounding his eyes and mouth softened as he gave her a sad smile. "I understand this is difficult for you being new in your service to the crown, but these concerns would better suit your advisors, not this Senate. We are not rulers, only enforcers of the Thirteen."

And spies. Margaret forced herself to nod. Though how they had seen her research, she had no idea. Could the orb see that far? Through castle walls? What else had they seen? Her cheeks grew hot.

Senator Montero took her flush for proper repentance and said, "As to the Shadian army, do nothing. If they proceed on this path, they will be dealt with."

Could the Senate see all the way to the border?

"T-thank you," she said, and the orb dimmed to black. Though she had no doubt their eyes remained watching as she slid the bookshelf back into place. Watching as she left the council chambers and sought her own. Watching as she curled up in her chair in the sun, which failed to warm the chill in her bones.

She needed to speak with Master Maurus. If anyone might know about the Senate, it would be the Order. Or so she hoped. But the talk could not happen in the castle.

Her home was no longer safe.

THE KNOWLEDGE THAT THE SENATE WATCHED HER terrified Margaret more than the Shadian army occupying the Meridi Pass, a fact that left her staring at the ceiling as she tried to sleep. Once the all-too-bright sun ceased glaring across her face, she gave up fuming about her "chat" with the Senator and her lack of weapons' proficiency.

The latter was fixable, though it was not the same without Adelei. Captain Fenton was certainly adept with his short sword, but his lack of patience had left her more bruised than the wooden practice weapons. At first it had been one mistake after the other. She didn't hold the hilt correctly. She held it too tight. Then she held it too loose. She leaned to the right too often, or she led with her right foot. Ask her to throw a chair at his head—*that* she could do! —but the art to sword work had eluded her.

Even worse, the good captain held back. No, she couldn't practice with an actual weapon. No, she couldn't practice with multiple assailants. No, he wouldn't attack her with earnest. Desperation had driven her to solo practice with a straw figure until she had demonstrated her ability to strike back, to see a blow, and some of the time, block it. All of which Captain Fenton had taken to mean she knew enough of sword work.

"You won't need to know more, Your Majesty. That's what your army is for," he had said before her father's death.

But with the Senate watching and the Shadians at the pass, the situation had changed. How would she ever survive if no one would show her how? Rather than counting time with her nerves, Margaret had ordered Leolin to meet her in the training rooms. If Captain Fenton couldn't help her, maybe Leolin could.

"You want me to *what?*" he said as his gaze traveled across her clothes: a pair of tight fitting breeches similar in style to the ones Adelei had worn, an undershirt that moved like a second skin followed by a tunic that fell mid-thigh, and a belt at her waist. His face flushed pink as he gestured at her. "A-And what's with...."

"The practice gear?"

"You look like a man!"

"Do you honestly expect me to fight in dress layers? Besides, this isn't much different from the clothes Adelei wore." When he scowled, she added, "Or those your mother wore for that matter. You offered to help me, Leolin."

His pointed nose, like his mother's, flared. "But you aren't my mother. *You* aren't a fighter, much less a warrior. You have guards to protect you—"

"A lot of good my guards did me against Gamun," she whispered.

His gaze fell anywhere but on her as he frowned. "A sword won't protect you against evil like that. Not in the way you hope. If someone sees you with a sword, they'll see you as—"

"An enemy or a target. Yes, I know. Captain Fenton has already been through that with me."

"Captain Fenton? He's been teaching you to fight?"

"Who do you think insisted I wear these ridiculous clothes?" she asked, and a genuine laugh escaped him. "I still don't understand how I'm supposed to survive if no one will teach me how. I'm not a crystalline vase to be displayed for the Little Dozen."

Leolin opened his mouth, then snapped it shut. He picked up one of the wooden practice swords and knocked it against hers. She gripped the hilt, but otherwise didn't move. "Good. I thought you'd drop it." When she scowled at his gibe, he said, "Not even a day back and already you test me, just like when we were kids."

He circled her, testing her with little jabs and feints, but he gave those away. His shoulders leaned, his heel twisted, and his eyes traveled across the path he would take. Leolin baited her, and her face flushed with heat.

"Don't toy with me," she snapped. "A killer wouldn't."

One corner of his generous lips tilted up in a smirk. Then he moved.

Speed carried him across the empty space and a fluid motion brought the practice sword across her ribs, knocking the breath out of her. Margaret staggered backward into the wall as her lungs burned. She heaved until the air returned, and all the while he remained silent. It had been a mistake a beginner would make, and as such, when she moved, her ribs smarted.

His gaze, still and serious, met hers. "Had this been steel, Alexander would be short a queen." Leolin tossed the wooden sword on the ground. "People treat you like crystal because you're all Alexander has. Your family's dead, Margaret, and you've no heir."

She ground her teeth in an attempt to keep her expression neutral and failed. Tears prickled her eyelids as she winced, both from soreness and embarrassment. If Adelei were here, she would raise the same points. Damn them both.

"May I?" he asked, and when she nodded, he poked her ribs a few times. "I don't think I broke anything, but you should have your physician double check it."

"I'm bruised, not broken, Leolin." The words were intended one way, but as she spoke them, his face flushed in response.

"Don't ask me to teach you again. We can't afford to lose you," he said before he strode through the door and out of the practice room.

Her cheeks grew hot, though she wasn't sure if it was from his chastisement of her or the images that flitted through her head. Images of his hands touching her ribs, hands that accidentally found themselves touching more.

But he was Leolin, her childhood friend. He would never take such liberties. Besides, who had the time with the threat of civil war, not to mention the ever-watching Senate?

Margaret leaned against the wall and sighed.

12

Three times the barmaid skirted by Bredych's spot in the corner, and three times a sly grin lit up her face. He was far too old for her to feel genuine attraction for him, so it must have been a ruse to garner an extra coin or three from what she assumed was an outsider. She was right about the latter, though he had no intention of paying more than a penny or two for his drink, especially since he only sipped it on occasion as he awaited Princess Margaret, and because it was little more than water with a splash of ale. Enough to keep the locals drinking, that is, if they had little desire to taste anything to begin with.

The absurdity of calling a meeting here of all places—a tavern labeled *The Rumeur Hoard*—left his nerves dancing like a mare in shifting sand. The name wasn't fooling anyone, though he'd yet to hear any rumors of consequence.

When Margaret pushed through the door, he'd noticed, but only because he'd been waiting and watching for her. Dried sweat and dirt clung to an outfit he well recognized: tight-fitting breeches that were tied at the waist and ankles, followed by an equally tight-fitting shirt bound at the wrists.

The boots didn't match the Amaskan gear, but no one in the tavern would notice the error. They weren't Amaskan. Margaret had skipped the hooded cloak and gloves, opting for a smudge or three of grease on her hands to detract from the lack of fighting calluses, and she carried a hilted short-sword at her waist.

If they weren't Adelei's clothes, Bredych would drink himself silly.

Unlike Adelei, Margaret wore her long hair loose—a style that would be used against her in a fight—and when she moved, her fingers tugged at the shirt's side. But not even the outfit could mask that she wasn't Amaskan.

She tried to glance around the room unobtrusively, but the way her eyes widened when she spotted him gave her away. Or it would have had anyone else been looking at her face. Most of the tavern's occupants were nose-deep in a tankard, and those that had noticed her entrance had either returned to their business or slunk away from what they had assumed was trouble.

If they knew their Queen was among them.... Bredych took another glance around the tavern and caught the shadow following a few breaths behind Margaret. So the boy had come too. Had that been intentional?

Margaret claimed the chair next to Bredych and attempted a scowl. The mix of wide-eyed nervousness and brow-furrowed determination was comical, and Bredych bit back his laughter.

Leolin claimed a nearby chair, his back to them both, and answered Bredych's question. "Thank you for meeting me, *Mentessa*," he said as he poured ale into a mug. When she frowned at the false name, Bredych gave a brief shake of his head. "The weather in this city is gorgeous. I haven't seen this much sun in weeks."

Her booted foot connected with his shin, but he continued on with idle pleasantries until he was sure that no one other than Leolin was listening, and that the barmaid had settled in for good with the scraggly man ten tables over. Bredych leaned across the table and whispered, "Were you aware that you were followed?"

Bredych resisted his brow's urge to ride high across his face when she didn't leap to her feet. He'd expected that, rather than the slight flinch he received. For a moment, fear and suspicion battled for control of her facial features, and when she settled for calm, his respect for her grew. She feigned a sip of the ale while searching the tavern through drowsy eyelids. No one Bredych could see paid her any mind, but he kept watch all the same. Shadows moved too easily in Alesta.

The last place her gaze settled was on the back of a hooded man whose body sat too still and too stiff for someone casually resting in a tavern. With the extended silence, the man tilted his head backward in their direction, and this time, Margaret succeeded at her scowl. She stood to move in his direction, but Bredych stopped her with a raised hand. "Allow me," he whispered before standing.

His chair didn't move nor did his footfalls make sound on the wood flooring as he approached Leolin. Whatever fool game the boy played, he was in for quite the shock.

Leolin leaned on his left buttock, his right foot digging into the floor and announcing his intention before he moved. As he leapt up, Bredych caught Leolin's arm as it swung behind him. When the boy caught sight of who held him, his eyes widened before he stumbled backward. "She's meeting you? Marg—"

Bredych interrupted him by snagging the boy's tunic and pulled him in the corner's direction. "Mentessa's not fallin' for ya, boy, but I'll let'er tell ya," he bellowed, and several nearby patrons tittered in response. Then he knocked Leolin into a seat across from Margaret before reclaiming his chair.

From the flush of her cheeks to the glare she gave Leolin, Bredych was glad he wasn't on the receiving end of her temper. Before she could belt out a litany of complaints, Bredych nudged the mug of ale in her direction with a slight glance at the barmaid, who now openly stared at the three of them. As Margaret pretended to sip her ale, Bredych offered his to Leolin. "Drink," he ordered.

"Why should—" the boy protested, and Bredych kicked Leolin under the table.

Three men entering the tavern distracted the barmaid. Margaret didn't wait much longer than a breath to slam her mug down, sending a cascade of watered ale over the side. "Why did you follow me?" she hissed to Leolin.

"You sneaked out of the castle without so much as a guard to keep you safe, dressed like *that* no less. Of course I followed you!"

"Where I go and how I dress is none of your concern!"

Had they been Amaskan, Bredych would have smacked them both for this foolishness. As it was, he was sorely tempted to do so now—royalty or not. Instead, he snapped his fingers in their faces. Both brows furrowed though their mouths closed. "If you're both done acting like children, I assume there's a reason you wanted to meet here of all places. The boy has a point—" When Margaret's mouth popped open, Bredych snapped his fingers again. "This isn't the safest place to meet, though I assume you have your reasons."

"I do. I could not be sure we wouldn't be watched," she said. Leolin stilled in his chair but said nothing as she continued. "Last night, I was having trouble sleeping, so I spent some time in my father's library."

"I assume you found something," Bredych said.

Margaret nodded. "The rumors are correct. The borders *have* been changing, for several generations at least. Worse yet, a particular group has crossed to the pass. Since I possessed proof of both, I decided to ask for assistance from —" She pursed her lips together, then whispered, "The group of people I'm supposed to call on when absolutely necessary."

The three men who'd entered earlier sat unusually still and stared at their mugs too long without drinking. The barmaid set another pitcher of ale on their table and scrambled away. Whoever they were, something about them set Bredych's nerves on edge, and he angled his body a fraction more in their direction.

To Margaret he said, "I've never understood how people in your position could speak to them so quickly." The lie rolled off Bredych's lips with ease. *It must be another orb.* No wonder she worried of being watched.

"They knew things," she whispered.

Someone's chair scraped against the floor, and Leolin flinched. Bredych followed his gaze to the three men who still appeared to ignore everyone in the room. Without shifting his eyes, Leolin asked, "What things?"

"They knew what proof I'd found."

One of the men stood and made a show of stretching as if tired. As good as Margaret had been at sneaking out of the castle, she hadn't spotted the false way one man coughed or how his friends stood too slowly, too carefully. As if straining to listen. Or if she did notice, she gave no indication. Bredych's finger brushed the throwing knife tucked into the belt around his waist.

"That doesn't mean anything. Maybe they already knew. They are the...them after all," said Leolin.

"It wasn't that they knew what I had found. They knew *when* and *where* I had found it, Leolin. They knew other things too. Things they would have no way of knowing unless they were watching me."

"And how could they do that, *Mentessa?*" the boy asked, stressing the false name as he rolled his eyes. "You sound as crazy and mistrustful as *she* did."

Her cheeks flushed, and the spark returned to her eyes. "My sister was not crazy. She had good reason to doubt them, as did my father."

"Mentessa, these people aren't all-seeing. They can't know every action and decision made. There's no possible way for them to do what you're suggesting."

"But there is—" The words had barely left her mouth when the standing men moved. The first, the larger of the three by half, made it two steps before Bredych was on his feet, his body between the would-be attackers and Margaret. Leolin rose only a second behind and drew his wide-bladed falchion.

The tavern's volume doubled with stools etching scratches in the wood as patrons fled toward the door. Mugs were abandoned as the tension in the room shifted, and the large man in gray dipped his gloved hand into a pouch. His gloved fingers now glittered in the light.

He never had the chance to exhale and blow the powder at them, as Bredych flicked his wrist and set his throwing knife in the man's throat.

Their friend's death bothered the other two only as long as it took for Margaret to go pale, then they rushed the table, their gloved hands glittering.

Barak. They couldn't touch Margaret.

The short sword at Margaret's waist slid free of its sheath easily enough, and Bredych brought it down to connect with one of the assailant's arms. "Don't let them touch you, boy," he said.

"I'm hardly a boy." Leolin ducked to dodge the knife thrown at him by the third man.

With Margaret tucked into the corner behind him, Bredych repositioned the blade in his hands. Expecting an old man and a woman before them, rather than two well-trained fighters, one man spun on his heel to retreat. Bredych grabbed him by the hood and pulled him backward. He ran the blade through the man's heart, then let the tainted body drop to the ground. He turned to find the boy standing over another corpse, his bloody sword having run the attacker through.

"What was that?" Margaret asked, eyes wide as she stared at the bodies.

"*Barak*," said Bredych as he rolled a body over with his booted toe. Avoiding the hands, he knelt down and wiped off the short sword on the man's cloak before handing it back to Margaret.

Pale though she was, she accepted it with a nod and returned it to its sheath. "What's *barak*?"

Bredych rifled through the man's now empty pouch with a gloved hand and pulled out an empty vial that glowed slightly in the light that streamed in from outside. "It's a cactus from Sadai. Flowers very rarely—seen it twice in my lifetime. Pretty little things, though deadly as poisons get." He pointed at the vial. "The flower petals glow in the light. That's the pretty. But the petals are delicate. They don't last long at all. But if one was able to obtain such a flower, the powder's lethal and very valuable."

Leolin retrieved a piece of folded parchment from the other man's pouch, opened it, and gasped.

"What is it?" Bredych asked, but the boy leapt to his feet, clutching the parchment in one fist. He held his sword in front of him as he stepped in front of Margaret, his gaze sweeping across the almost empty tavern. The barmaid huddled behind the counter while two patrons remained unperturbed on their stools. The rest had cleared out, leaving only the dead bodies behind.

The hairs on his arms prickled as several somethings approached the tavern door, and Bredych snatched the parchment from Leolin's hand. A rather detailed and accurate sketch of Margaret comprised the top while details about her habits and movements in the castle followed. At the bottom, a small reward was promised.

Bredych folded up the parchment and tucked it into his pocket. He retrieved two throwing knives from his booth sheaths as the tavern's front door opened. Both he and Leolin stepped forward, their bodies a shield. Behind them, Margaret sighed as Captain Fenton stepped through. While Leolin relaxed his stance, Bredych did so only marginally.

Someone not only had a bounty on Margaret's head, but it was someone in the castle. Someone aware of her movements, her appointments, and possibly someone who had followed her on her not-so-sneaky route out of the castle.

"Captain Fenton! Thank the Thirteen you've arrived," Leolin said as he nodded.

Whoever sought Margaret's head, they didn't have a large amount of coin to their name. The promised reward was barely worth the risk of attempting an assassination. They couldn't be too high up in rank. Perhaps someone on a captain's pay?

Margaret attempted to sidestep Bredych, and he pushed her back with his arm.

"What's the meaning of this? Unhand the Queen this minute," Captain Fenton ordered, but Bredych remained in front of her.

Leolin glanced between the captain, Margaret, and Bredych. "Wait, do you think the captain's behind this?" he asked.

"Behind what?" Margaret pressed her fingers lightly to Bredych's collarbone. "Hand me the parchment."

Bredych fetched it from his pouch and passed it over his shoulder. The silence that stretched between them was expected, though Leolin shifted from foot to foot like he awaited another attack. Rather than fainting or whatever in all the Thirteen hells the boy expected from his Queen, Margaret handed the parchment back to Bredych with fingers that didn't tremble so much as twitch the once.

Margaret stepped around Bredych and stood before Captain Fenton, her shoulders stiff and chin tilted upward. "Were you or were you not aware that there is a bounty on my head?"

"I was aware, though I didn't place it, Your Majesty."

"Was my council aware?"

Captain Fenton glanced at the dead bodies to either side of him again, his jaw clenched. When she repeated the question, he nodded briefly.

"Master Maurus," she said as she faced Bredych. "If you would escort me back to the castle, please. Captain, I'll leave you to dispose of the trash."

She didn't protest the guards who followed them out at the captain's signal, nor did she protest when Leolin led the way. Bredych waited for her to speak, but she remained silent as they passed through the third and second set of inner city walls.

Eight armed guards, a sergeant, and a "merc" escorting a woman in all black left most dawdlers afraid enough to find a reason to be indoors despite the warm sun that lit the late afternoon. As they passed through the last gate before the castle itself, Bredych spun in the *thwap*'s direction, but was too late to stop the blade that struck him in the shoulder. Margaret dropped to a crouch a moment later as the guards formed a tight-knit circle around her.

"Where'd it come from?" Leolin asked, his gaze studying the street.

Bredych pointed in the gate tower's direction. All that remained in the arrow-loop were deep shadows. Or that was what the attacker wished them to assume. It mattered little that his shoulder screamed in agony or that his old bones trembled at the tower's height. To allow the attacker to escape would sour Bredych's ability to gain Margaret's trust.

While guards stationed at the gate itself scurried about like angry ants, Bredych scaled the roughly cobbled wall until the blood seeping from his shoulder caused his fingers to slip. One hand dangled helplessly while the other clung to a lip of cobble, and he cursed the boots on his feet. The Order's toed slippers would have made short work of a rock wall like this. Hot and thick, blood oozed from his shoulder as he scrambled for purchase. With both hands on the wall, he climbed until he reached the lone window ledge.

His up-and-over wasn't nearly as smooth as usual. More a strain-and-fall than anything else as Bredych tumbled in through the window. So long out of the field he was that his nose itched incessantly, more so now that he'd had it buried in the dirt and dust that clung to the stone wall. He ground his teeth and dragged his tongue across the roof of his mouth to keep the sneeze at bay while his eyes adjusted to the light difference. The attacker had fled from the nearby arrow-loop. Besides the stairs that led down to armed guards, there was only one path they could have chosen, the path to Bredych's right.

In the darkness, anyone could be near him, so he tiptoed his way toward the flickering torch light near the narrow hallway's end. When the light disappeared, covered by something or someone, Bredych didn't wait for it to return. He ran toward the figure that almost blended in with the pitch. A hand connected with his shoulder, and he hissed before grabbing the figure's cloak. Coarse fabric pulled away from him as the cloak fell to the ground, and Bredych grabbed the torch from the wall and tossed it at the attacker's legs. The attacker—a woman—let loose a high-pitched cry as the flames narrowly missed her. Bredych shoved her to the ground, and she winced as her ankle turned.

A booted heel to the gut knocked the fight out of her, though when she caught her breath, she craned her neck to spit in his face. Bredych fetched a knife, which he jabbed at her. "Get up," he said, and while she moved slowly, she followed his instructions. As they neared the window, her pale skin showed the beaded sweat that decorated it. He couldn't check her ankle without looking away from her face, something he wasn't willing to do, but her exaggerated limp told him she probably hurt less than he did. She stopped at the top of the stairs, and he poked her in the back with his throwing knife.

"I won't talk," she muttered, and he kicked her calf. She let loose a shrillness that set his ears ringing and brought the outside guards running. With them was Leolin, and three steps behind him, Margaret.

At the sight of the Queen, the attacker lunged at her, and Margaret stepped forward, short sword drawn. By the way their eyes widened, it was a surprise to them both when the blade met resistance. The attacker's hood fell away and blood spilled from her mouth as she stared at Margaret. The woman dragged a hand across Margaret's face before her eyes closed and her body slumped forward.

Bredych nodded when Margaret stepped back but didn't drop the sword. Perhaps there was hope for her yet.

Moments after his thought, Margaret handed the bloody sword to Leolin and proceeded to lose the contents of her stomach against the stairwell wall. Leolin used the victim's tunic, a ragged black thing too long and too wide for her frame, to clean the blood from the sword, before he touched Margaret on the shoulder. She flinched, and he whispered something in her ear. Whatever he'd said, she shook her head and accepted her sword, which she returned to its sheath.

"Is this who hurt you?" she asked Bredych as she nudged the woman with a booted toe. "She looks so young."

Rather than answer, he lifted the woman's tunic enough to get at her waist. No pouch or purse was tied to her belt, though her breeches bore two pockets. He ran his hands across the pockets' exterior before gently probing their interiors. In one he found another parchment bearing the bounty's details, which he handed to Margaret before moving down to the attacker's ankles.

It wasn't a check he'd had the time to do on the three men earlier. Bredych removed the woman's boots, then rolled up her breeches to expose her ankles. On the left one, a hair beneath the ankle's bone was a fresh mark cut into her skin. The puffy, red triangle had oozed blood, leaving a trail down to the bottom of her foot.

"*Tribor*," whispered Leolin, whose gaze darted around the confined space.

Margaret's hand went to her sword hilt as she stepped closer to where Bredych crouched. "They recruit so young?" she asked.

Before Bredych could answer, Leolin said, "Like the Amaskans, they aren't against using people to get what they want." When the boy looked up, he met Bredych's gaze, lips pursed tight.

Nothing he said would sway Leolin, not yet anyway. Rather than refute the comment, Bredych gestured to the nearest guard. "Have the body taken outside the city walls and dumped for the scavengers." He turned to Margaret and said, "We need to get you back to the castle immediately."

"Ensure my safety as my guards have not, then you and I need to talk," she said before proceeding him down the stairs.

Leolin stepped forward, his body blocking Bredych's access to the stairwell. "I don't know what game you're playing at, Amaskan, but it ends today. We both know why the *Tribor* are here, and it has everything to do with your continued presence. If you really wish to protect Her Majesty, leave."

The boy was an idiot. A fool blinded by his feelings. Bredych followed him down the stairs, his ears straining for unusual sounds. *Tribor* never came alone. Where there was one, there was always another, and so far, this made a possible four. He didn't have to see the men at the tavern's ankles to know. The bounty was merely an excuse for them to do what the Shadians probably had paid them to do.

Itova be damned. I'm where Anur wishes me to be.

A few minutes later, they entered the castle's safety,

assuming the castle could be considered safe. Who had placed the bounty? Definitely somebody with access. Every person who passed them was a suspect, right down to Margaret's lady-in-waiting who stood inside the Queen's sitting room. Once inside, Margaret called for her personal physician, then dismissed everyone except Bredych and Leolin.

"Sit," she said to them both as she claimed the stiff-backed chair closest to the fireplace. No windows led to a darker, yet safer room as she held trembling hands out over the flames. "What I am about to tell you is a closely guarded secret. As far as my father knew, the only people aware of its existence are members of the royal family—at least those of age—and the Holy Few."

"Then why tell us? Why tell *him*?" asked Leolin as he pointed at Bredych, who sat in the chair beside Margaret. "You would trust him with such knowledge?"

"I don't know if you have noticed, but people I trust keep dying." Margaret's voice cracked as she stared at the flames. She opened her mouth to say more and a knock at the door announced the arrival of Master Roland. He bowed once and at her gesture, examined Bredych's shoulder.

The physician cut away part of Bredych's shirt sleeve to better see the wound. "The implement used to make the initial hole missed the important parts, but you'll be feeling the damage for a while. The wound looks stretched though. How long ago was the injury?"

"Unfortunately, Master Maurus took the wound saving my life, which he did twice tonight," said Margaret, and Roland inclined his chin.

"Our thanks then for the protection of our Queen." The

physician spread a powdery green mixture across a damp cloth, which he warmed near the fire.

Whatever was in the poultice numbed Bredych's shoulder to a mild throb rather than a sharp pain, and Bredych gave it a roll to test its movement.

Roland wagged a finger at him. "If you want it to heal, leave it be. No more heroics for you, though I suppose you'll listen about as well as Adelei did to my advice."

Bredych stiffened reflexively, then forced himself to relax. When he caught Margaret staring at him, her brows were furrowed, and she no longer held her hands over the fire but clenched them together in her lap. Roland wrapped a bandage around the wounded shoulder, then rolled up what was left of Bredych's bloody sleeve before he retreated from the room.

When he found his voice around the lump in his throat, Bredych asked, "Your personal physician attended an Amaskan?"

"She was more than an Amaskan. She was my sister."

Leolin ceased pacing and pointed at Bredych. "Your sister who was kidnapped by people like him."

"Enough," she shouted, clapping her hands together. "There are things I must say, and I need you both to hear them. Your distrust of my guest is noted, Leolin."

Leolin continued pacing, his hands buried deep in his pockets. The herbs' numbing affect had worn off, and Bredych's shoulder pulsed in rhythm to his heartbeat. He massaged it with his fingers. Did Margaret know something about the Senate? Something more than their obvious spying? Or was this something related to Adelei?

"The royal family has a way to communicate with the Boahim Senate, a way not known to anyone else." Bredych's arms prickled in response to Margaret's words, and he breathed deeply as she continued. "In every castle lies a magical orb; I say magical because I know no other way to explain it. When I speak a particular word in the old language, it comes to life. Inside the orb, I can see the senators and speak with them."

"You jest," said Leolin as he lowered himself into a chair.

Margaret laughed, a high-pitched laugh that chilled Bredych. "I wish I were. Life would be simpler without them looking on—"

"You believe they're using the orbs to spy on the Little Dozen Kingdoms," Bredych said.

"I do. They know things—information they have no way of knowing without sharing a room with me, and yet I know they have done nothing of the sort. The only time I have ever been in the same room with any of them is when they sentenced Gamun for his crimes."

And when they hanged my daughter, Adelei.

Tears bubbled up in Margaret's eyes, and Bredych's vision swam as well. He closed his eyes to hide the effect, and when he opened them again, Leolin watched him with a peculiar expression. Bredych waited for the boy to expose his cover or do something equally stupid, but the boy's facial muscles softened a touch before asking Margaret, "Why keep the orbs secret? What purpose do these orbs serve beyond spying on people?"

"The histories teach that they are a way for rulers to call for help, which is what I attempted to do when my father fell ill. Rather than offer assistance, they informed me that my father wasn't important. I contacted them again when I found records...records going back generations that show that the Poncett family has been changing our borders for decades. I thought perhaps they could tell me why. Not only did they know about the changing borders, but they knew the Shadian army occupied the Meridi Pass."

"Let me guess, the Shadian army isn't on your border at all, are they?" Bredych asked.

Margaret shook her head. "Not according to the original borders, and because of that, the Senate has no concern with their movements." She uncurled her clenched fingers in her lap and made to smooth a skirt she wasn't wearing. Halfway down her thigh, she tugged at the black breeches instead. "I have no doubt that the reason I still live is because of an Amaskan. The same thing that kept me alive when Gamun was here." Leolin opened his mouth, but she held up her hand. "I don't care what issue you have with Master Maurus. There is a spy in our ranks and a price on my head. If my sister were still alive, she would trust him, and so shall I."

She stood and walked over to a small wooden box that sat atop the fireplace mantel. It opened, then closed with a thud, and Margaret returned to Bredych with something in her hand.

Leolin's eyes snapped open. "No, please. Don't do this," he pled, but she knelt before Bredych just the same.

Margaret opened her hand to reveal a small brooch bearing a *kenturi,* and Bredych gasped. The creature was mostly a blot of white clay on such a small object, but its thirteen faces were recognizable to him—the same thirteen faces sketched in *The Book of Ja'ahr* and belonging to the Thirteen themselves. Its hooves glowed in the firelight, as did its eyes.

"When my father ruled, his *sepier* bore a different symbol, the star, but this brooch belonged to my mother. She was drawn to the *kenturi,* a creature my sister told me was sacred to the Amaskan, are they not?" she asked.

"Amaskans are tasked with serving Justice, of being selfless in the act of protecting the people of the Little Dozen Kingdoms." Leolin sniggered, which Bredych chose to ignore. "We believe that if we are truly lacking in self, we will be reborn at the feet of the Thirteen as a *kenturi*, tasked with leading those who are lost."

She reached out to take Bredych's hand and placed the brooch inside it. "I read once that the *kenturi* once represented the King's *Sepier* when the land was still Boahim. I find it fitting to use it once again. If you would be willing, I would have you as my *sepier*. I need someone trustworthy, someone who won't hide information from me and can help me make the difficult decisions ahead."

The look she gave the boy would have shriveled a cactus, and Bredych sighed. It would be easy to say yes. Doing so would give him access to all the information he'd wanted and then some, but his heart ached to see this child who resembled his Adelei kneel before him and offer him her life. And it would be her life. He would be tasked with the most important job in the kingdom.

He closed his hand over the brooch a moment, but her smile shifted to a frown when he opened it again and set the brooch back in her hand. "I know what you offer me, Your Majesty, and while it is a great honor, it's not one I'm worthy of."

"But you saved my life!"

"And so has Leolin and the good captain I wager. There are many who've done this and none of them have been offered so valuable a prize."

"Then you insult me," she said and stood.

"It's not my intention to insult. I'll remain here as an advisor to you if you can make use of such a role and in time, if I've earned such a position, I'll gladly take what you've offered, but not today. I'm no *kenturi*...not yet."

Margaret nodded, though her brows remained furrowed. "I gladly accept your proposition, though I believe you'll earn this title sooner than you think." She returned the brooch to its place and inclined her head, an obvious dismissal.

When he withdrew, Leolin followed him. Once the door closed with a soft thud, the boy shoved him from behind, sending Bredych forward a few steps more than intended. "I believe I told you to leave," the boy said.

Familiarity rested in his blue eyes, which flashed with hints of fire, and Bredych frowned. "Your queen isn't ready for me to leave just yet. Why not tell me what this is really about?"

The boy's hand gripped the hilt of his falchion until his knuckles were near white, and he growled. "The Amaskans ordered my father killed. For all I know, it could've been you!"

13

Even with the door closed, Leolin's accusation rang through the hallway, and Margaret winced.

"I wish I could deny it, but I've killed a lot of people's fathers in the service of Justice. I don't know if I killed yours. Who was your father? Why do you think Amaskans ordered him killed?" asked Master Maurus, though Margaret strained to hear him.

Sounds of a scuffle reached her, along with her guards' movements, and she opened the door in time to see Leolin's fist hit Maurus in the jaw.

There was no other way to describe it. The Thirteen knew Master Maurus moved with half the effort and double the speed of Leolin when he wished to do so, but he stood still as a stone as Leolin's fist cracked across his jaw.

Leolin acted the child. It wasn't the first time the thought had crossed her mind, and she suppressed the urge to throw something at his head. Rather than knock him unconscious, she sighed. Loudly.

Maurus pointed at Margaret, and Leolin spun to find himself nearly nose-to-nose with her. His cheeks flushed, then paled as he scrambled to bow. A few servants lingered in the hall, along with a few more guards, who openly stared at Leolin. "My apologies," he mumbled as he backed away from the scene to flee down the stairwell.

She didn't spare a glance for anyone as she followed after him. The footfalls behind her alerted her to her honor guard's presence, which she ignored as she climbed the stair's three flights. The door ahead shut as she reached the landing, and when she opened the door, Leolin was gone. The hallways were empty, but there was only one place Leolin would go—the gardens.

Margaret sprinted past a startled ambassador, and she made a mental note to apologize to the poor woman later. While the Amaskan-like fighting gear made it easy to move about, it screamed trouble in the castle as every person flinched or fled. The door leading to the interior gardens remained open a crack as she approached. When she pushed her way through, the sugary scent of wisteria and lilac tickled her nose, and for a moment, she was thirteen and hiding behind the flowers as Leolin called for her.

"Where are you? Maggie?"

She giggled as his tailed, black hair snagged in a rose bush, sending him squirming and spinning.

"I hear you laughing! Ow!"

If she didn't go untangle him, he would be stuck there all day...or at least until his shouts brought out the guards' pity. Three stood at the garden's entrance, their smiles visible from her hiding place. She extricated herself from the wisteria, sending a shower of purple petals onto the path. Their fragrance trailed behind her as she ran up behind Leolin. "Get stuck again?" she asked.

"No thanks to you." He held up a bloody finger, and

her stomach lurched at the sight of it. "If you're gonna get me tangled up and bloody, you should at least be able to look at it. Besides, one day when you're queen, you may lead people like me into battle. What then? Will you hide in the wisteria?"

Margaret stuck her tongue out at him. "That's why a ruler has a Grand Marshal," she said as she worked to untangle his hair from the rose thorns. His body went still as he stood upright, and a thorn pricked a new cut in his cheek. When she turned, his mother stood behind her, hands on her hips.

Even inside the safety of the castle, Ida Warhammer wore thick, leather armor and carried her short sword—a thick blade with a four-finger hilt that Margaret had touched once. Leolin had nearly leapt out of his skin when he had caught her. It had been the same day he had told her how she had received her name, and why she never carried a hammer.

Looking at the captain now, sweat beading on her brow as she frowned, Margaret dropped her shoulders and tried to make herself invisible.

"Where are ya supposed to be?" she asked Leolin, who tried and failed again to free himself from the roses. His mother snapped the offending branch, and he spared Margaret a glance before he nodding to his mother and running toward the garden doors.

"Thanks for freeing him. Some days that rose bush is his worst enemy," said Margaret. The warrior woman who stared at Margaret carried no warmth in her expression. Add to that the thick, puffy scar that traveled from ear to ear across her throat, and Margaret shivered.

As she turned away, the captain said, "A moment, please, Your Highness."

The voice was more gravel than silk, and she touched her own throat in response.

"Use it as a reminder, Your Highness."

Heat rose to Margaret's cheeks, and she dropped her hand. "A...a reminder of what?" she asked. No one spoke of the scar, nor how the woman had gotten it. Maybe the captain would be willing to tell her.

"Death," the captain whispered as she pointed at Margaret. "One day you'll rule Alexander, and Leolin'll serve ya in the Royal Army. But ya must remember—he's meant to serve, somethin' he'll never learn if ya keep distractin' him."

"Distracting him? I don't understand."

"Your tutors think ya in the library, yes?"

If the captain knew where she was, then so did her father. Margaret groaned.

"Like you, Leolin's got responsibilities. Yer both too old to be playin' like children. The sooner ya learn that, Your Highness, the better it'll be for us all. The better it'll be for Leolin too."

As the captain withdrew, her boots crushed the wisteria petals left on the ground. The sour smell flared Margaret's nostrils. Someone called her name from across the gardens. Probably one of her tutors. Probably on his way back from her father.

Margaret sighed.

"Margaret?"

She shook her head to clear the memory and found Leolin standing near the roses a few feet away. He avoided their thorny branches, choosing to stand outside their reach, and the corners of her mouth perked.

"What are you doing here?" he snapped, and her smile

faltered. He remembered his manners a few heartbeats later and gave a quick bow as she approached.

"I followed you, but when I entered the gardens, a memory overcame me." Margaret leaned in to smell a particularly pink rose. "Remember when things were simple?"

His frown deepened. "Nothing has ever been simple. That's the viewpoint of a child."

"That's what your mother believed as well," said Margaret.

He kicked a loose pebble at the garden bed's edge, then another one. Rather than further irritate him, Margaret sat on the wooden bench nestled between two rose bushes. Her father had carved flowers into its sides while her mother had paced the gardens late at night, pregnancy gifting her with insomnia as well as nausea. Margaret dangled an arm down the side and traced the carved wood with her fingers. The image of the dirt beneath her feet blurred. *Papa, how I miss you.*

Leolin sat beside her a few minutes later. "I'm sorry," he whispered.

Margaret kept her silence as she blinked back tears. If her father were here, he would know the words to heal whatever wounded her friend.

"Maggie, what did you remember?"

"The day you left."

He nodded. "I figured that was the one. Every time I smell wisteria, without fail," he said, then after a pause, added, "I didn't know she was sending me off to train under Lord Mellyn. I wish I'd known. I could've said goodbye."

"Goodbyes lead to people dying."

"Mine wouldn't have."

She glanced up to find his face closer than expected.

His blue eyes were clouded with emotions she could not read, and her breath hiccupped in her chest. When he kissed her, his lips tickled hers and a giggle escaped her. "That would have been an entirely different goodbye," she said.

"That would've been the point. Though if you'd giggled like that then, it would've crushed me."

"Your mother and I would have had an entirely different conversation if she had witnessed that," said Margaret as her insides tried to both dance and flee simultaneously.

His mother's words echoed in her mind, *Leolin's got responsibilities.*

She wanted to leap up and flee like her stomach, but she found her hand entangled in his as he watched her.

He asked, "What's wrong? Did I overstep—"

"No, your mother...."

"Maggie," he said as he released her hand. "What did my mother say to you after I left?"

The words spilled forth in a rush and when she was done, his temples throbbed all over again. Why did she always say the wrong words at the most inopportune time?

"My mother should've kept her peace," he said.

"But she was correct." When he opened his mouth to retort, Margaret held up her hand. "No, hear me out, please. I'm Queen. Your mother understood that one day, I would have to make difficult decisions, ones that might get you killed. Your training was important to the safety of not just the kingdom but of me and distracting you from that was irresponsible of me."

"You were a child!"

She shook her head. "It was not so long ago. I was

155

already promised to Gamun by then." His name soured the moment, and her tongue lay heavy in her mouth.

"Too young to know the world or what was to come," he whispered.

And now? Margaret stared at him. He did not understand. He couldn't. Leolin would never rule an entire kingdom full of people whose lives depended on him. At most he would command a small group of fighters. The wrinkles in her father's young face and his desire to flee inside his relationship with Ida made more sense now. Leolin was a man she could love but at what cost?

"This feud you have with Master Maurus—"

He curled his hands into fists. "He's dangerous."

"A fact that I am well aware of, but I have need of him. I need the information I can gain and the possible allies."

"You'd ally with those assassins?"

The last thing she wanted to do was hurt Leolin, but there was no time for personal dreams or wants. Yet she wanted nothing more than to send responsibilities to the Thirteen Hells. She had almost died today...twice. She sighed as she stood. "If that's what it takes to win this war, yes. And the sooner you learn that, the better it'll be for us all. The better it'll be for you."

His face crumpled, then froze as the crackling of cobble crushed beneath boots to her left announced someone else in the garden. Master Maurus stepped from between several trees and bowed. "Your Majesty, your council has need of you."

How long has he been there? Margaret shook her head. It didn't matter. None of it did.

"Escort me, please," she said to Maurus, then followed him from the gardens, leaving the wisteria far behind.

When the door opened to the council chambers, Grand Advisor Dumont Darras stood on the other side. His mouth fell open, then closed as he bowed. "My apologies, Your Majesty. I didn't recognize you in fighter's clothing."

"I had forgotten I still wore it as my day has been more eventful than anticipated. My apologies to my council for the casualness of my attire."

Her Grand Advisor's frown remained as he moved away from the door so that she might enter, and he kept his eyes downcast and away from her.

"Your Majesty, may I ask why he's here?" Captain Fenton asked and pointed at Master Maurus, who trailed into the council room behind Margaret.

"I've offered him the position of *sepier*," Margaret said.

Master Maurus took a standing position behind the chair she claimed at the table's end. "And I've said no, at least for the moment," he said.

Captain Fenton frowned. "Then what's his purpose here?"

Margaret slapped her hand against the table. "His purpose is my own," she said as the captain took his seat beside her Grand Advisor. Grand Marshal Doublis's seat was empty, as were the seats for Her Holiness of the Holy Few and her royal physician.

Before she could ask, Dumont said, "Marshal Doublis sends his regrets. The recent movement by the Shadian army has him elsewhere. Roland is treating the runner who brought us some news a candlemark ago, and Her Holiness is with him."

"The runner's wounds are severe?" she asked, and he nodded. "How was he wounded?"

Her mind painted gruesome images of some Shadian gutting her runner or dragging him through the rocky terrain, his body bouncing here and there as the horse galloped for the border. Not that the runner should have been in Shad....

"His horse spooked and threw the lad," said Dumont.

The news must be dire indeed for the runner to stress a horse so. "What news did he bring? I assume that is why I was called here?"

Captain Fenton fetched a scrap of parchment from the table and passed it to Margaret. Triangles and slash marks decorated the letters at seemingly random intervals. The words themselves made little sense as written, but the code was one she could decipher in her sleep and by touch if necessary—an old way of sending messages from a time of war that before now, Margaret had never known. Thankfully, her tutors had seen fit to ensure she could read it, though as she read the message, she wished it had remained gibberish.

Master Maurus leaned over her shoulder and stared at the parchment. "I've not seen those markings in a long while," he said.

"Can you decipher it?"

He shook his head. "It's not a skill I can rightfully claim, though there are members of my Order that do. I take it the news is not good?"

"The Halelindian army marches to join the Shadians at our border. Worse still, the Shadians have fortified the Meridi Pass. They intend to stay there or perhaps use it as a stronghold."

Dumont cleared his throat, then took a long swallow of water from his glass. "My apologies, Your Majesty, for being the bearer of bad news, but we received news this morning that the Monpolian army is at our northern border."

She pressed her fingers against the bridge of her nose as her heart pounded in her throat. The old man's chapped fingers patted her other hand, and for a moment, Margaret could imagine it was her father beside her. His chapped and roughened hands, his voice speaking to the council, and his wisdom guiding the kingdom.

But it wasn't.

The man might have been old, but he missed nothing as he tore his gaze away from Maurus and stared openly at Margaret, his brow furrowed. "I've done something to offend you."

"For a moment, I thought my father in the room."

"I believe he is, Your Majesty. As the Thirteen watch over us, so does he. Though he must wonder at the wisdom of having an Amaskan at this table." Dumont stared over Margaret's head at Master Maurus, his lips a thin line of disapproval. When the old man spotted Margaret's expression, he said, "I know you don't wish to hear it, but it *is* my job as your Grand Advisor to counsel you. No good has ever come of Amaskans, nor will it ever. He should be sent away. For the good of Alexander."

The old prejudice did not surprise her, though his insistence that Maurus leave did, and she shook her head. "Twice today Master Maurus has saved my life from a bounty on my head."

Rather than give him time to list a thousand reasons why the Amaskans were evil, she pulled the parchment from her pocket and spread it out in front of Dumont. The sketch of her was realistic enough she could believe it a mirror, and there was no mistaking the reward at the bottom for her life. "We were attacked by multiple assailants, all of them wishing to bring my life to a sudden end. If Master Maurus had not been there, I would be ashes like my father."

Dumont rose from the table and gave a brief, yet stiff bow in Maurus's direction. "Then you have this council's thanks for the life of our Queen, though I don't know what you wish to gain from such an action."

"Enough, Dumont. My own father held council with an Amaskan at this table. If anyone would understand the necessity of such an action, it would be him. If we are to win this war, we must use every tool at our disposal, including those who were once seen as enemies."

Her Grand Advisor kept his silence, but his face was ashen and his lips slightly blue. Margaret rang for a page and when the boy appeared, said, "Send for Master Roland."

"I'm fine," Dumont said as he waved at her. "Just old."

His chest labored as he breathed and even his nailbeds were blue-tinged. "Perhaps you should lie down," she said. Maurus reached out for Dumont, who jerked away, his eyes wide with fear.

"Don't touch me! I'll not be slain by the likes of you!" he shouted as he leapt up from his seat. The whites of his eyes shone as sweat prickled across his face, then he gasped once more before pitching forward across the council table.

Everyone moved at once.

Captain Fenton swept cups and parchment from the table as Maurus flipped Dumont on his back. Lord Cornish and Lady Mara backed against the wall as far as they could muster from Maurus, who leaned over to listen at the old man's throat. As Margaret stood, the door to the council chambers opened, and her personal physician rushed in.

"What happened?" Roland asked as he brushed aside Maurus.

"He's not breathing," Maurus said, and the unasked question hung in the air between them a moment before the Amaskan answered. "No, I didn't kill him."

"He grew unreasonably upset," Margaret said while Roland used a knife to cut open Darras's tunic. "His face was pale, gray like it is now, and his lips were blue. Then he fell across the table."

Roland pressed his hand against the Grand Advisor's heart, then his ribs as he listened at the man's mouth. When the chest didn't move, he examined the man's fingernails before opening the mouth and reaching inside. Margaret gripped the table's edge with her fingers as she waited, and the room spun when her personal physician shook his head.

"He stopped breathing, Your Majesty. Dumont was an old man. The stress of...the war was too much for his heart. There was nothing to be done. Itova required him," said Roland as he stared at the body.

"Surely there's something more we can do," said Margaret, but Roland shook his head. "But he was all I had left of my father. He was like a brother to him, like an uncle to me...."

"As with life, there is death. I am sorry, Your Majesty. I am no god to bring back the dead."

Maurus knelt beside the body and touched the man's hand. Words in the old tongue flowed like honey, their rhythm and cadence like the dance of bees, and when Roland moved to stop the man, Margaret took his hand and said, "No, allow him his ritual."

Once Maurus was done, he released Dumont's hand and took Margaret's. "There are openings and closings, and neither of us knows which will come first. Your loss is our loss, and the Amaskans grieve with you."

The room tilted and dimmed, and not even her fighting gear could help Margaret fight her sorrow as guilt and pain washed over her. Voices called out to her, then were silenced as the council chamber was no more.

14

When Margaret awoke, Leolin sat beside her, worry wrinkles marching across his face. She lay in her bedchambers, tucked under three quilts too many, and Roland stood not far away, mixing some concoction that was probably as foul as it was helpful. Captain Fenton stood guard at the door, though Maurus was nowhere to be seen. She sat up, and Leolin released the hand she had not been aware he held.

"You gave us quite a scare," Leolin said, and Roland rushed over.

The physician handed her the mug. "Drink all of this down. It will help you rest."

"What happened?" she asked. Roland and Leolin exchanged an odd look, and Margaret set the mug on the table beside her bed. "I'll not drink this until I know what happened and why I need it."

"You fainted, or that's what they tell me," said Leolin.

"We don't know that," Roland said and pointed at the mug. "You said yourself that someone's been trying to kill you, and while Dumont *was* an old man, he died rather suddenly. Soon after, you lose consciousness. For all we know, someone has poisoned him and has now tried to poison you. I suggest you drink the mug just in case, Your Majesty."

Dumont. He was dead.

Tears welled up in her eyes and blurred her vision. She blinked them back rapidly as she fetched the mug and gave it a good sniff. Nothing smelled suspicious, not that she knew what poison smelled like. As everyone kept reminding her, she wasn't her sister, Adelei. In fact, the warm liquid smelled faintly of cinnamon and cloves. It smelled good.

Was that good? Or did it mean something ominous?

Margaret studied the cup for a moment. She took a sip and gagged on the thick sludge. "If anyone is trying to poison me, I proclaim it's you with this...this...foul drink," she said.

"The herbs will help your body fight anything someone may have used to harm you and nothing more," said Roland.

She took another sip and swallowed, though the back of her throat tried to regurgitate the liquid. A few more swallows and her body adjusted to it. *As much as anyone adjusts to drinking a slug.*

"Where is Master Maurus?" she asked Leolin, who stared at his lap.

"It was for your own good—"

"What was? What have you done?"

Leolin glanced up at Roland, as if he needed support, but the physician wisely kept his attention on cleaning up his supplies. "Maurus is locked up in the dungeon. At least until we can be sure that no attempt has been made on your life."

The urge to throw the mug at him swept over her, and for a moment she considered actually throwing it. He wouldn't expect it. Not from her—the spoiled, defenseless princess that everyone had to handhold—

When the mug hit floor, Leolin flinched. "Leave," she ordered Roland, who scurried out of her bedchambers with no further prompting. When Leolin opened his mouth, she held up her finger and silenced him. She allowed him the silence for a handful of heartbeats and watched as he squirmed in the chair beside her bed. At one point, his protection of her had been something she had appreciated, even enjoyed. He was her best friend. It was his job. But now....

"You go too far," she said.

"I don't follow."

Margaret pointed at the mug on the floor. "You think the mug is me. Something fragile, something easily broken. Something in need of coddling and protection." Rather than allow him to speak, she shook her finger and cut off what he had been about to say. "How much did Ida tell you...about what happened when Adelei arrived?"

"Nothing much. It wasn't long after that your father sent her to Shad."

"How much did you hear though? Rumors and such?"

Leolin swallowed hard as he glanced down at the mug. "The rumors aren't the type to be spoken in front of your queen."

"Tell me." When she glared at him, she pretended her eyes were iron, like the sword she had carried earlier, and he acquiesced.

"The rumors were a jumble of words by frightened people. Some say Adelei killed Gamun, while others still say she wanted Gamun for herself."

Laughter bubbled up in her at the idea. Adelei had wanted Gamun like she had wanted a donkey. At Leolin's confused look, Margaret waved her hand for him to continue.

"Some say Gamun came here to seize control of Alexander. I overheard Lieutenant Thomas telling someone else that Gamun was here under orders from the Boahim Senate—something similar to what you mentioned before about your father changing Alexander's borders."

As she studied him, she regretted throwing the mug. Her childhood friend sat in the chair before her, so completely unaware of how much she had changed since that thirteen-year-old girl had convinced him to skip lessons. Letters written across miles and months did not paint the proper picture of their experiences or how those experiences had sculpted them. Even at twenty-three, a few lines burrowed themselves in his youthful face, especially when he looked on her just now.

"Leolin, you have been trained to protect and to serve, but I am not the same person you knew, and not just because of what Gamun...did to me. There are magics about that have tested my beliefs in our world. I've had my own husband plot my death and the deaths of those close to me, and I've watched my father make choices no father should have to make."

"In other words, you've grown up," he said and furrowed his brow. "But that doesn't change the need to protect you, especially when you insist on keeping an Amaskan at your side."

"How do I make you understand?"

A knock at the door announced her lady-in-waiting, who kept her eyes downcast when she spotted Leolin. "My apologies, Your Majesty, but Lady Mara sends her regards and wishes you to know that she will be returning to her home in preparation for the w-war." The woman's hands shook as she pulled the door shut behind her.

"My own council is leaving me, and you wonder why I keep Master Maurus close," Margaret said.

"Not all are gone."

"My council was to be thirteen, Leolin. When my father died, that number was eight. Now, Doublis prepares to lead my army for the border, and Lady Mara has fled. Master Roland and Her Holiness are busy treating those seeking refuge or healing here, and my uncle is dead. That leaves Captain Fenton, who trusts in my abilities to lead about as much as you do, Lord Cornish, who would rather rule in my stead, and a seat that awaits my *sepier*, should Master Maurus accept the position."

His cheeks were flushed, but Leolin held his tongue until she had finished. "You want people to treat you like a leader, but are you leading?" he asked as he stood. "Your council is only that—your council. *You* are queen, not them. You talk of your father making hard choices, but right or wrong, at least he made them. So far, you keep waiting for people to make them for you, especially your pet Amaskan."

"Get out," she growled, and he glanced once more at the mug. "And release Master Maurus once you leave."

Leolin opened the door, but before stepping through it, he said, "Stone, wood, even metal are shapeable, but they hold up under pressure while glass does not. When you figure it out, which will you be, Margaret?"

The door closed behind him before she could respond.

Stone. She would become stone. Like Adelei.

THE TRICKIEST PART IN BECOMING LIKE STONE WAS forcing her inward emotions to reflect the outward appearance Margaret portrayed three days later as she strode into her empty council chamber. Rather than her typical attire, she wore a simple silk skirt and tunic over her chemise. It lacked the typical embroidery or beadwork of most of her clothing, but the fabric moved freely, especially with a cloth belt around it rather than a proper bodice. She had been tempted to wear breeches, but the mourning ritual did not allow for such measures. Even if there *was* a chance of attack. Dumont's body had been given a full thirteen candlemark burn the day before and his ashes given to Her Holiness, where they would be formally added to the list of royal family members before being retired to the castle gardens.

What little remained of her council would meet her here in a candlemark, but for now, she used the silence to pen a message to King Havin. The chances of his listening to her request were about as great as the chances she would survive this war unscathed, but it was time for her to make the difficult choices, as Leolin had so bluntly reminded her. With him in mind, she spread the sheet of parchment before her and dipped her quill in the ink well.

To His Majesty, King Havin Bajit of Shad
   from the desk of Her Majesty Queen Margaret I,

Cousin, I write to you in hopes that whatever conflict lay between us is one that might be settled with words rather than with swords. The loss of Gamun at the hands of the Boahim Senate was unfortunate, as was the loss of my father. Both of us have seen no justice, though together, perhaps we could.

> *My Grand Marshal informs me that your army holds the Meridi Pass, which the Boahim Senate states is your land. My own delving into my family's records finds that they may be correct. I concede the Pass to your people and promise you that I have no intention of continuing to change my borders.*
>
> *Let us meet and discuss the future. There is no need for additional blood to spill across our lands.*
>
> *I await your response and wish you and family the blessings of Delorcini.*

Her Majesty Queen Margaret Poncett I

Margaret affixed her seal across the letter, which she handed to the page stationed outside the council room. "Take this to the pigeon master."

"Its destination, Your Majesty?"

"King Havin, Meredi Pass." *Knowing him, he's sitting on a tall horse amidst his army rather than hiding at the capital. The way I am.*

The members of her council arrived as the page set off down the hallway, and Margaret proceeded them into the room. With Master Maurus and Leolin present, the space was less desolate than Margaret felt. When Maurus refused the chair meant for her *sepier* and sat in Lady Mara's vacant seat, Leolin claimed the seat beside Margaret. She said nothing, choosing to maintain an expression of nonchalance, though her insides quaked with exhaustion and anger.

Margaret retrieved a piece of parchment penned the day before and dipped her pen in the inkwell before affixing her name to it.

Lord Cornish smacked his lips together once before he

asked, "Perhaps you wish to consider all options before making this decision?"

"I don't. Splitting the army is the only way to deal with the threats on both of our borders. The Grand Marshal will go toward the Pass while Captain Fenton will go north."

Captain Fenton frowned but nodded at Margaret.

"If Captain Fenton is going north, who will take his position on this council?" asked Lord Cornish. "I can recommend a few high class members who would be of use to Your Majesty—"

"That will not be necessary. If Master Maurus will not serve as my *sepier*, he will serve this council in the Grand Marshal's place and advise me on matters of war."

Leolin sputtered his drink, but before he could protest, Margaret turned her gaze on him with what she hoped was solid stone. "Before Sergeant Leolin can protest this, I have good reason for this decision. I do not need Sadai at my third border in this war—not as an enemy. They can hardly go to war with me with one of their own on my council and in my high regard. The Amaskans will serve me as Adelei did my father, as they do King Adir of Sadai."

The cacophony that met her statement was expected, and rather than try and speak over their protests, she waited. She poured herself a glass of mulled wine, though her hands shook despite her best efforts. She brought the glass up to her lips and sipped.

The last time someone drank in this room, they had died.

She took another sip and waited. Maurus said nothing. He watched the chaos with a similar look—his eyes flat and his mouth straight-lined—though one corner of his mouth twitched when he spotted her.

Leolin was the first to notice her silence as he paused mid-word. "Your Majesty's very quiet," he said.

"Are you boys finished?" she asked, pitching her voice a bit lower than normal. Indifference. Apathy. Boredom. Or that was what she hoped it portrayed.

"My apologies, Your Majesty, but what you're proposing isn't a wise course of action," said Lord Cornish.

"I wasn't *proposing* anything, my lord. It's already done."

His face, a brilliant spectrum of purples and reds, puffed up as he prepared to let loose with some unsolicited wisdom, which he swallowed when he met her gaze.

Perhaps she was better at this than she initially thought. Or maybe they only pretended complacency. Either way, this would do for now. "In addition, I'm promoting Sergeant Leolin to lieutenant. He will serve on my council in the captain's place," she said, and Leolin smirked at Maurus.

Margaret handed the document to the returned page. Her orders to leave for the Shadian border with all haste would go directly to the Grand Marshal. If King Havin disregarded her letter, the Grand Marshal would be ready. She affixed her signature and seal to another document, a similar one ordering Captain Fenton to the northern border, and handed it directly to him. When he left the room, silence descended, and Margaret found herself drawn to the Thirteen engraved across the council room table. Farimun, God of Journeys and Luck, appeared to stare back at her, his multiple chins and chubby cheeks shining in the candlelight.

"We could use some luck, couldn't we?" asked Leolin.

Something about the question brought up memories of a past long gone, and before she could stop herself, she smiled. The way he had made her smile—she was breathless as the remainder of the room faded away. Lord Cornish cleared his throat, and reality returned. "With three armies at our borders, we could use more than a little luck."

"About those armies—if Your Majesty intends to make use of the Amaskans, perhaps our *friend* here could prove his loyalties. If perhaps he would send a message to King Adir of Sadai and ask for assistance," said Lord Cornish.

Master Maurus nodded and when Margaret handed him a clean piece of parchment, the Amaskan scribbled out a short note before handing it back to her. The note itself was concise in its message, followed by a simple symbol that served as his signature.

She passed it to Lord Cornish, who frowned and said, "This message is addressed to the King himself!"

"It is," said Maurus.

"And why would the King of Sadai grant you such a boon?" asked Leolin.

Lord Cornish tapped his thick fingers on the table as he nodded. "Yes! Why not write to the Amaskans you serve?"

Because then we would know where the Amaskans are located, would we not? Margaret held out her hand for the parchment. She glanced at it a second time, particularly the symbol at the bottom. At first glance, it was a simple circle, but the circle's beginning and end went from narrow point to a thick brush as the writer used the quill's side. Pressure differences changed the smoothness and thickness of the circle, but that couldn't be the only distinguishing point. "There's no real difference in the symbol, so how will King Adir know which Amaskan this is from?"

Maurus smiled as his eyes lit up. "There are words within the message itself. Something in the way of the wording."

"What needs saying would change from message to

message. Are all Amaskans clever enough to reword the message so easily to say what needs saying?" she asked.

Lord Cornish rose from his chair unsteadily, his face flustered. "And who are you that a king would listen to you, Amaskan or no? Your Majesty, this man is a master of nothing. A charlatan! His promises mean nothing, and if anything, will lead only to the deaths of more honest Alexandrians!"

"My Lord, I acknowledge the wisdom in your words. Perhaps if you breathed a bit more and shouted a bit less, you would be with us long enough for Master Maurus to explain." *And explain he better*. Margaret inclined her head in the Maurus's direction.

"There are some things I can't say. The lives of others depend on such secrecy—"

"Of course you'd say that! Nothing more than a thief, I tell you," shouted Lord Cornish.

Master Maurus shook his head. "That's not what I meant, my lord. Please allow me to finish—"

"We'll not stand by as you lie to our faces—" said Leolin.

She could do this. What was it Adelei had said? Belief in the self is belief in others?

When Margaret stood, it was a slow, controlled movement—an intentional movement she had seen her father do a thousand times. The first time she had attempted it, members of her council had noticed, though only because honor bound them to do so. She had seen it in their eyes, their silent assent. And pity. The latter being the worst of those days when her father had been bedridden. But when she stood now, voices fell silent, though they trailed off rather than abruptly ceasing the way she had hoped they would.

"Each of you carries a wisdom I need. A voice that I believe is necessary for us to survive the upcoming battle. However, your voices are here at my discretion. It is I who wears the crown, and I who ultimately must make the decisions for the people of Alexander. If you cannot be the voice I need, then your voice will no longer be needed." She paused to glance at each of them for a moment. Her voice did not quiver, and inside she smiled. "Now, since I value each of you, you will work together or not at all. Swear it or forever leave this room."

Margaret turned to Leolin first, who swallowed hard before speaking. "I swear I will abide by your wishes to... work with the council, Your Majesty."

"I swear, Your Majesty," said Lord Cornish, though his eyes promised nothing of the sort, and she sighed before turning to Master Maurus.

She had expected him to be the fastest to answer not the slowest. As he stared at the table, the frown he wore deepened, and she said, "I would have your promise as well, Master Maurus."

"Your Majesty, I would gladly swear to work with your council, but what am I swearing to? I won't betray my allegiance to the Order by taking such oaths lightly." Maurus touched a wrinkled hand to the scar on his jaw, and before anyone could protest, he said, "As long as my actions do not endanger the lives of my Order or break my oath with the Thirteen, I will work with your council. War helps no one. After all, there are many little ways to peace, and none can be found at the end of a sword."

His wording withheld him from technically swearing, but Margaret let the matter pass. She needed the information and contacts he brought too much to press it.

"If you would finish your explanation, please," she said, and he nodded.

"Long ago, when I was new to the Order, I was tasked with finding the spy within King Adir's court. At the time, he was a young prince and full of the fervor and excitement of youth. Multiple assassination attempts had been made on his life, yet he shrugged them off with more bravery than most Amaskans. When I exposed the spy, I saved the lives of not just the prince but his father as well. Because of this, King Adir is someone I would consider a friend. If I support Alexander in this war, he will likely follow with his support."

The King of Sadai was a perplexing man. Margaret's father had known the man his entire reign, yet when it came to the man, King Leon had known him as well as a random river rock. "Are you satisfied, Lord Cornish?" she asked.

"I am."

"Lieutenant?" She turned to Leon, who furrowed his brows but acquiesced. "Good. It pleases me that we've made progress. I only wish our headway with the Boahim Senate were as good."

"You have news from the Senate?" asked Lord Cornish.

"Yes, though I wish it were good news."

"A moment please, Your Majesty," said Master Maurus, and she paused. "I will need something to guarantee the safety of this letter on its journey through your lands."

She turned to stare openly at him. He had Amaskans within her borders. There was no other explanation for why someone delivering a message would need her personal seal. "We have messenger pigeons that could deliver the message," she said.

"He will trust that this message is truly from me only if it is delivered through nontraditional means."

By an Amaskan, you mean. Margaret bit the inside of her lip. Once written, this letter would give the Amaskans free rein to travel through her country when and where they wished. Master Maurus met her gaze evenly and inclined his head the tiniest fraction. Such an admission was unexpected, and the ambivalence made Margaret's head whirl. She inhaled deeply and set her face to a calm she did not feel. Before she could rethink the decision, she scribbled a quick note on parchment and lobbed a melted blob of wax to the paper, which she stamped with her personal seal. When she handed it to him, she kept her eyes on him so she would not see her council's disapproval.

"The news from the Senate's not good," she said. Leolin and Maurus were already aware of the changing borders and the Senate's thoughts on the war, though Margaret repeated it for Lord Cornish, whose belly flopped with each harrumph and sigh he made. She left out the bits about the orb—no need to give him more than necessary.

"Your Majesty, these border shifts are perfectly natural. Over time, the land and the people change. Every kingdom in the Little Dozen Kingdoms has seen borders flex and move over time. I don't see how the Senate can use this as an excuse to not protect the people of Alexander," said Lord Cornish.

Margaret nodded, though the news surprised her. If every ruler were held to the same laws, would war be drawing closer? Was that not the purpose of the Senate? To protect everyone, farmer and king alike? "I wish to research the Senate's role and their history further. Perhaps if we can find something to force their hand, we can end this battle before it's begun."

As the members of her council rose to leave, Margaret gestured for Leolin and Master Maurus to remain. When the room cleared and the door closed behind them, both men returned to their seats.

"Perhaps the Senate's time comes to an end," said Maurus.

She glanced at the wall where the orb slept. Were the senators listening to them now?

Both men followed the direction of her gaze. "Is that where it is?" asked Leolin.

"Yes, though I doubt a wall will keep them from hearing what they wish." To Maurus, she said, "That which you speak of is sacrilege. The Senate has existed since the Little Dozen Kingdoms were formed. Their fall would be the fall of us all."

"Perhaps, but if they don't serve their purpose, then like all things old and decrepit, they must fade away." Maurus walked over to the bookshelf and ran his hands along the shelves. "I've heard rumor that orbs like this exist deep within the Order, though why, I wouldn't know. Perhaps we can find the answer in our research."

"*Our* research?" Margaret asked.

"Three sets of eyes will find information faster than one," Maurus answered before he faced her and bowed. "If there is nothing more you need of me, I would like to send this message to His Majesty as quickly as possible."

She nodded and when Leolin stood, she said, "Leolin, remain a moment more." Once Maurus had retreated, Margaret continued. "I realize that you dislike Master Maurus—perhaps *dislike* understates your feelings—but we cannot afford to allow petty differences to interrupt what needs doing. Besides, Master Maurus is far more than he has said."

Leolin frowned. "How so?"

"He's more than a mere Amaskan. He knows too much

and possesses friends and contacts much higher than he should."

"And what do you plan to do with this information?"

"Use it." *And him.*

Inside she winced. The old man had grown on her. He reminded her too much of Adelei and a bit of her father and Dumont tossed in for good measure, which made it more than difficult to do what she had planned. She would use Maurus to save her people, and Leolin, too.

"Maggie, are you sure you can do this?" Leolin asked. Like stone, the façade crawled across her skin as she lost her smile. He must have felt the shift as he tossed both hands in the air. "I didn't mean it that way. Damn it, I'm doing this all wrong. I used to know how to talk to you."

"You know how to talk to Princess Margaret—a spoiled brat who knew nothing and thought she knew everything."

Leolin ran his hands through his hair, then stopped to study her. His gaze paused at her eyes and the stress lines she was sure surrounded them. "Can I have my spoiled princess back?" he whispered.

If I knew where to find her, I might be tempted. To him, she merely shrugged. "That princess would get everyone killed, and I've lost enough people..." Tears blurred her vision, and she blinked rapidly to clear them.

"I didn't mean to bring up the dead," he said and reached for her hand.

She was so tired of being strong, of being what she wasn't. Given the time and opportunity, a good cry would do her wonders. He could hold her, and the world would be at peace for a moment. Like it used to be. But if she did, he would forever question her decisions and her strength. His calloused fingers traced a delicate line across her hand.

Rather than relax into his offer, she stilled and pushed aside the trembling in her gut and heart.

Leolin paused before withdrawing his hand with a sigh. "Tell me how you mean to use him."

"There are things I need to research and confirm—suspicions I have about Master Maurus—but if I'm correct, I am going to hold him to his oath."

"Which one?"

"The one that matters most to him."

15

As the majority of the Alexandrian army left for the borders, few people sought an audience with Margaret as they either fled or prepared for fighting. With the military decisions in more capable hands than hers, she found herself with plenty of time to examine the Boahim Senate. Her father's personal library had been a retreat, a private room where he gathered his thoughts and decided what course would be best for his kingdom, but rather than solace, Margaret had found only sorrow sitting in the room alone. A good night's sleep given by some concoction Roland mixed up made the difference, as did the presence of Leolin and Maurus two days later.

The room was as she had left it when she had learned the truth about her family and how the Boahim Senate possessed eyes and ears in unexpected places. Chances were they watched as Leolin and Maurus followed her into a place that held her father's touch on every book spine.

Leolin whistled at the walls full of books, while the corners of Maurus's mouth tilted up in amusement. He had seen larger libraries then. Perhaps at the Order? Margaret pointed at the corner closest to the window. "Most of the histories and treaties of Alexander begin over there and are arranged in chronological order. Some are missing. I think my sister and I may have destroyed a copy with a bucket of water once."

"And what were you doing with a bucket of water in a library?" Maurus asked.

Margaret smiled. "We filled a bucket with flowers from the garden, then realized they would need water to survive in here. Most of the water had sloshed over the sides all over the castle by the time we reached this room, but enough remained to destroy whatever book it was. I think it might have been a royal journal. I do not recall. Whatever it was, I thought Papa—my father—would kill us both."

"It's hard to think of an Amaskan hauling buckets through the castle as a child. I always thought she would've been killing bunnies or something," said Leolin.

"She was a child like anyone else," she said, but out of the corner of her eye, she glanced at Maurus. Ever since he had spoken of King Adir, her brain prickled with questions. He was much more important to the Amaskans than he let on. At the mention of Adelei, his face softened. It was a look she had seen often enough on her father's features. "Master Maurus, do you have children?" she asked as he browsed book spines, then felt the heat rise to her cheeks. "My apologies. I don't know if it's permitted of Amaskans to have families...."

"No apology needed, Your Majesty. Most Amaskans don't and for good reason. The life of an Amaskan is often dangerous and short-lived. But yes, I had a child."

Had. Past tense. Margaret took note of the fact and changed the topic by pointing at another shelf of books. "These books here are mostly treaties and agreements drawn up by my father and grandsire. Some precede the Poncett line, but they are in delicate condition. Before now, I have never thought to explore them or have them rewritten by scribes, though I'm reconsidering that now that I have need of them."

Leolin retrieved a heavy book with gold bindings as thick as his wrist. It was a book Margaret recognized from long sessions with tutors, and she groaned.

"Recognize it, I take it?" he asked.

Margaret nodded. "There may still be a few of my scribbles in that copy."

"I look forward to finding them." Leolin's lopsided grin made her heart race, and she glanced beneath half-shuttered lashes at Master Maurus. His focus remained on the books, and she sighed in relief.

"If you want information on the Senate, what better place to start than *The Rise and Fall of Boahim*," said Leolin as he settled into a chair near the window.

Her father's chair.

She almost ordered him out of it, but the thought was ridiculous. The room held exactly one comfortable chair near the window's light. Besides, he had to sit somewhere, though a piece of her wished he had chosen a seat in closer proximity to her.

The remaining space was crammed with books and two wooden chairs at a lone table, one of which Maurus claimed. He was already scribbling on a piece of parchment as his eyes scanned a book's page.

Margaret flipped through the bound treaties until she found one held together by ancient stitching. It was a copy of the original treaty signed by the rulers of twelve lands that bound them together under the Boahim Senate. The treaty made for dry material, even the fifteenth time reading it, but it was a necessary place to start.

"ANY LUCK?" ASKED LEOLIN AS HE LEANED OVER Margaret's shoulder. The boy was like a tracking dog with a scent he wouldn't relinquish. All day he came to her with useless tidbits that got them nowhere, all in hopes that this stone façade she wore would melt before him. Finally she wore the focus of the crown, and he wished to take that away. Bredych scowled.

The midday meal had come and gone, as had several pitchers of mulled wine and water, brought at Margaret's request, yet a handful of histories later, nothing explained the Senate's ambivalence. Margaret closed the bound document in front of her and shook her head. "The Boahim Senate was formed after the Fall of Boahim, in order to protect everyone, from prince to pauper. The documents all speak of the same ideas."

"Same here. They're bound by the Thirteen laws and answer only to the Thirteen themselves, and so on and so on. You'd think somewhere there'd be some document that actually stipulates their duties." Leolin pointed at the book to his left. "What about that one...*A Treatise on Senates and Rulers: Dissecting the Boahim Senate in a Modern World.* Have you checked that book yet?"

"Not yet," said Margaret.

Bredych picked up the text and thumbed through it until he spotted the passage he'd read earlier and smacked the table. "Aha! I knew I'd seen this book before. Look here," he said as he pointed at the page.

"It's an interpretation of the Thirteen laws," she said.

"More than that. It's an interpretation supported by treaties and peace agreements."

Leolin frowned. "Agreements? As in plural? The Fall of Boahim and the Little War of Three...right?"

Bredych riffled through a few documents on the table until he had the original document in his hands. He skimmed it, then he set it down in front of Margaret. "It's a translation of an agreement signed before your father was crowned, in which the Little Dozen Kingdoms reconfirmed their acceptance of the Boahim Senate as a governing body. All of this took place after the Sadai-Monpoli conflict. I knew I'd read about that somewhere," he said as he tapped the book. "Several kingdoms felt the Boahim Senate was unnecessary. They argued that the kingdoms could rule themselves without interference from the Senate. Sadai was one of those kingdoms, but Monpoli argued that without the Senate, what would keep a ruler from killing anyone who didn't agree with his or her way of ruling? Who would enforce the Thirteen laws?"

"I read about this a few years ago. A conflict broke out between Sadai and Monpoli, but was it war? I thought it nothing more than a scuffle," said Margaret.

"A scuffle that resulted in the death of Monpoli's king," Bredych said, and Leolin whistled. "The Senate used the death as evidence of why they were necessary. Without them, they argued, the Little Dozen Kingdoms would dissolve into another civil war, this one worse than the one that caused Boahim to fall."

Leolin dragged his chair away from the window and set it beside Margaret. "Master Maurus, Boahim fell because twelve lords couldn't agree, not because they needed oversight. Do these agreements give us anything useful though? Some random person's interpretations aren't exactly law."

Bredych held up his finger as he skimmed a second and third page. "Unless they are. This document—" he pointed again at the single parchment, "—is an agreement between the Senate and Little Dozen Kingdoms that says that any treaty ratified by all twelve is an extension of the original agreement that placed the Senate into power. And this book lists the last peace agreement as 'the last agreement that shall be made' because 'The Senate shall intervene in any conflict that would rip asunder what the Thirteen have created.'"

It was exactly what they needed. But if it were that easy to find.... Margaret held out her hand, and Maurus passed her the book. Her brow furrowed and her expression twisted as if she'd swallowed something sour. Maybe her thoughts followed his.

Leolin asked, "If they are meant to be the wall between any conflict or war, then why haven't they stopped this one?"

"Because something else motivates them," said Margaret. Her hands shook as she stared at the table. "Your mother, Ida, dead. My sister, Adelei, dead. My father dead. And for what? What purpose do they have in encouraging a feud?" she whispered, then stood.

Like a whipped hound, she fled to the door, where she stopped when its wood ceased her forward momentum. Her fingers curled around the handle at the same time that Maurus reached her. When his hand gripped her shoulder, she spun to face him. "They're dead. All of them. How many more will die in the name of their foolishness?" she shouted.

Her hand trembled as if she wished to strike him, to lash

out at something real, something present. It was a feeling he knew too well, and he was proud when she reined it in and her hand ceased shaking. It was natural to feel anger. Hell, if the Senate was doing half of what Bredych believed they were, she would be enraged by the time everything was said and done.

Her eyelids narrowed as she threw herself back against the door. "Is that how they knew? Was it you?" she asked. She hadn't buried her anger at all. Rather than adjust, she'd made him her target. Margaret shifted her weight to her right heel and angled her left shoulder forward—a defensive position as she readied for a fight.

"What? I have no idea what you're talking about, Your Majesty," he said.

"The Senate's been spying on all of us, remember? They knew things, personal things they should not, and how did they? Did they send you here to spy on me?"

He would have laughed in her face if she weren't ready to fight him. Not that she could hurt him, but it wasn't himself he worried about. He needed her trust. "You think me aligned with the Senate?" he asked, and when Margaret poked him in the shoulder, he pretended to wince.

"It's the perfect plan. Send someone with knowledge, with connections to kings. Someone who will remind me of my sister, someone who will feed me information just when I need it most and encourage me to make the decisions *they* want me to make!"

"I swear to you I have no love of the Senate, Your Highness. Greedy fools in need of power to make themselves feel important. There's nothing I want more than to see this war end before it begins, trust me on that. You're not the only one who's lost someone in whatever scheme they're planning."

"How do I know you're being truthful with me?"

Bredych held his hands out to her, arms spread in a vulnerable stance. "Have I lied to you once since I arrived in this city?" Margaret shook her head, and he leaned close to her ear. "Count the times I have saved your life, Your Majesty. If I'd wanted you dead, you'd be dead, yes?"

"Yes," she whispered.

"If the Senate wanted a spy, the last person they'd pick would be an Amaskan," said Leolin from where he stood at the table. In his hands was *A Treatise on Senates and Rulers*, which he held out to Margaret.

Her eyes flicked once in his direction, long enough for Bredych to step out of range of her anger. "And why is that?" she snapped at Leolin, who glanced back and forth between her and Bredych.

Leolin said, "It says here that the Amaskans sided with Sadai. They wanted to rid us of the Senate."

It was then that she noticed Bredych had moved away, and the way her eyes flashed was so similar to Adelei's that Bredych's knees shook. The candlelight left flicks of yellow in Margaret's pupils where Adelei's had been all soil and wood. She, too, would have questioned his motives. Adelei would have been ready for a fight sooner, but a fight it would have been.

"Master Maurus? Did you hear me?" asked Leolin, and Bredych blinked. "I asked you if Amaskans still believe the Senate serves no purpose."

"The Order views any who would tell others how to live by the Thirteen as enemies. What makes them more in touch with the Gods than the rest of the Little Dozen Kingdoms?" Bredych asked.

Margaret nodded, but whatever trust she'd had in him was shaken, and she eyed him like some slithering, scaled snake come in the night to poison her. Poison was the weapon of cowards and fools. Of the *Tribor*.

She walked over to the table and stood a touch too close to the boy. "Perhaps a break is needed. There is plenty to research and time to do it tomorrow...after I have thought on this," she said.

Bredych bowed deeply, then withdrew. That was fine with him. He had something in mind for the rest of his day as it was, and perhaps he could give her a reason to trust him once and for all.

As night settled across the castle, Margaret stood in her bedchamber wearing Adelei's clothes: black, silk breeches and tunic clung to her curves, while silk scarves bound the clothing at her waist, wrists, and ankles; rather than boots, she donned her sister's toed shoes, which left her footfalls a whisper on the stone floor; and her lengthy hair was bound in a knot at her nape, though a wisp escaped near her ear. If she squinted some, she could believe herself Amaskan.

Almost.

The way her scabbard hung slightly crooked at her side made her scowl. *Who am I fooling? I am little more than a lost queen hiding in someone else's clothes. Though they do fit better than when I wore them to my wedding...* Margaret ran her hands across shoulders more defined and muscular than a few years before, and with a deep breath, raised her head to look at the woman in the mirror. Maybe if she believed herself capable, others would as well.

When she stepped outside her chambers, the wide-eyed guards outside stood tall as she passed. When her honor guard made to follow, she dismissed them with the shake of her head. Halfway down the first flight of stairs, Margaret recalled the need to be silent and sneaky, though few were out to sneak past. Once she arrived at the second floor, she practiced walking heel to toe toward Master Maurus's guest room where she pressed her ear against the door. No sounds came from inside the room, and she tested the doorknob, which was locked.

Margaret retrieved the key tucked into her waist. At least she need not pick it. The key fit readily into the lock, but as she turned the knob, servants' chatter echoed up from the nearby stairwell. No one would question the Queen entering a room in her own castle, but an Amaskan— perhaps this had been the wrong outfit to wear. She ducked into Master Maurus's room before they reached the landing, then gasped when the man himself stared at her from the room's lone chair.

"May I help you with something, Your Majesty?" asked Master Maurus as he set aside the book he had been reading. Outside the room, the servants' voices passed, and Margaret remained silent. "I would assume by your attire that you came here with a purpose."

She had assumed he would be elsewhere. Margaret's heart pounded in her chest, and when Maurus stood, she backed up against the door. "Please—"

He reached for her scabbard at the same time she did, though his hands stopped on the buckle itself. Maurus tightened the buckle another notch and when he stepped back, she glanced down to find the scabbard no longer crooked. "If it's too loose, the short sword's weight gives the scabbard too much sway," he said.

Humor danced in his eyes and before she could halt its progress, a smile escaped in response. Her smile loosed his own and two breaths later, both held their sides as laughter broke the room's tension. Between giggles, she said, "I came here...to search your room."

"I expected as much, Your Majesty." Maurus gestured toward his room. "You're welcome to do so."

The laughter on her lips faded as she took a moment to assess the room. The simplicity of it left few places to hide much of anything, though the storage chest could hold whatever it was he wished to hide. He caught the glance and strode over to the chest, which he opened to reveal clothing, both his own and those articles he had borrowed from the seneschal. "Honestly, I'm not sure that I would find anything in a room this small," said Margaret as she closed the chest's lid. "If you have something to hide, I suspect it relates to who you are among the Amaskans rather than something physical. Who are you that you speak with royalty?" *Not to mention knew I was not Amaskan.*

Rather than answer, Maurus ran his hands across his head and paused. His fingers curled into fists, and she retreated a step toward the door. Seeing her response, he said, "Forgive me, Your Majesty. It's been a long time since I've felt the prickling weight of my hair."

"It's little more than stubble. No weight at all."

"To you, perhaps, but it's been over fifty years since I've allowed my hair to grow. For an Amaskan, to allow such hair to grow on our bodies is weighty indeed. I suppose it's not something you'd understand, but Amaskan is all I am. The feel of it...was startling," he said as he ran his hands through his head a second time, this time much more slowly.

"Adelei felt the same, though she noticed it less the longer she remained here. Perhaps it will be the same for you." Margaret's smile faltered as his shoulders stiffened in response to her words. "I'm sorry if I have offended you, Master Maurus. It was not my intention. The words from my mouth today are offensive to everyone it seems."

Maurus shook his head. "We are both prickly cacti this evening it would seem."

Margaret's gaze fell to the scar at his jaw. "She never adjusted to the scar either. I don't think she realized how often she touched it."

He reflexively moved to touch his, but stopped at his chin, though the movement brought back memories. Even the way he moved resembled Adelei. *Do all Amaskans move in such a manner? Though Captain Warhammer didn't move quite the same.*

"This may be rather forward of me, but you seemed rather shocked by the feel of your hair. Did you never run your fingers through the hair of a partner?" she asked.

"Yes, but she's Amaskan, too. If we're asking rather forward questions, if I may be so bold as to give you some advice, Your Majesty?" When Margaret nodded, he said, "Perhaps that outfit isn't the best one for you. Someone might see you and think you are what you aren't. Like your guards. You have enemies enough as it is."

"I thought it would help me sneak into your room better."

Rather than laugh at her, he merely smiled. "Your sister wore the silks of the Order and held a power and wisdom you now find yourself coveting. It's understandable that you would be drawn to that which was hers. I am old, Your Majesty. Older than your father was and old enough to have seen many Amaskans come and go. But wisdom doesn't come from the clothing. It comes from experience, something you're gaining with each day that passes. The only piece of information I can give you that will help you today is this: Queen Margaret is strong enough on her own for Alexander. She doesn't need her sister's help."

It was advice her father would have given had he been there, and tears blurred her vision. "Thank you. I apologize for the intrusion," she said as she gave him a slight nod before retreating from his guest room.

The servants were long gone from the hallway, a fact for which she was grateful as her tears escaped. Everywhere she turned, people around her died. Margaret lay her hands against her castle's stone walls, which were cool to the touch. "I will be like stone," she whispered as she brushed aside her grief.

The dead would be made to wait until times of peace.

Calmer, she approached the stairwell walking heel to toe, and when she reached the corner, she leaned her back against the wall. Nothing sounded around the corner, but one never knew who lurked in the shadows. Margaret peered around the corner and sighed when she found it empty.

Something poked her in the back, and when she reached for her blade, strong hands reached around her waist to capture her hands. "For a moment, I thought you the enemy, but no Amaskan would hesitate the way you did," whispered Leolin in her ear.

She tried to move and found herself unable to escape his hold—a hold she enjoyed—and her heart fluttered in response. "Since you know I'm not your enemy, release me," she said, though she regretted the words' necessity. His blade, while sheathed, continued to prod her in the back, though his grasp loosened a touch.

"If I were your attacker, you would be dead, Your Majesty." Her breath caught in her throat as he spoke.

"Might I recommend that you stop this foolishness? You're not her."

"Who?" she asked as she elbowed him in the ribs, and a slight *oof* escaped his lips.

Leolin glanced in the direction of Maurus's room before meeting her gaze. "You're no Amaskan, Your Majesty, no matter what he might tell you."

Before she had done more than open her mouth, Leolin retreated up the stairwell and into the shadows. He was right—she wasn't Adelei—but he had also been wrong. Maurus hadn't told her to be anything other than herself. *Unlike Leolin.* If anything, Maurus and Leolin were in agreement when it came to her attempts to emulate her sister.

But Leolin finding her vulnerable stung.

One moment I want him to kiss me, and the next, he opens his mouth and I find myself wishing his return to the border.

It was nothing like her experiences with Gamun, which left her flustered. She blinked back tears as she released the pins holding her hair in place.

To most, she still resembled an Amaskan, but perhaps she was less likely to be run through on the way back to her rooms. Deep breaths and thoughts of cool, smooth stone carried Margaret up the stairs at a slower pace.

By the time she reached the fourth floor, Leolin was thankfully elsewhere. Margaret stripped off her sister's clothes and tucked them away into the bottom of a trunk.

That portion of her sister was ashes. Laid to rest in the castle gardens.

16

Something about the way parchment burned always left King Havin feeling content, much like sitting before a fireplace on a cold day, but as the flames scorched and blackened Queen Margaret's letter, his bushy brows furrowed. There was nothing pleasant about this letter, nor its burning.

Havin gestured to an ancient mural on the wall as he turned to Rajami, a great hulk of a man with a scraggly beard the color of mud. "How nice of the Queen to grant me that which is already mine. She forgets that during Boahim's fall, my ancestor held the land from here to the Sadain Mountains to the west. During the war, a dispute between brothers divided that region into what would become Shad and Alexander. Besides, she's hardly the first to blame the Senate for Gamun's death, but it doesn't matter. Not one bit."

He swallowed a gulp of *surrah* from his glass, savoring the way it burned down his throat, but not even the intoxicating drink could numb the fire in his belly. "I was there, Rajami. I felt what that Senator did to my son. The way she toyed with his mind. Whether it was the Poncetts or that Amaskan bitch, Gamun's spirit is gone from the world."

Rajami tilted his head to meet King Havin's gaze. "And yet, something made you grin."

"Indeed. If I didn't know any better, I'd think the Queen was offering me a unique opportunity."

"For peace? That isn't your style."

Havin shook his head. "No, not peace—not while the Poncetts remain on this earth—but I think Queen Margaret's offering me the chance to stand with her against the Boahim Senate."

The *Tribor* leader stilled, the glass in his hand halfway to his mouth. When he set the glass on the table beside them, his blue-gray eyes darkened with shadows. "Feels like a trap. What would Shad gain from such an alliance?"

"Many things, Rajami. The Senate has long outlived its usefulness, though Senator Whitlen...the power that woman holds. Perhaps Queen Margaret has the right idea casting a light on the behemoth holding us all on a tight leash."

"And the Queen? What will you do with her?"

Havin clamped a hand on the *Tribor* leader's shoulder. "Keep your pets flying in Alexander, at least for the time being."

Rajami hoisted his lumbering frame from his seat and bowed, though Havin waited until the man had left the room to retreat to his private study. Shelves overflowed with books and his desk brimmed over with stacks of parchments. He ignored it all, seeking the rear wall instead. When he pressed his palms against it, they emitted a faint blue glow which spread to envelop the stones. His hands passed through the wall first as he stepped forward into the hidden room.

Candles lined the walls, and when he snapped his fingers, flames danced along their wicks. Etched across the wooden floor was a glowing triangle, and behind it the orb. A faint whine escaped from beneath the thick, black cloth enshrouding it, and Havin smiled as he fetched a tattered book from the shelf. His teacher's writings were illegible to those outside the school of Mystic Lago Turoth, but too many curious eyes would try if the book were stored elsewhere.

There would be no alliance with Alexander, not while Havin lived anyway, but the renewed idea of ridding the world of the Senate was encouraging. It was an idea his teacher had spoken of when Havin had begun his service to Itova. Twelve rulers pretended they ruled their lands, but not even royalty was protected from the mighty Senate.

Havin opened the book. For too long the Senate had held the power in the Little Dozen Kingdoms. All he needed was something to convince the others that his plan held merit. With the Kingdom of Alexander fallen and the other rulers supporting Shad, the Senate would fall. Boahim would be united once again.

Not even the *Tribor* felt it possible to remove such powerful players as the Boahim Senate, but that had been before the Senate's grave mistake. Their use of magic opened up many possibilities.

Perhaps one would lead to the Poncett family's end. Havin smiled.

17

_____

I appreciate your willingness to do this," said Margaret as she donned a dull-edged practice sword. Maurus held a similar one in his hand as he stood beside her. "I fear I am out of practice."

"How long have you been training alone?"

"I began training with Adelei, but after her death, I couldn't for a time." Sunlight filtered into the workroom through the open window, and Margaret adjusted her stance to keep it from her face. "I managed to convince Captain Fenton to train me for a time, but I reached a point where I needed to advance beyond wooden swords, and...."

"He refused out of fear of injuring his Queen. If I train you, you advance when I say you do." Maurus shifted his weight from one foot to another, then stilled as he waited for her to move.

Rather than give him what he wanted, Margaret watched with a patience she did not feel as her grip on the sword tightened and loosened. "Adelei tried to teach me some self-defense, though I admit to being an awful student at the time," she said as he flicked his practice blade to the right. Her sword flickered in response to his feint, but nothing more as they danced without stepping. "I didn't think it necessary for me to learn such things until I learned the truth about my former husband, Prince Gamun. Thank the Thirteen Adelei was there."

At the mention of her name, his shoulder muscles tensed and his fingers paled as they dug into the hilt. It was no coincidence the way he reacted to her name, but what was his tie to Adelei? How closely had he known her when she was at the Order? With as many Amaskans as she thought there were, she had assumed one could be a member and not know everyone. Perhaps that assumption had been wrong. He held himself stiff, giving Margaret an advantage, and she shifted her weight forward, thrusting her sword forward toward his sword hand.

Despite the tension he held, Maurus sidestepped her attack with ease. "You lead with your dominate side," he said as he tapped her sword with his. "And your grip is too tight. Sword-work requires flexibility and a flowing movement. Much like dancing."

Margaret nodded. "The grip is a flaw of mine."

"If I may ask, Your Majesty, what made you decide on a straight short sword? Did your sister recommend it?"

Laughter escaped her at the thought, and she shook her head. "Adelei felt I was as suited to a sword as much as a horse is suited to a dress, but if I'm on the battlefield, I can't rely on random objects around me to protect me from an attacker. Everything is a weapon in the correct hands, but sometimes there's nothing to use or your hands are already full."

She nearly missed the subtle shift as he turned heel to block her sword blow and grinned that she had spotted it at all. *Maurus may be old enough to be my grandsire, but he moves like he's my age and then some.* He did not stop with the block and continued his forward momentum to bring his own sword within her space where it *thwapped* against her thigh. She winced as he retreated outside the parring square. Thinking too much was going to leave too many bruises.

"If I may be blunt, I would agree with your sister's assessment. The short sword is not a weapon I would train you to use. I would rather train you in a ranged weapon. No need to put the Queen in the middle of a battle if it can be helped. That's what your marshal is for," he said.

Margaret pursed her lips as the sword hung loosely in her grip. When his eyes noted the action, he turned his back to her to set the practice sword on a nearby table, and she rushed forward until the dull blade rested against the side of his neck.

"Would you strike me unarmed?" he asked, and in response she nudged him again with the blade's edge.

His body relaxed, and she withdrew the sword. "How do you do that?"

"Do what, Your Majesty?"

"Relax in a moment of danger."

When he faced her, his face was alight with his grin. "I was in no danger. 'Tis but a practice sword."

She rubbed her still smarting thigh and said, "My leg begs to differ."

"It's good that you held to your decision to attack. An enemy cares not for your sense of morals. However, attacking someone in a rush of anger will only get you killed, Your Majesty."

Heat flushed her cheeks at his rebuke. She did not throw the sword, but her fingers ached as she squeezed the leather-wrapped hilt. "It is not *my* fault that no one saw fit to teach me to defend myself until it was almost too late! I know I sound like the spoiled princess everyone thinks I am, but people are dying. *My* people. An enemy marches on my country and rather than leading the charge, I am cocooned up in this castle like a delicate butterfly."

"You're a lot like her," he said, his voice barely audible over the sounds of blood rushing in her head.

"Who?"

"My daughter."

She had expected him to say Adelei, to confirm the suspicion buzzing around her head, but his daughter?

Tension returned to his shoulders, which crept a smidge closer to his ears. "She was stubborn to a fault," he said as he returned the practice sword to his hand. "I never wanted her to be an Amaskan—to follow such a dangerous path— but even as a child she was determined to follow me."

Maurus gestured for her to attack, and she stepped forward and jabbed at his stomach. When he blocked, she left her sword in place and stepped forward, driving him back a step until he nodded. "If someone's trying to kill you, you have to be willing to kill them first, especially if you have thoughts to lead your army."

She nodded as he brought his sword around to her side, a move she parried, then countered. "If need be, I will take a life," she said.

"And if there are multiple attackers?" He snapped his fingers, and the guardsmen at the door picked up practice blades. They formed a moving circle around her as Maurus stepped behind them to watch. "What will you do now?"

Rather than answer, she danced in small circles as she watched the three guards. One was taller than the other two by several hands and his stance broader. Margaret feinted an attack against the shortest, who easily blocked. The tall guardsman used the opportunity to lunge, and rather than meet him, she sidestepped and brought up her elbow into the shortest guard's chin. When he stepped back, shaking his head, she used the opening to flee the circle toward the door, a move that would have earned her a 'well done!' from Captain Fenton.

Rather than praise, Maurus blocked the door. "On the battlefield, you can't flee, Your Majesty." When he attacked, he used the same technique against her she had used moments before, driving her backward into the group of armed guardsmen. Three swords touched her back in various spots, though none of them hard enough to bruise. "I believe a sword through the kidney would be a fatal wound," he said.

"Our apologies, Your Majesty," the tallest guard muttered as all three guardsmen bowed before her.

"Again," said Maurus, and the three men set themselves to a rocking stance as they circled her.

When she blocked one, another two jabbed her from behind, and after a dozen pokes from practice swords, she let her hers fall to the floor below. "I yield," she said, and the circling stopped. "Without someone to watch my back, there's no way I can fend off three attackers. Perhaps you can, but I cannot."

Maurus entered the circle and retrieved her practice sword from the floor. "This is why most people learn to fight in twos. Amaskans are about the silent kill, the ability to sneak in and take care of what's needed, swiftly and without attention, but in a war, your Captain Fenton fights with a team. With more practice, you could learn to fight off multiple opponents, but without someone to watch your back, there're no guarantees."

This time when the guardsmen circled her, Maurus

stood behind her, his back close to hers. The first few times the guardsmen attacked, Margaret bumped into Maurus as she tried to step backward or she found herself stepping on his heels, an action that left him wincing, then limping as the lesson proceeded. Her awareness of his movements in addition to her own lacked finesse, and the metallic taste of blood soured her mouth from biting her lip.

"Did Captain Fenton never train *with* you against another opponent?" Maurus asked after she stumbled into him *again*.

She shook her head. "He only trained me because I ordered it. He never believed I would need such training."

Despite her clumsiness working with another, she blocked more hits then she took and for once, she allowed herself a slight grin. It was only when a page brought a reminder message of her upcoming appearance with her court that she stopped their practice. Margaret turned to set her practice sword on the table when one poked her in the back.

"Half a candlemark remaining until you are needed," he said as she spun to face him, her cheeks growing warm.

"Time I will need to appear presentable before my people, Master Maurus."

He poked her in the gut. Hard. "You say you want to fight, but wars aren't about looking presentable. They aren't about defense either. They're about fighting to the death. Blood. A man's guts spilling out across the field while the spray of blood soaks your cloak. The question is, when that happens, will you fight or faint, Your Majesty?"

Her fingers dug into the sword's hilt as she held it behind her back. He understood nothing of her responsibilities. Nothing. *As if meetings and planning were not a part of battle!*

The sword jabbed her in the stomach a second time, and on the third, she blocked it. By the fourth attempt, she stepped forward with her right foot and feinted. When he moved to block it, she spun on her left toe and thrust her sword lower than he expected. It jabbed him in the lower ribs hard enough for him to tuck his elbows in and bring his head down in a protective crouch. He managed to block the next jab, but missed the following, and her sword caught him square in the jaw. Margaret managed to collapse her elbow at the last moment so that the flat of the blade smacked him rather than the edge, but even as blunt as it was, his skin flushed red from the contact. Margaret opened her mouth to apologize, then snapped it shut as he smiled.

"You're stronger than you look," he said as he rubbed his jaw.

Margaret shrugged. "You're the only one who believes that. Besides, that was purposeful on your part."

Maurus nodded. "I needed to see if you'd attack when pushed. You defended yourself against your guards, but you never seized the opportunity. My daughter...she believed in herself too much I think, but you do yourself a disservice. I'm not saying you could withstand an army, or even a group of attackers—not yet—but you know what to look for when being attacked. You know how to move, how to defend yourself, when to run and when to attack."

When she shook her head, he let the sword clatter to the ground as he gripped her by the shoulders. A faint waft of mulled wine drifted up from his mouth as he stared at her. "When outnumbered, your first instinct was to flee. It's a good instinct to have. When faced by one opponent, you took advantage of weakness and attacked as necessary. I'm not sure what you expect of yourself, Your Majesty, but you did as well as anyone would with a few years' training."

"But—"

"Don't," he said.

"Don't what?"

"Don't come up with a reason why you aren't fit to be Queen."

As much as she wished to pull her gaze from his blue-gray eyes, she couldn't. Something about the way his nostrils flared told her that disagreeing with him would be a mistake, so she shrugged as she squirmed in his grip.

"I don't think my daughter believed me either, at least, not until she became a full Amaskan," he said, and before she could blink, he had released her shoulders, only to swing his palm at her face.

Margaret caught his hand with her own and bit back a wince at the sting. Better her hand than her cheek.

"If you won't trust what I say, trust in yourself, Your Majesty. Not even Adelei could have hit you just then."

It was the first time he had said her name, rather than calling her Margaret's sister, and the name lent a sadness to his face, similar to the one Margaret's father had carried. It was not until Maurus had bowed and retreated that she realized he had paid her a compliment.

Maybe she could believe it. *Maybe.*

She lacked experience—in both ruling and fighting—but Margaret's tenacity resembled Adelei's, and Bredych's heart sang in response. He left the practice room, but rather than return to the castle, he set out for the city proper. More people had gathered behind the city walls since the King's death, and while it slowed down his navigation through the city circles, it increased his ability to send and receive messages to the Order.

A two-story shack partially leaned against the city's outer wall, and Bredych pushed open a door whose hinges screamed in protest. Four people looked up from their business in the public house's back corner, and their gazes remained on him until he'd stepped inside and closed the door. No windows made for dim lighting, not that lighting was needed for such a place. The stout woman operating the bar nodded once in the stair's direction. The establishment had no name, nor did it need one in this portion of Alesta. Everyone knew Mademe Pouffaur, and Mademe Pouffaur knew everyone. *Though she still believes me to be a simple Amaskan,* Bredych thought as he climbed the stairs.

He rapped a short, detached pattern on the hallway's last door while various cries, grunts, and moans seeped out from behind other doors. A diminutive woman wearing a wool, sheer robe greeted him silently, a lazy smile playing across her face. Bredych followed her into the room where rosewood and cloves tickled his nose. Incense burned on the room's lone table, and the woman gestured for him to have a seat.

One side of the couch had a raised back that left little question as to its purpose, and Bredych shook his head. "I need a message sent," he said, and the woman's bottom lip stuck out in a pout.

"Ya sure that's all, honey?"

Bredych removed a rolled up piece of parchment from his pouch and handed it to her. "Noam, at the border. Same as before."

The woman tugged on the string holding her robe in place, and it tumbled silently to the wooden floor. She arched a brow at Bredych as she pulled on clothing from a nearby chest, then frowned when he stared blankly at her. For all that her curves were pleasant to watch, her obsession with men she assumed dangerous made her the wrong type of woman for any Amaskan to get involved with. She tucked the message into the pouch on her garter belt and once fully-clothed, stretched her hand out, palm up.

He placed half-a-notch, more than double what she made as a public girl into her waiting hand, and her smile returned. "And if there's a response for ya?" she asked.

"There won't be."

"But if there is?"

"Leave word with Mademe. She knows how to find me," he said.

Five minutes after he left the public house, a delicate hand appeared at the window shutter upstairs. The woman tied a pale-green scarf to its handle, then disappeared from view. Someone traveling to the border would offer the "poor girl" a ride, and his message would be on its way. Once in Breighton, Noam would see that the message continued across the chain of former clients until it reached the Order.

He wished he'd had more to report beyond Margaret's trust in him. As he turned to leave his hiding spot in the alley across the street, an older man wearing beggars' clothes and carrying a walking stick left the house beside Mademe's. No bulges or odd shapes betrayed hidden weapons, but the way the man moved said fighter, not vagabond.

As Bredych followed the man through the second set of walls leading toward the castle, Bredych rubbed a hand across his head. Several street vendors watched him pass, his hair still too short to pass as Alexandrian, and he sighed. In exchange for answers about Adelei, he'd left the Order behind when he'd come here. He didn't know who made decisions now, let alone what they thought of his reports, but perhaps it had been worth it to know Margaret.

She's so like Adelei.

Once the man posing as a beggar drew within sight of the castle proper, his stance shifted. He hobbled more than strode, and his shoulders slumped as he withdrew a ragged doll from a pocket. When the man asked for an audience with Her Majesty, Bredych's body tensed in response. Everything about this man elicited warnings in Bredych. Bredych drew his hood up over his head and followed the man into the line of people awaiting to see the queen.

IT WAS THE PORTION OF RULING SHE KNEW WELL— sitting before a trailing line of people, all wishing to speak with her on a matter of some importance to them. Whether it was truly important mattered little. What mattered was that she listen to them as attentively as her father did and if possible, help them with their problems. After the woman who battered her own child, Margaret's desire to help those who needed it had multiplied, and as word grew, the line of those wishing an audience multiplied tenfold.

Most wished assurances that Alesta was safe from the war or hoped the new Queen would perhaps extend them some coin for a wide range of "needs," but it was the old man with a gnarled walking stick that caught her attention as he approached.

The way his wrinkles curled in on themselves, much like the engraved lines of his walking stick, made him at least Master Maurus's age if not older. His shoulders hunched over as he approached the dais, and his bow resembled a nod more than a proper bending at the waist. He had been announced with a simple name and no title, though his ragged clothing spoke of his impoverished state more than any name could. Margaret gave a slight incline of her head, but he hesitated, his free hand shaking as he held it out, open-palmed, before her.

"No harm will befall you here, so speak and have justice," she said.

He flinched at the informal greeting and fell to his knees. Her honor guard rushed to her side as she left the dais. A foul stench burned her nose as she approached him, but she kept her expression in check. The moment her hand touched his arm tears ran down his gaunt cheeks, and when he turned to look at her, his eyes were the lake mid-winter, a pale-blue almost white with frost. He gripped her hands tightly as she huddled on the floor beside him.

"You honor me, Your Majesty." His voice was paper-thin and carried a rasp much like Leolin's mother.

Her gaze traveled to his jawline, but no scar or tattoo was present, nor did he bear the wounds at his throat like Ida Warhammer had.

"Any good voice I might've had left me in the womb, Your Majesty, along with my sight, though I see more than people believe." When he reached inside his vest, her guards' hands fell to their blades' hilts, and the old man sighed. "I'll not hurt you, Your Majesty. I only wish to fetch my granddaughter's doll."

She nodded to her guards and said, "Please, proceed."

The doll's wooden face had been carved with great care, and her clothing was finer than anything the old man wore. He placed it into her hand, face down, and said, "I made this when Mina was born. My first grandchild. She carried it everywhere from the moment she was crawling across the forest floor."

"It is amazing that...one such as you could carve something so accurately without sight."

When he smiled, his eyes did not light up the way most did, but his cheeks blushed as his gaze wandered. "There are many ways of seeing, Your Majesty, and not all of them require eyes."

Light bumps raced across her skin. Did he speak of magic? Or was he speaking in metaphors? "I apologize for my ignorance in such matters. Is your granddaughter with you in Alesta?"

A sharp pain curled her hands into fists around the doll and when she glanced down, a dark crimson covered her hands and marred the doll's face. The wooden doll clattered to the floor, the sound echoing in the hall's sudden silence. When she wrest her eyes away from the blood, she stood alone in the grand hall. Something grabbed her hands, and the room returned with the scuffling of feet and clearing of throats.

"What did you do to me?" she whispered as his hands scuffled across the floor until they located the doll.

"I allowed you to see. Nothing more."

Margaret backed a few steps away from the old man. "What did I see? What was that?" she asked.

"Mina." The old man's wandering gaze froze on Margaret. "She carried her doll as she wandered from the temple where we hid. I-I couldn't see how she escaped—it must have been when they opened the doors for those running to safety—but I heard her screams as those Shadian butchers cut her down."

"You came from the Pass?"

The old man nodded. "Aye, Your Majesty."

"And you know it was the Shadian army that attacked your people?"

"It was. I fled the temple when her screams started, and by the time I reached Mina's doll, she was quiet. Her body lay limp beside it, buried in the stench of death." The whispers in the room increased as he spoke. "The clash of metal on metal warned me of the fight nearby, and one of our men yelled for me to run. The Thirteen led me; I don't think I stopped running until I got here."

The hum of chatter increased, and Margaret gestured for her lady-in-waiting. "Have him clothed and fed, then shown to a guest room. I will wish to speak with him later." *Without prying eyes and ears to spread rumors throughout an already frightened city.*

Rather than continue onto the next citizen, she said, "While We appreciate every piece of information brought before our court, no word has reached us of an attack at the Pass." *Not yet anyway.* "Perhaps this man has suffered a loss and his brain has become addled and confused. Rest assured We will investigate his tale and ensure justice is done, if necessary. We require some time to look into his claims and wish for you to return on the morrow."

A few grumbles met her words as the guards escorted people from the hall, though one person remained. She caught his movement from the corner of her eye and rather than sit, she slid a hand into her corset to grab the dagger within.

"I request a moment of Your Majesty's time," a familiar voice called out, and when the figure grew closer to the light, Margaret slid the dagger back into its sheath.

"A formal audience is not necessary, Lieutenant."

She waited until the formal audience chamber had cleared to dismiss all but her honor guard. Leolin bowed, and she waved a hand at him as she stood. His eyes narrowed as she approached, and when she stood beside him, he frowned.

"You're hurt."

"I'm fine," she said as she walked. Sitting made for stiffened bruises that changed into painful reminders to dodge or block practice swords in the future. "Did you hear the story the old man told? Other than the woman who lied, I've heard nothing from the Pass about anything more than threats and feints. Surely if there had been an attack, I would know."

Leolin nodded, then touched his hand to her shoulder. She bit back a wince, though not soon enough as he clenched his fingers. "You're not fine. Who hurt you? Was there another attempt on your life?"

"No, no attack. Master Maurus was training me, nothing more."

His features froze in an expression unlike him as his nose flared and his eyes widened. "Of course it was him. I've told you before that he's a dangerous man. That's not the training you need, Maggie. In fact, you shouldn't need training at all."

"You're wrong, Leolin. Whether that old man speaks the truth or not, there *is* a battle coming. If I'm not able to lead my people, someone will lead them for me. Perhaps in the wrong direction. Too much of that has occurred in this family, and I will not allow it again."

The stiffness of her muscles set her to moving again, and Leolin trailed behind her for a time before he touched her again, this time gently as he turned her to face him. "Maggie, I don't mean to tell you what to do. I...I know you think this the best way to proceed, but I don't want to see you hurt. You've had enough of that in your life. Besides, there's more than one way to fight. Not every battle must be with your body."

Margaret pulled away from his touch, her face hot and cold at the same time.

"What did I say?"

"The truth," she whispered as she opened the audience chamber doors. He moved to follow her, but she shut the doors firmly behind her, leaving him alone in the hall. For all his words, his actions spoke louder. "I am retiring to my rooms and am not to be disturbed," she told a member of her honor guard. "Make sure the good lieutenant does not follow."

He had been correct that not every battle would be fought with bodies. Some could be fought with words. With magic.

It was time to have another conversation with the blind old man.

18

As the guards guided the old man to a guest room, Bredych stepped out of line and followed a few breaths behind the two. When traveling through the city's lower circles, the man had walked without a trace of his age. Now he moved like an ancient grandsire. While a snake might shed its skin, it was still a snake within, and the old man was no different. As he hobbled into the provided guest room, the guard took up station outside the doorway, and Bredych leaned against the wall near a statue down the hallway to wait.

Other than a few people who trickled from the Margaret's audience chamber, the halls remained empty outside the occasional servant. The guard was a problem. Getting past him would expose that Bredych had visited the old man. Farimun was with him as the old man opened the door and mumbled something to the guard. Soon after, the guardsman left his post, and Bredych rushed forward to the wooden door.

He knocked on it lightly, and when the door opened, he pushed his way inside as the old man cried out in protest.

Bredych kicked the door shut behind him, then clamped a hand over the old man's mouth. The walking stick leaned against the corner, and the old man's gaze darted between it and Bredych. "Move or cry out, and you'll decorate the floor with your blood," said Bredych as he removed his hand.

The old man frowned. "You'd harm an old, blind man?"

Bredych gave a quiet chuckle. "If you're blind, I'm the Thirteen. Raise your breeches. Slowly, mind you." One leg revealed wrinkled, old skin but nothing else, and he gestured to the other. "Both, please."

This time when the old man raised his breeches, a small triangle marred his skin, and the old man grinned. "Find what you were expecting, assassin?" he asked, and Bredych removed the small pouch from his pocket. A small triangle in green had been sewn into the wool, though no other marks decorated the pouch. The old man's eyes grew large and he asked, "Where'd you get that?"

"One of your colleagues tried, and failed I might add, to use it on Her Majesty a few days back, though I would love to know *where* he got *barak* from. I'm not even sure I could obtain this, and *I* know where to look."

The old man shook his head. "Look to your Order. They're the ones controlling its movements."

Whether or not the information was false, it shouldn't have made Bredych's heart race like a war steed. It was the old man's turn to laugh, and Bredych took a slow breath. "Why are you here?"

The old man pitched forward toward the staff, and Bredych punched the man in the chest a few fingers' width above the breastbone. While the *Tribor* gasped for air that didn't come, Bredych grabbed him by the shirt and pulled him close enough to shove the pouch under the man's open mouth. Frozen by pain, the old man couldn't move for a dozen heartbeats, and when his breathing returned, he gasped, inhaling a large dose of *barak* with the air.

Rather than allow the old man to stumble about and make noise, Bredych pushed him in the direction of his bed, where he fell down as tremors took him. Not long after, the poison halted his movements, and his eyes bulged as his face turned bright red.

Using the bedsheet, Bredych closed the pouch and tucked it into his pocket. Not enough remained on the bedding to be bothersome though the body itself presented a problem. He tore off a corner of the old man's ragged tunic and dipped it into the water glass before dabbing anywhere he spotted the glittering substance.

As long as no one inhaled it, the substance would at most give them a headache. Bredych tossed the scrap of tunic into the fireplace, then listened at the door. Hearing nothing, he opened the door a crack to find the guardsman hadn't yet returned.

Before anyone else spotted him, Bredych left the guest room and the *Tribor* assassin behind.

"HE COULD SEE WITHOUT SEEING, MASTER MAURUS, and when he handed me the doll, there was blood on my hands. For a moment, I was no longer with him but elsewhere, a place where I could see death. I don't know how to describe what it was like, but he has magic. He could be what we need to win the war," said Margaret as they walked together. He had arrived at his rooms with the city's dust on his clothes, but it would have to wait.

"You think he's a mystic?" Maurus asked.

"I don't know for certain that he is, but for a blind man, he certainly sees quite a bit."

As they reached the expanse of guest rooms, Maurus said, "Sadai doesn't share Alexander's aversion to mystics, though there are few of them these days. Still, I've seen one, and he didn't possess the skills this old man of yours claims to have."

The guardsman outside the door bowed briefly to Margaret. "How else do you explain his ability to make it from the pass to Alesta unaided?" she asked as she reached out to knock on the door.

Maurus gave a brief shake of his head to stop her. "How do you know he arrived unaided? For all we know, he's a spy sent here from Shad, meant to prey upon your wish to protect your citizens. It's what I would do if I wanted a way to reach an enemy ruler," he said.

While there was truth to his words, something about the man felt right. If she were wrong though.... "I would ask that you enter before me," she said to Maurus, who gave the wooden door a brief knock. When no one answered on the second knock, he tried the knob. The door swung open with ease to a small, empty sitting area.

Maurus took a few steps into the room before halting. "Your Majesty," he called out, and she followed Maurus into the brief bedchamber to the left. Something lay beneath the bed covers, and Margaret's stomach turned in response. Perhaps it was merely a blanket, and the old man had fled.

Through the nonexistent window? She held her breath as Maurus touched the lump which did not move.

He shook it, and when there was no response, he pulled back the blanket to expose the old man's body. He lay peacefully beneath the blanket, his fingers clutching his granddaughter's doll.

"Does he live?" she asked.

Maurus held his hand above the old man's mouth. Finding no breath, he shook his head. "He appears to have died in his sleep."

"Buried beneath the blanket?" asked Margaret.

"Maybe he took chill."

"You believe that as much as I do."

While Maurus remained with the body, Margaret retreated to the hallway and the guardsman outside. "Were any visitors received?" she asked.

"No, Your Majesty. The old man asked for some water, then stayed in his room."

"Who brought him water?"

The guard stared at his feet as he answered, "Lieutenant Leolin, Your Majesty. I ran into the lieutenant in the stairwell. He offered to fetch the water, and—"

She forgot to breathe for a moment as he continued. There was something off about the story.

"Is there something wrong, Your Majesty? Should I get the lieutenant?"

Margaret shook her head. "Why did you leave your post?"

"The man asked me for the water. I went in search of a servant, Your Majesty."

"The stairwell is not far from here. How long were you away?"

The guardsman stared at the floor. "I—I had to use the privy."

Master Maurus touched Margaret's elbow and pointed next door to the council room.

The orb. Pins and needles danced across her skin.

"Your Majesty? Are you ill?" asked the guardsman.

Maurus closed the guest room door. He said nothing, though the corners of his lips turned down as he tucked something into a pocket.

"I'm fine, but no one is to enter this room until Master Roland arrives," she said.

Once they escaped earshot of the guard, Maurus retrieved the piece of paper and handed it to her. The scrap had been folded many times over the years, leaving dust in the fold lines that decorated it. Odd symbols were scribbled across it, though none had any meaning to Margaret. "Do you recognize these markings?" she asked.

"I've never seen anything like them. Before you say they might have to do with mystics, there was nothing on his body to indicate he had any such powers. Just dirt and old age."

She lowered her voice and drew closer to Maurus. "Leolin came to visit our mystic, though I doubt he had anything to do with the old man's death. He came to give the man some water. I, on the other hand, am a fool." When Maurus tilted his head, she said, "I placed him in the guest room beside the council room."

"It's possible the Senate's responsible for his untimely death."

"They could have come and gone from the orb without my ever knowing," she said.

Maurus nodded. "The Boahim Senate may still remain. If they're using magics, they could be anywhere in Alesta for that matter."

"If you would, check the council room. If there are intruders here, I wish to know."

"Your Majesty, I can check the room itself, but how do I reach the orb? I can't check that room without you."

She shook her head. "For now, take a listen behind the bookcase."

"And the lieutenant's possible involvement?"

They stopped at the stairwell. "It may be harmless—delivering a requested drink—but if he had a role in the old man's death.... No, I don't believe it was him."

"If it was, we may have our traitor," said Maurus.

Margaret turned away from him to hide the tears that threatened to spill over. "I'll see to Leolin and notify Roland of the old man's death. We'll have our answers soon enough."

One way or another.

WHILE ROLAND SET OUT TO EXAMINE THE OLD MAN'S body, Margaret ventured forth to locate Leolin. Last she had seen him, she had closed the door in his face, but she doubted he had remained in the empty audience chamber. The guard stationed outside said he had left shortly after her, though to go where, he did not know.

Leolin was not in his rooms, nor was he waiting for her in her sitting room. He was not in the council room where Maurus examined the orb, nor had he left the castle grounds, at least not that the palace guards had seen. There remained one place to search.

He sulked beside the garden's blooming roses. The seriousness of her visit almost kept her from smiling at that pout. It *was* rather handsome the way his bottom lip jutted out a hint as his blue eyes stared off at nothing in particular.

At first he didn't notice her arrival. It was not until she sat beside him that he flinched. "I suppose you've come to ask me if I killed him," he said.

Those were *not* the words she had expected, but rather than give herself away, Margaret leaned over to smell a rose. As she pulled away from its sweet fragrance, the doll's image washed across her mind. Like the rose, it had been coated in an unusual shade of crimson red. "I was not aware you knew of the old man's death," she said without looking directly at him.

"After you closed the door in my face, I followed your lady-in-waiting hoping to find you, and instead, found an old man asking for water. By the time I returned with it, he was already dead."

"How did you find him?"

"Dead."

Margaret shook her head. "That is not what I meant. How was the body arranged?"

"He was sprawled in bed with that doll," said Leolin. A butterfly landed on a rose nearby, and he flicked the rose's stem. "When I realized he was dead, I covered him with his blanket. I was going to mention it to you, but your guards told me you didn't wish to be disturbed and that I would need to 'request an audience' to speak with you." He scoffed as he flicked the rose again. "The day I need a formal audience with you is the day I know we're no longer friends."

"Is that what we are, Leolin? Friends?" Margaret's face warmed, and she stood to hide her confusion. "Never mind. Did you notice anyone in the room before you? Someone leaving perhaps?"

"No, why?"

"Nothing."

His skin was electricity when he took her hand, but when she turned to face him, his eyes narrowed as he stared at her. "You know you can tell me anything, right, Maggie?"

She nodded, but her insides threatened to bleed across the gardens. They were not children anymore to blindly trust one another. Things had been simpler then—before the war, before the confusing feelings that left her unsure of herself and their relationship.

If the old man didn't lie dead in his guest room, his killer unknown, she would have kissed Leolin. Instead, she forced a smile upon her lips. If he was the traitor, she would need to tread carefully with him.

"I'm sorry for earlier," he said as she returned to her seat on the stone bench.

"All is forgiven."

He reached out and plucked a rose petal to hold against her cheek. "You turn a brilliant shade of crimson when you're angry. It becomes you. Now tell me about this old man. Did you find any clues to how he died?"

She would need to tread very carefully indeed.

WHILE HE KNEW THE WORDS REQUIRED TO ACTIVATE the orb, uncovering it remained beyond reach as Bredych stared at the bookshelf. When he'd arrived, the council chambers had been empty. If the silence behind the bookshelf was to be believed, the hidden room was empty, too. Rather than wait for Margaret to make her way to him, Bredych sought her out. Four questions and a dozen guards later, he located her in the castle's inner gardens.

Margaret and the boy sat side by side, their hands intertwined as they talked, and Bredych frowned as he stared across the flowers. For all she knew, the boy could have killed the old man, yet her love for him blinded her. Or perhaps she played a more complicated game with the boy.

Not that the boy *had* killed him, but Margaret didn't know that, and Bredych bit back a curse. A quick glance revealed ten guards in the gardens. They'd have to be enough. He retreated into the shadows and left the gardens before she could spot him.

When Bredych approached the old man's guest room, a tired, pale Roland was closing the door behind him.

"I assume you've examined the body?" asked Bredych, and the physician nodded. "What say you as to how he died?"

Roland opened the door again, gesturing for Bredych to follow him inside. The body remained on the bed, though the blanket no longer covered the old man. The cup of water sat on the bedside table, and when Bredych leaned closer, the physician said, "Be careful. Smell gently."

"You suspect poison?"

"While the old man was exhausted, there are no signs of why or how he died other than this." Roland pulled up the tunic to expose the old man's chest. Pink streaks ran across his pale flesh. "These have faded from when I first arrived."

Bredych feigned shock and brought the candle closer to the body. A few specks sparkled in the candle's light. "Definitely some type of poison. I would be careful handling the body."

"It's *barak*, if I recall. I've seen it once before near the border. It's derived from a Sadain plant." Roland gave him a pointed look.

"I've heard it's difficult to obtain. I'm not even sure where to get it to be honest, although I can look into it." *And I will be, on that you can be sure.* "Anything else of note on the body?" he asked.

Roland rolled up the man's breeches up to expose the

triangle tattoo on the old man's ankle, then allowed the leg to fall back into place.

"So the old man's *Tribor*. Probably here to harm the Queen."

"I'll have the body disposed of—carefully—and recommend that Her Majesty stop all audiences for the time being," said Roland.

Bredych nodded. "I would recommend against telling her about this. At least until the person behind the attacks is caught." Or at least until the evidence was destroyed. The last thing Bredych needed was for Margaret to have yet another reason to doubt him.

When the physician nodded, Bredych left the man to do his work. It had been a pity to kill the old man before gaining any information, but the *Tribor* rarely spoke of their employers. Whoever had hired them for this job had paid them well, though sending an old man... Whoever it was had grown desperate to have used someone who could so easily fail. Or perhaps they had known Margaret would feel sorry for an elderly, blind man and set out to exploit the vulnerability.

When he reached his own guest room, Bredych fetched the bag stowed in the chest and shoved his clothing inside. It wasn't that he wished to leave—far from it—nor did he wish to leave Margaret susceptible with an attacker on the loose. But if the Order controlled the *barak* trade, his people were on their way to the Thirteen Hells without him, and if they didn't, then the information available at the Order might help find out who did. No one had returned any of his messages to the Order, leaving him little choice. Besides, if he returned with valuable information, Margaret might trust him enough to give him the answers he needed.

Bredych removed a piece of parchment and scribbled a

note to her, which he handed to a page running past him as he took the stairs to the first floor. "Please give this to Her Majesty on the morrow with my apologies," he said, and fled the castle.

Maybe there was still time to catch a ride with the public girl to the border and hand deliver the letter to the King himself.

19

The guard outside nodded at Leolin, then opened the door to allow him access to what formerly had been King Leon's private library. Margaret sat at the table, buried in books as she had the day before, although this time there was a desperation to her efforts as she flipped through one book's pages, only to snag another book from beside her and flick through it. Without a word, she glanced up as he closed the door behind him but otherwise gave no indication that she cared that he was there, and he frowned as he claimed the chair across the table from her. Twenty minutes passed in silence before she stood and paced in the narrow space between the bookshelves and table.

"What's wrong?" he asked, and she paused long enough to stare at the ceiling.

"What *isn't* wrong? We are no closer to understanding the Senate's motivation than before. Even worse, I received this note this morning." She fetched a small scrap of parchment from beneath a book and passed it to him. When he opened it, the bottom of it bore the same circular symbol Maurus had used to mark the note to King Adir of Sadai.

Queen Margaret,

You don't trust my loyalties, nor do you trust me. If we're to defeat our enemies and move forward, we must have a relationship built on trust and openness, which isn't something I can give as I am. I've returned to Sadai to speak personally to King Adir and to see if I can find information that will be of help. I hope to bring back not only good news, but someone who can provide the help you need.

Leolin handed the note back to Margaret with a shrug. They were better off without the Amaskan.

"He left, Leolin! The guards found no trace of him in his room, nor did they find him in the city. By all accounts, he's vanished," she said, her voice rising to a pitch.

"Good! You're safer without him here." *Much safer.*

Margaret shot him a look that made his insides shiver. "There's a bounty on my head, and the one person who's protecting me is gone."

"Didn't it ever strike you as odd?" he asked, and she shook her head with a slight frown. "Think about it, Maggie. He arrives and suddenly you're in danger. Someone tried to kill you during your father's burial ritual, or so *he* says." When she opened her mouth to protest, he held up his hand. "No, hear me out. How do you *know* he wasn't the one after you? Or maybe the attempts were by people Maurus hired, another Amaskan perhaps. Every time you're with him, someone tries to kill you, and you never stop to wonder why?"

"B-but there were things he said... the way he looked at me. It was as if he cared about my well-being. Sometimes he looked on me as if he saw a spirit, Leolin. While I'll admit that he *is* hiding something, I don't believe it to be what you think it is. Besides, the same arguments could be said about you."

Except I'm not Amaskan. Rather than say it, he asked, "Did he tell you?"

"Tell me what?"

"The old, blind man was *Tribor*."

Margaret gasped. "Why didn't he report this to me? Who else knows?"

"Roland found the tattoo when examining the body, and after Maurus swore him to secrecy, he reported the information to me. 'To keep you safe.' As to the real reason he kept the information from you, Maurus probably enjoyed the fact that I'd been painted as the old man's murderer."

She resumed her pacing, then stopped to frown. "It's not outside the realm of possibilities that you played a role in his death, whether or not that man was *Tribor*."

"I had no part in it, I swear it." The idea that she questioned it wounded him, and he fought to keep the pain from his face. "Look, Master Maurus is Amaskan. They're masters of deception and lies. He would say anything to take advantage of a new queen amidst a war, including whatever it takes to make you lose your trust in those around you. Your trust in *me*."

Despite the stern look that furrowed her brows and thinned her lips, moisture gathered at the corners of her eyelids as she listened, and Leolin added, "Look, I know you have a connection I don't understand with this old man, but if your sister were here, what would she think of this scenario?"

A deep sigh escaped Margaret's lips. "She would be asking the same questions as you, especially the Adelei I knew."

"What do you mean?"

"She grew to doubt the Amaskans. The things they did to her, Leolin." Margaret shook her head and a wisp of black hair fled her braids; he reached out to tuck the escaping strand behind her ear as she continued. "Before she died, Adelei wasn't sure of anything anymore."

What could her own people have done to make her doubt them? As far as Leolin knew, once an Amaskan, always an Amaskan. Maybe once the threat was abated, Margaret would be willing to tell him. "Come sit down. Focus on the task before you rather than what's outside your control."

"Maurus said that," she whispered and picked up a book. "Never mind."

Amaskans and their mind games. They'd all be better off once the Amaskans were long dead and burned, their ashes scattered across the Little Dozen Kingdoms. Assuming the Little Dozen Kingdoms survived the coming war.

The kind of war that broke apart kingdoms. As it had once before.

Leolin picked up another book with a sigh.

STARING AT THE SKETCH, MARGARET BROUGHT THE OLD tome closer to study it. They *had* to be ancestors. There was no other explanation for it. She walked over to one of the shelves and ran her finger across the spines until she found the book she had passed earlier that morning. A history book, like so many others on the shelves, but this one was penned at the start of her father's reign.

"Did you find something?" Leolin asked.

She set the book down on the table and flipped through the pages until she found the earlier entry. "This here," she said and pointed at another sketch.

"The Boahim Senate? What about them?"

"Now look at the sketch in this book."

Leolin studied both, brow furrowed. His eyes widened when he spotted it, and Margaret nodded. "Are they the same?" Leolin asked.

"That's not possible. This sketch here," she said, pointing at a book so old that many pages hung loosely from their bindings. "This one is a sketch of the original Boahim Senate at its forming. This other one was sketched when my father was crowned king. I thought them perhaps ancestors, but that makes little sense. The Boahim Senate is supposedly formed of representatives from each of the Little Dozen Kingdoms."

When he blinked at her and said nothing, she added, "As in each senator is chosen by the royal family. It is not supposed to be an inherited position."

He glanced back and forth between the two sketches a second time. "I hate to mention it, but there's no way the senators are being chosen, unless they're choosing people of a certain blood," he said.

Senator Whitlen's face was the same stern face but amassed with a lifetime of wrinkles and stress lines, right down to her squinting green eyes that stared through Margaret, even in sketch form. When she compared it to the original Senate, a woman of similar build and stature with piercing eyes stared back at her. Bumps rose across Margaret's arms. The two women could have been twins.

"Leolin...." Margaret nudged him with her elbow, and he glanced up from the book in his hands. "What if they're mystics?"

"You mean, they're using magic to appoint the people they want in power?"

She shook her head. "What if they are using magics to live longer?"

The color fled from his face as he set the book down on the table. "That style of magic doesn't exist, at least not anymore. Not since before the Fall."

"Supposedly magic was outlawed as against the Thirteen, but who originally said that? How do we know that is what occurred?"

"The Boahim Senate."

"Exactly," Margaret said, and she poured herself a glass of mulled wine. "Mystics are forbidden in Alexander, but some other kingdoms employ them to use the healing arts of Sharmus. What if the other magics are still exist?"

Leolin spoke but the words were a whisper compared to the roaring in her head. "What is it?" he repeated, louder.

At first she could not speak. Fear rooted her to her chair and sent her brain spinning in panic. She took a sip of her drink and said, "When Gamun was tried for his crimes, someone or something attempted to gain control of him in order to kill Senator Whitlen. It only stopped when Adelei killed Gamun. It was real magic, Leolin. Magics only talked about in rumors and ancient histories. The same magics they used to keep my sister's corpse on display after they...."

Despite the warm sunlight that streamed in through the

window, he shuddered. "Do you have any idea what that makes the Senate capable of?"

She had been absent when her former husband, Gamun, had been hauled before the Boahim Senate, but the picture Adelei had painted for her had left little to the imagination. Not only could they control people, but perhaps they could extend life itself. When the tears blurred her vision, she couldn't stop them. No amount of imagining stone could harden her and shape her into what she wanted to be. What she would need to be to survive if the Senate possessed that power.

Leolin lay his hand gently on her shoulder. "We'll figure this out, Maggie."

"It's not that," she whispered as she stared at her hands. "I've.... So much death."

"Your father?"

He didn't understand. *If he did, would he still sit beside me? Would he still care for me?* Margaret faced him as tears rolled down her cheeks. "If they have this power, then they hold terrible secrets. Secrets worth killing for, Leolin. And I helped them."

"I doubt that. You couldn't hurt a leaf, let alone a person."

The images came fast and brutal. Amaskans tossed from a wagon and into a clearing where they were beheaded at her order. One screaming for the life of his colleagues before he was beaten and tossed outside the castle walls. Their blood was on her hands, theirs and many more. The light lunch she had eaten sped upwards, and she stumbled away from the table and toward the door. She was halfway to it when her meal escaped her, and she cried as she heaved. Her body fought her for each death: the Amaskans, Adelei, her Papa, Ida, Gamun. All of it her doing.

His footfalls were mostly masked by the sounds of her sick, so when he touched her, she scrambled away from him, her skirt leaving a trail of vomit across the floor.

"Maggie, it's just me," he said as he held out a hand toward her. She allowed him to touch her this time, and he lifted her gently from the stone floor.

"No, I can't go out there. Not like this," she said when he neared the door. Instead, she pointed at the chair near the window. "Take me there."

Leolin placed her in her father's chair, which stood in the sunshine, and then fetched her glass from the table. "Here," he said, placing it in her hand. "Drink this."

Warmth was life. It was the continuation of the tasks ahead, something she was not worthy of, but she closed her eyes a moment to soak it in all the same. Leolin stood beside her, his fingers twitching and his eyes searching the room for answers it did not hold. Margaret took another sip from the glass before braving the truth. "When Gamun...when he killed all those girls, I helped convince my father to call the Boahim Senate. I don't mourn my former husband, but his trial cost me my sister. The arrangement with Shad cost me my family and led to the death of your mother."

He frowned but said nothing as she continued. "I was so angry, Leolin. I thought the reason everyone had died was the Amaskans, so when more crossed our border, I ordered them killed. I watched from the safety of my balcony as they were murdered. *I* did that. The Senate has made a monster of everyone, including me."

Her tears renewed at this, and Leolin crouched down beside her. "Maggie, you thought they were a threat. What else could you do?"

"I could have questioned them to discover why they

were in Alexander. I could have done anything else, but I called for their deaths. I sinned against the Thirteen."

"You didn't kill those...assassins. That isn't on you. It's on Maurus."

Margaret frowned. "I don't understand."

"You know he's more than some simple Amaskan named Maurus. You figured it out before I did. Why else keep him here? You spoke of using him, which only makes sense if he's valuable, so who is he?"

The wine soured in her mouth as she swallowed. "I'm not sure. I believe I know, but no matter how much I look for confirmation, there's no description of their leader."

Leolin bolted upright. "Bredych. Leader of the Order of Amaska and my mother's brother."

"It's only a suspicion. I can't prove it, Leolin."

"And yet *you* feel guilty for killing those assassins? He sent them here to get answers any way possible, including by killing you. If nothing else, this should be the evidence you need that the bounty's being paid for by him. It's the evidence needed to finally stop the Amaskans once and for all." He paced the short distance between the bookshelves, every muscle tense.

He would not understand it—not now, maybe not ever —but making peace with the Order was something she had to do, if not for Adelei then for herself. "That's not why I need him. All my suspicions prove nothing. There is no evidence that he's Grand Master Bredych. Did your mother ever tell you about him? Describe him?"

"No, but the similarities are there. His eyes are grayer than hers, but the sharp nose, the tilt of his chin, his dark hair—those could be descriptions of my mother. I don't know why I didn't think of it earlier," he said and ceased wearing a path into the stone floor long enough to meet her gaze. "You've heard the stories of what he did to her?"

She nodded. "Adelei told me, as did my father."

"Yet you'd keep this vile being here? In your confidence?"

His face hardened as he clenched his jaw, and she stepped forward until she was close enough to touch him. She placed a trembling hand on his woolen shirt. "That vile being may be your uncle," she said, and his heart pulsed rapidly. It hurt to see him in pain, yet she had to ask. "There are blood stains on my hands yet you wish to add more deaths to my conscience. Why?"

Leolin took her hand in his. So gentle a touch and yet his muscles screamed for death. For justice.

"Vengeance."

"'The temple is a gift from Adlain. To kill another is to kill yourself,'" she said, quoting the Thirteen. "Something I've learned is that life is precious, Leolin. Who are we to decide who lives?"

He stared at her hand, his face drooping. "And yet you do. All rulers do. Besides, who are the Amaskans to decide it either? Look, I don't want to argue with you. I...It's not your fault that people are dead." Leolin pointed at a crease that split one side of her palm from the other. "Do you know what this is called in the old tongue?"

Margaret shook her head.

"It's called *ka haimhut*, or the life path. It's said that in the beginning of time, only Silence lived, until it stretched across the darkness and seeped into every curve and corner of time. It grew too large to be contained by a single word and in Her expansion, She sang like the rustling of trees and the shaking of ground. Yet She needed a name, so she settled upon *Luthia*, the first of all things," he said, his gaze following the path on her hand.

It wasn't the first time she had heard the story of the Thirteen, though Leolin told it with small word changes that gave it a slightly different flow, though not altogether unpleasant to listen to.

"A passenger in the night, Luthia could only watch as candlemarks and years and eons passed, and in her loneliness, she birthed Adlain, the All-Father of creation. Despite the frost of silence, his birth brought light to the darkness of Luthia's heart. And in the illumination hid a pocket of life, Agaia. With the fragrance of tulips damp from the rains, she burst forth and left a trail of light across the heavens." Leolin traced the path of her *ka haimhut* with a finger. "It's said when Adlain created us, he spread Agaia's light across our lives, which left the lines of our lives forever engraved in our flesh as a promise to us."

"That 'Winter would fade as the flowers grew, war would never remain when peace was found, and the sun would always shine for the world's born anew,'" she said.

Leolin nodded. "This is not your doing, nor will it last."

The way his eyes softened when he looked at her relaxed the tension and fear that gripped her.

One moment he was smiling, and the next, his eyes closed as he slumped forward across her. Margaret staggered under his weight as she fell to her knees. The creak at the door and slight hiss registered as the sounds they were after they sounded, and a shadow crossed where one should not. Leolin groaned in her arms, and she nearly fainted with relief. When she pulled her hand away from his dark hair, her hand was covered in blood.

She feigned closing her eyes and swayed once before taking them both to the floor. Margaret used the cover of his body to retrieve the dagger tucked in her corset's boning. Her body screamed for her to move, to flee, but running meant death. Gentle footsteps approached them—black boots and above that, black silk breeches. She dared not look up without risking her cover, but whoever it was, they wished her to believe them Amaskan.

Had Leolin been correct? Was Master Maurus behind the attempts on her life?

The attacker's boots stopped a mere inch from her nose, and the figure crouched down, their hands shoving Leolin aside. Margaret reached out and slashed the dagger across the attacker's right tendon. The man's ankle gave out as he fell to his left, and she used the distraction to grab the nearest book from the shelf and throw it at the man's head. First one, then another and another. She did not stop throwing books until he held his bloody face in both hands and screamed.

Pounding feet somewhere outside meant the guards would arrive soon, a fact that must have occurred to her attacker at the same time and he crawled toward the open window. Margaret pursued and before he could do more than rise to his knees, she dragged her dagger across his throat, sending a spray of blood across the stone wall.

If there had been anything else in her stomach to empty, she would have done so. Instead, her guts twisted and lurched as three guards burst through the door to her father's private library. "Would someone fetch Master Roland, please? The lieutenant's been injured," she said as the edges of her vision went dark. Margaret gripped the dagger still in her hand and blinked. Breathing came next, and the darkness retreated.

She was still standing near the body when Roland arrived, then multiple voices assaulted her at once. What had happened? Who had killed the attacker? Was she injured? The last from Roland as he pointed at the blood that trailed down her arm. When she dropped the dagger and held her hand up to her personal physician, he winced at where the dagger had dug into the palm of her hand.

"I'm not the superstitious type, but you missed your *ka haimhut* by a few hairs, Your Majesty," said Roland as he pressed a rag against her wound.

Margaret gave him a gentle push in Leolin's direction. "I am fine. Please see to Leolin."

He hesitated for a heartbeat before he crouched down beside the lieutenant, whose head bled profusely. The darkness encroached on her once again, and she removed the bandage from her hand to stare at the cut that ran parallel to her life path. "I will not faint," she whispered as she stared at it. "My *ka haimhut* will light my way."

Roland glanced up at her, a puzzled look upon his face, and the room faded away.

20

Before today, wearing the clothes of a fighter had left her at odds with herself. She was not her sister, Adelei, or the well-known warrior, Ida, both women who could demand respect with a single look. She was not her father, a man whose mental and physical strength carried sway with the royalty of most of the Little Dozen Kingdoms.

Before today, she had been only Margaret—pampered princess turned queen who had no idea what a real battle looked like and until today, had never killed a man. She swallowed back the bile that burned her throat. Margaret turned to the left, then the right as she studied the woman in the mirror. Dark circles hid beneath powder, and a war between fierceness and fear battled in her brown eyes.

Today, the fighting clothes she had ordered fit more than her figure: sapphire blue enveloped her with a knee-length tunic over breeches, both of which molded against her slender frame, a belt encircling her waist carried her short sword, followed up with brown leather boots. A few throwing knives were hidden on her as well as her dagger, which carried an extra shine after having the blood removed from it.

Maurus had been right. *I am capable of defending myself and others.* A picture of Gamun popped into her mind, and she closed her eyes until the image faded.

Braided hair tucked neatly beneath her cloak's hood, she gave herself one last look before exiting the room. Her honor guards followed her down the stairs to the first floor and down a lengthy corridor. Margaret stopped before one of the empty rooms that normally housed guests. "Wait here," she said, and both guards took up positions outside the door.

According to the Lord Stewart, this was the one unoccupied room on the first floor, and the reason why Margaret had chosen it. She entered the room, then closed and locked the door behind her.

He's suffered a concussion but is otherwise fine, Your Majesty. Roland's words a candlemark before had done little to calm the chaos that drove her now to flee the castle. If she thought about Leolin.... Stone did not fear an attack. It did not bend beneath light pressure or cry out when thrown. She pushed the flood of images aside without a second thought.

She opened the window that led to the courtyard. Her blood hummed as she clambered out the window, though the drop was a foot larger than expected, and she landed on her rear in the bush below. The palm of her hand smarted where the bush's scraggly leaves scraped it, but otherwise, the drop left her unharmed.

A line of people stood at the castle gates awaiting entrance, their belongings strapped to their backs. *More people seeking shelter.* Margaret tightened the hood across her head as she passed. A child waved at her as she walked by, his dirt stained cheeks reminding her of her own cleanliness. Every fighter she had ever seen carried stains. Once out of view, she scurried over to one of the smaller gardens and snatched a small handful of dirt from the ground and smeared some of it across her face and clothes.

The moment she passed through the gates, the scenery changed. Travelers lined the streets. Tired women carried children while older men stood nearby, their gazes settled on the castle. Even with the smudge of dirt, a barefoot little boy ran up to her and tugged on her breaches. "Spare? Spare?" he said as he pointed at the coin purse on her hip.

If she gave him a coin, it would never end. Margaret shook her head. "I'm sorry—"

A glob of spit landed on her tunic before he broke away from her and ran. Rather than touch it, she left it be. Another stain to be added to her fighter appearance. Margaret remained on the street's edge as she passed through the second and third set of walls until she reached the city's outer circle.

It was not until she stopped near the gate that she noticed one of the guard's gestures. She frowned as she approached and spotted the tankard of ale in his hand. "Ar'ya in th'wron place?" he asked.

"Are you not drunk when you should be keeping the city safe?"

Sour ale and the rank smell of rotten meat washed over her as he laughed in her face. "And who's here ta tell me otherwise? You?" The guardsman jabbed her in the shoulder. "Li'l woman witha big sword."

Rather than turn her back to him, she stepped backward, and he followed her, mimicking her exaggerated steps. She continued to retreat, and when he followed her still, she touched the hilt of her sword.

"Antoine! What'd I tell you about showing up for duty drunker than a bard?" said someone behind Margaret, and she ground her teeth to keep from flinching.

She was armed. She was safe.

When she turned, she stood before a lieutenant she did not know. He scowled at her once before his gaze slid away, and he continued berating the guardsman. Three dozen steps took her away from the main road and into the residential streets of Alesta. If she wished to hire an assassin, where would she go? Pieces of patched-over roof sheltered crammed together buildings, but none of the houses fit the description of evil.

"Lookin' for someone?" a young woman with a toddler strapped across one hip asked as she stared at Margaret. She shared the same bulbous nose as the toddler, though her dark eyes were a contrast to the baby's sky blue.

"Um, yes, yes I am. Where would I find—"

"Oh!" The young woman pointed at the way Margaret's sword hung slightly crooked at her waist. "Ya must be needin' the swordsmith. He's down yonder, past the farrier."

"Well, no, I was hoping...." The young woman dipped into an open doorway, then closed the door behind her, leaving Margaret alone on the street.

How foolish was she to look for an assassin on the streets? Besides, what would she do if she found one? How would she question someone with more skill than she? The adrenaline that had fueled her escape from the castle drained out of her, and she melted against the side of a house.

Leolin lay in the castle, his head bandaged as he slept, but her mind pictured him draped across her, blood pouring forth from his head wound. At the time, all she had thought about was how much she wanted to drive her sword into whoever was behind the attacks. Whoever it was had harmed Leolin, had *tried* to harm her. He deserved to die.

She was not aware that she had unsheathed her sword until a foot scraping across the dirt road sounded nearby. An old man, all bones and teeth, stood across the road from her, his eyes wide as he stared at the sword. He backed up one step and another, and she followed him until he reached the corner.

"Please, beggin' yer pardon. I mean no harm," he said. He held out his walking stick to her. "It's all I have, but it's yers."

He was an old man. No danger to her. The image of him dead, his blood splattered across the house behind him made her hands shake as she forced herself to step backward. Dead. Like the man who had attacked her. Attacked Leolin.

"Go," she muttered, and he hobbled down an alley, leaving his walking stick behind.

Margaret dropped her sword and fell to her knees, the hard dirt digging holes in her skin. She retched, her stomach upending its contents across the ground as the images skittered across her mind. Death surrounded her, leaving her weak and alone.

When all that was left was dry heaves, she retrieved her sword from the dust and vomit before standing. "This was a mistake," she whispered.

"Drinkin' usually is," called out a voice from down the road.

I could have been robbed. Or worse. Margaret shivered as she drew her hood back over her head. Eyes followed her as she returned to the main road, but no one stopped her or harassed her. Perhaps that was what her look had needed —vomit.

The absurdity made her giggle as she approached the last gate before the castle. A guard held up a hand to stop her. "Milady, you'll need to get in line w'the rest," he said.

She pulled out a piece of parchment from her pouch and held it up for the guard. He probably couldn't read it, but it held the Queen's seal, and he waved her through with wide eyes. The guards at the castle entrance were not so easily fooled and stared at the document a few heartbeats longer before they had her escorted inside.

When she approached her honor guard still stationed outside the empty room, one bowed, his nostrils flaring from the sour smell of vomit that still clung to the hem of her cloak. "Y-Your Majesty?"

She shook her head, then motioned for them to escort her to her rooms, where her lady-in-waiting helped her undress. "I'll have these clothes given to those in need," the Lady Claretta.

"No. Clean them gently and hang them to dry."

"Yes, Your Majesty."

Despite the warmth outside, the air chilled her bare skin as Lady Claretta turned the lever on the wall. Several minutes later, warm water heated from fires below spilled out of the tap above the bathing tub. Her lady-in-waiting offered her arm as Margaret sank into the tub. "Is Lieutenant Leolin awake yet?" she asked as the woman picked up the offending clothing from the floor.

"I will find out, Your Majesty."

"Leave me," she said, and her lady-in-waiting withdrew. Margaret's nose burned as bile rose in the back of her throat. How had Adelei dealt with the blood on her hands?

Margaret hugged her knees to her chest and shivered until it the warm water grew cold.

PART II

21

Margaret pointed at the drink on the table and said, "Drink."

While the chair the servant had hauled into the library moments before was comfortable, Leolin grimaced as he shifted in it. Padded with more pillows than necessary, he sat at the long table with Margaret, his hands already on a book. His head was no longer bound by bandages, though a chunk of hair was missing where Master Roland had cut it away to examine the initial head wound.

At least the attacker had used an improvised sling rather than throwing knives. Access to a sharp weapon would have left Leolin dead and possibly Margaret along with him. She reached out to brush her fingers across the fresh growth, and her heart trembled. If she had lost him too....

"If I have to drink another of Roland's brews, I'll sleep my way through this war," he said, interrupting her thoughts.

That isn't a bad idea. Although she didn't voice the thought, she didn't have to as Leolin scowled.

"You need me, Maggie. Alert and able. Your capable

physician has declared my addled brain healing. The wound's gone and look," he said as he pointed to his head. "Besides, it's been three weeks since I was injured. My hair's growing back, as you well know. I'm fine." He pushed the cup to the table's edge. "I can drink one this evening, *after* some reading."

Margaret crossed her arms over her chest. "Drink it now or back to your room you go."

"Yes, Your Majesty." He grimaced as he swallowed the bitter drink, then set the cup in front of her. "Can we return to searching for something to take to the Senate? Or is that something to use against them? Thirteen Hells, I don't know who to trust anymore, Maggie."

She glanced over at the open window. Though the room no longer reeked of blood and vomit, the wall's stone still bore a pinkish hue in a few spots despite copious scrubbing by servants. Margaret could have argued that she survived the attack without him, that she had killed the attacker without him, that she needed his complaints as much as he needed another head wound, but it would have stirred up another argument. What he *didn't* need right now was another headache, a leftover side effect of his head injury. Though if he continued to push himself before he was healed, she might knock him over the head herself.

His gaze traveled across one page and then another. "It says here that people stopped using magic after the Fall. At least, non-healing magic. But Alexander doesn't use mystics at all, do they?" he asked.

She shook her head as she retrieved a small, leather bound journal she had brought with her from her rooms. "Those kingdoms that follow the Holy Few's teachings believe all magic to be against the Thirteen. Only the Gods should have powers of that nature."

"I thought everyone followed the teachings of the Holy Few."

There was no readable title on the small journal—only four words in the old tongue scribbled on the front page. It didn't matter that Margaret didn't recognize the words. The book had been tucked beneath the mattress in Adelei's former room. Whenever her hands touched its cover, pinpricks of lightning danced across her skin the same way it did when someone watched her.

"Maggie?"

She glanced up to find Leolin staring at her.

"We were talking about the Holy Few?" he said.

"There's a group of people who believe the Holy Few are no more aware of what the Thirteen want than any of the rest of us. Rather than follow the advice of the Holy Few, they believe in reading the *Shlosheser* and interpreting the Thirteen's intent for themselves."

Margaret flipped past the first page, but not fast enough as Leolin leaned across and snatched the book from her. "What has you distracted so?" he asked. His eyes widened as he spotted the symbol. "Is this...did this belong to your sister?"

She nodded. "She brought a few books with her from the Order, this being one of them."

"This could give us answers," he said as he turned another page then swore. "What language is this?"

"The old tongue."

His fingers ran across the letters as he shook his head. "No one knows the old tongue. Not anymore."

"It's said the Holy Few still use it, though I doubt they would be willing to translate an Amaskan text for us no matter who threatens our borders," she said. When he handed the book back to her, she stared at the first page.

The letters were handwritten, the ink pressed into the page with a heavy hand. Small symbols decorated the pages' edges, and as she flipped through the journal, the occasional scribble in her sister's hand marred the journal. A particular word caught her eye, and her skin prickled.

"What is it?" asked Leolin. She pointed at the word, and he shook his head. "I don't know what that says."

"I do. *Shataf.* Kidnap in the old tongue."

"Is there something particularly ominous about the word kidnap? And how did you read that?"

It was not a memory she relished, but the thinned hair on Leolin's head taunted her. "There was this horror of a child I knew who used to tease me relentlessly because his tutors were teaching him about weaponry and tactics and mine were not."

Leolin stuck his tongue out at her and for a moment, she was ten again and running through the gardens, tears running down her face.

"I'm sorry, Maggie. What did I do?" he asked.

"I hated that you were encouraged to learn sword-work whereas I was not. My father would marry me off to someone, and I would be taken care of. A nice, pampered princess to look pretty on the throne." Margaret frowned. "After you left, I lost myself in the library. No one cared if I read books."

"You taught yourself the old tongue from books?" He leaned back and whistled. "I'm lucky if I know a few words, and I had a teacher."

Margaret shook her head. "I don't know the old tongue. Just a few words here and there, and only because I wished to know something you didn't. I taught myself what others would not. What teacher could you have had though? I searched for a tutor who could teach me, but few speak a dead language, and I had no interest in joining the Holy Few."

"Not a tutor. My mother."

"Ida spoke the old tongue?" she asked.

"Most Amaskans speak a smattering of it. Some more than others." Leolin pointed at the journal. "If their texts are written in it, I can see why. I used to hate her for making me memorize it."

"Maybe between the two of us we can piece together what this says," said Margaret as she slid the book between them. He leaned closer to her, a piece of parchment nearby. When she found a word she knew, she marked it on her page as he did the same.

By the end of three candlemarks, they had made a dent in the transcription but nothing more, and Margaret scowled. "This is another of my sister's personal journals and nothing more. It won't help us."

"She may have written down something important," he said and pointed again at the word *shataf.* "Someone was kidnapped. It might be important to know who."

"I already know the answer to that one. This page I was working on is dated a few days before Adelei arrived in Alesta. This is an entry about Ida and my sister—the day when she found out who stole her from us and why."

The memory of dust and horse sweat tickled her nose as panic and bile rose in her throat. Running. There had been so much running as her horse had carried Margaret along with her mother's corpse all the way back to Alesta. The memory made her dizzy as the image of her sister's face overwhelmed her. Adelei must have been so scared when they had bound and gagged her....

When he kissed her, his lips tasted of the herbs Roland had used in his foul drinks. She wrinkled her nose at him, and his laughter tickled her ears. The distraction had swept the memory away, though her throat remained dry like the dust. "Lieutenant, that was entirely inappropriate," she said as she pursed her lips together. His eyes fell to her lips and when he leaned forward to kiss her again, she placed a hand on his chest.

"Why did you kiss me?" He flushed and muttered something unintelligible, and she repeated the question.

"You had this expression on your face, like you were in pain. Sometimes you fall into the past, and what you find there isn't...something you want to remember. I figure if I kiss you, I'll give you something else to think about."

It was an acceptable answer, and inside Margaret beamed. "We have a task before us, and you aren't helping by distracting me."

"And what task is that, because I have a few in mind myself."

She halfway ignored his playful response as she shook her head. "I had this plan. A way to win the war." Leolin sat up straight in his chair, all humor lost in a moment, and she regretted her choice of words. "I'm saying this incorrectly."

He fluttered his hand out in a faux bow like the lords at high court. "Please carry on, Your Highness of the Old Tongue." She froze open-mouthed and eyes wide, and his hand fell to his side. "What did I say?"

"Highness of the Old Tongue. Leolin, King Dama."

"Who?"

"King Dama Yachad, the King of Boahim." When he stared at her blankly, she wagged her finger at him. "Don't tell me your tutors skipped the histories on Boahim before the Fall."

Leolin shrugged. "Or I've forgotten. Unlike you, I'm not much of a book person. So what makes him important?"

"He was the last king before the Fall. When the nobility decided to overthrow King Dama, they believed that only war would resolve the question of who would rule. After armies and civilians died by the thousands, King Dama suggested Boahim split once and for all. It was his suggestion that the Boahim Senate be formed to enforce the will of the Thirteen."

"So if we find information on King Dama, we might find more information the Senate, and from there, what happened to magic." When she nodded, he said, "You said you had a plan on how to win the war. What was it?"

She could become like stone. She had done it before in the council room and then again when she had killed their attacker. It would be what Adelei would do.... But this was Leolin. Could he be made to understand? Margaret inhaled deeply to clear her lungs of dust and horse sweat.

"Maggie, it'll be okay," he said as he rested his hand against her cheek.

There was no queen in the room when he looked at her then, only someone he cared about and perhaps even loved. Her heart beat awkwardly in her chest—half fleeing horse and half butterfly—and she leaned close enough to smell the bitter drink still on his breath. It was better than the smell of horses.

"I don't want to be like stone," she said. His confusion was cut short when she kissed him, a passionate plea to feel anything other than the fear and confusion and numbness that warred within her and had since the day the crown had come to rest upon her brow. He winced when her fingers brushed the bruise on his head, which he then ignored as her hands brought him closer. Close enough to feel the warmth of her body.

He pulled away for a moment, his brow furrowed. "Maggie...."

In the recesses of her mind, the horses approached—dark nightmares that carried fear and stank of blood and death. They encroached on the daylight, and the memory of her mother's screams pierced her ears.

She was tired of people looking at her and seeing someone weak, of seeing a pampered princess who knew nothing of the world around her, she was tired of being manipulated and controlled, and beyond anything else, she was tired of trying and failing to be like stone. Margaret shook her head at whatever he might have said and dug her fingers into his shoulders.

"Make me not stone."

"Yes, Your Majesty."

22

The horse he'd stolen from Alesta's stables hadn't been the best of beasts as the horse had complained every five steps once Bredych reached the Sadain Desert. Carrying the note from the Queen, originally intended for his messenger, had gotten him across the border and into Bredych's homeland; although once there, his breathing had hitched in his lungs with each sun that set between him and Queen Margaret.

Maybe it had been a mistake to leave, but she needed the time and space to think on the words that dragged like heavy sand between them. *Besides, I need information. It's the only way I'll get information from her.* Adelei's face appeared in his mind—one where she frowned at him like only she could, her eyes saddened by whatever made her soul ache, and when Bredych shook his head to clear the image, her face morphed into that of her sister, Margaret.

So alike and yet so utterly different.

His horse harrumphed as he picked up the scent of something ahead. Three weeks' travel and he was as ready as his horse for the Order's comforts, which would be quite comfortable after desert and mountain travel. The first reminder of home was the crooked tree left bent from a lightning storm. The second was the sound of waves crashing against the rocky coast in the distance.

But the third was the eyes that followed his travels as he approached, invisible eyes in the foliage that never left his back as he rode toward home.

Bredych smiled at the sight of smoke up ahead, and his mouth watered at the thought of something other than smoked deer meat for a meal. In response to his mood shift, the gray and white dappled horse picked up his pace. No walls were necessary here. Anyone foolish enough to approach would have been turned back half a candlemark ago, and anyone strong enough to make it this close was someone possibly worth talking to.

Another set of hoofbeats approached behind him at a gallop, then slowed as it reached Bredych. The Amaskan riding a black and white spotted horse bowed from the saddle. "Grand Master, we've been awaiting your return." The man handed him a scrap of parchment. "You're needed by the masters as soon as possible."

The man moved on as Bredych glanced at the parchment.

You were missed.

No signature, though none was needed. He smiled as he tucked the piece of parchment into his borrowed saddlebag and nudged his horse forward. It wasn't long before he'd passed the familiar trails leading to the coast and then those that led to the training grounds and stables. The large building that housed trainees and those Amaskans not on a mission loomed ahead, its gray and white cobble walls covered in more ivy than when he'd left. As much as his old bones ached for home, he turned his horse toward the path leading to the stables.

Several horses had been turned out to the paddock to enjoy the afternoon sun, and Bredych's horse whickered a greeting upon their approach. A lone trainee waited outside and took the reins from Bredych when he dismounted.

"And who's this beauty?" the trainee asked.

"No clue as to his name, but he hates the desert and spooks too easily. I've got the bruises to prove it." Bredych left the saddle bag for the trainee. Nothing inside it carried any personal sentiment, a habit from a life of service to the Order, and the clothes had long since needed replacing. He gave the horse one last pat. "After he's recovered from the journey, tell Master Marash to sell the beast. No use to us here."

He left the trainee to his business and followed the path that led back to the main hall. Several Amaskans gave partial bows to him as he passed, and Bredych quickened his pace despite the hitch in his hip. As much as his body yearned for the comfort of his rooms, he bypassed the stairwell and followed the long hallway to the room where the masters waited. Carvings of the Thirteen in the wall's blues and greens smiled at him with a joy he reciprocated, but when he reached the council room, he hesitated outside the doorway.

They hadn't understood his reason for sending Amaskans into Alexander, so why would they understand what he had done? What he was planning to do? He took a calming breath and passed through the doorway. The first master to greet him was Miriam, a calculated move on the masters' part. If *he* were delivering bad news, he'd put a friendly face before him as well.

She scoffed at his hair, but when she caught a glimpse of

the scar on his jaw, she rushed to his side. Her fingers lightly brushed the scar where his tattoo once had been. "Was this necessary? I was quite fond of your face the way it was," she said as one side of her mouth tilted downward.

His muscles tensed as the chatter inside the second room died, and Miriam gestured for him to pass beneath the arch first. For all that he was her superior as Grand Master, he understood their reticence. He had returned months later, tattoo-less, and riding a horse bearing the markings of Alexander.

The blue archway tingled as he passed beneath it, and the tension he carried melted away like snow. A dozen faces watched him from their seats at the table, waiting for some indication that he wasn't who he claimed, that his loyalties had shifted, and when the arch released him without issue, they dipped their heads in unison until he claimed his seat at the rectangular table's end. "It's good to be home," he said and dismissed the room's formality with a hand wave.

"Grand Master, your...journey was quite sudden," said Miriam. Her blue eyes cut through him as she narrowed her eyes. "Did you find the information you sought?"

He nodded. "If what I've learned is the truth, the Boahim Senate's behind Adelei's death."

"And the rest of our brothers and sisters?"

"I have yet to uncover this, but I don't believe Alexander is responsible." It wasn't exactly the whole truth, but it was true enough. Had the Senate remained on their little island, Adelei would still be alive and so would the others.

Twelve masters listened as he explained the Senate's role in Adelei's death, the way they'd frozen her body and used her as an example of their power, and their apathy toward the threat of civil war. "I believe the senators wish to use this war as a means to place the Little Dozen Kingdoms solidly under their control." When Bredych said the words aloud, their absurdity stood out like an Amaskan at the daytime market, yet he could see no other rationale for their actions.

"The Boahim Senate enforces the Thirteen. In some ways, you could say they already control the Little Dozen Kingdoms," Miriam said.

Several masters nodded their agreement, and Bredych sighed. They didn't know about the orbs.

Miriam laid her hand on his a moment before placing a cup of mulled wine beside him. He took a swallow as she plucked grapes from a bowl and set them, along with some cheese and bread, where he could reach. While their relationship wasn't a secret, she'd never shown him affection inside this room. Not here where they decided who lived and who died by Amaskan hand. The change in demeanor left him more on edge than when he'd walked through the door, and he said as much.

"There's so much I haven't said, things I can't say, but I ask as your Grand Master that you trust me. Know that I have your lives in mind when I make the choices that I do," he said. A dozen sets of eyes looked anywhere but at him, and he chewed on a wedge of sharp cheese. "So when did you take the vote?" he asked.

Heat rushed to several faces, but it was Miriam who answered. "A month ago. When you didn't return, we thought you dead. No word came from you or of you. The last Amaskans who traveled to Alexander—"

"Died, yes, I know. I sent several messages."

"We never received them."

Bredych narrowed his eyes as he stared at Miriam. Did she speak the truth, or had his leaving merely given them the opportunity? "Who did you name my replacement?" he asked.

"For now, we voted to make decisions together rather than one master over all."

They've had enough of me, I suppose. Bredych clenched his jaw. Perhaps it would be better this way. He was old and tired. Without the future of Amaskan lives weighing him down, he could do whatever he wished. He shook his head. "I'm obviously not dead, and since you didn't receive my messages, there's much to discuss. But first, we will take a small journey of our own," he said as he rose.

The blue arch settled their confusion as they passed beneath it and into the front room. They followed him into the outer chamber, where pictures of the Thirteen decorated the walls. When he approached the statue of Anur, God of Justice, Miriam cleared her throat. "This is a short journey, Bredych. I assume there's a point to it?"

The corners of his mouth tilted up as he depressed one of Anur's eyes. As before, a click sounded within the wall to his right, and several masters flinched. Bredych pushed against the wall until it slid open to expose the dusty room that held the now dead orb.

"What is this place?" she asked as she held out a lit candle. Without the orb's glow, the room's darkness left the masters straining to see until Bredych lit the torches along the wall. One of the masters reached out and touched the orb with a single finger. When nothing happened, the group turned to him, puzzlement on their faces. "It's pretty, but I was expecting something more I guess. Does it power the arch?" asked Miriam.

Bredych shook his head. "To my knowledge, no one knows what powers the arch. It's old though, as old as this orb. Fifteen of these orbs exist that I know of—one in each kingdom, one in the Boahim Senate, and this one."

Miriam gasped. "Is this how rulers are able to summon the Senate so quickly?"

"Yes, though there's more to it than that." When he told them of Margaret's suspicions, the masters turned their faces away from the orb's view. "This one's dead, though it's probably best to retreat from here before we discuss this further."

Only when the room was sealed and the group firmly past the blue arch did they speak—a dozen questions or more as they inquired how he had known of the orb, what its true purpose was, and why he'd waited so long to tell them. "There's so much we don't understand about magic. As a new Grand Master, the last thing I wanted was to expose this Order to danger, so until I knew more about it, it remained a secret, as it has been for at least a century or more. The words used to activate the orb are carved into these very walls. I only tell you this so that once I'm gone, you won't be left without information that could prove vital in the coming years."

"How did it die?" This question from Master Sarra, the only Amaskan older than Bredych and one well-versed in the Order's histories.

"I used it to contact the Senate." Bredych held up a hand before their protests began. "I did so in search of answers. Or to attempt to find them anyway. Senator Whitlen confirmed a suspicion I'd held for many years— and when I asked her about the coming war and the death of Adelei, she destroyed the orb's connection."

"Let me guess," said Miriam, whose dark complexion paled. "The Boahim Senate uses magic."

"We always suspected they used some, yes. Perhaps as

physicians, healers, or maybe mystics, but this goes far beyond that," Bredych said as his gaze traveled around the table. "They used powerful magics in Alesta to destroy Prince Gamun Bajit of Shad. While I've gained Queen Margaret's trust, she's not told me every detail, but judging by her reaction, the magics used were quite powerful. Adelei's body was held in a protected state after her death. No one could move or harm the body until they allowed it. Worse still, they can use the orbs to travel instantly between their island and another orb."

Miriam leapt to her feet, as did three other masters. "We must destroy the orb and do it now," she cried as she strode toward the other room.

"It can't be destroyed," said Bredych, and she paused beneath the blue arch. He gestured for her to return to her seat, and when she and the others did so, Miriam bowed her head.

"My apologies, Grand Master. My actions are those of a trainee rather than a master. Please, tell us what you know of these orbs."

Bredych paused several heartbeats as the others slowly dipped their heads in submission. "Being made Grand Master was a promotion my sister didn't approve of and as such, she worried that perhaps she had made the wrong choice in joining the Order. In her search to find evidence that Amaskans were defiling Justice rather than upholding it, she found the orb."

"But how?" asked Master Sarra.

"She was angry with me. We argued, and after I left these chambers, she punched the statue. Broke two fingers in the process, but it exposed the orb. It wasn't until much later that I realized the words on the walls were important. It took some doing to discover which ones woke the sleeping orb, and when a senator appeared, I tossed a black scrap of cloth over it and fled. Until I understood more about it, I couldn't trust the information to leave my head."

He paused to sip from his cup and glanced around the table. While confused, they waited for him to continue rather than questioning him. His sister, Shendra, used to do that. At least she'd done so before she had fled and become Ida. Bredych shook his head to clear the memory. "Certain questions plagued me. When someone committed a crime against the Thirteen, how did the Senate know? How did they travel so quickly within the kingdoms to dole out justice, and how did rulers communicate with them without being intercepted? No matter how many times I sent Amaskans to places where I suspected the Senate would be, there were no runners, no messages by torch tower or pigeons. Nothing that would explain these answers other than magic."

Miriam tapped her finger on the table as she frowned. "That explains their magic use but not the orb. How do you know there are others throughout the Little Dozen Kingdoms?"

"Adelei," Bredych said.

The masters held their collective breath as he took a larger swallow of wine. "King Leon of Alexander entrusted her with this knowledge. She spoke with the Boahim Senate through the orb in Alesta. When she realized they could use the device to travel in an instant, she left an encoded message in Alesta with one of our contacts."

Bredych pulled the piece of parchment from the pouch at his waist, unfolded it, and set it on the table. "I left for the wrong reasons, I admit," he said as they passed the message around the table. "Vengeance isn't our purpose or our path. But when I learned of this, I knew I had to remain in Alesta and get closer to the Queen. We needed answers about what and who it is we face."

"We?" asked Master Sarra.

"We sit on the cusp of a civil war that could tear the Little Dozen Kingdoms apart—a war being encouraged by the Boahim Senate. It won't stop with a few kingdoms. If we're to survive, we must discover the Senate's true purpose and how to stop them. The Senate must go the way of the old tongue—something whispered about by old people fascinated with histories and nothing more."

Miriam remained silent as she glanced his way, her shoulders inching upward as she breathed. She had to understand. They all did. Bredych had made plenty of mistakes in his life, but this couldn't be one of them. "I plan to spend a day or two looking for answers in our archives before traveling to King Adir. I bear a message and proposition from Queen Margaret," he said.

"And does this proposition involve the Amaskans?" another master asked.

Bredych nodded. "I propose that the Amaskans and Sadai side with Alexander in the upcoming war, and that we rid ourselves of Boahim's spies once and for all."

"We will follow where you lead, Grand Master," said Miriam, though the words were hesitant. She waited as the other masters left the room, and once they were alone, she pursed her lips together and glared at him. "Are you sure you aren't jumping from one firepit to the next, Bredych?"

"Explain."

She set her wrinkled hand over his and grasped it tightly. "Your sister. I was there that day, remember?"

"I do, but I fail to see what that has to do with this."

"Shendra was the weakest point of your leadership and

your largest critic. Family's never easy, especially when they're younger and think themselves wiser than Anur."

Bredych chuckled softly, then poured himself more wine. Shendra was the only one who could make him wish for a horse and a straight road to anywhere else.

"When she killed her Amaskan brothers, she required punishment. No one questions why you killed her, but you acted so swiftly. Rashly, some would say. Much like you're doing now."

"Did you know she survived?" he asked.

Miriam held her breath a moment before the air rushed out of her with a single word. "How?"

"How does anyone survive a wound like that? It had to be magic."

"You don't know?"

He shook his head. "I only know that she survived. She's how King Leon discovered Adelei's whereabouts. Shendra...or Ida as Leon knew her, was his *sepier* and before that his Captain of the Royal Army."

The candlelight wavered before him, and when Bredych brought his hands to his eyes, moisture gathered on his fingertips. He was not a man given to tears, but his heart burned with a history he couldn't escape and a decision that kept him awake long after the sun set. "I never wanted her dead," he whispered. "Not really. She was my world for so long after our parents' murders, but she questioned my authority too often. To then kill fellow Amaskans...I had no choice. Or I felt that I didn't at the time. Looking back, I suppose I could've confined her to the Order...."

"She was never the type to be confined. You knew that. Regardless of your rationale then, you've never been one to relinquish control. Today was an example of that." When he raised an eyebrow, she added, "You know what I mean,

Bredych. That was quite the coup you used to regain your position."

"A position I never lost."

"A position you lost because you disappeared," Miriam said as she released his hand. "If you keep everything from us, you might not like the way we're forced to act in your absence. We've had this conversation before, Bredych. We can't make the choice you want if we don't know what it is you want."

If her aging body had allowed for it, she would have paced as the old debate burned between them. Some years it erupted hotter than others, and when it did, their relationship crisped until it cracked and crumbled, only to renew again at a later time when they'd forgotten the angry words spoken across the table.

It was a pity she would never understand the conflict he carried with so many lives in his hands. Rather than set fire to the room, Bredych stood with a curt nod to her, then strode through the blue arch. He kept walking until he'd left the chambers altogether.

In the back of his head reverberated Shendra's deep, melodic laughter. *You're a fool*, she said, and Bredych dug his nails into the palms of his hands. He'd intended to tell Miriam about his other discovery—Leolin—but at this point, perhaps it was better if his secrets remained his own.

They soured less that way.

23

The scars across his shoulder blade had stretched and grown with him as the years had passed, but seeing them as he slept reminded Margaret how fragile life was. Leolin had been ten or eleven when his mother's horse had kicked him into a pitchfork. As Margaret traced the old puncture marks with the tip of her finger, his chest moved with each breath as he lay sleeping in her bed.

With Gamun, she had grown to wish for his breath to cease, especially when he had been particularly cruel. Whereas with Leolin, the need to count each breath and ensure their continuance held her a different form of hostage, a pleasant one, and she smiled.

Reality would insert itself into her world soon enough, but for the moment, she was content to be soft and alive rather than the stony, brave façade she attempted to wear these days.

It wasn't until the barest hints of pink punctuated the dark skies outside that she slipped from beneath the blankets and wrapped a robe around her naked body.

Quietly, so as not to wake him, she gathered clothing and weapons discarded the evening before and donned them in her bath chamber.

The castle lay quiet in the pre-dawn candlemarks as she strode through nearly empty halls and then outside toward the Holy Few's chapel. Seeing it empty brought comfort to Margaret as she approached the stained glass windows toward the front. Scenes of the rise and fall of Boahim were displayed across several panes, and sunlight streamed through them, casting colors and shadows across the stone floor. Beneath the windows were small statues of the Thirteen, and before them, thirteen red candles. None were lit, though a white candle nearby held a flame. She lifted the candle while she stood before her gods.

"I submit to this temple seeking guidance. May the Thirteen bless me this day," she said and held the candle's flame against a red candle's wick. She lit a second candle, then set the white candle aside. "Asti, bring me peace. Let it carry my hand and guide my actions, despite the war in my soul." Her army would arrive at the borders—possibly today or on the morrow—and breath trembled in her chest. The three candles cast an eerie light upon the small statues, and rather than comfort her, their eyes watched her. "Do not judge me. I was never meant to lead," she whispered.

Her vision strayed toward a third candle where she hesitated a moment before fetching the candle again. "Cerci, still the war within my heart. What I want, I'm not sure I can have. Not right now, but...I wish it nonetheless," said Margaret. The creaking of wood behind her startled her, and she spun on her heel to find Her Holiness standing near the chapel's rear doors.

"The Thirteen lead you, Your Majesty," the woman

said as she approached. "It was not my intention to startle you."

Margaret glanced over her shoulder, though she could not tell if the third candle burned. "The Thirteen lead you as well, Your Holiness."

"All three candles still burn, never fear," Her Holiness said as she lifted the long, red robes to climb the dais steps. When she reached Margaret's side, she pressed two fingers against Margaret's brow in blessing. "Is there a way for me to assist you further, Your Majesty?"

"Not unless you can dissuade the Shadians from war." *Or help me figure out what lies between Leolin and me.*

Her Holiness took the white candle from Margaret's hands and lit Adlain's candle. The largest of the thirteen candles, its long tapered appearance clashed with the All-Father's strong frame, if the statue's shape was to be believed. The holy woman said nothing, merely closing her eyes in brief prayer before she returned her attention to Margaret. "The Thirteen will decide whether the Little Dozen Kingdoms fall, though the Fall of Boahim brought forth twelve kingdoms, including your own. Not every death is something to be mourned."

Had the candle still been in her hands, Margaret would have crushed it between her fingers. "While I understand your intent, Your Holiness, I thoroughly disagree. I'm surrounded by death and constantly reminded of the painful absence of those who should still be here. Itova has had her fill of my family."

"Your grief is new, Your Majesty, but death brings forth life. Change brings new opportunities. Gamun's death kept you from a harrowing fate and—" Her Holiness glanced toward the candles, "—has brought you someone who truly cares for you."

Margaret's cheeks grew warm, though her fingers remained chilled. "And my father's death? And that of my sister?"

"Your father carried an illness that weakened him. He wouldn't have carried Alexander into war, not without great cost. As Queen, you will accomplish what he could not. As to your sister, her loss brought you to this moment."

"I don't understand."

Her Holiness tilted her head as she stared through Margaret. "Who were you before, and who are you now?"

"I...I know what everyone sees when they look at me, and who they wish I was." Margaret swallowed the lump in her throat. "But who I am remains shrouded in fog. One moment, I feel ready to lead my kingdom, and the next I'm stumbling through a rose bush where a thousand thorns pierce my skin. Somewhere in all of this, I'm supposed to make decisions that won't result in the deaths of my people, but I'm not my father. I'm not my sister."

"You're many things, Your Majesty, but no, you aren't your father. He wouldn't wish you to be. Nor are you your sister. She shut herself away from others. How can you rule if you're sequestered from those who need you most?"

"Adelei was stone."

The holy woman shook her head. "She may have wished to be, but not even the All-Father Adlain could keep stone from changing. 'Be wary of that which would harden you, as hardened rock is prone to cracking under pressure. If you would be like stone, be like those of the river, malleable and shaped by that which flows over and through you.'"

The hair on the back of Margaret's neck stood up as Her Holiness quoted *The Book of Ja'ahr*, and she asked, "How....When did the Holy Few begin reading Amaskan texts?"

"Their Order has stolen much from us, including our holy words of the *Shlosheser*."

Margaret inclined her head a moment as her thoughts chased one another. There was little time to think, yet time was what she needed. To the holy woman, she said, "I appreciate your advice, Your Holiness. I leave you to your day."

Her Holiness remained beside the candles as Margaret walked through the chapel, but when she reached the door, the woman's words reached her, though they were but a whisper. "The Thirteen lead you, Queen Margaret. May your Way guide you."

With Maurus returned to his Order, she needed all the help she could get.

Thirteen be with me.

THE BOOKS IN BREDYCH'S SADDLEBAGS WEREN'T THE sort to have ever left the Order—rare volumes that were few in number on purpose—but within them held histories about the Fall of Boahim and the Senate's forming. Each day he was away from Margaret, the more his muscles tensed as he waited for word of her death to reach him. Word of the bounty lingered on Sadain tongues. Bredych had wrapped the four volumes in thick woolen fabric to ready them for travel.

His hand lingered on an old, leather bound journal. A woven, well-worn bracelet marked the pages that he'd read many an evening in the past few years, a journal entry from Adelei when she advanced from journeyman to full membership in the Order. More recent journals were missing—likely taken with Adelei to Alexander—but to see her life here might help Margaret understand the good her sister had done. Bredych's lips fell into a sad smile as he tucked the journal away in his saddlebag. Along with the books went some of Bredych's personal notes, including those he'd taken on the *barak* trade— though truth be told, he suspected the *Tribor* of laying a false trail.

Another set of clothes followed, and when he gave his bedroom another glance, his gaze lingered on the emptiness of it. A full life of serving Justice had left little time for the acquisition of the usual knickknacks and personal trinkets. Other than a painting Adelei had done as a child, one too fragile for the trip, he could think of nothing else worth taking. His foot caught on the chest at the bed's foot, and he winced.

He opened the chest and fetched a pair of throwing knives Miriam had gifted him years before. As he hefted them both, their lightness reminded him of how well they split the air, and he set them on his bed. Too lanky to use a broadsword, the weapons chest held an arrangement of daggers, throwing knives, and a single crossbow. One dagger slid into the sheath at his waist. The crossbow and bolts would go with him as well. He rooted beneath a blanket and found the smooth pebble Shendra had given him when they were younger. *How long ago was it when you gave me this? Four decades at least. Remnants of a time when things were simpler between us.* His hand lingered over the bed before he released the stone into the pile of belongings that would return with him to Alesta.

As he closed the chest, someone knocked at his door, and he crossed the ten steps to open it. Miriam stood outside, a bottle of wine in one hand and a plate of varying cheeses and fruits in the other. Her gaze traveled to the saddlebags on his bed, and she smirked. "I see you're already packing."

Bredych stepped aside to allow her entrance, and she set the wine and food on the side table. Small though his room was, it was nestled at the top of a tower off the main hall. High enough that the lone window wasn't much threat, especially not when he was surrounded by Amaskans.

"You always did have a beautiful view," she said as she stared out the window. Off in the distance lay the coast and the Harren Sea. Miriam settled into one of two chairs and without looking, gestured at the wall shelf. "Be a good lad and grab two cups."

Aged and well-used, both wooden cups wobbled a touch, but as they had on many evenings with Miriam, they would serve their purpose. He set them down, and she poured wine into them without a word. When he claimed the chair across from her, tears gathered at the edges of her eyelids.

She plucked a grape from the plate and ate it. "When did I grow this soft?"

"You've always been this soft," he said, as she swallowed another grape. "I won't be gone forever."

The unspoken *I hope* lay between them as they sipped their wine, but it was small bits that saddened him most as he shared a piece of cheese with her: the way she leaned to her left because the ache in her right hip, the subtle way her fingers worried the hem of her shirt, and the almost invisible fear that enshrouded her as she sat at his table.

"Bredych...why leave?"

"We need answers."

Miriam shook her head. "You say that, but I think your priorities have changed. You return because of her."

"Adelei?"

"No, her twin. Don't think I don't see it. The look you get when you mention her. She's in your heart, which is a dangerous place to be," she said.

"So are you, my dear. Does that make you dangerous, too?"

While the corners of her mouth tilted up, the smile never reached her eyes. "Deadly. You best remember that, Bredych, but this Margaret; she's not Adelei."

She grew silent as they sipped wine, while outside, waves crashed upon the cliff side. The rise and fall of it and the rumble as the waves peaked was a sound he would miss almost as much as Miriam. When his vision blurred, he changed the topic and asked, "How much do you remember from before Shendra left for Alexander?"

Her shrug came too fast. "Over a decade ago? Some mornings I can barely recall what happened the day before. Why?"

"Is it possible Shendra was pregnant when she left?" he asked. Only decades as an Amaskan kept the surprise from her face, though her fingers twitched as they picked at the cheese. "There's a boy in Alexander who claims to be her son, though I can't imagine who the father is. Most Amaskans' lives are too short for families."

"There's nothing to say the father was Amaskan."

When would she have had time to fraternize with anyone else? Bredych shook his head. "I suppose not. I can't help but wonder if the man's still alive, whoever he is. If she was pregnant with this boy, that might be why she couldn't do it."

"Do what? Murder a child?"

"Yes," he said.

Miriam swallowed hard. "She couldn't kill Adelei

because it was the wrong call, Bredych. Amaskans aren't murderers. To have sent Shendra on that mission was a mistake, and we both know it."

"I can't undo the past, Miriam. What's done is done," he said as he offered her another piece of cheese.

She shook her head. "You might not be able to undo the past, but you can make the future right. If this boy's her son, that makes him your nephew. He's family."

All of my family is right here.

As if she'd read his thoughts, she said, "I know you've never given much credence to blood connections. Hells, in this profession, who would? But he might be all that you have left of her in this world."

"The boy makes my head ache."

"Family usually does."

He sipped his wine silently as she gazed out the window. It would be simpler without the boy in the picture. As it was, he swayed Margaret too easily, which wasn't going to make the choices in her future any easier.

Miriam spoke, though the sound was muffled by his thoughts. "...you leave, they may make you pick someone. Even if you return from this war, you won't live forever."

Bredych opened the single drawer on the table's underside and withdrew an envelope. He passed it to her, and when she opened it, she withdrew a single piece of parchment and read it.

"Me?" she asked.

"It's always been you."

A tear escaped her, and she brushed it away with the back of her hand. "I never wanted to be Grand Master. Not even after we...."

He reached out to take her hand. "That's why it must

be you. You never wanted it." He had every intention of returning, but like her, his gut told him it was unlikely.

"You just be sure those Alexandrians know that you're mine," she whispered as a few more tears appeared. "If you fall, I want your body brought home."

"They don't know where the Order's located. That's not something I plan to tell them either." Miriam closed her eyes as he leaned over and kissed them. "I appreciate the sentiment though," he said.

"Have your body sent to King Adir. It'll make it home. To me." She ran her fingers across his head. "You know, I might grow to like you with hair."

The corners of Bredych's mouth twitched upward as she dropped her hand to his scar, which tickled as she caressed it. Outside, the sun kissed the shore, scattering reds and oranges across the sky, but Bredych barely noticed as Miriam painted a picture of her own for him long after the wine was gone. He would see plenty of sunsets when he returned to Alexander.

And with hope, plenty of sunsets with Miriam upon my return.

24

Y our Majesty, though your council dwindles, I offer whatever advice you need. As I did for your father," said Lord Cornish, who sat alone at the council table with Margaret.

Despite the numerous lit candles, darkness huddled close by as she counted the empty chairs. One for her late Grand Advisor, Dumont Darras, and another for Lady Mara, who had returned home. A third for Captain Fenton and a fourth for her Grand Marshal, both of whom fought battles she could not...at least not yet. Her Holiness and her personal physician, Roland, had more pressing matters. Bredych had returned to his Order, and Leolin lay recovering. Eight out of a possible thirteen and only one of them before her.

The one whose opinion mattered least.

"Your Majesty?"

Margaret glanced across the table at Lord Cornish. "My apologies. It seems my mind is elsewhere today. I appreciate your willingness to help as needed, though I'm not entirely sure why you wished to meet."

"To speak about the attack...attacks on you, Your Majesty. If this bounty is being funded by someone within the castle, we must find out who and immediately. This most recent attack.... I can't imagine what would've happened if Lieutenant Leolin hadn't been there," said Lord Cornish.

Heat rose to her cheeks. "Lord Cornish, I assure you—"

"It's a blessing that you have someone to rely on now that your father's gone."

When he waved a hand in her direction, the flab under his arms jiggled, and she glanced away. He rambled on about the necessity of support for her, and she was content to let him, if only to get it out of his system. He ran out of words a few minutes later, and she clapped her hands once to regain his attention. "The lieutenant was knocked unconscious, Lord Cornish. Who do you think killed the attacker?"

He frowned, then paled as comprehension flooded through him. "Surely not you, Your Majesty. A gentile breed like yourself...."

If Adelei were here, she would run a blade in his jowls for such a remark. The knife tucked in her corset brushed against her as she sighed. Perhaps she could throw it at the wall to make a point, though if she missed.... Margaret shuddered.

"Are you all right, Your Majesty? It's a bit chilly in this room."

Of course she was not all right. She had killed someone. Attacker or no, his blood still burned her fingers at night when she woke up shaking. Would the Thirteen forgive her for taking a life? Or would it haunt her through the afterlife?

When she glanced at Lord Cornish, his fat tongue

licked his lips as he blabbered on about her innocence and upbringing. Like two sides of Echana, the Goddess of Chaos, the same fear that kept her awake fueled her with a power she didn't understand. "Have you ever held a blade, Lord Cornish?" she asked, interrupting him.

"Of course, Your Majesty. Weapons work is taught to most young men who are of noble blood."

Margaret rose from her chair and removed the knife from her corset. "Do you know what it feels like to slice open flesh, Lord Cornish? To watch someone's life spray across the wall and know that they will never see another sunrise or speak another word because of an action *you* took?"

He shook his head, his gaze steady on her knife. She stood beside him, her backside against the table as she turned the blade in her hands. She had killed a man. Gamun's face popped into her mind—the way he had snarled when he hit her, the way he....

No one will take advantage of me again.

To Lord Cornish she said, "The servants have failed to remove his blood from the walls completely. Little pink splotches—reminders that I killed someone, Lord Cornish. I slit his throat and killed him."

The words tumbled out, and she stared at him until he reached out a chubby hand to take the knife from her. "Your Majesty, if there's any advice I would give you, it would be to let us help you. You're not alone. A Queen should never be placed in the position you're in. Let me find the person who has called for your death."

"You believe yourself capable of this task?"

"I do," he said as he nodded. "A man in my position has faced many peasants bearing whatever weapons they could amass. Unhappy with their lot in life, they come seeking vengeance, much like an Amaskan."

Margaret clenched her jaw. *Little toad of a man he is. How did my father ever put up with such a weak fool?* She held out her hand for the knife, which he gave back with a trembling hand. He glanced away when she returned it to the hidden sheath tucked into her corset. She couldn't trust this man to find her enemy. He wouldn't recognize an opponent if they carried three swords and a battle axe. But he was correct about one thing: the person within her castle must be found.

"Lord Cornish, when Master Maurus returns, we will discover who is behind this bounty." *I hope.*

"You would trust an Amaskan?" he asked.

"An Amaskan who is a member of my council, yes, and I would ask that you do the same, Lord Cornish."

His face flushed as he wrung his hands. "Your Majesty, if I may be so bold...I wish to ask...."

"Yes?"

"Has it occurred to you that perhaps this Maurus is the man behind the attacks? He knows your schedule and your movements. As an Amaskan, he's trained to find the flaws in any defenses and extort such things."

She waved a hand at him to dismiss him, though his words remained with her. *Damn him for being correct. Again.* Master Maurus or whatever his true identity could remove her from the throne without blinking. It was entirely possible, if not probable, that he was behind the attempts on her life. But something about him told her he was safe. Once the man returned, he would answer her questions once at for all.

Assuming he returned.

Hips barely recovered from the lengthy trek to the Order, Bredych set out again, this time toward the capital city of Sadai. At least this journey he traveled on an Amaskan battle steed rather than a random horse who spooked at the slightest wind. The mottled mare carried herself like silk on desert sand as she maneuvered the packed dirt that led into the city. Six days' travel inland, the city of Aruna rose up from the mountainside, its castle protruding from the rock itself.

Unlike his travel through Alexander, he wore the black, silk wraps of his Order. While his tattoo was gone, the guards throughout the city recognized him on sight and waved him through the outer gates. A falcon passed overhead, its cry ringing in his ears, and he smiled to be home.

His family's cottage no longer stood, but Bredych could find the corner blindfolded during a storm. Vendors lined the streets as he passed through the city's central plaza, and he nudged his horse forward, past the clatter of coin and scent of bread. Ten minutes later, he dismounted before the castle and handed his horse off to a stable hand with a whisper of old tongue to keep his steed's manners in check. A line twenty solicitors long stood outside the royal hall awaiting their chance to speak to King Adir.

"Name?" the guardsman asked as Bredych approached.

"Bredych."

The guardsman glanced back and forth between the scar on Bredych's jaw and his face, then stepped through an archway and out of sight. When he returned, he scowled at Bredych and asked, "What does an Amaskan need with a King?"

The test was an old one, but one of many protocols used between the King and Bredych, and he leaned close to the guard's ear. "My business is my own, and my own is Justice," he whispered and was waved through, much to the chagrin of those in line.

When King Adir saw him, he gestured for Bredych to approach, then rang a small chime on the table beside him. Guards cleared the room of people until they were alone. "It's been too long my friend!" the King said.

Ten years had passed since Bredych last had walked these halls, yet the King remained the same. From his small posture and jet black hair that bore little gray, to his dark skin marred little by wrinkles, his friend still resembled the young boy he'd known in many ways. Adir's throne, carved of polished stone, dwarfed him, and Bredych smiled. "It is good to see you are well, my King."

"You don't visit often enough, so if you're here personally, you have news that can't wait. What say you?"

Bredych bowed to the King. "May I approach?"

Adir nodded, and Bredych handed him the letter from Margaret. His friend's eyes narrowed as he read it. "This would be quite the boon to grant you. The rumors from the East are that Alexander is vastly outnumbered. How do you know the Senate won't yet intervene?"

"They've been given the opportunity to do so thrice now, yet they choose the path of silence rather than ensuring the people's safety. If they continue with their ambivalence, the people may rise up to protect themselves, which is what Queen Margaret is proposing, Your Majesty."

King Adir chuckled, a deep rumbling sound that bounced around the empty hall. "You always did have lofty ideas, my friend. All right, suppose I lend my support to this new queen. What reassurance do I have that our side will be the winning side? I'll not lead my people into a war I can't win."

Bredych knelt before the King, turning his face into the light, and exposed his lack of tattoo. "This isn't a favor I ask for my Order, but one I ask for myself. As payment for your life."

He flushed, his hands still in his lap as he stared at Bredych from his stone throne. "I owe you a great debt for saving my life, but the favor you ask is not just of me but of my people as well. Many of those I serve might die if I agree to this. Surely you understand my hesitation?"

"Adelei died at the hands of the Boahim Senate."

King Adir's shoulders slumped. "That is sad news indeed. I know your daughter was your world."

"As your niece was yours." The reminder was a dangerous one, but it was the dance of court politics. The pleasuring or threatening of the crowd in order to win favor and fear. Either the King would agree or he wouldn't, and if the latter.... Adir scowled at his friend, and Bredych continued. "They used evil magics to kill my daughter and kept her body on display as an example for those who would resist their will. I know exactly what I ask of you, Your Majesty, but civil war's eminent whether or not you agree to participate. Would it not be better to 'pluck the evil from our brow before it overgrows our sight'?" Bredych asked.

"That you would use my niece against me wounds me deeply. Friend you may be, but remember whose coffer funds your Order."

Had he pushed too far? Bredych remained on his knees as the King stood and approached. Smooth hands gripped his jaw, and the King turned it until he could look better at the scar.

"Was this by choice?" King Adir asked, and Bredych nodded.

"I needed a way into Alexander without arousing suspicion."

"And what did your Order think of such betrayal by their leader? Was your welcome back the reception you had hoped for?"

Images of the council flashed through Bredych's head. Something had the King walking along a cliff's edge, something that made him wish Bredych unsettled. His jaw ached from clenching it, and he cursed Adir's ability to rattle him. "My people are prepared to follow me in the fight to free us of our bonds. Are yours?"

A piece of fabric fell to the ground in front of Bredych— a splash of burnt red that popped against the gray stone floor. "Pick it up," said King Adir.

Bredych's fingers ran across the silk, and when he brought it up to the light where he could better see it, dark crimson decorated it in splatters. "Whose?" he asked.

King Adir's face crumpled, his words choked by grief.

It must be his niece. "I'm sorry for your loss, Your Majesty." Bredych folded the cloth into a square, which he returned. "If you don't mind the intrusion, may I ask who?"

"I don't know. I left a message for you in the normal spot a few months ago, but when I checked it, my message was still there. Now I know why."

"I apologize that I was unavailable to help you, but it was critical that I travel to Alexander," said Bredych.

The King sighed. "I suppose it was. If you cared for Adelei as I cared for my niece, I'm sure you rode with the winds of Agaia at your back. You said the Senate killed your daughter, so I assume vengeance has not tempered your soul?"

"It has not."

"Is this your real reason for waging war upon the Senate?"

"I won't be shackled, Your Majesty. That's my reason. That and the armies crossing into Alexander's borders while the Senate does nothing," said Bredych as he stood. "I understand that I ask much of you, Your Majesty, but I don't have time for doubts. Either you pay your debts or you don't. It's your choice."

King Adir cocked an eyebrow at Bredych. "And if I don't?"

"Then you will be labeled an oath breaker by the Order."

"And risk losing your funding?"

He nodded. "Money's not required for service to Justice, and you are not our only client. We'll survive with or without Your Majesty's patronage." When his friend sighed, Bredych's shoulders relaxed a fraction.

"Tell Queen Margaret we will side with her in this war. I'll send some of my army to the border to help defend against whatever happens next, but should we lose, I hope she's willing to house the Amaskans, as I no longer will."

"One more question if I may, Your Majesty?" When King Adir waved an impatient hand, Bredych asked, "What do you know of *barak*?"

"It's a difficult to obtain poison. What of it?"

When he removed the pouch from his pocket, the King retreated several steps. "Someone mentioned to me that it might be traded again, and since I encountered it in Alesta, I wondered who controlled its movement."

"I've not seen or heard of its use in over a decade. If that is all, you may leave."

Bredych inclined his head once more before withdrawing. Sweat broke out across his skin as he stepped into the hallway, and tucked the pouch away before wiping his forehead with the back of his hand. Nothing at the Order had pointed to their involvement in the harvesting of *barak*. If his friend was to be believed, the poison's trade came from neither the Amaskans nor the King. While he had never heard of *barak* growing in Shad, it wasn't impossible. *The mountains are the right elevation for it.*

He bit back a curse as he headed toward an inn. Now that his friend had agreed to help, there was a more difficult task ahead—assassinating a king.

25

_____

It wasn't something Bredych had mentioned to Margaret, especially not with her doubts about his character and motives, but as the events unfolded, the idea brewed in his mind. Something to stop the war before it started. He left a single, black pebble beneath a shrub's roots outside the inn in town. When it disappeared, he left a second and then a third. On the fourth night in the place the stone should be, a man in ragged clothes sat. The smell of manure drifted up from the man, and while his hood covered most of his face, Bredych would be willing to bet the man sported a circular tattoo where his jaw met his ear.

"Anur's blessing this night," Bredych said.

The man stretched his legs out in front of him, then resumed his cross-legged stance. "Asti's blessing this night," the Amaskan corrected. "May blades find evil in its height."

Bredych gestured for the man to follow him. Rather than meet inside the inn, he led the Amaskan down an alleyway and through another before he stopped. "You know who I am?" asked Bredych.

"Yes, Grand Master."

A piece of parchment came out of Bredych's pouch, which he handed to the Amaskan. "Memorize that sketch, then destroy it."

"Last location of the mark?"

"Drehsma, Shad, though it's possible he's at the Meridi Pass."

The Amaskan flinched. "It's a long ride to Shad, Grand Master. Especially in these uneasy times."

He passed a second set of papers to the Amaskan, and when he moved to open them, Bredych placed a hand on them to stop him. "No. Use them only if you must. They'll grant you safe passage through Alexander." The man's eyes grew wide as he stuffed the paper inside a hole in his tunic, but he asked no questions. "They bear the official seal of Her Majesty, Queen Margaret of Alexander. If you make it to Shad, you'll need to destroy the papers before you cross the border. I can't guarantee your safety once across the Shadian border. Check the Pass first."

Bredych handed a smaller coin pouch to the Amaskan, which also disappeared somewhere beneath his tunic. "That should be enough coin to buy your way past most situations, though I'll trust you not to get into anything you can't afford," said Bredych.

"The mark's the King of Shad," the Amaskan whispered.

"Is that a problem?"

"No, Grand Master. It's an honor to serve Justice in any capacity. Though if I might beg a request?"

"Yes?"

The Amaskan took hold of Bredych's hand. The weight of something metallic and heavy dropped into it, and when Bredych looked, he held a long, silver key. "In my room at the Order is a box. That's the key. When I don't return, my sister'll be worrin' 'bout me. Give her the box and key if you would."

His stomach twisted, but he nodded. "I'll deliver it myself," Bredych said as he tucked the key away.

A moment later, Bredych stood alone in the alley, his plan set in motion. In the morning, he would ride for Alexander. With hope the Queen would still be alive when he got there.

Might Margaret never know what he'd done with her letter.

Or whose life it would cost.

It was a foolhardy idea.

Margaret chafed at the very idea as she sought out the council chambers that early morning, but if she was going to declare the Boahim Senate her enemy, she must give them one last opportunity to protect the people of the Little Dozen Kingdoms. It was a chance to redeem themselves in her eyes and the eyes of her people, the latter of which would fail to understand why they had been abandoned.

The sun slept, as did most of Alesta, when she crept from her bed chamber in formal attire. Tightening the corset herself had taken an overabundance of time and contortion, but waking her lady-in-waiting would have meant questioning looks and gossiping tongues. Since sleep had abandoned her, leaving ghostly voices of dreams behind, Margaret sought her council room. She allowed one guardsman to escort her as she made her way down empty stairs and the long hallway.

"No one is to enter," she said to the guardsman before she closed the door. Margaret stood at the front of the council table for a moment and breathed deeply. When she tried to still her facial expressions, her eyebrow twitched as her nerves ran races around her mind.

It's Leolin's fault. Adelei must be laughing at me right now.

She slammed her fist against the table harder than she had anticipated and winced as her hand screamed in protest. She couldn't even hit the table correctly. There was no use in delaying things if her nerves were going to run rampant.

The bookcase slid with the ease of common use, and the orb glowed faintly as it waited. Margaret lit a single candle to take with her inside, then closed the entrance behind her. The orb brightened in response to the darkness.

"*Ta'asor Ley,*" she whispered, and the orb pulsed once before it returned to its normal dim. Margaret frowned and repeated the phrase. Once again it pulsed before fading. "Hello?" The orb remained silent, and she returned to the bookcase. A sudden light glinted off her ring's jeweled signet, and when she turned, she threw up her hands to block the bright light emitted by the orb.

A popping sound, much like uncorking a barrel, echoed in the small room, and the orb's light reduced. Margaret uncovered her face to find Senator Whitlen scowling at her. Several senators scurried in the background as dust rained down on the Senator's head.

"Now's not a good time, Queen Margaret," said Senator Whitlen as the sound of thunder reverberated from the orb.

"Is there a storm on your island?"

The ground appeared to shake as the Senator grabbed something out of view for support. The rumbling growl ceased, as did the cascade of dust, and Senator Whitlen wiped the debris from her shoulder with a shaking hand. "What can I do for your kingdom, Your Majesty?"

Speak plainly now, or the chance will dissipate like whatever storm holds them in its grip. Margaret cleared her throat and asked, "Have you heard of the text *A Treatise on Senates and Rulers: Dissecting the Boahim Senate in a Modern World?*"

"An interpretation of older texts by a half-drunken fool in love with power. Why do you ask?"

"It states that after the Sadai-Monpoli conflict, an agreement was signed—signed by my grandsire and other rulers—that confirmed the original agreement created the Boahim Senate. The agreement states that 'The Senate shall intervene in any conflict that would rip asunder what the Thirteen have created.' May I ask why you have failed to uphold the very agreement that gives you purpose?" Margaret asked.

The ground shook beneath Senator Whitlen's feet and behind her, glass shattered on the stone floor. "What do you think we're doing, child? Do you speak to the leaders of your army?"

What does she mean? "I do, but I don't understand. How are you helping? People will die if you don't stop this madness. Several armies gather at my border, and what does the Senate do? Ride out a storm?"

Senator Whitlen's wrinkles gained wrinkles as she peered into the orb, her lips pursed together. "This is no storm! What exactly would you have us do?"

"Send their armies back where they belong. Hold King Bajit responsible for the deaths of *Sepier* Warhammer and the other deaths after hers. You and I both know you can walk through this orb, so what's stopped you from doing so in Shad? In Monpoli? In Halelind?"

Someone shouted something indiscernible in the background, and the Senator's face flushed. When she turned back to the orb, she jabbed her finger at Margaret. "Look to your own people, and take care before you call on us again."

"Wait! I'm sorry, but you *have* to intervene! To ignore this is pure madness! What kind of person leaves tens of thousands to die—"

Senator Whitlen's green eyes burned with an eerie light, and the room temperature dropped. When she exhaled, her breath floated in front of her. Inside the orb, the ground shook once more as the Senator glared at her. "Who do you think you are to speak to me about death? You who has twenty-one years in that skin and so much to learn. You know nothing of suffering. I—"

A chunk of stone fell from overhead and for a moment, Senator Whitlen disappeared from view as she was pulled away. Margaret stepped back from the orb and pushed the wall open behind her. Something odd was happening on that island, something that left Margaret's stomach tilting and turning as if she were being tossed about on a ship.

"Make sure no one else is wounded," someone called in the background, and Senator Whitlen returned to view. When she spotted Margaret shivering, her brows bunched together as she limped forward.

"Itova has nothing on me, child. Go see to your people before there's naught but cinders before me," said Senator Whitlen, and the orb darkened.

For a moment, Margaret gripped the bookshelf's edge as her body trembled. The room's temperature rose, but nothing warmed her as her mind repeated the Senator's words. Bile burned the back of her throat and nose as her stomach pitched. *Why am I still nauseated?*

As the question rolled through her mind, the ground beneath her rolled.

Spiderwebs spilled their way across the smooth stone floor, and Margaret clung to the bookshelf, which slid back and forth along its rail. The guard stumbled into the council room. "Your Majesty?" he called out as he glanced around the seemingly empty room. When he spotted her clinging to a moving wall, his eyes widened a moment before he staggered over. "Are you hurt, Your Majesty?"

"N-no," she said.

He took her by the arm with an apologetic look. "We need to get you out of here. This room's not safe."

A wood beam from the ceiling creaked overhead as they passed beneath it, and Margaret hurried her steps. In her entire lifetime, she couldn't recall the earth ever having buckled in this region. As they passed through the doorway, the shaking stopped.

"Margaret!" Leolin's voice came from down the hallway in the stairwell's direction. He bolted half-clothed and barefoot toward the council room, and when he spotted her, he slowed to a light run. "Are you hurt?"

"If I may be excused, Your Majesty? Others may be injured," the guard asked, and Margaret nodded.

Once the guard was away from earshot, Margaret leaned closely to Leolin's ear and whispered, "The earthquake began on the island—*their* island."

"You think they created it?"

Margaret shook her head. "I was speaking to Senator Whitlen when it shook them. A stone fell from the ceiling and almost crushed her. She looked too startled for this to be something of their making, at least not on purpose."

He opened the council room door, then gestured for her

to follow him inside. When she did, he closed the door behind her, then held up her arm.

It was the first opportunity since the earth stopped moving for her to access her body's reaction, and when she glanced at her arm, the skin was red and chafed. She rubbed it with a finger and winced as it burned. "How did I get burned?" she asked.

"I was hoping you'd tell me." Leolin touched a crack in the wall, then spotted the orb that lay exposed. "Was it the Senate?"

"One moment I was talking with the senator and the next, it was cold. Bitter cold. I could see my breath. Then the orb went dark, and the earthquake began here."

Magic. There was no other explanation. To Leolin she said, "No matter how many times they prove their power, it's surprising that there are magics out there that can harm or kill people from afar."

Leolin tugged at the bookshelf, but it did not budge. "Damn. The earthquake must have knocked it off its rail." He turned toward her, his brow furrowed. "Why were you talking to the Senate?"

She opened her mouth, then stopped as the thought knocked loose. The senator kept mentioning the need for Margaret to look after her people. Her full skirts did not allow for fast movement, but she walked as quickly as she could to the door and outside into the hallway.

"Wait, what's wrong?" Leolin asked as he followed behind her.

"When I asked Senator Whitlen why she wasn't helping prevent the war, she was offended. Made comments about my needing to see to my people and how I was misinformed. What if some of the Senate is at the border? Or in Shad?"

He shrugged. "That would be good, right?"

"That depends on what action they're taking." *Or not taking.* Her skin tingled and chafed as she moved toward the stairs. "We need to know what's happening at the border, and we need more information on magic. How does it work? Where does the power come from? And we need more information on the senators. Something Senator Whitlen said...."

Her lady-in-waiting stood outside her rooms, and the woman practically fainted when she spotted Margaret. "Your Majesty, thank the Thirteen you're unharmed—"

"I need my advisors in the council room in a candlemark and a list of any injured or dead in Alesta compiled. Also, a list of damaged structures," she rattled off.

"Roland should see to your wounds," said Leolin, and she shook her head.

"I'll be fine. I'm sure my physician has others more in need of his care. Leolin, I need you to send messenger pigeons to the borders. Find out what happened out there," Margaret said as she opened the door to her rooms. She stepped forward and something crunched beneath her slippered foot.

A cup's clay pieces lay on the floor, along with a few other decorative objects. A book had been overturned, its pages splayed like a wounded bird. Margaret inhaled deeply to calm herself. Her eyes widened as the thick smell of smoke tickled her nose.

Her room was on fire.

26

There was only so fast and so far one could push a horse, even a battle steed trained for endurance and fighting. Once the earthquakes began, Bredych's horse reared, almost throwing the Amaskan from the saddle. The candlemark's ride until the next town left them both frazzled, and Bredych in need of a strong drink. Little town or no, he stopped early to give them both a rest, though Bredych's body was more weary than sleepy.

He'd not had the opportunity to give the books he'd brought with him more than a cursory glance, but as he settled into a room at the town's lone inn, he pulled out a book as thick as his forearm on the Order's history. Too many possibilities whirled in his head as he read. How much did the Senate know about the Order? How were new senators chosen? Was it based on familial ties as the sketches suggested? Then there was the Senate's rampant use of magics that had been forbidden for centuries.

The Order itself had been a protective measure put in place by King Dama Yachad after the Fall. Thirteen people agreeing on its creation didn't mean all thirteen continued to trust the Senate once it was formed. Former Grand Masters of the Order noted their distrust as the decades passed, though none of them had acted on their fears. Someone needed to ensure that justice was served.

At least, that's what the Order taught.

Bredych continued to read until his eyes and shoulders drooped, and when he startled himself awake for the fourth time, he closed the book with a snap and sought his bed. Nothing of note appeared in the book, though it was possible Margaret and the boy had found something in his absence. Although, it was possible he would arrive and find the castle in chaos. Or in ruins.

His mind wove nightmarish tapestries as he stared, suddenly awake, at the wooden crossbeams on the ceiling until the sun blushed pink upon the horizon.

"DAMN IT!" LEOLIN SHOUTED AS HE BRUSHED PAST Margaret into her sitting room where a table burned. He ripped the rug from the ground and beat the flames with it.

Margaret's lady-in-waiting wobbled on her feet, and Margaret snapped her fingers in front of the woman's face. "Go get help! Now!" she ordered, and her lady-in-waiting stumbled off in the direction of the stairs. Margaret pressed her skirts closer about her body as she entered the room and grabbed the pitcher of water sitting on the table across the room from the flames. She tossed it at the fires, which flickered but remained burning.

"Do you have any more water?" Leolin asked.

She fetched the water basin and passed it to Leolin, who upended it across the table. The sudden water sent a billow of smoke and ash across the sitting room. Leolin stamped out the few bits that smoldered nearby with his boots as she stepped out of the water's pathway.

It was then that she glanced around the damaged sitting room, a room she had spent many evenings in with her father. The table had been ordered built by her grandsire. The chair had been his and later her father's as he read in the evenings near the fireplace. Margaret's legs wobbled beneath her as she stared at dirty, melted wax, all that remained of the candle that had been burning when she had left to seek the orb.

"T-The earthquake must have knocked over the candle," she said as she pointed at the wax.

"Probably. We were lucky to catch the fire when we did. Otherwise this whole room would have burned."

Margaret leaned back against the wall, and Leolin stepped over the table's remains to reach her. "The fire's out. You're safe."

"Leolin, if...if I hadn't sought the orb, I would have been sleeping. The flames would have spread and possibly trapped me," she said as she gripped his arm. "But I couldn't sleep. Something woke me."

The color drained from Leolin's face. "You said something woke you. What was it?"

"I heard...I must have been dreaming, but I could swear I heard Senator Montero's voice."

His eyes widened as he wrapped an arm about her shoulders. "He was calling for help," he said.

"How do you know that?"

Leolin shook his head as he stared at the remains of her grandsire's table. "I heard it, too," he said as footsteps pounded in the hallway.

Help had arrived, but too late for the table and chair. Guards rushed in carrying buckets of water as her lady-in-waiting shouted behind them. "I hope those pigeons fly fast," she said to Leolin, though whatever help Senator Montero needed, whatever news the pigeons returned with would likely not help him.

"Remove the remnants, please," she asked as she strode out into the hallway. Leolin followed her down the hall toward the stairs. "With hope the drawing room's still intact."

"I don't know whether I want to talk closer or further away from that orb," he said as they walked down the stairs. "Were they watching us? Is that why he called out to us? And how is that even possible?"

Margaret's hands trembled. "I wish my father were still here."

"So do I, Maggie. So do I."

27

B redych sighed with relief when as he passed through the city walls and spied the castle ahead. Houses and buildings spilled a few innards into the streets, and a few thatch roofs had collapsed on the outskirts of the city, but the closer he traveled to the castle, the less damage was obvious to him. Sweat gathered beneath the mercenary clothing he donned, and he gripped the reins tighter to resist the urge to scratch the small of his back. Summer's heat approached, and he nudged his horse to a trot. Even with the few inches of hair on his usually bald head, his scalp itched in the humidity.

He followed the path to the castle stables where a man met him with a grin and a sugar cube. "Master Maurus, Horsemaster Will at your service." The man held out the sugar cube and whispered to the battle steed, who relaxed and stepped forward to nibble on the treat.

"How did you—"

Will grinned at Bredych's shock. "Our former *sepier*, Captain Warhammer, had a horse like this, as did the

Queen's sister. Between the two of 'em, I've picked up a few tricks over the years."

Bredych dismounted and handed the reins over to the horsemaster. His fingers touched the saddlebag's buckle when Will asked, "Would you like someone to take your bags to your room?"

A book corner poked out from the top of one bag, which Bredych removed. "Please, though I'll take this one with me if it's all the same." All he needed was for some page or servant to take a tumble and spot the contents. While the Queen and her council knew he was Amaskan, no one else did. Best to keep it that way. He tossed the bag over one shoulder, leaving the larger one behind. At least the news that he traveled with food, water, a blanket, and some clothes wouldn't set the city on edge. Rather than head straight for the Queen, Bredych passed the front entrance and continued along a stepped path leading to the buildings housing the Holy Few.

The idea had come to him while staring at the ceiling. If anyone knew about the histories of the Senate, the Order, and Boahim, it would be the men and women who dedicated their lives to the preservation of information, one of several tenants followed by the Holy Few. Whether they would share this information with him was the trickier piece of the plan, but perhaps they would be willing to trade. Bypassing the chapel, he followed the trail along the side until he reached the smaller one-story building made of simple stone and wood. Its front door, a solid wood piece, was carved with words from the old tongue.

"Beautiful, isn't it?"

Bredych turned to find a man wearing a red robe not three steps behind him. "It is, though I don't recognize most of these words. I see unity, as well as life and death, but what are the rest?" he asked as he pointed at the sentence.

"'Those who submit to the way of the world, find unity in both life and death.' The words of—"

"Itova." The word soured on Bredych's lips.

The disciple nodded and pushed open the door. Its hinges squealed as the man said, "Spoken like someone who's suffered recent loss." He gestured for Bredych to follow him inside. "Without death, life has no meaning. Even Itova serves a purpose in our world, though few are willing to admit it."

The Tribor are. They worship Itova and flock to do her bidding. Or what they perceive to be her bidding anyway. Large skylights brought light in from outside, as did the large windows alongside one wall. Two benches and tables sat closest to the windows while the remainder housed a small kitchen area, a dozen cots, and a door leading elsewhere in the building. No ornate decor graced the dwelling. Everything from the blankets and pillows to the rugs was in deep shades of red, like the disciple's robes.

The disciple led Bredych to one of the benches and gestured for him to sit. "Do you require any refreshment? You've the look of someone well-traveled," the man asked.

"Water or wine if you don't mind."

He nodded, then wandered over to the small kitchen where he opened a hatch in the ground and removed a small bottle. The disciple set the bottle on a tray with two wooden cups.

Had the room been larger or the disciple elsewhere, Bredych would have explored the room, but he waited with a false patience as the man returned. Even the pouring of wine stretched into eternity as the man made idle chat about the earthquake. When Bredych's finger tapped on the cup's side, the disciple gave him a thin-lipped smile.

"My apologies, Master...."

"Master Maurus."

"Ah! Our Queen's newest advisor. An honored role to be sure. I apologize—my mind wanders from time to time, and I forget that others don't have a lifetime in which to sit and think. What may the Holy Few do for you?"

Bredych opened the saddle bag beside him and retrieved one of the books from the Order. "I am in need of information. Historical information. In fact, I'm willing to trade for it."

The disciple's eyes widened at the circles on the book's cover, and he rose from his seat. "I will fetch Her Holiness at once," he said before rushing over to the closed door at the room's rear. He knocked at it, and another disciple appeared. They whispered to each other before the second one disappeared behind the door. The first waited, his eyes on Bredych at all times.

Damn. They left no opportunity for him to do more than look at the place with his eyes.

Only a few minutes passed before an imposing woman in almost crimson robes arrived. When her gaze locked with Bredych's, her eyes narrowed a moment before her face fell into a smooth, serene look. Her silk robes trailed behind her, almost dancing across the stone as she crossed the room. She didn't glance so much as once at the book but stared openly at the scar on his jaw.

He stood and gave a partial bow before her. "I appreciate your willingness to—"

"Willingness has little to do with our meeting. Thirteen candlemarks since the earth silenced, and an Amaskan comes before us with knowledge. The Thirteen steer us where they will, and I'm happy to hear what you come to offer us."

Thirteen candlemarks? But the ground shook last several days ago. Bredych shook his head.

"This is a holy place aligned with honesty, so if we are to enter into an agreement, I require the name of the man I am dealing with," she said.

When he glanced at the disciples still behind her, she held three fingers in the air over her head. The disciples retreated behind the closed door, which was locked behind them with the thudding of a wood bar. "My name is Master M—" His lips touched with every intent of saying the name Maurus, but the word refused to leave his tongue.

The corner of her mouth twitched at his discomfort. "May I remind you that this holy place is one of the few inner sanctums of the Thirteen. To lie would be to lie before Them."

Her fingers didn't move, nor did she whisper or chant or do anything else that would suggest magic, yet his brain and mouth were at odds with one another. His shoulders slumped in defeat before he answered honestly. "I am a man of several names. While I've been using the name Maurus here, and the Amaskans know me as Eli Bredych, my name is Malaki Abner of Sadai." Bredych curled his hands into fists. That name was long dead to anyone that mattered, including himself, and its utterance sent a revulsion through him. "What magic is this to force a man to divulge privacies best kept between himself and his gods?" he asked.

Her Holiness claimed the chair previously occupied by Her disciple, then gestured for Bredych to join her. When he remained standing, a slight frown flittered across her face. "We who serve the Thirteen give up our names as these bodies are merely vessels given to us. Names are unimportant when one can see all," she said as she refilled his cup of wine.

"If names are unimportant, why ask me mine? Why require me to divulge it?"

"It was a test of honesty. A way of seeing what breed of man stands before us in our holy place."

If he continued standing, he would pace, giving her knowledge as to his mental state. Bredych took the seat across from her. "What sort of test is it when magic forces the answer out of me?"

"You were compelled to speak truthfully, but once done, you could have left this place. Yet here you sit with me, sharing wine with someone you may wish harm upon. That speaks to your character much more than the words that were released."

Wrapping his hands around his cup kept them out of his lap and kept them from being fists as he took a deep, slow breath. He took another before he trusted himself to speak. "I came here to trade information. I'm not looking to harm anyone, let alone be harmed," he said.

"Of course. Though I would ask you something first if you don't mind." When he nodded, she asked, "There are some magics known to the Amaskans as well, are there not? Certain suggestions that make someone compliant and ensure information isn't divulged that could cause harm to the Order, its members, and its clientele."

If the cup in his hand had been made of glass, it would have shattered. As it was, he gripped it white-knuckled as he glared at her. *How did she...? Of course. Adelei.*

Despite decades of practice keeping emotions from his expression, his body betrayed him, and Her Holiness set her hand over his. "I will call you Master Bredych, as I know it's the name you prefer. Your daughter struggled over which father to love. Was there not room enough for her to love both men who shaped her? Yet this mental conditioning left her feeling exploited, similar to how you felt a moment ago when compelled to speak the truth."

"That's not the same thing." He said the words, but they were a lie. His hands trembled at the truth's weight as it hung between him and every Amaskan he'd shaped and every mark he'd killed.

"I don't wish you harm, Master Bredych. Much the opposite. Did you know that many people come here at the end of their days to seek penance for all the little slights that are meaningless before the Thirteen? It matters not if one called their sibling a name or stole a loaf of bread to feed one's family. It's the acknowledgement of one's mistakes that grants the penance, not me, yet people come all the same."

The wine in his stomach soured as her hand remained on his. "Do you think me at the end of my days?" he asked, and she shrugged.

"That is up to the Thirteen, but you approach a darkness that clouds us all. Who's to say whether any of us will survive what's ahead?" For all that Her Holiness appeared youthful and light in that moment, a shadow was cast across her features. Her skin sagged, and her eyes dulled. "Dark days come. No one's safe. Not even the Thirteen."

He shivered in the darkness as doubt circled him like an angry wolf. Who was he to determine who lived and died? Who was he to know what was and was not Justice? Amaskans had been tasked to protect and serve, yet was that what he had done?

Was this how Adelei had felt at the end?

"There can be no darkness without light," Her Holiness said, and when he glanced up, the shadow over her was gone.

Don't, his mind cried. *She can't be trusted.*

Why not? came the response from his heart. If it truly was the end of things, what harm would come from sharing his soul with another? Perhaps she would then trust him with the information he needed. An exchange of truths.

Words wrapped around his head and heart like a vice. He expected it to squeeze until he burst out with what Her Holiness wished to hear, but when the pressure gripped him, the poison poured forth from him without hesitation. Whether it was magic or the Thirteen, he cared not. His body slumped forward as he stared at his cup. "I've killed so many that even if I knew it, I couldn't give you a number. I don't regret the majority—they were rapists and murderers and twisted people who would've hurt others had I not sent them to Itova—but there was one who did nothing to deserve...what I did."

"Do you speak of Adelei?"

Bredych shook his head. "No, I speak of my sister, though I wronged Adelei as well. Everything I've ever loved has fallen away from me like dried leaves from the branch. When our parents died, I was all Shendra had. I swore to her that I would protect her, which I did until the day she betrayed me."

"Was it really betrayal? Or was it something else?"

"She disobeyed me."

"And like a parent, you punished her," she said.

"Like a monster, I slit her throat." He raised his head to look at Her Holiness, whose pale blue eyes looked on him with a patience he didn't understand. "I left her to die! I became the monster we seek to kill, the man who would kill his sister because she refused to murder a child!"

Her Holiness touched his jaw where only a scar remained. "And in turn, created a woman who showed our King a love and a mercy he deserved. A woman who showed your daughter there could be room in her life for two fathers."

"No," Bredych whispered. "Don't."

"Don't what?"

"Don't pity me. Don't turn what I've done as if the aftermath somehow makes up for my actions because it doesn't." He took a long swallow of wine before continuing. "I've carried this weight a long time. Most days I thought it behind me, but in the silence it whispers to me, Your Holiness. I came here with every intention of killing King Leon and his daughter. I came here to bathe in their blood, because I thought it would wipe away my pain."

She tensed at his words, but made no indication of moving from her chair or crying out. "What stopped you?" she asked.

"What makes you think I've stopped?"

Her Holiness smiled at him. "You're here with me. You've had countless opportunities to kill the Queen. Instead, you've saved her life several times. You left this kingdom and could have remained in Sadai, yet you returned. If you wanted Her Majesty dead, she would be dead, so I ask you again, what stopped you?"

"I thought it was Leon. I sat with him before he died, and he spoke of my daughter's love for both of her fathers. He also spoke of my sister. He was a man I'd misunderstood, like possibly many men, but that wasn't what stopped me." His mind sped back to the funeral, to Queen Margaret standing beside the burning bodies. So fragile and alone, yet she had stood tall and strong. Enough that she could have been Adelei in that moment. "She could've been my daughter. When I ordered Adelei here, the way she looked at me. She thought I didn't l-love her anymore." Tears spilled over his eyelids as Bredych spoke.

"Yet you did. You sent her away to keep her safe."

Bredych nodded as a cry escaped him. "L-Leon said I didn't understand the why, but I did."

"Only another who has sacrificed can understand the sacrifices people make," Her Holiness said as he cried.

"The more I spoke to the Queen, the more I understood. I don't regret raising Adelei—never that—but what I did wasn't in the service of Justice. It was selfish and vengeful." He touched his scar with a trembling hand. "I am undeserving of the tattoo I wore. Miriam knew. Somehow she knew."

Her Holiness tilted her head. "Miriam?"

He bit back a curse. It was one thing to confess his doubts and fears to the Holy Few and quite another to bring another Amaskan into it. "Someone I know—knew. The way we parted, she spoke as if I wouldn't return. I thought she worried I would die, but perhaps she knew I couldn't return to the life...the lie I've led. How could I return to serve that which I'm not sure I believe in anymore?"

"Justice?"

"How can I? Amaskans formed to ensure Justice for all."

"I thought that the Boahim Senate's duty," she said, and he shook his head.

Bredych leaned over to retrieve the book he'd first shown the disciple. "That's the problem. Our histories state the Amaskans developed a distrust in the Boahim Senate, that they worried corruption would poison them the way it had the King before them. We're taught that Justice is Justice, and we're all in service to Anur, yet how was it Justice that Adelei die? How was it Justice...what I did to my sister? I'm no less corrupt than the Senate I now fight against."

"Saying it aloud doesn't rid us of the pain or the doubt, Master Bredych, but acknowledging the part we play in this world helps us to atone for past mistakes. There's nothing I can do to remove the darkness that plagues your dreams. That's something only you can fix."

"'During the darkest moments of our days, only then will we be made to see the light,'" whispered Bredych.

Her Holiness nodded. "The *Shlosheser* says something similar, though I wonder who took it from the other. It also states that 'there are two ways for light to remain in the world. We must either burn ourselves in order to be the candle's light, or we must be the water that reflects it.' Some of us are able to reflect that which is wrong, while others, we destroy ourselves so that others may live purely."

A great sorrow swept across her face as she spoke, and she turned, drawing her face away from the window's light. Whatever secrets this woman held were as deep and dark as his own, that much he was sure. "May we light the Way for whatever may be," he said, and when he smiled, he hoped a flicker of light reached his eyes.

"You had questions for me," she said.

"When Adelei spoke to the Boahim Senate, they knew information that I thought known only to the Order. I need to know about the history of where we come from, and of how the Order was formed."

"And this information will help you light the world?"

Bredych frowned. "I don't know if it will, but Her Majesty and I found information about the Senate that causes us concern. I know your allegiance lies with them as well—"

"Our allegiance is with the Thirteen, where it has always been."

"My apologies, Your Holiness. We have reason to believe the Senate is encouraging the upcoming war. If I knew more about the Order's connection with them, perhaps there would be something to explain their actions and help us stop whatever's coming."

"Our memories are long, Master Bredych. Every text ever written resides within the mind of someone in the Holy Few, even books whose pages have scattered in the flames, but the answers you seek may not give you the answers you hope."

He brought the cup to his lips and found it empty. "Whatever you know can't be much worse than what I've imagined."

Her Holiness closed her eyelids, though her eyes moved rapidly back and forth beneath them as she spoke. "After the Fall, thousands upon thousands died as war ravaged Boahim. The King suggested the split into individual kingdoms with the Senate as mediator. He was dragged into the streets of his city and burned to death as his own people tore the city apart. Once a grand capital, most of Alesta was reduced to mounds of ash and cinder before night fell. Upon the dawning sun, thirteen men and women climbed the hill to meet with any who would listen—"

"Thirteen?" he asked.

"One would assume they chose the number on purpose. This text isn't clear. It only states that they met with those who would be kings and queens and those who would serve. They agreed upon splitting Boahim into the Little Dozen Kingdoms, and the Senate's creation to ensure that the

Thirteen Laws would always remain in place. That our world would never fall again."

"And the Order?"

The eyes beneath Her lids paused for a moment. "I don't have this information," she said. Bredych sighed, and she shook her head. "There is one here who does, if you would permit."

"I do."

She stood and approached the door, which opened when she tapped thrice. The disciple he had spoken to before followed her into the room, where he nodded once to Bredych. "This disciple speaks the text known only as 'The Circle,'" Her Holiness said.

There wasn't enough wine in the place to calm the way his skin crawled. The only pieces that remained of that text were whispers and conjecture. How the Holy Few knew of it....

The man took on a posture similar to that of Her Holiness as his mind saw the words written across the ancient pages. "One of the texts written after the Senate's establishment says that two decades after the Fall, the Boahim Senate with the help of the Holy Few, wiped magic from the land and forbid its use in anything other than for healing."

"Why would they do that?" asked Bredych.

"Many journals written by former Holinesses state that magic is what caused the Fall. Powers meant only for the Thirteen were never intended for us to use. In order to ensure the safety of the Little Dozen Kingdoms, magic was removed by the Thirteen," answered Her Holiness.

"By the Thirteen?"

"That's what the histories of the Holy Few say. They rose from the ashes of Alesta and decreed it to be against the

Thirteen. 'Sharmus blessing upon those gifted with the ability to heal others. All other 'gifts' be an affront to the Gods and evil in their nature.'"

And yet the Senate themselves used this evilness to enforce the Thirteen. The Little Dozen Kingdoms' rulers possessed magical artifacts, as did the Amaskans and the Holy Few. *If the Thirteen believe it evil, why has it been allowed to exist?*

The disciple cleared his throat and continued at Bredych's nod. "One King, a King Tamandani of Shad refused to surrender his powers. The Senate executed him. I believe there is more. One moment please."

Bredych opened his mouth to ask a question, when Her Holiness set her hand on his shoulder. She shook her head against his words, and he traced his cup's lip with his finger while he waited.

When the disciple spoke again, his brow furrowed. "Some of the descendants of the original Senate were in service to the Senate. Disciples if you will. But they worried that a darkness lived within the senators. That perhaps the same darkness that drove men to split Boahim by force had twisted the Senate. They formed a secret order, the Order of Amaska, to ensure that the Thirteen would never be corrupted and that Justice would be served no matter servant, king, or senator."

"They broke away from their family to protect the people of the Little Dozen Kingdoms," said Bredych.

"The Order remained hidden while they brought others into their service. I-it...says 'Until the day of Truth, we shall remain in darkness, but on that day, we will be the Light.' Perhaps you understand, Master?"

All the wine in the Little Dozen Kingdoms wouldn't be enough for Bredych. Her Holiness touched his shoulder again, and he leapt out of his chair with a howl. "I-I thank you for this information," Bredych said as he pulled the other books from his bag. He dropped them into the chair he'd abandoned, then strode for the door.

"Please return if you require further information," Her Holiness called after him.

He had no intention of returning. Her Holiness had known what information he needed and had fed it to him in trickles—enough to convince him to trust her—and what had it gotten him? The promise of death.

If the disciple's book had been right, this war was destined no matter what action Bredych took, and with it would come the Order's fall. All that talk of light. She wanted him to be the spark that began the end.

The end of everything.

Her Holiness be damned. She could rot in the Thirteen Hells before he'd allow that to happen.

28

THE MERIDI PASS

As tall as he was, King Havin didn't need his horse's seventeen hands to add to his magnificence. Especially not with the silver threads' angular patterns running across his purple cloak. From the cliff side, the fighting in the valley below reminded him of wild dogs in a scuffle as bodies surged forward, then backward at irregular times over some prized tidbit.

The Alexandrians had arrived the day before, their encampment a mere pebble's toss from his army, and while he had made no immediate move to engage them, close proximity to one's enemy left many men on both sides chafing to take up arms. As he had planned the morning's attack from his tent, fighting erupted near the bridge as calls for justice and revenge clashed with the clanging of swords.

The war had officially begun.

Somewhere below, his son led the Shadian army, though Amar was invisible in the mass of bodies. A messenger brought updates from Havin's Grand Marshal, while the King waited from the cliff's safety. Once

Halelind arrived and flanked the Alexandrians, he'd lead the second half of his army in a southern approach to surround them.

Assuming the Halelind army arrives on time.

Light glinted from the swords below as a beam of light appeared in the sky, and Havin brought his hands up to shield his eyes. Even with his hands before him, the sky glowed with a sun's intensity despite the overcast day. Pressure built up in his ears, which suddenly dissipated when the light flashed once and disappeared. When he glanced below, several people glowing with faint silver light stood not three feet from both armies. They must have spoken as he spotted Amar ride forward, his head shaking from side to side as he replied.

Havin urged his horse down the trail that led to the valley below. He was halfway down when someone shouted. A senator fell to the ground, and another flash of light blinded Havin. When the spots disappeared from his vision, the ground began to shake. It was a low rumble at first, and his horse stepped sideways as he whinnied. The shaking intensified and rather than be unsaddled, he dismounted moments before the horse reared in panic.

Cracks of earth erupted in jagged lines, and those fighters who weren't swallowed up were burned as flaming boulders the size of his horse's head rained down on them. He clung to a nearby tree as the shaking intensified.

"Sharmus protect me and Itova spare me," Havin whispered.

A few of his guards down the path cried out in terror, and he snapped his eyes shut as he repeated his prayer. The ground buckled beneath him, and old bones cried out in protest as he fell on all fours. When his arm grew warm, he opened his eyes to find a flaming rock had landed a foot away from him. He grabbed a handful of dirt and used it to tamp out his smoldering sleeve.

While the earth had ceased shaking, fire still danced in the valley below. Havin stumbled his way down the path in a rush of dust and debris. Blood trickled down his forehead, sticky and warm, but the cut was nothing compared to the scene before him. Large fissures rendered the valley a nightmarish scene as charred remains littered the ground red and black. Those who lived cried out for help or for mercy, but he offered neither.

"Your Majesty! Are you hurt?" called out a guard.

Havin brushed him aside and cried out in a cracking voice, "Amar?"

Survivors stumbled toward the cliff, some offering support to those who could walk. In the distance, the bridge had collapsed into the river, and Havin winced. How many of his people had fallen to the rushing waters below? Had his son been on the bridge? "Amar? Has anyone seen my son?" he called out, and in the distance a faint cry answered him.

Havin tripped over a tree branch. Beneath it, a boy lay dead, and his heart seized in his chest. When he listened, someone called for him to his right, and he followed the sound. A hand moved from beneath several bodies. He tugged at the corpses to find the source, but when he reached it, the hand belonged to his captain, not his son. "Have you seen Amar?" he asked.

The captain nodded, then pointed in the direction of a crevice. Tears streamed down Havin's cheeks as he stumbled toward the chasm, and when he reached it, his knees trembled. He couldn't look down.

"Father?"

He remained frozen until the voice called out again, and

he glanced into the fissure to see Amar huddled on a ledge seven feet down. "Can you stand?" Havin asked, though his voice trembled.

"If I do, the ledge may collapse beneath me."

"Captain, get rope...and anyone able-bodied!" Havin shouted behind him. "Don't move. We'll come to you."

Someone tapped him on the shoulder and rather than his captain, an Alexandrian handed him a coil of rope, one end of it burned but otherwise functional. "We'll tie it 'round me. Then have him tie it 'round his waist, and we'll pull'im up," the man said.

Havin nodded and tossed one end to his son. "Amar, tie this around you."

It would have been easy for the Alexandrian to use the opportunity to kill him. *Had our roles been reversed...well, let us say the Alexandrians would've been short a ruler.* But the man helped pull Amar to safety in spite of painful burns across his arms. Once his son reached the top, Havin hugged him tight to his chest. "Itova passed you by," he whispered as his son nodded.

The Alexandrian continued down the fissure to look for other survivors as King Havin examined his eldest son. Burns and scrapes and a sword wound to the shoulder, but otherwise, no major injuries. "What happened? My view from the cliff was obstructed once the earthquakes began."

"The Senate."

"Those were the ones glowing, yes?" asked Havin.

Amar nodded. "They commanded us to cease fighting. Someone shot an arrow a-and hit one of them. Father, the look in that senator's eyes when the arrow hit her...."

"Then the Boahim Senate was responsible for this?"

His son nodded. "The woman—her hands burned with

flames. When the ground shook, she disappeared and fire fell from the sky."

"Disappeared? Where did the senator go? Did she fall into one of the crevices?"

"I-I don't know, Father. She appeared to vanish. One moment she was there and the next, she was gone."

The hair on Havin's arms stood up. *Magic.* There was no other explanation for what had occurred. As he helped his son toward the cliff, he gripped his sword until his knuckles ached. Not even the magic *he* knew could reproduce what the Senate had done today.

Maybe Queen Margaret had been correct about how dangerous the Boahim Senate was.

"How do you know they were senators?" asked Havin.

"They wore silver cloaks bearing the tree of life, and all six were old, Father. As old as grandsire." When Havin glanced at his son, the smoke and grit lent hard angles to his otherwise boyish looks, and his blue eyes held tight to the firelight around them. "When Alexander's wiped from this land, the Senate will pay for this, Father."

The way his son stared across the corpses backlit by small fires, Havin didn't know who he feared most in that moment: the Senate...or his son.

29

Tales reached Bredych about a fire in the Queen's bedchambers. That and the damage done to the castle left his heart pounding. Most of the structure bore cosmetic damage, but here and there stone had shaken loose or a crossbeam had fallen. Builders and servants scrambling to repair the damage ignored Bredych as he made his way toward the second floor and the council room. The guards outside nodded at him as he approached, but when he opened the door, the room stood empty.

"Where's Her Majesty?" he asked a guardsman.

"Her Majesty is among her people, touring the city's damage."

Bredych cursed. Of all the fool things to do. Wandering about when there was a price on her head. "Is there a particular place she can be found?"

"Her Majesty did not disclose her plans."

Smart of her. He nodded his thanks and set off down the hallway toward the castle stairs, which he took until he reached the fifth floor bower.

A stern guardsman stepped in front of the door. "No one is permitted entry without word from Her Majesty."

"I don't need entry, just a vantage point," said Bredych as he wedged his shoulder into the tiny window.

His chin scraped the stone as he leaned as far outside as his body would fit. He couldn't see the outer walls or much of the middle circle of Alesta, but guards lined the inner walls in increased numbers. From this height, a large group of people gathered around something east of a guard station, and he tugged his body back through the window before setting back down the stairs.

By the time he reached the inner walls, the gathering had shifted a few houses down, and a tall man in bright green silks stood outside a house with three children. In his hands he carried a loaf of bread as big around as Bredych's thigh, which he kept pushing in Queen Margaret's direction. She shook her head once, then nodded as one of the children said something unintelligible from the distance.

He angled his way through the loiterers until he neared the front, and Margaret's eyes widened when she caught sight of him. Leolin found him a moment later, and his blue eyes narrowed.

"Thank you," said Margaret to the man in green as she stepped away from him. She gestured for Bredych to join her as she continued down the street, her entourage trailing behind. "It is good to see you returned to Alexander, Master Maurus."

"It's good to be back, Your Majesty. I have news—"

Margaret held up her hand as she stopped outside a house whose wooden door hung crooked. Several large cracks ran up the cobble side toward the roof, and when she pointed, her lady-in-waiting made a note on a piece of parchment. "Your news will have to wait a moment longer," Margaret said as she continued walking.

Bredych slowed his pace until he was shoulder to shoulder with Leolin. "How long has Her Majesty been out here?" he asked.

"Maybe a candlemark. She's determined to help anyone who suffered damage in the earthquake."

A foul smell like sun-warmed dung and beer burned Bredych's nose, and a raggedy woman with sharp features bumped his shoulder. "Iffen she truly wished t'elp, them in t'outer circles could use 'er 'elp more 'an these highborns," the woman muttered through blackened teeth. Leolin tensed as the woman stumbled into a guard.

One moment, the group following Margaret was calm and the next, they pushed forward toward the Queen. Where there had been a dozen people, there were now several dozen. The raggedy woman rushed toward Margaret, her hands outstretched like jagged claws. Bredych rushed forward and pulled his dagger from its sheath. "Get back!" Leolin yelled as he held his hands in the air before those struggling forward.

The raggedy woman froze as the crowd behind Bredych bumped against him. "No 'arm, no 'arm," the woman chanted.

Bredych grabbed her shoulder, his hand sinking into a mound of crispy cloth that sent a whiff of waste his way. Margaret held her own sword steady in her hand, her body tense as she glared at the woman.

"No 'arm, no 'arm, just wanted t'touch a pretty thing, no 'arm." The sing-song chant continued as the raggedy woman reached out for Margaret again, this time slower.

Margaret's sword remained firmly before her as she shook her head. "Perhaps it would be best if you left."

"My Queen! Help m'boy!" someone yelled behind Bredych, and another three people shouted similar statements.

"Where's my help?"

"Will there be war? Are we gonna die, m'lady?"

Shouts rose in volume and intensity as the crowd swelled. Margaret's eyes widened as she wrested her gaze away from the woman and spotted the mass of bodies behind Leolin, Bredych, and her guardsmen. "What have you done?" Margaret shouted.

"Help 'em, she could," said the raggedy woman, who stuck out her bottom lip in a pout. "Pretty thing. Help 'em."

A guardsman pushed someone back, and the group surged forward. "Get her out of here," shouted Leolin, and Bredych pushed Margaret forward, his body between her and the maddening crowd.

"I don't understand," she said as he led her through an empty alley.

One way in and out. He scanned the rooftops of nearby buildings, then studied the alleyway's shadows. "You offered help in a time of intense fear."

"I thought that's what was needed," she said.

A deepening shadow moved at the alley's end, and Bredych pushed Margaret behind an empty crate. "Can you defend yourself?"

Margaret glanced down the alleyway, her nostrils flaring as she breathed. "Yes."

"Stay here and be ready," he ordered. From the cries behind them, Leolin and the guards were keeping the crowd from the alley, with hope, long enough for Bredych to deal with whoever waited ahead. The length of the shadow cast by the sun made the man a giant. Either way, he stood taller than Bredych's six-foot frame. A sword glinted in the sun, and when the man stepped forward, his hood fell away and Margaret gasped.

"Who is it?" Bredych asked.

"It's the Grand Marshal's son, Philip."

With his free hand, Bredych palmed a throwing knife as he waited. Philip shifted his weight from side to side, and when he spotted Margaret's face peeking out from behind the crate, he charged forward, his face a snarling jumble of pain. The alleyway's narrowness left little room for a fight, nor did it leave many options to defend Margaret. Bredych threw the knife in his hand.

Philip grunted upon its impact but the knife only slowed his rush. A small flush of red seeped into his blue tunic at the shoulder where the blade protruded, and when he swung his sword at Bredych, its arc fell short as he cried out in pain and frustration. Another shadow fell on the road, and when Bredych glanced hurriedly at Margaret, he found her standing beside him.

"Philip, stop," she said, one hand held in front of her.

His young face contorted in an angry mess, though his steps forward stumbled in his hesitation. "It's your fault," he cried as his sword wavered before him.

While Philip's attention was distracted, Bredych stepped around Margaret until he stood beside her sword hand. *He's little more than a boy, really.* Bredych's fingers found another knife just the same.

"Put the sword away, Philip," said Margaret. When she reached forward and touched his sword with her free hand, Bredych held his breath. A droplet of blood fell to the paved road below, and Margaret's eyes widened as she glanced at her hand.

It was little more than a pinprick but an attack against her person nonetheless, and Bredych grabbed hold of her sword a finger span above her grip. She released it, and he stepped forward. Philip's eyes narrowed as he studied Bredych, and when his gaze landed on Bredych's scar, he paled.

"You're Amaskan?" Philip asked.

Bredych nodded and said, "And you're the man who's injured the Queen. If you'd like to remain breathing, I would heartily suggest you put your sword away."

Philip's sword wavered as he glanced at Margaret, and Bredych seized the opportunity to toss another throwing knife with his free hand. It embedded itself in the top of the man's hand. He dropped his sword with a curse, and when it clattered to the cobble below, Margaret kicked it away. Bredych shoved Philip against the building, where the man slid down until he sat on the ground.

"Philip," said Margaret as she crouched beside him. "What entranced you to attack me?"

When the man lunged forward, Bredych used his forearm to knock him back against the stone wall. "Answer her."

"Has she told you yet? How her incompetence cost my father his life?"

The color drained from Margaret's face. "How—"

"How did I know?" shouted Philip, as he stared at her with open hostility. "You sent him to the border, t-to a war he couldn't win, and s-so I waited. A few coins in the right palms will get a noble son time alone with the messenger pigeons."

"You intercepted my messages," said Margaret, and Philip nodded. "But those messages are sealed."

"By my father. I've access to the extra seal and wax he keeps in his desk, not that it matters to you. You're still the reason he's dead." Despite Bredych's arm against his chest,

Philip strained against him. Footsteps sounded at the alleyway's end, and Bredych glanced up. His attention shifted for a single moment, but it was all that was necessary for Philip's hand to reach his boot top.

It was only a sliver of a blade, but lethal just the same. Philip threw it at Margaret, where it embedded itself in her left shoulder. Her eyes widened at the impact, then she reached up and yanked the knife from her shoulder. A red circle spread across her light blue tunic, and while the strain made wrinkles around her eyes, she crouched down beside Philip until she could touch his face. "Your father understood something that you don't, Philip," she said.

"What's that?"

"Honor. And loyalty."

Philip pursed his lips together and a wad of spit landed on Margaret's cheek. Bredych raised his hand to slap the young man, but Margaret shook her head.

"My father was loyal to the King, not to some pampered royal playing at Queen," said Philip. Her fingers tightened around the knife's hilt, the knife covered in her blood. Philip grinned as he caught the reaction. "When the Shadian army arrives, I hope you die as slowly as my father did."

If I knock him out, he might live through this. Bredych raised his hand, but before he could hit the young man, Margaret stuck the knife in Philip's chest. A gurgling sound escaped the young man's open lips, painting his teeth a dark crimson as he grinned at her. His body shuddered once before the spirit left his eyes, which stared unseeing at Margaret.

The guards stopped beside them, one of them removing his sash. "Your Majesty, you're hurt!"

She stared at the knife in Philip's chest, her face emotionless. Bredych grabbed the sash from the guardsman and wrapped it around her shoulder, tying a knot across it to help stem the bleeding. "We should leave," he whispered to her, but she remained transfixed upon the blade. To the guards he said, "Dispose of him. I'll get Her Majesty to safety."

As the guards gathered up the body, Bredych pulled Margaret up by her shoulders. "Time to move," he said, and she blinked at him, her face as pale and still as marble. The briefest hint of color appeared on her cheeks as Leolin's voice called out nearby. Bredych glanced over his shoulder to see the boy running to catch up to them. The way his eyes narrowed and his jaw tensed as he spotted the blood at Margaret's shoulder—there was no doubting the boy was Shendra's.

"What happened?" asked Leolin as he took Margaret's free hand.

"Philip, the Grand Marshal's son. It's been taken care of." Her voice was distant and hollow as she spoke, and Leolin frowned.

He glanced at Bredych, who gave a brief shake of his head. Now wasn't the time to go into details, not with so many potential dangers remaining on the streets. The alleyway's end let out on another street, this one lacking in townsfolk and vendors. Its silence made Bredych's skin prickle, and he stopped. "Stay with her," he said to Leolin before sidling along the walls and doorways of the street. He was all the way at the end when the ground began to shake.

Cobblestone cracked and buckled as the ground pitched and rocked, and a chasm opened up beside him. Bredych fell to his knees, his stomach roiling out of rhythm with the ground. Finding his footing much more secure on all fours, he crawled in Margaret's direction. The shaking stretched out in front of him like the long trail through the Sadain Desert. Several awnings collapsed, and behind him, cracking timber split the air. Margaret and Leolin huddled together under an empty cart, and as Bredych crawled up beside them, the shaking ceased.

"I must reach the castle," said Margaret.

"We'll need to move quickly. There may be more earthquakes," said Bredych as he stood. He and Leolin flanked Margaret as they moved through the streets toward the castle. As people escaped their homes, the streets filled as the uninjured searched for those missing or injured. So many bore injuries that no one looked twice at Margaret's blood-stained tunic, nor the two men who escorted her.

They might have made it to the castle unscathed, but as Bredych watched the way Margaret answered her guards in clipped sentences, her body held stiff, he frowned. As an Amaskan, he was intimately familiar with what she was doing—separating the trauma in order to make the necessary decisions—but there was a price to it. A steep one.

No one could be stone forever.

30

Reports from across the city arrived from breathless guardsmen as Margaret's personal physician treated her wound. Mostly caved in roofs, cracks in walls, broken household objects, and a few crevices in the ground. An old woman living on the city's outskirts died when her roof collapsed but otherwise, human damage was limited to broken bones and concussions. Leolin remained behind with Margaret while Bredych climbed the steps to the pigeon house. Several messages awaited Margaret, which he fetched before returning to the castle. When he entered the council room, his muscles tensed in response to the look that passed between Margaret and Lord Cornish.

Bredych set the messages on the table, and Margaret gestured for him to sit, wincing with the movement. He claimed the seat and waited as she opened the messages one by one.

"The earthquakes began on the Senate's island, but spread from the Harren to Prespen Seas."

Margaret paused as Lord Cornish cleared his throat.

"Forgive me, Your Majesty. It appears I have been wrong today about...many things," he said, his eyes staring at the table.

He followed Lord Cornish's gaze to find it rested on the carving of Itova. High cheekbones and a sharp nose gave way to a narrow chin. For all that she was feared, her beauty was striking. And familiar.

When Bredych dragged his gaze away from the carving, Margaret frowned at him. "I'm sorry, Your Majesty. Too many days on the road," he said.

"I spoke to the Boahim Senate minutes before the first earthquake here, though the shakes had already begun on their island. People were injured, though it's unclear if the injured were senators or others living on the island. Senator Whitlen mentioned many times that I should see after my people. It was as if she knew the earthquakes would strike here next," Margaret said.

"'Strike here next' is an interesting way to phrase it," said Bredych.

Margaret exchanged a glance with Leolin before responding. "I believe the earthquakes unnatural. That they were a direct result of what was happening at the Pass."

"Magic happened at the border, didn't it?" Bredych asked, and she nodded.

Lord Cornish wrung his hands in his lap though he remained silent, glancing now and again at the table's wood inlay.

"We sent pigeons to the Monpoli border as well as Meridi Pass." She swallowed hard as she held up the first scrap of parchment. "One of the lieutenants reports that a 'large light appeared in the sky moments before the earth began to shake.' When the first quake stopped, members of the Boahim Senate stood on the Pass between the Shadian and Alexandrian armies."

"That's impossible!" shouted Lord Cornish. "Magic like that hasn't existed for centuries."

Margaret slapped the paper on the table with her good arm. "Tell that to my sister, who watched King Havin control his son's body as Gamun tried to kill Senator Whitlen. Or tell it to my sister's corpse, which they froze in place." She pushed back the sleeves of her tunic to expose arms red and chafed. "Or tell it to me when the Senate tried to freeze me to death for daring to question them. Believe me, Lord Cornish, I wish to the Thirteen that it's impossible for fire to rain down and kill my people. If I ignore the evidence in front of me, more people will die. Possibly me. Probably you. Do you wish to withdraw from this council?"

"Your Majesty?"

"Do you wish to withdraw, Lord Cornish? I've little time to deal with your inability to process the truth."

The color fled her cheeks as she stared at the papers before her. It was a familiar look—the withdrawn, haunted face of loss, but before Bredych could ask, Lord Cornish cleared his throat. "My profound apologies, Your Majesty. I'll do my best to counsel you in these changing times," he said.

She nodded and returned to the message. "The Senate ordered both sides to return to their lands when a member of the Shadian army shot an arrow at a senator. The lieutenant had done little more than blink when fire rained from the sky. Then the quakes began again. Both the Shadians and our army suffered heavy casualties at the Pass, and...." Margaret closed her eyes. "And Grand Marshal Doublis is dead."

"His son died today." When Lord Cornish tilted his

head, Bredych added, "In the earthquake."

It was a little lie, but the man had no need to know the truth. Margaret swallowed hard before she continued. "When the fire fell from the skies, people panicked—everyone running in every direction—and when the earthquakes began, the ground buckled and split. He was one of the first to be swallowed by the earth. By the time the shaking stopped, the Senate was gone, as was most of our army. It's unclear if the members of the Senate live or perished with our people."

They live. If what I suspect is true, they live.

Margaret took a drink from her cup before picking up a second piece of parchment. "News from Captain Fenton at the Monpoli border was better. The Senate appeared there as well, though neither side was stupid enough to ignore their warning. For the time being, both armies have pulled back half a day's ride from the border. We suffered injuries there as well, though no deaths. There was only one earthquake there, and it was minor in comparison."

Bredych found himself drawn again to Itova's carving. Her smug gaze as she reaped people from their world left him breathless for a moment. "When you speak to the Senate, Your Majesty, does the ground ever shake?" he asked, and she shook her head. "What about when the Senate came here, for...Adelei?"

"No, not that I noticed. But I will admit I wasn't present at their arrival."

"Who was?"

The corners of her mouth fell as she stared at him. "Only the dead now."

"Your Majesty, if I may ask, how do you speak to the Senate? Is it some form of magic? Did speaking to them perhaps trigger the earthquakes?" asked Lord Cornish.

Margaret stood and walked over to the back wall where a blanket had been draped across the bookshelf. When she pulled it back, the orb pulsed lightly, and Lord Cornish covered his eyes. "What evil is this?" he asked as she returned the makeshift drape to its place.

"It's knowledge passed to me by my father on his death bed. A magical means of calling for help when the time arrives," she said as she returned to her seat. "It is also a means for the Senate to watch and listen."

Lord Cornish rose up from his seat. "B-but they could be here, now, listening to us discuss them!"

"Yes, they could. In all likelihood, they are. Assuming they're still alive," said Leolin. He turned to Bredych and pointed at him. "While we don't have time to argue the existence of magic, we also don't have time to waste with lies and secrecy."

"I will keep no secrets from this council." He couldn't. Not after hearing the words of *The Circle*. "What would you ask of me?"

It was Margaret who responded, her voice small and tinny as she rubbed her shoulder. "Who are you? Be truthful."

Like sitting before Her Holiness, his tongue thickened in his mouth as he pondered over what he would say, what he *could* say to make her understand. "My name is Eli Bredych, Grand Master of the Order of Amaska."

She nodded slowly, then glanced at Leolin. His eyes flashed in the candlelight as he shifted in his chair. "You are responsible for a great many deaths, Master Bredych," whispered Leolin.

"I am. There is naught I can do about past deeds, though I can control what future path I carve into the land. You seem unsurprised by this announcement."

Margaret touched a finger to the scar at his jawline. "You're not the first I've seen with that particular scar, Master Bredych. Though you gave yourself away in more ways than that," she said. When he frowned, she tapped his heart once. "Every time someone said her name, your face... it was a look my father gave only to me."

"Her?" He asked the question, though the answer was sewn into his soul. Perhaps it had been a mistake to come here, to assume he could hide among his enemies, but when he looked on Margaret, for a moment *she* sat before him again. Whatever the cost, it had been worth it.

"Though she felt betrayed by both of her fathers, I think she loved you most," said Margaret.

Lord Cornish rose slowly from his chair and backed away from the table. His eyes glazed over as he stared at the Thirteen. "They speak in riddles," he whispered, and then he shook his head. "I'm sorry, Your Majesty. I can't remain in this room. By your leave?"

When Margaret nodded, the man fled, leaving the three of them alone. "He said, 'they speak in riddles.' Who is 'they'?" said Margaret.

"The Thirteen? Or the Senate?" asked Bredych, and he sighed. "I think it's time I share my news. Unless you have more questions for me?" He asked the question of Margaret, though he looked at Leolin. The boy shrugged, though the way his eyes narrowed, the conversation was far from over.

"I assume you bring news from King Adir?" asked Margaret.

"I do. Should civil war erupt across the Little Dozen Kingdoms, he pledges his support, as does the Order." Though whether the support would be needed was still unknown. His Amaskan might have rid them of the problem, but with fire falling from the sky and the earth trembling, he might be as dead as the Grand Marshal. At some point, he would need to check in at Mademe's.

Assuming it still stood.

"Finally, the light shines into all this darkness," said Margaret as the makeshift curtain fell, exposing the orb behind it.

"There is more to tell, but perhaps it would be best if we took this conversation elsewhere," said Bredych as he glanced toward the orb.

Leolin followed his gaze, then approached the sliding bookshelf. The boy leaned his shoulder into it until it moved forward an arm's length. "Help me out with this," he said to Bredych, who joined him at the wall.

He crouched down at floor level, where the wheels underneath the moving shelf sat crookedly in their track. "Stop pushing for a moment," said Bredych, and he shoved a wheel with the butt of his hand.

It fell back into place, though the second wheel remained stuck. Wedged behind the wheel was a rusty silver key the length of the wheel itself. He stretched out across the floor and braced his feet against the wall. "Move out of the way," he said to Leolin, and when the boy stepped aside, Bredych stretched his fingers out and palmed the key. He gave the shelf a good kick with his booted heel. The wheel rolled back into place with a thunk, and Leolin slid the bookshelf shut.

"I would still recommend we take the conversation to another room," Bredych said.

He followed Margaret into the hallway. A flurry of activity outside covered their passage up the stairs where they sought privacy in the private library. The blood splatter's paleness hid it a little from someone used to seeing such things, though Bredych blanched. "Your Majesty, I fear I've missed something of importance," he said and gestured toward the window.

Her explanation of the attack was succinct and distant, and she kept her gaze firmly on him rather than looking about the room. When she was done, he repressed a shiver. Trained as he was, his first and second kills had shaken him. She leveled a look on him that spoke of a confidence she didn't have. "Your Majesty, I...I'm sorry you were put in such a position that you had to take a life, two lives as of today," he said as they gathered at the small table.

"Is it not my job?"

Beside her, the color fled Leolin's face, and Bredych thought, *So the boy didn't know it was she who killed Philip.*

"Maggie, self-defense or not, the Senate won't like that," said Leolin.

"Damn the Senate and their false ideals of justice!" Margaret struck the table with her fist and winced as it jarred her shoulder. "Every ruler before me has found one reason or another to use corporal punishment, let alone kill in self-defense. Why am I suddenly held to a higher standard? Philip intended to murder me, Leolin. Had his knife hit a few fingers lower, you could be planning my burning."

Bredych cleared his throat, and both Margaret and Leolin flinched. "I only mentioned it because I understand what it means to take a life...and the pain and guilt that comes after. Should you wish to talk about it, please seek me out, Your Majesty. For now, I must warn you against making such comments against the senators."

"Why?" she asked.

Bredych flipped open one of the books on the table, a recent tomb detailing information about the current Boahim Senate. He stopped on the page of information about the life of Senator Whitlen and pointed at the image of her face. "Does she look familiar?"

"It's Senator Whitlen," said Leolin as he cocked an eyebrow. "Why?"

He pulled a piece of folded parchment from his pocket, one he'd torn from a book he'd left with The Holy Few. When Bredych unfolded it length wise, sketches of the Thirteen stretched across the page, which he spun to face Margaret and Leolin. "These are the Thirteen. Drawings passed down from generations ago, back when the Gods still walked among men."

"The sketch appears in several of our books as well. My great-grandsire used it when he commissioned the carvings of the Thirteen in the council room," said Margaret.

Bredych nodded. "That's what made me tear this page from the book at the Order. When I saw Her, I knew."

"Her?" asked Leolin.

When Bredych pointed at the sketch of Itova, Goddess of Death, Margaret leaned across the page and studied the drawing. Her eyes widened, and she dragged the open book closer, laying the torn page on top of it. Side by side, there were subtle differences. Senator Whitlen's cheekbones were a touch lower than Itova's, and her face a touch fleshier than the Goddess, but the nose was the same sharp nose, the chin the same narrow chin that jutted out when she grew irritated.

"It's not possible," whispered Margaret. "We suspected they might be mystics and long lived, but if...if they are the same, they would never age. 'The Thirteen are ageless. They have always been and always will be, until the end of time itself.'"

"The *Shlosheser* is not impervious, Your Majesty. Human hands and voices narrate the copies made. No one owns the original text, despite what the Holy Few would tell you. Perhaps even gods age. Perhaps they grow tired of the ways of man." Bredych pointed at the sketch again. "Think on this—we find ourselves amidst a Senate who possesses magics long thought dead. Who better to ensure people follow the laws of the Thirteen than the Thirteen themselves?"

"We move like pawns at their bidding," said Leolin.

"Until they position us in such a way that civil war threatens the Little Dozen Kingdoms. But to what end? If they are as you say, Master Bredych, what do they gain by this war?" asked Margaret.

"I may have an answer to that question as well."

She stared at Bredych, the whites of her eyes visible around brown irises. "What you're suggesting is madness. This war might mean their destruction as well!"

"Maggie, the other day you said you couldn't remember who'd been the senator before Whitlen. Maybe that's because there wasn't anyone," said Leolin as Margaret flipped through the book's pages.

When she landed on another set of sketches, she said, "Look, this is the senator before Adela Whitlen. Senator Ada Whitlen, her grandsire."

"Who we thought looked too similar to be coincidence," said Leolin.

"And before her?" asked Bredych as she flipped backwards through the book. Each time she stopped, the senator was a woman. The names changed and each sketch was a touch different, a touch older. "This is more than similarities. More than coincidence."

Leolin nodded as he glanced back and forth between the book and the loose page. "Either Whitlen comes from a long line of senators who live much longer than anyone we've ever known, or...."

"Or the Boahim Senate *is* the Thirteen."

"Maybe it's only Senator Whitlen who's a god," said Margaret.

Bredych pointed at Asti, The God of Peace. "Look like anyone you know, Your Majesty?"

When she sighed, her shoulders slumped forward. "Senator Montero of Alexander, right down to his kind smile. Why has no one noticed this before?"

"Perhaps someone did. Perhaps they were silenced. This book is rare, so it's possible no one has had the resources to make the connection before. Honestly, if you don't know to look for it, you might not recognize what you're seeing," said Bredych.

"Who would think the senators were the Thirteen? It's not something most people going about their day-to-day lives would think about. Most commoners don't interact at all with the Senate." Leolin paused, then smacked his hand against his forehead. "The orbs! If they truly are the Thirteen, they can see everything without the orbs. That's how they knew Maggie was looking into the Senate's founding."

"And they can hear everything we say." While she leaned closer to Leolin, her voice surprisingly didn't waver. "But I still fail to understand why someone didn't notice. If they are...oh."

Leolin tilted his head. "What? What did you remember?"

"The senators are representatives for each kingdom, representatives the people think are elected, but the truth is, the Holy Few choose them. Senators serve until their death at which point a ruler suggests a replacement. Her Holiness or whoever serves the Few in that kingdom can appoint someone else. Leolin and I found this information while you were gone. But that means the Holy Few *know* the senators are the Thirteen."

"I'm not sure that they do." Bredych closed his eyes a moment. If he told them, it would be a betrayal to the Order, but if he didn't.... Images of flames erupting from jagged holes in the ground filled his mind. When he opened his eyes, they both watched him—Leolin with suspicion, if his narrowed eyes were any indication, and Margaret with a concerned look she wore more and more every day. "Before returning to the castle, I spoke to Her Holiness in hopes of finding information on the Boahim Senate and their connection to the Order. By telling you this, I am breaking vows that would label me an Oathbreaker to my people."

Margaret shot a quick glance at Leolin, whose lips thinned as he frowned. "Master Bredych, you don't have to break your oath. If you give this information, please do so because you choose to, and not because you feel I require it."

"But if he's half the man you claim he is, Maggie, he'll tell it anyway," said Leolin.

Bredych fished about in his pouch until his fingers found the smooth, cold stone within it. Soon, he and the boy would need to have a conversation. *I can't keep referring to my nephew that way. His name is Leolin.* He cleared his throat and left the stone in his pocket. "I part with this information willingly, because it could be critical to our survival."

"Please continue," Margaret said.

"The Holy Few are carriers of memories, of texts and histories that would make this library a pebble in an ocean of pebbles. The Order has a similar purpose."

"You mean killing isn't the only skill you have?"

When Bredych glanced at Leolin, the boy's muscles tensed as he ground his teeth together. "We don't have time for pettiness, Lieutenant. If you have something to say to me, let it out so we can move past it," said Bredych.

"Speak," ordered Margaret.

Leolin gave her a curt nod. "You're more than the leader of the Order of Amaska. My mother told stories about her time with the Order. If you're the Grand Master, then you're my mother's brother. The one who slit her throat and left her for dead."

Ah. There it is. This was what had been chewing at the boy since Bredych had revealed his identity. By Margaret's lack of response, she'd already known. "I am. What would you do with this newfound information?"

The boy tossed a small dagger onto the table, and Bredych retrieved the stone from his pouch. When he set it beside the dagger, Leolin asked, "What trickery is this?"

"It was your mother's."

The boy stared at the round, gray stone. A normal river rock with nothing marring its smoothness, but still a plain stone beside the small sapphire gem on the hilt of the boy's dagger. "I don't understand."

"When your mother was young, we used to argue. I was older and thought I knew the way of everything, as many children do. I thought it was my responsibility to be the adult, especially when our parents died. Your mother didn't understand why I...why I joined the Order. It was something I did for her, for us. Without them, we would have died on the streets. Two more starving street rats to be found in an alley come spring thaw. It only took her disappearing once for me to understand how a parent feels when their child goes missing."

Margaret's face bunched up as she tilted her head. "And yet you didn't use this knowledge to rethink your plan to kill my sister?"

"I'm not perfect, no matter how much my younger self believed it. Leading the Order came early to me, earlier than most. Power changes a person, as well you know, Your Majesty. When Shendra, Ida to you, disappeared, I thought my world would end. I found her candlemarks later near the river with this stone in her hand. She'd felt bad about what she'd said to me and had been searching for 'something pretty' for me as an apology." Bredych ran his fingers across the stone, which blurred as unbidden tears gathered in his eyes. "I-I haven't thought on this in ages, but perhaps it's time I do so. Every time we disagreed, I'd leave the stone for her as an apology, or she would leave it for me in return."

Our last argument was over the kidnapping of Adelei. Bredych blinked rapidly to push aside the tears. *Mourn later. 'Truth leads in times of war.' Or that was what she always had said.*

"I went back to...where we left her body, intending to leave the stone for her, but when I returned, her body was gone. Someone had dragged it away. I always assumed it was someone at the Order, someone close to her that wished her to be burned, but I had no idea she'd survived. Or how."

Leolin's face was a mess of emotions as his nostrils flared and mouth grimaced, but unlike Bredych, no tears gathered in Leolin's eyes. "And what? Now you offer me this stone as an apology? Like you did with her?"

Bredych nodded. "It doesn't make up for—"

"Not even close, old man. You killed my parents. That's not something to be forgiven." Leolin shoved the stone away with the butt of his palm. "Ever."

"This isn't the first time you've accused me of killing your father. Do you know who he was?" Bredych asked.

"He died before I was born, murdered by the Order because he dared love my mother."

"If it's as you say, I would have his name."

Leolin scowled but answered. "His name was Samuhel Banach."

The stench of rotting flesh burned Bredych's nose even now, some fourteen years later, and when he managed to shake off the memory, he found Margaret's hand on his as she said his name.

"That's a name I've not heard in many years. Samuhel was one of our best Amaskans, next to your mother that is, though it wasn't the Order that killed him."

"You lie!" shouted Leolin.

"How old are you, Lieutenant?"

The boy's fingers gripped the table as he stared at the dagger. Margaret nudged him with her elbow, and he said, "Twenty-three. Why?"

"Your mother wasn't pregnant when she left the Order. If that's truly your age, you were born seven years before she left, before I...tried to kill her. I never knew Shendra had borne a child, much less that she had a relationship with Samuhel. He died a year after your mother tried to leave."

One moment the dagger lay on the table and the next, it whizzed past Bredych's head, where it embedded itself in a book's spine. Leolin, his face a marble slab, stood, sending his wooden chair stumbling backward. When Margaret reached for his hand, he wrested his away from her and leaned across the table. He jabbed a finger in Bredych's face. "You are a murderer and a liar. There's nothing you can say that I'll believe."

"Your father was murdered," said Bredych.

"I know. By your orders."

Bredych shook his head. "No, not mine. There's no crime or sin in the Order for having a family, so there was no reason to kill him. His body was brought home to the Order by one of our traders after being found in the streets of Tarmsworth. Someone removed his tongue before killing him. They wanted to be sure he'd be unable to talk in the afterlife. There's nothing I can do to convince you I tell the truth beyond sharing with you the information I brought with me from the Order. But first, I must tell you about *The Circle*."

"Leolin, sit. Please." Hearing her plead lessened some of the pain around the boy's eyes, but while he returned to his seat, his jaw spasmed at regular intervals. "What's *The Circle*?" asked Margaret.

"In the Order, there are different levels of Amaskan, from the trainees and journeymen all the way up to the Masters."

"And you," she said.

"And me. While the learning of information is... encouraged, there's a private library accessible only to the masters, and some volumes are readable only by the Grand Master. One of those texts is a journal from a Grand Master many generations ago, which quotes *The Circle* extensively. I thought the text a myth until today, until I spoke with Her Holiness."

Margaret frowned. "How is it that the Holy Few have access to Amaskan histories that you don't?"

"I assume it has to do with how the Order and the Senate are connected. *The Circle* dates back to before the Fall, and according to it, the first senators' descendants served the senators as disciples. Many of them worried that a darkness had corrupted the senators, so they founded a secret order to ensure that Justice would be served, no matter servant, king, or senator."

"The Thirteen had children who became the Order of Amaska?" asked Margaret.

Bredych shrugged. "The creation story of our world speaks of the Thirteen creating new life. Who's to say they didn't continue to do so?"

"So Amaskans are gods?" The words were followed by Leolin's sharp laughter. "More lies from an Amaskan."

"The Amaskans aren't gods, boy. The Thirteen bred with humans. Somewhere back in our histories, we might once have been close, but that's long lost to us now. Inside this Grand Master's journal is a prophecy, copied from *The Circle*, and the prophecy is supposedly from the first Amaskans, otherwise known as—"

"The Circle. What did this prophecy say?" asked Margaret.

Bredych closed his eyes a moment. The longhand writing of an ancient Grand Master splashed across the pages as he recalled the words. "'Upon our honor, we will uphold our secrets and serve Justice. Until the day of Truth, we shall remain in darkness, but on that day, we will be the Light. We will brandish our Light before us like an ever-burning torch and battle the corruption in our midst until everything before us burns. No corruption, be it man or king or god will destroy Boahim again.'"

She frowned. "The day of Truth...what does that mean?"

"It's a quote that's been studied for decades by many Grand Masters. Before this year, I had no idea what the day of Truth was, but in light of the knowledge we have, I believe the 'truth' refers to the fact that we now know the senators to be the Thirteen. A truth like that can't be kept in the shadows. It's a truth that could start wars. The very people tasked with helping and protecting us are using a corrupted magic they 'wiped from the land' and declared a sin. As for the rest of the prophecy, I believe it means that we Amaskans will play a pivotal role in the war against the Senate."

An entire day of bravado, and it was then that Margaret's shell cracked as she stared at him. "War against...the Thirteen?" she said, her voice trembling.

"This war will happen whether you or I want it to. It was destined to be, written by the Gods themselves."

"But for what purpose? If the Thirteen have fallen to corruption, this war would be the end of them, and if you're right, the end of the Amaskans as well. Why begin a war that means your own death?" asked Leolin.

"I think they're tired," said Margaret, and when Bredych frowned, she continued. "Senator Whitlen was afraid when the earthquakes began, and she appeared...old. Every line and wrinkle was carved into her skin in ways I've never seen before, like cracks in the land itself. What if the Thirteen *want* to die?"

Bredych opened his mouth, then closed it. Perhaps she was right. Perhaps centuries of living in human form, if not longer, had grown exhausting to them.

"I've got more questions than answers," said Leolin, and Margaret nodded agreement. "Do gods age, or is it merely magic? Why were the earthquakes a surprise to them? What caused the earthquakes if not the Thirteen? Most importantly, how do gods die? I don't suppose *that* was in your findings?"

His bones ached as Bredych shook his head. He'd served as Grand Master far longer than his predecessors.

Far too long. This is a battle for the young, for those with less blood on their blade.

"Do we have to go to war with the Thirteen?" It was a child's voice, tight and small, that asked the question, and once out, Margaret pursed her lips together against whatever would have come next. Leolin patted her hand, but even he trembled as he did so.

Whatever the answers, they wouldn't come by them amidst fear. They needed something to shake them from their melancholy. Bredych retrieved the key from his pocket and set it on the table beside Shendra's stone. "This key was stuck under the orb room's door. Any idea what it goes to?" he asked.

Margaret picked it up and turned it in the sunlight streaming in from the window. "This mark here," she said, pointing at a mountain shape etched into the key's bow. "I've seen it before, but I can't recall where. Somewhere in the castle though."

"Perhaps in the orb's room?" asked Bredych, but she shook her head. "Did your father have any other rooms like this one where you and he spent time? You may have seen it there."

"I'm sure it will come to me. Probably candlemarks before the sun rises when I'm staring wide-eyed at the ceiling. In the meantime, I need to get a message to Captain Fenton about his...promotion. I'm going to send him to Meridi Pass." Margaret picked up the key from the table and tucked it into the top of her corset.

"Who will you elevate to captain in the North?" asked Leolin. When she smiled, Leolin waved his hands in the air. "No, Maggie. Not me. I'm needed here."

"I have to agree with the lieutenant. If the Shadian armies break through the Pass, their next stop will be

Alesta. Leolin will need to command your armies stationed here," said Bredych.

She frowned but said nothing more. Bredych's gaze returned to the gray pebble. It was too bad the boy didn't see the gift for what it was. Perhaps a little time would help him see reason.

"Lieutenant, if you would excuse us, please, I need to speak with Master Bredych for a moment."

Leolin flinched at the formality, then stood and bowed before retreating. Once the door closed behind him, Margaret pressed her hands against her cheeks. "Master Bredych, tell me honestly. Is this a war we can win?"

"No one wins in a war, Your Majesty, but perhaps we can end the golden shackles that bind us to the Senate."

"You're not afraid? The Thirteen—they're *gods*."

"Aging gods who fear earthquakes, which means they have worries like we do. I like our chances, Your Majesty. I like them very much," Bredych said as he smiled. He kept the tremor from his voice by pure effort as the words of *The Circle* echoed in his mind.

We will brandish our Light before us like an ever-burning torch and battle the corruption in our midst until everything before us burns.

Margaret smiled in response, her face so like Adelei's, and his heart twinged in response.

If I can help it, the only thing that will burn is me.

31

"I appreciate your willingness to meet with me, my lord," said Leolin as he entered Lord Cornish's rooms. Unlike most of the guest rooms in the castle, his were intended to be used on a semi-permanent basis and as such, contained a small sitting area in addition to living quarters. Lavish amounts of color decorated the numerous chairs, and Leolin claimed one sporting a grain-colored cushion, accented by glass beads of pale green.

"By the frown you wear, I suspect you come bearing ill news. I admit, I'm not surprised. Nothing good can come of all this magic," said Lord Cornish.

"I come with a different problem. One concerning our queen and...and the Amaskan."

"Go on."

When the three of them had discussed the possibility of the senators being the Thirteen, it had sounded plausible, but as he recounted the tale, Leolin found himself pausing to consider the believability of his words. It didn't help that Lord Cornish wasn't the calmest of men in the best of times and a seed of worry pitted itself in Leolin's stomach.

The way the man's eyes bulged as Leolin spoke and the way his lips curled up lightly at their corners.... While disclosing their discoveries hadn't been the best idea, what Bredych suggested was treason, not to mention suicide. How could anyone think they stood a chance against the Thirteen? If it put Maggie in danger, Leolin couldn't proceed with whatever they planned.

"If the queen relies so heavily upon the Amaskan, so much that she would stage a coup against the Boahim Senate, perhaps it's necessary, our duty even, to consider further measures," said Lord Cornish.

"Such as?"

"Perhaps we should report her actions to the senators. No ruler is impervious to the laws that bind us all, and if what you insinuate is true, then Her Majesty's not well." When Leolin frowned, Cornish quickly added, "I only mean that perhaps she needs more help than her advisors, few though they are, can give. She's suffered great losses. Her Majesty wouldn't be the first ruler to be found unfit to rule."

"Wait a minute, I wasn't implying she's unfit. Only that she needs our help. We're her council, so we should, I don't know...counsel her."

Lord Cornish set his meaty hand on Leolin's shoulder. "And counsel her we will. We will explain that if she wishes to keep the Senate out of her kingdom, she may wish to listen to wiser, more experienced shoulders."

"And if she doesn't?" asked Leolin as he glanced up at the old man.

"Then perhaps someone with more experience should wear the crown, someone more equipped to deal with the coming war."

Leolin stood more abruptly than he'd anticipated, and

the chair's garish, golden cushion tumbled to the floor. Lord Cornish knelt to retrieve it but stopped when he caught sight of the grimace Leolin wore. "I came to you for help, my lord, not to help you plan a coup of your own."

He towered over the old man, whose face paled as he waved his hands in front of him. "A coup is such a strong word, but think of the future. This Amaskan, this *murderer* has convinced our queen to declare war against the Thirteen themselves! That's simply not done. It's not a war anyone can win, much less begin. With someone more levelheaded and less emotional in place, the Kingdom of Alexander would have the respect it deserves," said Lord Cornish.

This was the opposite of what he'd wanted. *Damn it. Maggie even warned me about him and his ambitious drive to rule.*

Sweat trickled down the folds of Lord Cornish's face, and when Leolin stepped close enough to smell the sweetness of honey on the man's breath, Lord Cornish's complexion paled to that of candle wax. He tried to step backward into the wall behind him, and Leolin tapped a finger against the man's collarbone. "You'll do nothing with the information I've given you. If I find out you've even sneezed in the Senate's direction, you'll find yourself a lord of little more than a chamber pot, do you understand...*my lord?*"

"I u-understand, Lieutenant."

Leolin turned heel and strode shoulders straight from the room, though when the door shut behind him, his knees wobbled. How was he going to explain this to Maggie?

BETWEEN THE LINGERING SMELL OF SMOKE IN HER sitting room and the ever-present gaze of the orb in the council room, Margaret found herself in the gardens more and more, though sitting among the flowers brought up their own hellish thoughts as her mind lingered on all those lost. Then there was Leolin.

He had gone from childhood friend to something more, but was there time for *more* when it was possible the Thirteen encouraged war? Assuming they really were the Thirteen. Every time she thought of Leolin, thoughts that plagued her sleep crept into her days. Margaret crumbled the rose petals in her hands, turning her fingers slightly purple.

"Maybe I should come back another time."

She flinched at the sudden voice, and the crumpled petals fell to the dirt below.

"I didn't mean to startle you," said Leolin as he approached. "You look like you've had the morning I'm having."

Rather than his typical smile, a relaxed grin that brought out his high cheekbones, the one he wore now stretched his lips too thin as it forced its way across his features. Margaret gestured for him to join her on the bench. "You're either bringing me bad news, or you have swallowed something foul. Perhaps rotten quail eggs."

His lips twitched, but he did not laugh. The former then.

"You and I haven't talked about...us. About the future," said Leolin.

Margaret curled her hands in her skirt's layers. "With an impending war, it's difficult to think about a future. Everything's uncertain, i-including us."

"I understand that, but...well, we aren't kids anymore.

You aren't promised to some maniac, and I'm not stationed at some tiny town near the border. What I'm trying to say is, you're more to me than just someone I knew in passing."

She jabbed him in the shoulder as she laughed, though her throat felt tight around her words. "I should hope so! I know your secrets, like where you buried the hunting pup who drowned and how many days you cried over him."

Leolin's eyes tightened as he swallowed. "Maggie, I-I love you. You know that, right?"

The air evaporated for a moment as she stilled. There was knowing it and then *knowing* it. Her heart sang in response. She couldn't trust her voice, so she nodded while she stared at her hands.

"Do you love me? It's okay if you don't. I know there's been a lot for you to deal with—"

Rather than answer, she leaned over and kissed him.

When they parted, his muscles were tense as he looked at her. "Maggie, that didn't answer the question."

"It didn't?"

He shook his head. "Love isn't a requirement for kissing, or sex for that matter. At least not for most. While I know you're a hopeless romantic, I need to know how you really feel about me."

"Why the sudden urgency?" she asked.

"I...I did something incredibly stupid, and I need to know if I can trust you. *Really* trust you. Like partners do."

Margaret frowned. She thought she loved him, but how did one know? Was it the way her words to him were never germane? Or the way he made her forget Gamun existed? Was that love?

"With everyone around me gone, I didn't think I had the strength to rule, but with you and Master Bredych here —" When his face flushed, Margaret took his warm hand in hers. "Hear me out, Leolin. When you both arrived in Alesta, it was easy to lean on you—to allow you both to make the decisions for me—but I can't do that. The crown is mine to wear."

"No one's arguing that."

She squeezed his hand gently. "But when I'm with you, I don't have to be Queen. I can be me—Margaret. If you had asked me this even a few weeks ago, I'm not sure I would have been capable of an answer. Not because I don't care for you, but because I didn't think myself capable of love. With Gamun...there was no love, and before him, the only love I had known was that of family—something also ripped untimely from me. As much as you dislike Master Bredych, he taught me that I'm capable of much more than I knew."

"Is that a really long way of saying you love me?"

"If never having the correct words when I'm with you, or the idea of my life without you being like living underwater without air, if that's love, then yes, I love you. But I've not forgotten that you have done something 'incredibly stupid.' What is it that you came here to tell me looking like a hound that missed the kill?"

Leolin released her hand and stood, then began pacing before her. "You aren't wrong about my hatred toward Bredych."

"Your uncle."

"Uncle or not, he tried to kill my mother and murdered my father—"

"Which he says he didn't do," said Margaret.

He stopped pacing and stared at the sky for a moment. "Thirteen help me, you're frustrating sometimes, Maggie. Whether he did it or not, my mother told me he did. I've spent my entire life hating a man for something he might not have done. It's not something you wake up one morning

354

and forget. You know this. You went through this with your sister when she returned."

"True. I'm sorry. Please continue."

His pacing resumed, slower and more precise as he created a circle-eight in the dirt path. "We don't *know* for a fact that the senators are the Thirteen. I mean, it's possible, but think about what that means, Maggie, and what that means in terms of this war. You'd be fighting gods."

"We would."

He skidded to a halt and knelt down in front of her. "Maggie, you'd die. No one can defeat a god, much less thirteen of them."

"I don't have the answers yet, but to ignore the evidence before us is folly. We will find a way." *I hope.* "But what does any of this have to do with this stupid thing you've done?" The air rushed out of her lungs as she drew her hands together into fists. "Did you contact the Thirteen? But how could you? You do not know the words—"

"No, no, I didn't do that. But...look, I was worried about you. I don't want you do die."

"What did you do?" she asked, her voice sharp.

"I told Lord Cornish."

She did not remember standing, only the tension that carried her away from the bench and where Leolin now stood. Her feet tread a similar path to his until she stopped, her hands crossed over her chest. "You told the man who wishes to wear my crown that we were going to declare war against the Senate and thus, the Thirteen?"

"I—well, yes. I was hoping he'd have ideas on how best to help you."

"Let me guess. This conversation didn't go as planned." When he shook his head, she added, "He probably mentioned some ultimatum or another about doing what he says, wise man that he is. Leolin, you gave him exactly what he wanted. Doubt."

"I thought he'd do the right thing. That he'd have some way out of this mess that didn't involve you dying."

Margaret shook her head. "Why are you so convinced that this plan means I'll die? Do you have that little faith in my abilities?"

"It's not you I doubt, Maggie, but no human can defeat a god. Are you not frightened?"

"Terrified."

She held out her trembling hands where he could see them. When he stepped forward to claim one, she stepped away. "My father had a saying he used to tell Iliana—I mean Adelei—and me when we were young, something I didn't understand until after his death. He said, 'The difference between a ruler and one who rules is that the first worries none for fear, while the second is crippled by it.' Of course I'm afraid, but I don't have the luxury of being afraid for myself when so many are in danger. Besides, as Master Bredych says, 'Fear is a temporary feeling. Regret, though, will follow you a lifetime.'"

"Can we have a conversation that he isn't a part of?" Leolin asked.

He didn't understand. Hatred blinded him, and as much as she wished to point out his mistake, doing so wouldn't convince him that Bredych meant well. Leolin's posture relaxed when she stepped forward and kissed him lightly on the cheek. "I do love you, you know, but your hatred of Bredych is a problem I can't afford. He was my sister's father, and despite his mistakes, he's been an ally in a time when allies are few and far between. We need him in this fight. Don't ask me to make a choice."

"I won't, I promise, but if your life's in danger, I'll do

whatever's necessary to protect you. The only choice I'll ask you to make is to take care of yourself. Don't take unnecessary risks, and don't let him force you to do so either."

Margaret nodded, but her insides knotted themselves. He said the right words, but did he mean them? What he had done was treasonous, yet he had done so out of fear for her life. The way her insides squirmed...was this part of love as well? What she needed was answers. Now would be the time to pray.

If only the Thirteen weren't listening.

THE PARCHMENT IN FRONT OF MARGARET LAY BLANK. How did one phrase the words to properly express the crown's condolences over the loss of someone's son or wife? No one had ever divulged this part of ruling—the writing of such letters to families who would care very little about her apologies.

When the proper death counts from the Pass had arrived, Margaret had hidden in her council chamber, her face in her hands as she cried. It made little sense why the Boahim Senate would kill large swaths of people, yet kill they had and indiscriminately. Perhaps Bredych was correct —perhaps they *were* tired of living. Or perhaps they were merely twisted beings who wished to rain down terror on the people of the Little Dozen Kingdoms.

The faces of the Thirteen mocked her as they stared at nothing and everything, their almost garish smiles exposing their smooth teeth. As a child, she had loved the carved relief across the council room table, little fingers brushing the oak, but now it served as a constant reminder that nowhere was safe. Nowhere was sacred.

Even here she wasn't alone.

One hundred dead with another hundred missing from the Alexandrian army alone. Presumably, if one gathered up the various body parts scattered across the valley, thoroughly described in the notes from Captain Fenton, perhaps then a hundred bodies could be cobbled together from the chaos. Margaret shivered at the thought.

Whether it was one or two hundred dead mattered little. They were still dead. And the Senate were still gods. *They must be. No one else has the power to wreak such havoc and destruction in a few heartbeats. Not even the magicians of old.*

Perhaps they had been gods as well. Who was she to say who was or wasn't a god? Margaret stared at the parchment, which remained blank. If they were gods, why not use their powers to create beauty in the world, to help those who needed it most or perhaps heal the sick?

Tears pricked her eyelids and swayed her vision a moment as her father's debilitated body tore at her mind. He had lain in his bed for months, unable to use a chamber pot without assistance. His hands shook as his lungs burned, erupting in a hacking cough that left bruises across his chest and back.

They could have stopped it. Whether it was mystical or natural, they could have. And yet the Thirteen chose not to remove the malady from him. They let him die.

The candle before her flickered as if brushed by a gentle wind. Margaret snatched the silver candelabrum from the table and slammed its base into Itova's high cheekbones.

The wood chipped, and she struck it a second and third time, knocking away pieces until the goddess's face was little more than a sunken pit among the twelve other gods. If only it were that easy.

She touched her free hand to her cheek to find it flushed with warmth. Another breeze moved through the room, flickering the remaining candles, and Margaret set the now-bent candelabrum on the table beside the parchment. A high-pitched whine tickled Margaret's ears, its pitch sharpening the louder it grew. Beneath the bookshelf, a bright light glowed, and her skin prickled in response.

The Senate. Or the Thirteen. Whatever they called themselves, they wished her attention, and despite the little jolts that coursed through her body, warning her against such an action, she stood and approached the bookshelf. Cold air seeped out from beneath it, chilling her toes through her slippers, and the light pulsed in rhythm to her heartbeat.

Everything is a weapon. Always examine your surroundings, especially in enemy territory. Adelei's words were loud enough that Margaret winced before glancing around the council chambers, but her sister remained a memory.

Like their father.

She gasped as she touched the wooden shelf, only to find it as cold as a morning's frost. Using her sleeve like a glove, she pushed the shelf along its track. The orb glowed, and she shielded her eyes until they adjusted to the room's brightness. When she removed her hands, the expected face awaited her in the orb.

"Senator Whitlen," Margaret said as she inclined her head. "What can my kingdom do for the Senate?" She dropped her hand to her side where it waited within easy reach of her short sword. It would do little against a god but if anywhere was enemy territory, this was it.

Dark circles buried themselves beneath the Senator's eyes. Her pale skin stretched too thin over her frame as she leaned closely to the orb. "I think it's you who has something to say to me. Perhaps an explanation—"

"I-I know who you are." Margaret's hand squeezed the fabric of her skirt and the flush across her face grew hotter.

"I should hope so considering how often we've spoken."

"That is not what I mean, Senator. Or should I call you Itova?"

The Senator smirked, her thin lips almost disappearing in wrinkles. "Ah, I tired of that pretense a century ago. Since we speak plainly now, may I ask why you felt the need to destroy my face? That carving has been a part of your family since the beginning of Alexander."

For all that she thought herself brave, in that moment, Margaret's legs trembled beneath her as she stood before the Goddess of Death. "You're gods, and yet you allowed hundreds to die. No, not allowed—you killed them. My people. Explain yourself."

A piercing gaze was Itova's only response, and Margaret repressed the desire to shudder.

"You will answer for your crimes."

"Crimes? What crimes do you propose we committed?"

Margaret removed the parchment from her pocket and unfolded it. "Shall I read the names of the men and women you murdered? Or is it only mortals who must follow the Thirteen laws?" The orb's light flared and the parchment she held dissolved into specks of light that fluttered to the ground where they dimmed until they were little more than dust.

"We do not answer to you, Queen Margaret."

"But you do!" she shouted at the orb. "You sit on your island, year after year, watching as the world drifts by and expect us to follow your rules. But when we come to you for help, you do nothing. Perhaps you're as helpless as we are. Dying gods in a dying world."

The room's bitter cold intensified until Margaret's teeth chattered, but when the faces of the dead flashed across her thoughts, she stepped close enough to the orb to touch it. "Bring them back," she growled.

Itova blinked. "Bringing back the dead won't prevent the war that—"

"Not them." Margaret shook her head. "My father. My sister."

The Goddess of Death grinned, her dark eyes glistening as she stared across the distance. "I told you before that we couldn't save your father—"

"You're a god! You have powers and magics I don't even begin to understand. If there were ever someone in this world with the power to do what I've asked, it's you. I am not *asking* you. This is something you will do, or I will—"

"You'll what? Send your pet Amaskan after me?"

Margaret frowned. "If you don't do as I ask, I will ensure that every ruler and citizen of the Little Dozen Kingdoms knows who and what they serve. I will see your name a footnote in history, something people utter when they remember the old ones we worshipped before the awakening."

The very air in the room stilled with the flash of light, and Margaret inhaled nothingness. Her lungs seized, and when she sought the orb, Itova's face swirled in a cloud of icy mist. "You think me powerless, little queen? I am the Goddess of Death and Winter. The cold answers to me, as it was I who brought forth growth after the long war...."

As the Goddess spoke, her hands—more like ethereal claws than fingers—reached for Margaret, who unsheathed the short sword at her waist. The Goddess laughed as Margaret swung the sword in an arc where it passed harmlessly through her ethereal claws.

"Did you really think you could harm a god?" asked Itova.

The knowledge that she couldn't chilled Margaret more than the frost that developed around the orb. Itova's face, more solid than before, shifted through the glass as she leaned out from the orb the way one would lean from a window. The temperature in the room plummeted. Margaret's vision swam as her lungs cried for air, and she slammed her sword's pommel into the orb.

For a moment, there was only the cold and the burning of her lungs as glass shards rained down from the orb's pedestal. Then oxygen rushed into the room, filling her lungs as she gasped in the sudden darkness. Her hands trembled as she stumbled into the council chamber where the sudden flood of candlelight made her wince. Margaret wrapped her fingers around the dented candelabrum, but try as she might, she could not turn to face the destruction in the orb's room.

Or what it meant.

32

Bredych kept to the night's shadows by habit as he crept across the courtyard. Sleepy guards were stationed at various junctures, though if they spotted him, they paid him no mind as he made his way to Mademe's and the messages that awaited him.

It wasn't that he needed secrecy to receive them—their codes ensured their safety—but he wished the silence of late night to read them. Based on the news from the border, the King of Shad remained unfortunately alive—a fact that would complicate whatever Queen Margaret decided to do moving forward. At the bar, Mademe retrieved a short stack of notes and passed them to Bredych. Each one bore a single circle scratched onto the folded parchment.

The first message, from a contact he had in Tarmsworth, was confirmation that the Order hadn't killed Leolin's father. He scanned the notes, and then tucked them into his bag. The second message bore a spot of blood at its corner. Whatever news this brought, it came at a cost. His fingers unfolded the message, and he frowned.

The king lives. I have failed. He marches on Alexander.
–G

Bredych cursed. The very action he'd hoped to avoid by killing Adir now spread-out before him. He opened the third and final message.

Master,

Word's reached me that you're in Alexander and are advising Queen Margaret. I hope that this information's accurate and that this message finds you before the battle arrives in Alesta, as it soon shall. Word in the Halelind Court is that King Marco has answered the Shadians' call for assistance. Their armies can be seen preparing for battle and just this morning, they began leaving in small clusters—presumably for the border. Lorcliff's ambassador speaks of his kingdom's support as well, which is bad news for Alexander.

May Asti bless and keep you, and may Anur's Justice prevail.

-M

He laughed, though his heart wept. *I've spent my entire life in service to a corrupt god who knows nothing of Justice. But I will protect the people of the Little Dozen Kingdoms as I have always done.* His cloak billowed behind him as he fled Mademe's, his fingers shredding the messages as he went. *Margaret must be warned.*

The guards noticed his swift motion across the courtyard upon his return, their eyes snapping wide as they observed the tenseness of his movements, but Bredych didn't stop until he stood outside Margaret's suite. "I must see Her Majesty immediately," he said to the guard outside.

"My apologies, but Her Majesty is elsewhere."

"Where?"

The guard shook his head, but Bredych didn't wait beyond half a heartbeat as he sought the council chambers, but they too were empty.

She wasn't in the audience chamber, nor the drawing room. The royal library was empty this time of night, as was her bower. Even the gardens were eerily silent. Bredych ran face-first into Leolin as he strode through the archway leading out to the stables.

"Leaving us so soon?" asked Leolin, the corners of his mouth tilted up in a false grin.

"Have you seen Her Majesty?" When Leolin shook his head, Bredych brushed by the boy and was stopped two footsteps later by a hand on his shoulder. "If you wish to keep that hand, I suggest you remove it."

Leolin released Bredych's shoulder and asked, "Why do you need to see Margaret?"

"I have news for her. News that is critical. Now unless you know her whereabouts, you'll have to scowl at me later." When the hand returned to Bredych's shoulder, the man dipped the shoulder and spun on his heel to face Leolin. "I don't have time to worry about your petty jealousy. Either leave me be or go mope in the gardens."

"Damned Amaskans are all the same," Leolin muttered. "Always convinced they're the center of the world."

"If it weren't for those 'damned Amaskans,' you wouldn't be here, boy."

The boy froze, one foot toward the gardens, and faced Bredych. "And what's that supposed to mean?"

Bredych unbuckled the clasp of the bag strapped to his belt and riffled through it until he found the scrap of parchment. When he shoved it in Leolin's direction, the boy frowned.

"What's this?"

"The answer."

"To what?" asked Leolin.

"Your questions. When I was at the Order, I wanted to know more about...well, you, which led me to Tarmsworth. I just received this message. Details on what happened to your father."

Leolin unfolded the parchment, his gaze scanning over the words. A storm gathered across his face and when he spoke, his words were soft like the clouds before the darkness broke over them. "I don't know what you're playing at, but this—"

"Is the truth."

"It's a lie. The Amaskans ordered my father killed. They used the *Tribor* to do it. My mother told me as much."

Bredych shook his head. "When will you wake up? The *Tribor* are the sworn enemies of the Amaskans. We'd never use them for anything. Besides that, your father was an Amaskan, one of many who visited Tarmsworth. I never could figure out why Sam was convinced the *Tribor* had a foothold there, but by his own words he was visiting a woman with whom he had fallen in love, a woman who had born him a son."

"But you have no proof that woman was my mother."

When Bredych snatched the paper from Leolin's grasp, the boy flinched. Bredych stabbed a paragraph with his finger. "Look at the description, boy. A warrior with black hair and blue eyes. Tall with a scar from ear to ear. Sound familiar?"

"But my mother...she said—"

"Your mother was an Amaskan. A trained liar. An assassin," said Bredych. The boy swallowed his words as he stared at the parchment. "Now why would she lie to you?"

The boy leapt at Bredych, who grabbed his outstretched arms and pulled the boy forward until their noses almost touched. "What purpose would I have to kill one of my people, hmm? Until this note, I had no clue your parents were together. Until I came to Alexander, I had no idea they'd had a child, and that you were he. Back then, I thought your mother nothing more than bones picked over by scavengers, so I ask you again, what purpose would I have to kill your father?"

Tears welled up in Leolin's eyes as he glared at Bredych, but he said nothing in response. Bredych released the boy's arms, and the boy staggered back.

"I don't know why your mother killed him—perhaps he threatened to tell me of her existence...or yours even. Perhaps it had nothing to do with the Order at all. Or perhaps it was the triangle that marked his ankle."

"My father was no *Tribor!*"

"Perhaps not. We thought him dead by *Tribor* hand as much as you did, so it's possible your mother marked him as such to distract us from discovering the truth. I can't give you all the answers, not yet, but perhaps this is a place to start in your search." *And a way to burry your anger toward me.*

Leolin snatched the parchment from the ground where it had dropped in their brief struggle. "I haven't seen Maggie since this morning," he said before disappearing into the darkness of the gardens.

Bredych frowned. At first, he wasn't sure which bothered him more, the ease with which he'd shaken Leolin or the knowledge that no one had seen the Queen all afternoon, but as he left the castle proper, the hairs on his neck stood on end.

Now was *not* the time to have a missing monarch.

33

F ather, I don't understand."

King Havin sat in one of the surviving tents as the shuffling of feet kicked up dust outside. "The Boahim Senate possesses powers unlike anything you and I have ever seen, Amar. While I'll not mourn the end of the Poncett line, I believe Queen Margaret correct when she says that your brother's death was their doing. Besides, I thought you said you wished them to pay, did you not?"

"I do, but frankly, splitting the army is a horrible strategy."

His oldest son paced before him as he tucked a curly lock of dark hair behind his ear. Havin stood and placed a hand on his son's shoulder. "Amar, the Pass wasn't the only place the Senate appeared. They also turned up before our Monpolian allies, who have now retreated. How will we take Alexander if our allies turn cowards?"

"Who will go north, and who will ride for Alesta?" Amar asked.

A shout rang out, and Havin strode forward to open the tent flap. Several wounded limped by as they followed a healer toward the opposite side of the encampment. One of them bit back a swear as he rubbed his arm, which hung from a sling made of someone's shirt. Havin allowed the flap to fall back into place before answering. "If the Senate remains in the North, I would see them destroyed. Besides, there's no one I trust more to ensure that whining bitch is removed from the throne than you, my son."

Amar grinned a rather boyish grin, a look Havin had missed of late. His son placed his fist on his chest as he gave a brief bow. "We will leave as soon as the men are able."

Once his son was gone from the tent, Havin spread out his map across the rickety table. Half his army dead, missing, or wounded, and while the Alexandrians had suffered similar losses, splitting their numbers further would leave the Shadian army on potentially equal footing with the Alexandrian army. At least until Halelind arrived. Havin sighed as he stared at the map. Too few people spread across too much land wasn't a way to win a war.

Where in the Thirteen Hells is the Halelind army? Only thirty would ride with him north to Monpoli while twenty worked on finishing the replacement bridge. Assuming his allies arrived before the war's end, they would require a way across the Pass. *Anur, let the senators remain in Monpoli so that I might crush them beneath my horse's hooves. I will have justice for those who died by their cowardly hands.* The remaining men would follow his son toward Alesta. Havin grinned as he stared at the city on the map.

And if they should discover what remains of the Alexandrian army along the way, so much the better.

34

————

Perhaps it was the ale talking, or perhaps it was the sheer terror that coursed through Margaret's veins as she brooded in the back corner of the *Hanged Man's Tavern*. Either way, she smiled when she spotted Bredych hovering near the door, his expression unreadable for a moment before it fell.

He eyed the surrounding patrons, most of whom were face down in their own pools of misery before sliding into the empty seat beside her. Up close, the lines in his face burrowed deeper than normal. "I've been looking for you for candlemarks. There is news we must discuss and it can't be here."

"Whatever news you have can wait. I'm enjoying a nice bit of ale if you don-don't mind."

His face blurred a touch around the edges as Margaret studied him. Had he always looked so...stern? She reached out a hand to touch the scar at his chin, and he caught it in the air before releasing it. "How'd you find me?" she asked. When Bredych tapped a finger to the black silken fabric that clung to her frame, Margaret frowned. "Oh. I'd forgotten I was wearing them."

"When word arrives that there's a drunk Amaskan in a tavern, one tends to investigate."

The barmaid brought another pitcher of ale along with another glass, the latter of which Margaret passed to Bredych. He refused to meet her gaze, and she asked, "Did you think me *her*?"

"For a moment."

"What changed your mind?"

It was then that he glanced up at her, his eyes full of pity. "Her smile was genuine." She frowned and took another sip. Bredych tilted his head toward Margaret's shoulder, where the clothing's threads had begun to unravel. "I thought them merely based on our silks, but they were hers, weren't they?" he asked.

"Adelei had several of these, though she burned in one. I...I don't know why I kept it. After the orb broke, I needed to get away, and they a-allow me to do that." Margaret reached for her glass of ale, but Bredych intercepted her.

"You've had enough," he said as he slid the mug away from her.

She could have protested, but the way the room moved if she turned her head too quickly left her stomach less stable than she liked. Instead, she stared at her hands. The black cloth wrapped tightly around her slender wrists, but rather than roughened hands bearing scars and scratches, soft, pale skin covered her hands. The image did not mesh with the symbol she wore, and Margaret frowned. Wearing her sister's clothing may have expedited her escape from the castle, but it had not given her bravery. Not even the liquid courage had truly done that.

"What did you mean by 'the orb broke'?" asked Bredych.

Her tongue stumbled a few times as she recounted the experience. When she had finished, Bredych eyed the glass of ale. "I've taken away our one means of calling for help. Not that help's coming from them," she said, then frowned. "Even worse, I tried to kill Itova. How long do you figure it'll be 'fore she comes for me?"

The hum of conversation in the tavern ceased as many heads tilted in their direction. Not even the ale's slight intoxication effect could muffle the severity with which the bar matron peered at them. After a pause, the tavern's occupants resumed their drinking and light chatter. "Before the Amaskans entered my life, my world was much simpler. Certainly shallower and safer. But Adelei saved my life and without her, I'd still be married to a prick who'd break me and steal Alesta, assuming I lived that long."

"If there's anything I've learned, it's that nothing's certain. Nothing's what it appears to be." With that, she tapped her finger on the table in front of Bredych. "Perhaps I should hear your news, but first, a question! You've had free movement through my city. Naughty you—my guards've reported you coming and going from...an establishment of ill repute." She slapped his arm with a playful hand. "You move like shadows through my world. What was I saying? Ah, the question! The way the blind *Tribor* died...did you kill him?"

His face remained an expressionless wall as he met her gaze. "Yes, he was *Tribor*."

"Leolin doesn't trust you—says you'll be the death of me —but I've seen goodness in your heart. You loved my sister and would do *anything* to serve Justice,. Prove him wrong by being—by telling the truth. Is there anyone else you've killed or attempted to kill while in my service?"

"Yes."

"Who?" she asked.

"Is this information you really wish to know? And if so, is it information you wish me to disclose...here?" Bredych glanced out of the corner of his eye around the tavern. Rather than a cough here and there or a mild mannered disagreement, a moderate din of chatter now hummed in the background.

A man in a long gray cloak stared at them beneath long lashes from his spot at the bar. Margaret met his gaze for a moment, but no tattoo marred his jaw that she could see. Still, the fresh fuzz of hair across his head was circumspect, and she tilted her chin in his direction. "He one of yours?"

"Yes."

Only the ale's warmth kept her from frowning at this news. How many Amaskans did he have in Alesta? In all of Alexander? To him she said, "Tell me who."

Bredych poured some ale into the empty glass and took a sip before he answered. "I sent an Amaskan to kill the King of Shad. I thought if he were dead, we could end this war before it began."

Suddenly the ale did not feel like such a good idea as her stomach churned and bile burned the back of her throat. "Was this person...successful?" she asked.

"No."

"Does the Amaskan live?"

"Unlikely." With that, Bredych closed his eyes a moment as he swallowed another mouthful of ale.

On the one hand, Bredych had attempted to end the civil war in order to protect her, a gesture her father would have appreciated, but on the other hand, someone had died to try and save her people. She swallowed some ale to cover the foul taste in her mouth.

As much as the thought disturbed her, her father's journals had laid out plans to eliminate those he had thought a threat. How many of those plans had he had carried out? Had anyone been killed before on her behalf? Could she hold Bredych to a higher standard than her own father?

She closed her eyes briefly a moment before she said, "The Book of Ja'ahr says some very specific words against seeking vengeance."

"Indeed it does, as does it comment on the necessity of sacrificing a few in order to protect the many," said Bredych as he frowned. "I'll not apologize for my actions. They were necessary in an attempt to protect—"

"To protect me, twin to the daughter of your heart."

"Of course. And I would kill again if I thought it would protect you."

"Don't."

His sudden laughter left pinpricks across her flushed skin. "What do you think it is an Amaskan does? We make the choices others cannot. We take the sin upon ourselves so that Justice prevails. This war began long before your father's death. Long before you were born, I wager. No matter who Anur might be or how corrupt he may be, I serve Justice. You can sit helpless upon your throne and watch more die if you wish, but I refuse to allow more to die over a border squabble and petty gods who refuse to uphold their end of the bargain," said Bredych.

Her cheeks grew hot and she squelched the urge to dump her remaining ale on him. "You're right, but what can I do? The Thirteen'd strike me down."

Bredych touched a finger to her pale, smooth cheek.

"You wear the clothing of our Order and quote our holy texts as truth, and while you lack the mark, you serve Justice as honestly as any I have trained. Yet you forget the discovery that drives us now. 'Upon our honor, we will uphold our secrets and serve Justice. Until the day of Truth, we shall remain in darkness, but on that day, we will be the Light.'"

"I'm no Amaskan," she whispered.

"Perhaps not. Either way, everything has a time and a purpose."

Margaret shook her head, and the world swam. "They're gods, Bredych."

"Everything can die as death's a part of life. 'Created from the gods' fear, Itova ushered forth the death of a long year. All around her, green things shriveled and died, and the great beings that swam in the seas and roamed the lands lay down to sleep. But with the energies that flowed through the cold, Agaia honored her parents with a single blossom, one so beautiful that the world awoke from its slumber. For even in death there is life.'"

As Bredych stopped speaking, the world around Margaret grew hazy, and she mumbled, "I think your news'll have to wait."

A frown met her words, which she caught a brief glance of before the world grew dark once more.

The rest of the words eluded Margaret as bits and pieces chased her in her dreams. She chased a light beam through a field covered in black cloaks and blood until she stumbled upon a grave. Itova's face stared down at her from atop the stone, mouth wide as she screamed, yet no sound reached Margaret's ears. As she turned away, her skin burned.

There was more to what Bredych had said, something more about being the light, but no matter how far she ran, the light refused to spill its secrets. Like the Amaskan, the light remained enshrouded despite its goodness. Her skin burned as if a hundred suns spilled their rays across it, and when she dug at her skin with sharp fingernails, the field faded and with it, her skin.

Much like Itova, she screamed without sound as the world around her spun until she thought she might retch, and when she did, light burst out of her until there was nothing more to give....

Margaret opened her eyes to a room too bright as the sun beat down on her arms through the open window. It was her room, but the blaring light left her eyes gritty and sore as her head pounded in rhythm to her heartbeat. She was alone, a fact for which she was grateful a few moments later when she availed herself of the basin beside the bed.

There is being sick and then there is this.

Bits and pieces of the dream danced in her skull, keeping time with the events from the night before. If she moved carefully and slowly, she could function without vomiting, a feat she managed long enough bathe. By then, her lady-in-waiting stood outside the bathing chamber with a cup of something from her physician.

What she swallowed was almost as vile as what she had thrown up, but if it was anything like the concoction Adelei had given her the last time Margaret had drunk too much, it would be well worth the foul taste. A simple dress the color of new leaves lay waiting. For a moment, she considered wearing it—perhaps looking a little less like the fighter she was not would help—but where she was going required free-flowing movement, so she opted for a pair of riding breeches and a silk tunic the red of fall leaves. Too bad the majority of its beauty would be covered by the light leather armor. Better that than dead.

Not that she was likely to die in a forest, but.... Margaret shook her head to clear the grim thoughts. She allowed her lady-in-waiting to dress her and braid her long hair while she sat with her back to the window, then she left the room behind as she sought out the stables. One guard was all she allowed as she rode through her city and into the woods beyond the city walls. It had been sixteen years since her mother and she had fled Alesta, but the forest creaked and swayed even now, casting shadows across Margaret as she passed.

Her horse picked her way through a canopy of trees that grew so thick her horse's shoulders often brushed against their bark. Only when her horse balked did she dismount and hand the reins to her guard. "Remain here," she said.

The memory of the day her mother had died grew fuzzier and the trees changed with each passing year, yet she trudged her way through the dimness on instinct alone. *If I'm to wage war against the gods, I would say goodbye to my mother first and be at peace with Bredych.* Margaret pushed her way through the underbrush and into a clearing where a small stream trickled. Despite the peaceful water's sound, the canopy overhead blocked out the majority of the light, leaving the clearing dim and brooding. Exactly as she wanted it.

Dirty leaves clung to the hem of her long, belted tunic like moss clung to the surrounding rocks. The lightweight silk left her chilled as she lowered herself to her knees on the forest floor.

"This is my kingdom's darkest hour...or perhaps it only feels this way with the weight I bear," she whispered as she stared at the tree branches overhead. "I would say goodbye to my mother and ask her to understand the decision I make. I...I do not know to whom I pray or that my prayers will be heard by anyone."

Or that I even want them heard. It would depend solely on who is hearing them.

"If it is necessary for me to die, I can hope only that I find my end as bravely as my sister, but I would ask that my people not suffer. The King of Shad's conflict is with me and me alone."

Nothing moved in the forest—no birds sang or mole burrowed, nor did the wind blow or the fish splash. If anything, the water seemed to slow as time passed beneath the trees' shade. A stone dug its way into Margaret's aching knee, and she plucked it out from the soil and tossed it into the stream where it sank unceremoniously. "Adelei, if you can hear me—tell me what I should do. How do I keep my people safe?"

She waited until her teeth chattered from the cold before she stood. *No one's coming to save me. No apparition of a loved one will give me the knowledge I need to save the day, no matter how much I wish for it. Nothing but cold and darkness here. And me.*

This time when she stared at the trees, something stared back. Branches swayed in no wind as two eyes met hers, though whether foe or friend, she couldn't say.

We'll hope friend.

A voice smooth like silk tickled her ears with its sound, and she spun in a circle as she searched the trees for the source. The eyes had moved, this time to a bush a mere forty feet from her. Laughter danced in those eyes, and she frowned. "Who are you?" she asked.

"I would prefer not to say if you don't mind."

379

His voice, definitely male by the pitch and timbre, reminded her of someone, though *who* escaped her. A light tingle, like pinpricks, danced across her flesh for a moment before fading away. "How can I trust that you're a friend?"

"You asked for help, did you not?"

As she nodded, a flicker of light fluttered down from the canopy overhead. Halfway down, it sprouted wings and a beak, then feet, which it used to land on the ground before Margaret. The messenger pigeon bore Captain Fenton's bands on its leg, but how did it come to be here rather than the castle?

"Perhaps it's the help you seek."

Margaret flinched as the voice sounded over her shoulder, but when she spun, whatever watched her was gone. The bird waited as she removed the message. While it bore Fenton's signature at the bottom, it was the message itself that caught her attention. Three words—enough to make her blood run cold.

Shad and Halelind attack!

Halelind? That made three kingdoms with armies in motion. Margaret curled her fingers into fists. *I have no choice. Not if my people are to live. I was born of darker blood than this—blood meant to protect. My blood will have to be enough. I will be the light Bredych and Her Holiness spoke of.*

She tucked the message into a pocket as the forest sighed, a deep groan of wood and leaves. In the distance, a horse whinnied.

"Your Majesty!"

Her guard's panicked call sent her into motion as she

fled the clearing for the shadow's safety. She was a dozen footsteps from the guard when an arrow struck him in the chest, sending him to the ground with little more than a thud. Who attacked mattered little as she mounted her horse. What mattered was that she escape. The thud of an arrow embedding itself in a tree sounded somewhere to her left as she urged her horse through the trees as fast as she dared.

There was no person in front of her to cling to, nor rain to chill her skin, but for a moment the ride through the trees transported her to that day, and she was five again and afraid. Something wished her dead like before. Dark memories of her past tore at her bravery, and Margaret crouched down as close to her horse as she could get while branches slapped at her arms and face. She followed the light ahead where the trees thinned. One last *thwap* sounded off to her side as something stung across the top of her shoulder.

Margaret clenched her teeth against the stinging wound and pushed her mount faster as they broke clear of the thick forest. As they turned to the road, smoke burned her nose. Not Alesta. It billowed further to the east than the capital city, but not too far as the smell increased. Her horse slowed as they encountered a mass of people at the outer gates, all clamoring for the guards' attention.

"Let us in!" a woman yelled as she held a crying baby in one arm and a basket in another. The cries were echoed by many as they pushed toward the guards who stood in front of the gate. Margaret's horse danced sideways with the press of bodies, then reared up as she clung to the pommel.

One of the guards made a grab for the reins and pulled the horse to the front of the crowd. "You'll have to wait like the rest," he said to her, as he led her horse closer to the wooden gate. "But perhaps we'll have you wait here—" He paused as his gaze found the deep blue castles embroidered into her saddle blanket, the castles small replicas of Alesta's castle, and his eyes went wide.

She held a finger to her lips, and his head wobbled as he leaned in closer. "Why are the gates closed?" she whispered.

"There's been an attack on the farmlands to the southeast, Your—" He swallowed her title at the brief shake of her head. "Orders came to bar the gates."

"Orders from whom?"

"Lieutenant Leolin."

While the mass of frightened people scared the guardsman, it was only a few dozen people. An amount the city could handle easily, and Margaret gestured at the gate. "Open it. Once these people are through, close the gates behind us."

"But they could be here to attack the city!"

She gestured to the people behind her. "Do these women and children look like soldiers to you? Do they look armed and fighting ready? They're farmers, sir. Folks who are fleeing the coming army. Now open these gates."

The guardsman nodded, then whistled. Several men scrambled on the other side to unbar the gate. When it opened, those behind her touched a hand to her horse or her booted feet as they passed. "Thanks be to you and yours," one woman murmured before she scurried into the city. Margaret urged her horse forward and once clear of the mass, she set him to a fast trot through the city. The war had reached Alesta whether she wanted it to or not.

Where were the Sadains? Perhaps Bredych had more

Amaskans in the city than she suspected. Perhaps they were not as outnumbered as she feared.

Perhaps the Thirteen will show up, and none of this will matter.

She pushed her horse harder.

35

A page found Margaret before she had a chance to locate either Leolin or Bredych, though the message he carried did not change her destination. In fact, it only hurried her steps toward the council room. She sent the page off to find both men and settled in the chair at the table's end to wait. With the orb smashed, the room's silence took on a protective sense, whereas before it had felt overwhelming with the knowledge that someone *could* be listening. For the first time since her father's illness had sent him to his bed, she leaned back against the chair's deep cushion and relaxed...at least until her gaze fell on the messages in front of her.

The first message was a plea for help from Estona, a panicked cry from their queen that left Margaret grateful she had not eaten anything. The Monpolian army had engaged Estona at their border, leaving Estona unable to come to Alexander's aid. Her eyes fell to the shift in penmanship, rapid scribbles made in low light. Probably sent before the ink had dried if the smudges were any indication.

I worry greatly for my people as not even the Boahim Senate can save us. Before his death, did your father speak to you of the magical orbs used to call them in times of need? These orbs use a power understood only by the Holy Few. If he spoke not of them, speak to Her Holiness for guidance.

When I called for help, no senator answered my pleas. A mere servant crouched fearfully before the orb and when I spoke, he screamed as if my words flayed the skin from his bones. I know not what it means, only that the Senate cannot save my people.

I implore you—send aid! Else I fear Estona will fall.

If Margaret sent troops to assist, she would spread herself too thin and leave Alesta exposed. Margaret laid the message aside and rested her head in her hands a moment before splitting the next wax seal.

The second message confirmed what she had learned in the forest—Halelind had joined Shad in the civil war. Their troops had crossed over the Pass a week before and now sat posed to ride on Alesta alongside a portion of the Shadian army.

The third message merely cemented her resolve to leave Alesta, a decision her council would not take well. Word from Captain Fenton placed King Havin's son at the head of the Shadian army. Whatever his plans, Margaret should be there. Leading her people as a leader should. The only purpose she served in sitting idle in Alesta was to make a target of the city and further endanger her people.

She nearly dropped the fourth message, another from Estona, as the words made little sense.

Queen Margaret,

I implore you, please send assistance as my people cannot withstand the combined armies of Monpoli and Shad. Worse still, I fear the Boahim Senate has fallen.

Words to the orb fell on destruction and darkened halls until the representative from Alexander appeared early before this morning's dawn. I know not how it happened, but cousin, Senator Whitlen is dead. My representative to the Senate has fallen. What am I to do? Who will stop this war on behalf of my people?

Rumor is that others of the Senate have fallen. If you can't end this conflict with Shad, perhaps you could lend your assistance and keep my people safe. Perhaps we can help each other.

Signed,

Queen Catia Racci II

Whitlen is dead? But how? How does a god die? Something hummed in the background—yammering fragments of words that were all vowels and made little sense as her brain whirred. It wasn't until Bredych's voice cut through the din that the world shifted back into sharp focus.

"Your Majesty?"

Margaret folded the message and tucked it beneath the others. "I'm sorry, Bredych. I must not have heard you come in."

"You called for us."

When she glanced over his shoulder, Leolin stood nearby wearing a slight frown. "Messages have been arriving for most of the day," she said as she pointed at the short stack. "I need to see Her Holiness, and while I'm speaking with her, I have tasks for you both."

"What news from the good captain at the Pass? From your face, I'd call it grim," said Leolin as he took in the leather armor she wore.

"Specifics will wait. Leolin, please send half our remaining army to the north. Monpoli has attacked Estona, and Queen Catia requests aid," she said.

He shook his head, his black hair reflecting the candle light, and for a moment, her stomach lurched as she stared at him for a moment longer than necessary.

I might not see him again. She tucked the messages into her pants' pocket. *I won't be here to defend, and thus, there will be no reason to attack Alesta. I have no other choice.* "While this leaves us spread thin, we need all the allies we can get, which brings me to your task, Bredych."

He ran his hands through his hair. "I worry what task you have for me with a decision like that, but I am yours to command nonetheless."

"King Adir of Sadai and your Order have pledged their support. I would call upon that support now. We need every available Amaskan and as many of King Adir's troops here as he can spare. Bring them in from the border."

"Even if every Amaskan in the Order were here tomorrow, they couldn't fight an entire army, let alone several. It will take a few days, but the Sadain army can be on the move tomorrow," said Bredych.

"We must help Estona. To ignore their plight is to lose another ally to the Shadians."

Bredych nodded, though his wrinkles wore wrinkles as he scribbled notes on a scrap of parchment. "May I ask what reason you have to seek out Her Holiness? Have you found something new regarding the Thirteen?"

"Senator Whitlen is dead."

Both men froze, though Leolin recovered first. "How is that possible? She's one of the Thirteen."

"Unless we were wrong."

Even speaking the words sent a chill of excitement through Margaret. "Not that I relish the woman's death, but if the Senate is mortal...."

"That could change everything! We might have a chance—"

Margaret held up a hand to interrupt Leolin. "But we won't without help," she said as she rose from her chair. She didn't wait for them to respond. Once they did, they would pull the truth from her. Then they would spend the evening debating her plans, and by the time she escaped them it would be morning and more of her people would be dead.

She closed the door behind her, but rather than take the main hall toward the Holy Few's chapel, she stepped into the shadows of the empty Great Hall. Back to the wall, she waited as footsteps came and went.

One hundred heartbeats, then other hundred passed before she dared step out into the hallway. With Leolin and Bredych distracted, she sought her rooms where a small saddlebag was tucked into the corner. Another was stowed in the stables with her horse and carried her formal armor. Rather than start servants talking by stepping foot in the kitchens, Margaret sent her lady-in-waiting for food that would travel well. A simple note left on her desk would explain things after she was long gone from the city, and as she glanced at it, her heart grew heavy in her chest.

May Leolin forgive me.

Without another look back, she left her rooms, saddlebag slung over her shoulder. A few minutes' walk through the courtyard brought her to the stables where Her

Holiness waited. "Thank you for agreeing to meet me here," said Margaret.

"An odd choice of venue."

Margaret shrugged. "I needed to ensure privacy. Not many would think to look for me here."

Her Holiness turned her gaze on Margaret—an inquisitive look that left her shifting her weight from one foot to the other. Though she wished to look away, Margaret refused to give into the squirming of her stomach. A tingling sensation like sewing needles prickling her flesh danced across her body—similar to the way the orb had made her feel.

"You've spoken with the Thirteen."

When Her Holiness spoke, the words were a statement of fact rather than a question, and Margaret nodded. "I think so. Though I'm not sure why I'm still alive."

"And why would the Thirteen wish you dead, Your Highness?"

The prickling sensation returned, and Margaret said, "Whatever it is that you're doing, stop."

Her Holiness flushed, a rare reaction in Margaret's experience, and the feeling of needles disappeared. "How did you—never mind. What reason would the Thirteen have to kill you? What message did you receive?"

A horse nickered in response to the tension in Her Holiness's voice, and child stepped through the doors at the stable's end. His eyes grew wide when he spotted them, and he ducked out again before he had done more than blink. "I need to be quick." Margaret sighed. "Whoever it was came shrouded, but warned me that Halelind and Shad have attacked some of the nearby towns. They march for Alesta. As to why they would want me dead, I was hoping perhaps you would know the answer to that. What reason would the

Thirteen have not only to orchestrate this civil war but to murder hundreds of their followers in the field?"

The look Her Holiness turned on Margaret could have shriveled the hardiest of flowers, yet she met the woman's gaze firmly. "Your Highness, the Thirteen cannot be held responsible for the actions of its people. What the Boahim Senate has done—"

"Your Holiness, I would know the truth of this. The Holy Few have access to information—histories and stories well beyond any record the royal family has access to, so if anyone would know, it would be you. Are the Boahim senators the Thirteen?"

"You speak in riddles, Your Highness."

"Do I? Even the histories available in my father's library speak of the possibility."

Her Holiness shook her head. "There are stories, written by men laced with evil or touched by insanity. Pay them no mind."

The words were evenly spaced and almost monotone, and Her Holiness's posture was calm, almost relaxed as she scratched a horse above his nose. Nothing about her gave Margaret any indication if the woman told the truth, and Margaret clenched her teeth.

Rather than give Margaret the answers she sought, Her Holiness gestured at the bag Margaret held. "Taking a ride somewhere?"

"I already have." The lie fell easily from Margaret's lips. "The forest was where the Thirteen found me, followed shortly by an assassin who killed my guard and tried to kill me. I had wondered if the Thirteen sent the assassin, though it made little sense. Why warn me of an attack only to attack?"

"Only Itova knows the time and manner of one's death."

Unless Itova is dead. But gods do not die. Margaret frowned. "Your Holiness, do you believe the Thirteen are truly immortal?"

The prickling sensation returned with an intensity that left her breathless. Her feet refused to move, as did her arms and hands. "What have you done to me?" Margaret asked.

Her Holiness placed her thumb between Margaret's brows, and the spot burned slightly as the woman spoke in the old tongue. Margaret's vision dimmed, and she dug her nails into her palms. The stable returned with a flash of light, and Her Holiness stepped away from Margaret. The horse behind her whinnied while dancing in his stall.

"How did you do that?" asked Her Holiness.

"Do what?" When Her Holiness reached out to touch her, Margaret knocked her hand away. "Your Holiness is a much respected leader of the Holy Few, but despite my upbringing telling me I should bow to your wishes, I'll not allow you to touch me. You're doing something to me, something that burns of magic."

The woman should have flinched at the word, but Her Holiness merely sighed. "I am but a servant of the Thirteen. Yes, there is information known only to the Few, and skills practiced by the Few in service to the Thirteen. I believe that the Thirteen are gods, yes, and thus immortal. Their existence since the beginning of life tells us this."

Margaret frowned. "But how do we *know* for certain? Senator Whitlen is dead—"

"Making her a mortal, yes?"

There was that stillness again in Her Holiness—a calmness that baffled Margaret. If the Boahim Senate was mortal and not the Thirteen, how had they killed so many at the Meridi Pass? "They used magic, like you," she whispered.

"To use magic is a slight against the Thirteen. Only those healers and Few chosen would attempt to harness the Gods' power, Your Highness. What happened at the Pass could only be at the hands of a great evil, one I fear may be leading you toward decisions that will harm more than just your person."

The thought had not occurred to Margaret, and her breath caught in her throat. Gamun, her former husband, had been evil. Perhaps his touch had changed something in her, led her down a path of questioning that would lead her people to ruin. Even Adelei, by the Senate's reckoning, had been an evil doer, though Margaret pushed that thought aside.

"May I?" asked Her Holiness.

When she reached forward to touch Margaret's forehead, Margaret leaned forward in acceptance. Albeit brief, the tingling left her ears ringing and her toes curled in her boots. The lines around Her Holiness's mouth deepened as she stared at Margaret.

"He blessed you. Did you know?"

"The Thirteen? I don't understand. You said evil—"

"I was mistaken. His blessing has been guiding you, not evil. I wish you light feet and safe travels, Your Highness," said Her Holiness as she strode away from Margaret, her robes leaving slight swirls in the stable's dirt floor.

Margaret's heart pounded in her chest as she tread the ten feet to her horse's stall where she grabbed the waiting saddle bags. *I don't know whose blessing I have, or how she knew I was leaving, but I'll accept it. We need all the help we can get.* Rather than take her pony—a prancing mare of gentle breeding and easily recognizable—Margaret carried her bags further down to Leolin's horse.

Dark, black eyes stared at her from a golden brown stallion a good four hands taller than her pony, and she made a mental note to thank Master Bredych for encouraging her to train on horses other than her own. She offered up a dried apple chunk from her pocket, and the horse whickered as he tickled her palm with his lips. He eyed her as she entered the stall and set about saddling him, and another apple piece was offered and accepted before she tied the saddle bags to the saddle.

From the stowed packs, she removed a simple head scarf, which she tucked her brown hair beneath, and a leather helm, which she donned before offering the third and final apple piece to the horse. He munched on it as she led him out into the courtyard, where a stable hand gave her a leg up into the saddle.

It was time for her to be the leader her kingdom needed, and to do that, Margaret had to be *with* her people. Not hiding in the castle to tremble with fear but riding with her army as they fought to protect the Little Dozen Kingdoms. Her stomach trembled at the flood of pictures her mind painted, grim images of blood and body parts as people cried out in pain, the clinking of metal on metal, and the smell of rotting flesh. For a moment, Margaret almost dismounted.

She was no war queen. That would have been Adelei had she ruled.

"Is there anything else you need, milady?"

The stable hand hovered near her ankle, and she shook her head. Before she talked herself out of it, she urged the horse forward at a slow trot. Margaret rode through her city in armor that had never seen battle, with a horse that was not her own, and a tremor in her chest that left her flinching at every sound.

Too bad blessings don't give you answers. I could use some about now.

The guards didn't stop her as she rode through the gates, though a part of her wished they had. She knew how to sign treaties and how to ask her advisors what she should do, but no one had taught her how to lead or wage war. Smoke snaked its way through the sky as something burned in the distance. The clouds overhead gave way to rain as Margaret urged the horse forward toward the smoke.

I guess it's time I learn how to do both.

36

The acidic taste of burnt wood increased the further Margaret traveled from Alesta. As the sun approached the horizon, she rode through the town of Antines. Those who weren't walking or riding to Alesta, burned their food stores. The sight of these men, dark circles beneath their eyes, destroying that which had sustained them, left a hollow pit in her stomach. One of them paused as she approached and when he held up his hand, she slowed her horse.

"You don' wanna be headin' that way, milady. Them Shadians, their army isn't more than a day's ride from here," he said.

"So close?" Margaret urged the horse forward at a steady pace. When had the Shadian army made it this close to Alesta? Where was Captain Fenton and the rest of her army? The horse shook his head at her mixed signals. Every snapping twig left her glancing this way and that, yet she pushed on as the sun fell asleep. Darkness threatened to rob her of the trail, and she dismounted to lead her horse on foot.

Glowing embers greeted her before the moon did as she approached a small village. Muffled chatter reached her a moment before an arrow landed at her feet. The horse reared back, and Margaret fought not to lose the reins.

"Who goes there?"

The low timbre was strained, though oddly familiar. Shadows narrowed his wide nose and equally wide jawline as he stepped out of the shadows beside her horse.

He reached his hand out until Leolin's horse snuffled his palm. "Woah, woah. Easy now," said Captain Fenton, then he bowed. When he rose, dark circles warred with bruises for dominance beneath his eyes, and the corners of his cloak were tattered and charred. "Your Majesty, why are you riding this way? And without guards?" he whispered.

"I was looking for you. My place is with my army—"

Captain Fenton pointed at the encampment ahead where several dozen men and women gathered. "You've succeeded. Other than those to the north, you're looking at what is left of your army, Your Majesty."

For a moment she forgot to breathe. Three hundred went to the Meridi Pass, and this was all that remained? Margaret's legs trembled, and Captain Fenton tightened his grip on her arm to steady her, a necessity that set her teeth on edge. *They flee with the Shadians behind them, so why is it that I am the one relying on him for support? This is not how I intended to lead my army.*

The world swam, yet she squared her shoulders and shook off his helping hand. "Captain, how did our army come to such a state? Did so many die in the Senate's attack?"

"Many did, yes. Please, Your Majesty, come sit by the fire."

Margaret led the horse into the village, taking care to

step over the charred remains of what had been someone's home. Whispers spread through the makeshift camp, and a soldier, not much more than a whip of a boy, offered to take her horse. The men and women at the nearest fire shifted to make room and from somewhere, a mostly clean blanket was spread on the ground for her. Tired and wounded, they gave her what little comforts they had, and she blinked back tears as she took a seat beside them.

When Captain Fenton spoke, his voice crumbled like the town's burned remains they camped in. "You have no idea the destruction the Senate wrought at the Pass. It isn't possible to put into words. At this point, it's less a 'pass' and more a chasm. I've never seen anything like it."

"Your message spoke of fire that rained from the sky and earthquakes, but what did they do exactly?" asked Margaret.

"I'm not exactly sure, Your Majesty. One moment, we were engaged with the Shadians and the next, it was like we stood in a firestorm. I still bear the burn marks. The ground shook and split apart as people attempted to flee, but no one could move. We were frozen in place while white hot light tried to rip us apart. The ground opened and those who weren't burning were swallowed up. I don't think I'll ever get the images out of my brain. When the screaming stopped, the senators were gone along with most of your army."

"Why begin a war only to end it?"

Captain Fenton frowned. "I...I don't know, but that was magic, Your Majesty." He placed two fingers against his forehead before taking a swig of water from his waterskin, which he passed to her. She followed his example before asking for him to continue. "At first, no one did much of anything. We were all too busy helping those who survived, which wasn't much, Your Majesty. Then the Shadians attacked."

"And it weren't just the Shadians, Your Majesty," said a soldier to her left. "There were many colors on the field."

"The Halelinds. Monpoli, too, I would guess," she said.

"Monpoli's still engaged in the north, but the Halelinds arrived soon after the Pass fell. They didn't seem to lose as many as we did. With no help coming, I ordered the retreat." Captain Fenton shook his head as he stared at his hands. "I'm a coward, and I'm sorry for it, Your Majesty."

Margaret reached out and patted his hand. "You aren't a coward, Captain. You were surrounded and outnumbered. Had you stayed, I'm sure you would be dead, too."

Words of agreement and encouragement spread through the camp, and the captain gave a faint smile. "It's polite of you to think so, but my job is to protect this army and this kingdom. So far I've failed. Worst yet, half the remaining Shadian army's only a day's ride behind us. If we weren't so damned exhausted, we'd still be running toward Alesta."

"You said 'some,' but not all?"

Captain Fenton shook his head. "King Havin went north with some of the army. The rest followed us under his son's command."

"Havin rides for Estona," said Margaret.

"If that's true, we're in trouble. With no help from them, they'll crush us."

"Monpoli engaged Estona before they could send help, though the Sadain army should arrive in a week." *If we survive that long.* She didn't speak the words, but those seated at the fire heard them as their shoulders fell.

Fenton elbowed a man to his left and pointed at a bag in the distance. When the man handed it to Fenton, he fetched a scroll from it, which he unrolled in the fire light. A rough map of the Little Dozen Kingdoms spread out before her, and Fenton pointed at the Meridi Pass. "With the Pass gone, any support we were going to get from across the river is cut off. The Halelindians were delayed as they took the northern bridge. The good news is support can't reach the Shadians either."

"Thank you," said Margaret. When the captain glanced up from the map, his brow furrowed, she added, "I've spent the past few months surrounded by those who think me incapable of strategizing or planning."

"No one rides into danger without a plan. If your advisors don't see it, perhaps it's time for new advisors." He pointed at Sadai and shrugged. "You said the Sadains reach Alesta in a week?"

Margaret nodded. The grim looks at her confirmation made her stomach turn, and she forced her mouth into a smile. "We've the help of King Adir and...a spectacular group of fighters, not to mention those under Lieutenant Leolin's command. You have survived more than most, which means the Thirteen surely smile upon you."

Little words offering little hope, yet her army carried her name in murmurs and whispers as night settled in around them. A lean-to tent was offered to her for the evening, and the survivors gave hearty handshakes and deep bows to her as she passed by. Many of them injured and all of them blood stained, they looked upon her like a beacon of hope, and as she lay on a blanket on the ground, her stomach twisted and writhed. Captain Fenton had said no one rode into danger without a plan. They trusted her to save them. To save Alexander and the Little Dozen Kingdoms.

To have a plan.

But she had nothing. Certainly not against the Thirteen who wielded forbidden magics. A rock poked through the thin blanket, digging into her shoulder, and Margaret blinked back the tears that threatened to spill. What right did she have to complain about a rock? The people—her people—slept on little else while their injuries cried out for relief.

Margaret sat up and pulled her knees against her chest. Every cough and groan added a stone's weight to her shoulders as sleep eluded her. Sometime after the camp quieted, she lay back down to stare at the stars overhead as the sky grew darker, then lighter again as predawn approached.

Sometime after, she drifted into a half-sleep where she walked across a valley of charred ash. Up ahead, someone in black leather armor knelt before a stone cairn. The rocks crumbled as Margaret approached, and the figure spun on her heel to glare at Margaret.

"It fell because of you." Like looking in a mirror, the figure stared at her as it unsheathed a short sword.

No one else could look at her with such disappointment, and Margaret said, "Adelei, I'm sorry. I didn't mean to destroy it. Whose cairn is it?"

The figure tilted her head, then closed the distance between them. She stopped a few inches from Margaret, their noses almost touching. But the nose was too long, and it was narrower than Adelei's. The furrowed brows on her face were less dense. The figure held out the sword to Margaret, and when she accepted it, the figure smiled.

"You're not Adelei," said Margaret, and the figure shook her head. "Are you...me?"

"Yes."

Close up, the armor was certainly hers, as was the

sword, but the woman wore a confidence Margaret did not. When Margaret frowned, the figure said, "If you wish to fix it, you must pull it together."

The words dimmed, and she strained to listen. *Pull it together?* Margaret glanced down to the stones, which glittered in contrast to the ashy earth. "I am doing the best that I can. Papa never—"

"Pull it together!" her other self shouted, and Margaret winced as the sound bounced inside her head. The figure placed strong hands on either side of her face and stared at her a moment.

"Pull them together."

Something touched her shoulders as hoofbeats crunched debris, and she shook her head against a sound that made little sense. Margaret closed her eyes, and when she opened them, the makeshift tent surrounded her once more. A rock dug into her shoulder blade, while outside a horse dug at the charred remains of a trough. When their meaning hit her, the words stung like an unrelenting splinter. It was a dangerous idea, but one that might work.

Assuming she could get to the Pass.

Assuming they would meet her there.

There were many assumptions in her plan, but she smiled as the first hints of true sunlight touched the horizon. It could work...assuming she didn't die first.

THE RETURN RIDE TO ALESTA REMAINED QUIET WITH the exception of occasional muttering once the rain began. The gates opened to a flurry of activity, and as they entered the city proper, Leolin stood nearby, his face haggard and pale. "What were you thinking, leaving Alesta—"

Before Margaret could do more than open her mouth, Captain Fenton held up his hand to interrupt Leolin. "Lieutenant, I would remind you who you're speaking to."

While the comment stopped his words, they didn't stop Leolin's forward momentum as he rushed to Margaret's side. Looking down at him from his horse, she frowned. Captain Fenton believed her capable, so why didn't Leolin? The question rankled her, and when he offered his hand to help her dismount, she ignored it. "I have need of your horse a moment longer, Lieutenant. Captain, if you would see to organizing what troops remain here, I will ensure that our injured are looked after."

Those who were able followed their captain, while the injured followed her to the castle. For once, Leolin held his tongue as he trailed along behind her as they passed through the city's interior walls. Refugees huddled in corners or in homes overflowing with people, and she glanced toward the forest she could not see. *Whoever you are, if you really mean to lend aid, my people could use some about now,* Margaret thought.

At the castle, she sent a page for Roland, then pointed into the entry hall. "Leolin, please see that these injured are set up in the Entry Hall for Roland."

"Yes, Your Majesty. Master Bredych is awaiting you in the Great Chamber."

"The Great Chamber?" she asked.

Leolin nodded, then motioned for the injured to follow him. Margaret hurried toward the stairs. If he waited in the Great Chamber, there were important guests awaiting her. *Perhaps the Sadain?* When she reached the third floor, she paused at the top of the steps to catch her breath before entering the large room across the hall. Two dozen heads swiveled in her direction, then bowed as she entered.

She motioned for them to rise, and Master Bredych held out his hand in the direction of a tall and slender man in gray robes. "Your Majesty, may I introduce Shai Hauman, Leader of the Mystics of Sadai."

Margaret inclined her head to keep the man from seeing the shock on her face. There had been rumors that Sadai employed not only healers but actual mystics. To stand before one left her both awed and terrified. "I am honored to have you in Alesta, Mystic Shai," she said and gestured for him to take a seat in one of the blue embroidered chairs toward the room's front. The others, all wearing similarly plain gray robes, claimed spots on benches or leaned against the walls as they waited.

"The honor is mine." Shai's Alexandrian was fluent, though rather than falling off the tongue like water, his words were slightly clipped and guttural. "Your Majesty, King Adir of Sadai sent us to you in hopes that we could be of use. Master Bredych has told me of the battle at the Meridi Pass, as well as the Boahim Senate's use of magics."

When she glanced at Bredych, he gave a slight shake of his head. So he hadn't told them of her suspicions regarding the senators. A servant poured refreshments for the gathered group, then exited at a gesture from Margaret. Curious as to his beliefs, she asked, "Are the senators mystics? Or something else altogether?"

Shai frowned. "Are you familiar with where the term 'mystic' came from, Your Majesty?"

"I assume sometime in Boahim's history it was used to describe those who use magic."

"True, but its roots come from the word *mysticos* in the old tongue, meaning secret. While not public knowledge, the mystics originated from within the Order of Amaska. The first Boahim Senate ruled that magic was of the

Thirteen and thus, for the Thirteen to use alone. The Order of Amaska disagreed. Partly because too many could be helped through magical healing but also out of fear. If someone chose to use it against the Senate, who would have the ability to stop them with magic mostly removed from the world?"

He took a sip of his drink before he continued. "The Little Dozen Kingdoms agreed with the Senate and time passed, leaving magic to disappear from the lands as the Order feared would happen. The mystics left the Order to practice what would appear to be healing magics, though we practiced other magics in secret. Our members spent many decades hiding in many kingdoms, afraid for our lives and the lives of our children. We were seen as vagabonds and thieves. We gained a reputation as 'those without a home,' though we are fortunate that King Adir favors us. He's given us a place to call home, and so we will defend it with all that we are."

"That does not answer my question."

Several mystics to her left bristled at Margaret's words, but Shai merely smiled. "But it does, Your Majesty. A mystic is only someone who uses magic. You've already seen the powers wielded by the Senate."

"You mentioned knowing more than the healing arts. We'll need that if we are to defeat the Senate."

"I thought you at war with the Shadians," said Shai.

"Yes, but what happened at the Pass cannot be ignored. The very people who are supposed to protect us have slaughtered hundreds of innocent people. I can't ignore that."

When the mystic nodded, she glanced around the room to count the number of gray robes.

Eleven versus thirteen. *Or is it Thirteen?* Margaret ground her teeth.

"I don't know if we'll be enough." Well-worn wrinkles like cart tracks deepened themselves across Shai's face. "They're powerful, Your Majesty. More powerful than anything I've seen. We know magic, yes; there's magic and then there's *magic*. We had no knowledge that spells that powerful still existed. If I'm honest, I don't think we can help much more than healing your wounded, but we will try."

The momentary surge of hope she felt crashed to the wooden floor, and when Master Bredych spoke to Shai, the words were little more than a muffled wah-wah as Margaret drowned beneath them. Half of the Shadian army would reach Alesta today, and she had little more than a city of scared farmers and eleven mystics. "Mystic Shai, I would see you help Captain Fenton. While we've wounded, the Shadian army will arrive at our doorstep soon enough. You may not be able to defeat the Senate, but for the time being you can help us keep the Shadians at bay."

Margaret rang a small bell on the table beside her, and a servant entered the room. "Please see Mystic Shai and his people to Captain Fenton."

As the trail of gray filed out of the room, Master Bredych sat down beside Margaret. "When was the last time you slept?" he asked.

"Two days ago maybe. I don't sleep well these days."

"Your Majesty, may I speak honestly?" When she nodded, Bredych cleared his throat. "In these months, you've become...important to me. You are so like your sister, Adelei, and yet you aren't. She would have left for the Pass as well, I imagine."

"She would have left before I did."

"Perhaps. You certainly left me with the same pit of worry in my stomach that she did many-a-time."

His laughter echoed in the empty room, and for a brief moment she could imagine it was a happier time and allowed herself to smile. "I suspect that's the duty of all children," she said.

"When you left, I worried I would lose you as well. I-I have something for you," he said as he dug through the pouch at his belt. When he removed the woven bracelet, Margaret gasped.

"Where did you get that?" she asked.

Bredych placed it in her hands. Faint though they were, the various grasses still held most of their coloring as she held it gently. "Adelei was wearing it when she arrived at the Order. I thought you might like it," he said.

Margaret tucked the bracelet into the armor she still wore where it settled close to her heart, and she blinked back tears. "I made that for her a few days before she... before she was taken. Thank you for its return and for her return."

He nodded. "I'm sorry for my role in taking her away from you. When I thought you might not return...well, I understand why you feel the need to lead your people. It's what you've been trained to do since you were a child. But I would ask, if you decide to put yourself in battle, that you would allow me at your side." He paused for a moment as the door opened. "I would accept that *sepier*'s pin you offered me before."

"Done."

There was a gasp, and Margaret glanced up to see Leolin's slumped frame bracing the doorway. "I came to tell you that the injured are being seen to, and that Captain Fenton is looking for you. Your Majesty." The last word was an afterthought as Leolin spun on his heel to leave.

"A moment, Lieutenant," she said. His shoulders tensed, but he remained in the doorway until she reached him. When she rested a hand on his shoulder, the muscles beneath it quivered in response. "Leolin, I—"

"Don't. There is nothing you can say that will make me accept him."

"I'm not asking you to accept him. I'm telling you to, Leolin. There are things that need doing, and I need to know that when I make the choices no one else can, my *sepier* will do what I say when I say it, without question."

Leolin glanced over his shoulder at her. Blue eyes that were normally open like the sky were shadowed by anger. "I would do anything you asked of me, Maggie. *Have done* everything you asked. Yet you would prefer a murderer be your protector."

"You may have done what I've asked, but you've questioned every choice I've made every step of the way. In the Senate, we have a common enemy that can apparently be killed. I must lead my people to a resolution that means saving more than Alexander. One that means saving Boahim."

"Boahim is long dead," he whispered.

"It doesn't have to be."

"It's foolish...." His words trailed off when she frowned at him, and he shrugged off the hand on his shoulder. "He's going to get you killed."

As he turned to leave, she wedged herself between him and the door. "Much like you, he would die before seeing me harmed. I know you hate him, but we need him to stop this war."

"You may need him, Your Majesty, but *I* don't."

Margaret did not stop him when he brushed past her, nor did she flinch when the door slammed shut in her face. He was acting the child, something she was intimately familiar with, but damn if she didn't need Leolin, too. With a groan, she turned to Master Bredych, who remained seated behind her. "Meet me in the gardens in ten minutes, please."

"Are you going after the boy?" he asked.

"No, but he'll meet us there nonetheless. I have an idea, but I'll need both of you to pull it off." Before the gardens, she needed to make a quick stop in her rooms. If she couldn't change Leolin's mind, perhaps a ghost could....

37

The well-worn leather brought tears to Leolin's eyes when Margaret handed it to him. Here amongst the roses his mother had loved, seeing her journal was like losing her all over again. "Before she'd earned the name Warhammer, my mother fought her way to her position as your father's *sepier*, often literally. But most evenings, she would write a little something in this journal. I never knew what she wrote about," he said as he flipped through the pages.

Mostly random thoughts or a few sentences about events in her life, the book held less than he thought it would. But seeing the slant of her writing, the occasional ink blot where he'd interrupted her thoughts—he could almost see the laughter in her blue eyes, and he blinked back moisture from his eyes.

"There's something I thought you should see," Margaret said. His shoulders tensed as she touched his mother's journal. When she pointed at a bookmarked passage, he clenched his fist at his side.

"When I arrived in Alesta, this should've been given to me with the rest of my mother's things."

"I'm sorry, but it wasn't with her belongings. It was with my father's."

Leolin pursed his lips together. It was possible his mother had given it to Leon—probable really, if he was honest about their relationship. "And you read it?" he asked.

"Yes, but only because it was unclear at first who wrote it."

He glanced at the passage she had pointed to, one written shortly before her death.

If there is nothin' else I've learned in this life, it's that love and trust can carry one through the darkest of days. I once had both, and while I think, in time, Leon'll forgive me, I suspect like most things in my life, that forgiveness'll come too late for me. Where Leon's concerned, I've been foolish and stubborn. The Book of Ja'ahr, which I'll admit I haven't read in too many years, speaks at length about trust. Leon says I'm still an Amaskan, but trust is everything to an Amaskan. Perhaps I'm nothin' but an old warrior now. But if I remember it right, the book says 'To Trust is to Love. How does one know if another is worthy of trust? By trusting. Only then will you know love.' It's somethin' I used to understand. May Delorcini help Leon to love and trust again.

This time, he couldn't stop the tears that spilled from his eyes. Somehow his mother knew her time had come, and even still she thought of how to make things right with Margaret's father. Leolin stared at the empty pages that followed her last entry. Nothing written to ease his mind or say goodbye, and he shoved the book back into Margaret's hands. "Why show me this?" he asked.

"Did you see the quote about trust?"

"Yes, and if you plan to tell me to trust Bredych, don't bother."

Margaret let out an exasperated sigh. "No, but I would ask you to trust *me*, Leolin, and before you say you do, take a moment to think on what it means to trust someone. You say you love me, but I have to wonder how much you can love someone when you don't trust them."

A bee landed on a nearby rose, and Leolin studied it rather than look at her. Maggie was as likely to befriend the King of Shad as Leolin was to accept Bredych.

Even if Bredych didn't kill Leolin's father, how could she ask him to forgive the man who attempted to murder his mother?

"I read through *The Book of Ja'ahr*." When Leolin frowned, Margaret added, "It was Adelei's copy—one she brought with her when she was sent here. I used to hate the Amaskans for taking her from me, but the more I learn about them, the more I realize how similar they are to the rest of us. Like us, they want justice to prevail and to live a life that is worthy of love and trust."

He scowled. Something moved across the gravel to his left, and when Leolin turned, Master Bredych approached. "Worthy of what? Nothing good has ever come from the Amaskans," said Leolin.

"You did, boy," said Bredych. The old man held a piece of parchment in his hands that was heavily yellowed with age. He didn't offer it to Leolin, but he glanced between it and Leolin as they stood in the gardens.

"Why is *he* here?"

Margaret rested her hand on Leolin's forearm. "We need every ally we can muster. Master Bredych is not our enemy. You must make peace with yourself and him before you can make war."

"I messed up, boy," said Bredych as he clutched the parchment. "I once was young and brash like you. It was that same anger and fire that's eating at you now that led me to slit your mother's throat."

While she meant well keeping a firm grip on his arm, her touch made Leolin's skin bristle. The way she adored the murderer made his stomach churn.

"There's much I never knew about...my sister. I never knew she loved." Bredych swallowed hard, his eyes glossy with moisture. "Your mother was damned good at her job—and because of that, she spent more time away from the Order than I liked. She was constantly traveling. Samuhel makes sense as your father, but what I couldn't figure out was how he died."

Like the gnarled roots of a rotting tree, Leolin's stomach twisted with each word. There was an odd logic to it, and bile rose in the back of his throat. "And? I assume if you're here that you've figured it out."

"For a while, as part of his cover, Sam ran a small inn in Tarmsworth."

Fuzzy memories of a small inn filtered through Leolin's brain, and of a man with a dark, scraggly beard. "Describe him," barked Leolin.

"He was a tall, quiet man, posing as barkeep. His appearance was changed as part of his cover, so he let his hair grow long and had a rather bushy beard to hide his tattoo. The Order managed to track down a record of your birth, though it only says you were born to a sword-for-hire sometime after the autumn festival."

"I...I remember something, but that still doesn't clear the Amaskans from killing my father. Bredych's already proven that he will kill whoever, whenever if it serves his purpose." Leolin threw his hand in Bredych's direction, upsetting a rose and sending a bee buzzing away angrily. Several pink petals fluttered to the ground, and he dug his boot heel into them.

"Look, boy, I don't know what happened between your mother and Samuhel, but I didn't order him killed."

Bredych shoved the parchment at Leolin, who took it with a scowl. The paper's corner crumbled in his grasp as he stared at a list of names, numbers, and scribbled notes in cramped handwriting. "What am I looking at?" asked Leolin.

Margaret leaned over to study the document. "I've seen these before. Reports from local constables on reported crimes are sent to the capital city." She pointed at the royal stamp at the document's bottom. "This one was sent from Tarmsworth to my father, though I doubt he gave it more than a glance."

Another scan through the list brought Leolin halfway down the page where the name *Sam Barach* was scribbled. The date was his birthing day....

Deceased male, possibly Tribor. Woman and child at scene. Woman states the man beat her before falling and hitting his head. Cause of death: accidental fall. Body taken for group burning. Discovered with additional body mutilation.

"On occasion, Samuhel was known to have a temper. It didn't manifest until his thirties, otherwise he never would have been taken into the Order, and once it did, he was given positions where his temper was less likely to cause a problem," said Bredych as Leolin stared at the parchment. "Maybe he threatened to tell me she had lived or maybe he threatened to take you away. I don't know what they argued about, but his death would bring questions. It's likely she used the *Tribor* tattoo and the cutting out of his tongue to try and hide what happened, including her involvement."

"No."

"Knowing Samuhel, she was probably well within her right mind to kill him."

Leolin shook his head as the garden blurred in a garish mash of too-bright colors. "I don't believe you," he muttered.

"You don't have to, but I've no reason to lie to you, boy. What would it gain me?" asked Bredych.

Something dark stirred within his mind, and he was eight and crouched in the corner of a room. His mother yelled at Sam, who shouted back and made to grab for Leolin. He had screamed, or had he only mumbled to himself as he shut his eyes? The bits and pieces were jumbled out of order, and he clamped his hands over his ears in an attempt to shut out the sound.

"Leolin? What is it?" Maggie's voice spun in the maelstrom of his mind, and he began humming a loud, obnoxious song he'd learned somewhere out near the border.

Something grabbed his arm, and he threw it off with a shrug. "Make it stop," he whispered.

"Make what stop? Talk to me."

Her voice again. "Make her stop."

A buzzing noise near his face set him spinning until he fell to his knees. When Leolin opened his eyes, Margaret crouched beside him, her eyes wide. "Make it stop," he whispered again, and Margaret frowned. "The sound. Can you make it stop?"

Bredych swatted the bee away from Leolin. "Is that better?"

The sound outside had ceased, but the sounds within his head looped until Leolin thought his head would split. "I can still hear it."

"Hear what?" asked Margaret.

"The sounds of her killing him."

"You were right to bring him to me, Your Majesty," said Mystic Shai as he opened his eyes and removed his hands from Leolin's head.

Margaret held his hand in her lap. Though he slept now, Leolin's sleep was uneasy as his facial muscles spasmed, and she winced when he squeezed her hand too tight. "Will he be all right?" she asked.

The mystic rubbed his temples with his fingers a moment before responding. "He doesn't recall more than bits and pieces of what happened, Your Majesty. His memories play like someone shattered a stained-glass window and hid the pieces throughout this castle. You might find one or two, but without looking at the larger piece, you'd never see what picture the window created to begin with."

"Someone messed with his memories."

Mystic Shai flinched. "How did you know that?"

"Something similar was done to my sister...by the Amaskans." A million questions ran through her head as she suppressed the urge to glance at Master Bredych, who stood guard at the door to her chambers. *That* conversation would have to come later. For now, she would listen to what the mystic could tell her. "Can you tell who did this to him? Or why?"

Mystic Shai kept his gaze on his patient but lowered his voice when he answered. "Your Majesty, I've been ordered by my king to give you whatever knowledge and skills we have that might help you win this war. I...I would have you know that the skill you speak of, the one used on your sister, is a skill known only to mystics. It's a powerful spell that few can manage."

"Are you saying the Order employs mystics to cast this spell?" He gave a slight tilt of the head, so slight she thought she had imagined it until he spoke again. "I was sworn not to tell you of this, but perhaps knowledge of such a skill could be of use to you as well."

"To toy with one's mind like that is...is evil!" she hissed.

"That depends upon your point of view, Your Majesty. What if a boy saw something so horrible that it left him broken? What if you had the power to help him forget so that he might heal? So that he might grow and live as a normal child should?"

Margaret squeezed Leolin's hand to keep from striking the mystic. "It's not your decision what a child should and should not remember. How dare you do something like this to him? To anyone!" Her voice rose as she spoke, but Master Bredych remained at the door. "Get out."

The mystic hesitated for a moment, then rose to leave. As he passed by Master Bredych, the Amaskan's gaze followed the man, though he said nothing. Once the door shut behind him, Margaret left Leolin's side, outrage in every step as she strode to Bredych's side. "How dare you play god, erasing and changing people's memories as if we're nothing more than playthings for the Amaskans' amusement," she said, and when he said nothing, she asked, "Was it you?"

"Was *what* me?"

"Was it you who had Leolin's memories erased?"

Bredych shook his head. "I didn't know the boy existed. How could I order it? What purpose would I have in giving him the answers he's sought if I were the one who removed them?"

"And Adelei?"

He closed his eyes a moment. "Your Majesty, there are things about the Order you do not and could not understand. Have I employed mystics? Yes. Have I ordered them to do things to protect my people? Yes. While I've not always made the correct decisions, I'll not apologize to you or anyone for those decisions I've made to protect them. Nor will I go back and ask forgiveness for every murderer killed or life saved."

"How do I know you're telling me the truth?" she asked as she studied his blue-gray eyes. Once she had thought them kind like her father's, but the calmness in them now sent a chill across her skin. "How do I know you haven't changed my memories, Grand Master?"

"I would never—"

Margaret jabbed her finger into his chest. "But you did it to *her*! You say you would never do it to me, but you played with your own daughter's mind." Like a child, he fell in on himself as he backed away from her, face and shoulders slumped. "She hated you for that, you know."

"I thought it necessary to protect the Order."

Hollow words from a hollow man. Margaret shook her head. "The Little Dozen Kingdoms are at war, Master Bredych, with an enemy more powerful than we understand, and you would have me add you to the war. I'll not battle a fourteenth enemy. Not today."

She turned her back to him—a brave move knowing what he was capable of even at his age—and returned to Leolin's side. "Tell your king I will use whatever military assistance he can provide, but we will not need the mystics' assistance."

"Your Majesty—"

"I'll not have my people or any others twisted by magic," she said.

"There are healing spells that could benefit your people. At least allow them to help with the injured."

She gathered Leolin's hand in her own as she watched him battle whatever shadow walked through in his memories. "And how would I know they were actually healing my people?"

"You're more like your sister than you know."

The words were a stabbing whisper to her heart before the door closed behind him. *Every time I think I can trust him, I learn something else to make me doubt him. Both of you*, she thought as she stared at Leolin.

A brief knock at the door interrupted her thoughts, but when she opened it, it was not Mystic Shai come to change her mind. Only a page bearing a slip of parchment. Her fingers shook as she opened it.

Senator Montero's arrived. He's with the mystics in the Entry Hall. -Captain Fenton

She was running down the stairs before the fear caught up with her, and when it did, she stumbled at the steps' base. Margaret caught the railing with an arm, then rushed down the hallway. At first, she wasn't sure what to make of the scene in the hall. Despite all the sick and injured who lay scattered in makeshift cots across the room, her physician Roland knelt beside a single cot. Mystic Shai and a dozen of his people gathered around it, obscuring the identity of the person who lay upon it, but nowhere did she see the senator who represented her kingdom. It wasn't until she drew closer that she saw the senator, his skin almost white next to the blue blanket that served as a pillow beneath his head. "What happened?" she asked as several mystics stepped aside to make room for her.

"Captain Fenton said the senator just appeared. Like magic," said Roland, who glanced sidelong at the mystics. "He opened his mouth to speak and then collapsed. I've been unable to wake him, Your Majesty."

Thinking about it made her stomach crawl, but Margaret asked, "Have the mystics tried to help him?"

A half-cry, half-cough escaped Roland. "Your Majesty, 'tis madness to use magic. Surely—"

"Mystic Shai, if you would try to wake him...and *only* to wake him," she said, and the mystic lay his fingers across the senator's forehead. The moment his skin made contact, the senator lurched awake with a wild gasp, and the mystic stumbled backward.

"That was not me, Your Majesty," said Mystic Shai as his hands trembled in front of him.

Senator Montero's eyes flitted back and forth in a panic until they found Margaret, and the man grabbed her hand. "Whitlen is dead," he cried.

"I know, Senator."

The man fell back against his makeshift pillow and closed his eyes. "She was beheaded. You were right, you know."

"Right about what?"

He inhaled sharply as his eyes snapped back open. When he looked at her, her nerves tingled as if her muscles were being tugged in several directions at once. "I tried to help you in the forest, but I've failed."

The room darkened, and Mystic Shai clenched his hands into fists. "Something is here," he said as he searched the room for the intruder.

Senator Montero pulled her attention back to him as he tugged at her hand. "I'm sorry, Your Majesty. I tried. I'm sorry."

The words made no sense, but she nodded as he searched her face. Whatever he sought, he found as he took one last breath and with his exhale, died. The hand that held hers shriveled, and she dropped it. Like a husk, the shell crinkled to the cot where it disintegrated into a powder, and she stared at it in horror.

It wasn't until she pulled her eyes away from the dust in her hand that she found his entire body had done the same, leaving nothing but clothing and dust where he had lain. Margaret screamed, or she attempted to do so, but her lungs burned, leaving her choking on air.

Mystic Shai dragged her away from the remains. "Stay back," he ordered as light returned to the room. He mumbled some words under his breath as Margaret's lungs cleared, and he edged forward to place a hand upon the dust. A faint yellow glow exuded from his hand, and when it disappeared, the mystic frowned. "There was great magic here, Your Majesty. I-I've never seen anything that powerful. Ever. Whatever power was here is now gone, along with our senator."

"What happened to him?" she asked.

"As near as I can tell, he died of exhaustion and...old age. His heart stopped suddenly."

Margaret frowned. "Senator Montero *was* an old man, but his body shriveled up and disintegrated into dust."

When Mystic Shai leaned close to her ear, her first instinct was to flee. If he touched her, Thirteen only knew what he could do to her, and her hand moved to the sword she carried. His gaze followed the movement, and he whispered, "I'll not hurt you, but what I need to say is for your ears only."

"Come with me," she said to him as she led him across the hall to a corner that was empty of all but an ornate vase on a pedestal. When he arched a brow at her, she added, "I'll not be alone with you, so you can speak here or not at all."

"What he said to you, did you understand it? He mentioned helping you in the forest, but he'd only arrived."

The forest! It had been Montero who had warned her, who had saved her life, but what had he meant by the rest? To the mystic she lied. "I'm not sure what he meant. Very little of it made sense."

"Your Majesty, he was old. Older than I can imagine. When I touched the remains, it was like touching the very bones of the earth, and then when the room grew dark, every living being mourned for his loss." Mystic Shai swallowed hard. "I know this is going to sound crazy, but...I think he may have been a god. With that much power and age and...I don't know, connection, I don't know how else to describe it."

You were right, you know.

He had answered the debate in Margaret's mind, and she hadn't even seen it. They were gods.

"Thank you," she said to Mystic Shai. "If you would excuse me...."

Gods who are dying.

Since the arrival of the Shadians at the city gates, Alesta had become Margaret's prison, though it would not be for much longer. A meeting with Captain Fenton that morning left her more than aware of the fighting outside the walls that had protected her and her family for generations, not to mention how difficult it would be to reach the battle outside.

Difficult, but not impossible.

Captain Fenton wished her to flee the city and she would leave, but not for the reasons he wished. Master Bredych had been scarce since their argument, not that she blamed him. The man had saved her life countless times and yet she doubted his motives and his sincerely. *Just as Leolin doubts mine. Broken people trying to save the world. Perhaps we are made for each other then.* Leolin remained silent, unable and unwilling to think about the fractured memories he held and what they meant. Not that she could blame him either.

No guard stood outside her council room. Every person who could be spared to fight was elsewhere, though Margaret paused at the door just the same. When she entered, silence was her only companion, and she held her candle out before her as she stared into the darkened orb's chamber.

"We've always had you to lean on. To call on in our time of need," she whispered, though the Thirteen could surely hear her thoughts before she lent them voice. "Even when you refused to save my father, the fact that I could ask, gave me more comfort than I knew at the time. It feels like a lifetime ago, and yet it wasn't even the turning of a year."

Margaret stepped closer to chamber's doorway, though

her candlelight did not protrude beyond the bookshelf. Perhaps magic prevented it from casting its light into the secret room, or perhaps the room was as broken as the orb.

"The time for indecision is over. Everyone must grow up sometime, myself included. Maybe the Little Dozen Kingdoms, too. Maybe we've outgrown our need for the Thirteen." When she crossed over the threshold into the room, candlelight flickered off the broken orb. "I've avoided this room out of fear that you still watched me, that perhaps you waited for me. That you would punish me for my insolence, Itova, but you can't. You're dead."

A few inches from the orb, glass crackled beneath her shoes. She brought her candle closer to the broken orb. Something dark coated its edges. With a trembling hand, Margaret touched the sticky substance, then brought her fingers closer to the light. A dark, reddish-brown liquid clung to her fingers.

Blood. But from what?

She was beheaded.

Montero's voice whispered in her head, and she tumbled back against the bookshelf where she leaned for more heartbeats than she could count. When the trembling stopped and her breath did not gasp, she knelt down beside the orb, candle held aloft.

There was more than glass on the floor.

38

Montero, whatever god he had been, had died to bring Margaret the information she had needed. It was not a sacrifice she could dismiss lightly, though she shoved away the image of Senator Whitlen's shriveled head. *That* she would deal with when this was over. For now, she sat at her desk with an inkwell and a stack of parchment. Well-armed with her notes on the Senate, she set about her next task—perhaps her final task as queen.

Writing a dozen compact messages left Margaret's hand cramped, but as she sealed the last scroll closed with her personal seal, she sighed with relief. A quick meal to replace the one she had lost in the orb's chamber, and it was time to send the notes to their destinations. She was halfway to the messenger pigeons when a tired but awake Leolin caught up to her.

"Why are you out of bed?" she asked, and when he held out his hands to help her carry the messages, she handed him half the stack. "Your orders were to sleep and keep sleeping until—"

"Until what? The Shadians overrun the castle? I'm fine."

Margaret shook her head. "'Fine' is not a word I would use."

"The memories aren't attacking me anymore, if that's what you're asking. One of the mystics gave me something to help mute them a bit."

She halted her steps to better look him in the eyes. There were worry lines around the corners but otherwise, he still appeared to be himself—right down to his usual smirk. "Leolin, the mystics are the reason you couldn't remember in the first place. They played with your brain the way they played with Adelei's. Why in the world would you allow them to do that to you again?"

"I know that I need to...deal with what I can only partially remember, but as you said, now's not the time. Not with a battle going on right outside," he said as they passed the lone guard outside the pigeon coop. "Now's not the time for a lot of things, including my overly stubborn attitude. I don't like Bredych. That won't change, even if you ask it of me, but placing you in the middle only serves to hurt this kingdom. And you. I really came to find you to say I'm sorry."

A cold knot rested in her belly as they approached the pigeons, and Leolin's words did little to thaw it. "Leolin, may I ask your advice on something?" she asked.

"As long as you tell me why we're carrying all these messages."

The goofy grin he wore was so reminiscent of his childhood self that she almost dropped her pile of scrolls. "While you were sleeping, Senator Montero arrived in the city."

Leolin's dropped the messages he carried, sending them

splaying across the table. "Thirteen Hells, d-did anyone die?"

"Senator Montero," said Margaret as she began inserting the messages into their color-coded bags. "He came to warn me...again. I don't have the time to explain the details, but the Boahim Senate *is* the Thirteen. Better yet, they can die. I've not figured out the how, only that it's possible, meaning my plan might work."

"The plan being what you need advice about," he said.

Margaret nodded as her fingers fumbled with the string. She had seen it done a dozen times, but for all that she tried, her trembling fingers could not attach the thin bag to the pigeon's back. Rather than strain the poor bird's wings, she ushered the bird back into its cage with a sigh. Perhaps not involving the pigeon fancier had been a bad idea.

Leolin placed his hand over Margaret's. "Whatever it is, it can't be any worse than the current state of things."

He had meant it as a joke, but the words stung. "I'm leaving for the Meridi Pass. These messages are a peace offering to each ruler of the Little Dozen Kingdoms." As she spoke, the color drained from his face. "Our enemy is not each other, but the Senate themselves. The Thirteen. Everything that's happened since the moment my sister was taken has been instigated by them. For what purpose, I don't know, but if we're to survive this, we must do it together."

"Maggie, no. Sacrificing yourself won't fix this. Your sister...that was Bredych and the Shadians. My mother was Bredych and the Shadians. Gamun was the Shadians. The Senate or the Thirteen or whatever the hell they are—blame them for what happened at the Pass, but this isn't some grand scheme."

"Then what is it?" When he shook his head, she said,

"You're not seeing the entire picture, just the frame, Leolin. Besides, I don't plan to sacrifice myself at all. These pigeons will go out ahead of me, inviting all rulers to meet me at the Pass in parley. If I can convince them to unite against the Senate, perhaps the Little Dozen Kingdoms will survive."

"You would make peace with the man who sent a scorpion into your bed? The man who had my mother killed?"

Margaret swallowed the lump in her throat. "There's a difference between peace and acceptance. I would have peace to protect the lives of all, whether or not it's easy."

"And if you're wrong? If you can't convince them?"

She gave a light laugh as she stared at her hands. Young hands, so unlike her father's. Inexperienced hands but not clean hands. Her hands had blood on them now. "My father never wanted me to rule alone. Honestly, he never wanted me to rule at all. He never thought I was capable, Leolin. Whether or not I want this crown, it's mine, and at some point, I have to wear it. If this is a mistake, it's mine to make. No one else's. Do you understand?"

"No, I don't. Maggie, you don't have to do this alone. You asked me for my advice, but it sounds like you don't really want it. What did Master Bredych say?"

"I didn't ask him."

The pigeon fancier approached and bowed before nodding once to Leolin. Margaret spread the bags out across the table so the fancier could see them. "There are twelve messages total that must be sent with all haste," she said to the man, whose gentle hands set about swiftly attaching the bags.

"Please, don't do this," said Leolin as she watched the first bird fly away, bag tied to its back.

She held her breath as the birds flew. As the last one left

427

the castle, the weight on her chest remained the same. No relief flooded through her, nor did any messenger appear to tell her she had made the correct decision. "If—I mean, when the replies arrive, send them to the guard tower at the Meridi Pass," said Margaret.

"Yes, Your Majesty. It will be several days for most, depending upon the weather."

Margaret nodded before leaving the room and the pigeons behind. The very walls of Alesta held her in her own cage as the Shadians camped outside. When she glanced at Leolin, she was reminded of another cage that had bound her. "Leolin, I know you mean well. You always have," she said.

"But...?"

"When I leave for the Pass, I need you to stay in Alesta."

"No."

The word's solidity almost rooted her in place, but she continued the path toward the stables. When he figured out her destination, he grabbed hold of her forearm to stop her. "Let me go," she said.

"Maggie, if you're determined to go through with this, let me accompany you. I can't lose you."

"I need you here in case my plan fails."

Leolin shook his head. "To what? Stand watch over your body as it burns through the night?"

"To keep the Shadians from seizing the throne." She stopped in front of the stables and ordered a horse saddled. "I understand you don't like this plan, but I need someone here that I can trust."

"I'm surprised you didn't ask Bredych."

Margaret growled at him. "I didn't ask him because I

need someone I trust completely. Damn it Leolin, I don't have time for you—I mean, for this."

"No, you meant what you said the first time, and we both know it."

The stable hand busied himself adjusting the horse's saddle, his cheeks flushed, while the other disappeared around the corner. The horse's nostrils flared as Margaret patted its nose. Would the wall between them always be there? Margaret took the offered reins from the stable hand, and the stable hand tied several saddlebags to her mount.

She led the horse to the side gate where six guards waited. One of them offered her a leg up into the saddle, which she accepted. "Leolin, maybe after all of this is done...."

Hollow words for a hollow moment, though she offered them nonetheless.

"If we're still alive," he murmured as he turned away from her.

For a moment she hesitated, ready to rush into his embrace and calm the fear that held him prisoner, but it would do neither of them any favors. An eruption of sound exploded as the city walls were breached—a small breach, but the distraction needed to allow her escape the city. Somewhere ahead, her plans unfolded as Captain Fenton and the rest of her army engaged with the Shadians. Before she could change her mind, Margaret urged her horse forward while six guards formed a protective circle around her. Provided they made it past the fighting armies, it would be a hard four days ride to the Pass.

As they moved through the narrow road that led to the rear gate, sounds of battle drifted toward them, though none of it nearby. It wasn't until they passed into the third ring of Alesta that they hit a wall of terrified citizens surging away from the gate. Crying children mixed with hushed whispers as they pushed forward. A man wearing little more than rags made a grab for her horse's reins, and she kicked him away with a booted heel.

For a moment, as he blundered backward, Margaret froze. This wasn't a Shadian but her own people. But as his panic returned and with it his need to escape on her horse, she withdrew her blade and swung it once to scatter the crowd. War had turned them into monsters, and the truth of it left her breathless.

She pushed forward to the gate, though the panic throughout Alesta had been nothing compared to the cacophony outside the city walls. From the moment the gate dropped shut behind them, pure chaos surrounded them, both maddening and deafening as horses and swords and people clashed.

Outside, her people engaged the Shadian army, though the combat spilled over the city walls like a flooding riverbank. Six guards formed a tight circle around Margaret as they pushed their way through the choppy sea of blood and steel, and for a moment, she glanced back the way they had come. It was only a moment's look—one that resulted in a sword too close to her person—and the first of her guards fell to an enemy blade.

Here her actions had life and death consequences. They always had, though it had been easier not to think on it when sitting in her castle. This was the correct action, no matter what her advisors believed. As long as she remained in Alesta, she would become what they shaped her to be, and that would result in the deaths of many more Alexandrians.

As she withdrew her sword and drove it into the Shadian beside her, Margaret returned her sights on the narrow trail leading north. The Margaret Leolin remembered had died while her father and sister had burned. The Margaret Bredych wished to see had never been. She never had been and never could be Adelei.

Bile burned the back of her throat, but with each Shadian she killed, with each blade that reached out to steal her life, she pushed forward toward the path leading away from the city. If she could reach the Pass, she could stop the war before others needlessly died.

Later she would deal with the war's cost. Later she would deal with her advisors' need to control her. Later she would deal with Leolin's inability to trust her. It would all come later.

If we're still alive.

EPILOGUE

257 Atlinas 5th,

I realize the precariousness of such a letter when my castle is under attack, but I am hopeful that this letter will stop further bloodshed. The Kingdom of Alexander is *not* your enemy. The Kingdom of Shad is *not* your enemy. Our kingdoms have been pawns in a game much larger than any one kingdom by a group originally created to protect us. A civil war such as this will end only when every man, woman, and child is dead. This is not an image that I would take with me to my grave.

The people we refer to as the Boahim Senate are not who we believe them to be. Perhaps it's power that has corrupted their hearts and minds, or perhaps the magics they use to control us have twisted them into wishing us harm. Whatever their rationale, the Boahim Senate has arranged this war.

It was the Senate who encouraged my late father to help those struggling at our borders by bringing them under our protection. This action increased conflict with various kingdoms, including the Kingdom of Shad.

It was the Senate who then encouraged my marriage to Prince Gamun Bajit of Shad, knowing full well that the Prince sought my crown for himself. This action led to the death of my late husband, which heightened tensions and began the war between Alexander and Shad.

Rather than help them in their times of need, it was the Senate who killed Prince Gamun Bajit and my sister, Adelei, as punishment for their crimes.

It was the Senate who thrice ignored my pleas for help in avoiding this war, and when the battle at the Meridi Pass began, it was the Senate who killed indiscriminately, who murdered men and women where they crouched in fear.

Every moment of this war has been driven by *their* wills and *their* desires.

When the Senate first formed, Boahim had fallen to greed. Civil war ripped it apart into twelve separate kingdoms, each one losing people to war's blade. The Senate's purpose was to unite the Little Dozen Kingdoms and ensure that no one was above reproach. They were our neutral allies who would ensure that our kingdoms remained safe against tyranny and oppression.

Now we find ourselves fighting once again.

These senators have a power I don't understand. It's a power capable of ripping apart the very ground we stand on and swallowing us whole, and the only way we can survive such an onslaught of magic is to unite. Powerful though they are, they can be killed.

I call on you—all of you—for a truce.

Meet me at the Meridi Pass under a banner of peace that we might have a chance of surviving the coming months—that our families and our kingdoms are not ripped apart by those who would have us dance to their drums. I am no man's puppet, nor is Boahim. Let us be as we were meant to be—twelve rulers talking peace. No armies. No senators. Only us, the people of Boahim.

Let us unite against our true enemy,

Penned by the hand of
Queen Margaret I of Alexander.

The story of the Poncett family will continue in Book III,
Amaskan's Honor.

Please enjoy this sneak peek at *Amaskan's Honor*, Book III
in the Boahim Trilogy.

Upcoming 2019 from Grey Sun Press.

EXCERPT FROM AMASKAN'S HONOR

The smell of cooked, rotten flesh reached her long before the Pass came into view, and Margaret ground her teeth to keep the bile in check. Six guards had accompanied her, though three had fallen in their fight to escape Alesta. The three who remained among the living followed her as she nudged her horse forward. Her thigh burned where a *Tribor* sword had grazed her a few days back, and she shifted her seat in the saddle. For seventeen days they had camped in the mountain's shadow, and her lungs still burned from the stench.

"Any sight of our guests?" she asked Sergeant Malcolm as he returned to her side.

"Not yet, Your Majesty, though they could be hiding as we are."

"Then we'll have to get closer." Margaret continued her horse forward at a slow walk, and the guards kept their hands on their swords as they neared the valley. As they cleared the trees, her skin crawled as if she were watched, and she glanced over her shoulder as they proceeded. Despite the gory scene ahead, she brought the spyglass to her eye to search for evidence that any of the Little Dozen Kingdoms' rulers waited for her.

Ten minutes left nothing visible but the dead, and she gestured to her remaining guards. "Now is as good a time as any other."

Most of the bones were sun-bleached and charred, though bits of shredded blue and green fabric accented the blackened earth. A large chasm split the ground, and Margaret dismounted. "We'll have to proceed on foot. Too many crevices make for slick footing for the mounts," she said as she handed off her reins. A guardsman led the horses back to a remaining tree while they rest followed her into the valley proper.

She donned leather gloves as did the others, and they picked up the remains as they passed. Whether they were Shadians or Alexandrian, Margaret and her guards worked their way through the valley, piling the remains into thirteen cairns. Scavengers had picked most of the remains clean, though a few bodies held fast to their rotting flesh, and she gagged as she and Sergeant Malcolm carried one.

Nothing marked their ranks or their names, and every body resembled every other as they worked. Somewhere in one of the chasms lay her Grand Marshal, and Margaret paused at the edge of one to look down. Darkness answered her, and she stepped back as she heaved the remains of a meager breakfast onto the ground. The sun had long since passed midday, and Sergeant Malcolm passed her a waterskin, though nothing rid her of the taste of bile and dust that coated the back of her throat. By the time they had gathered what remains could be reached, sweat dripped from her forehead and the muscles across her shoulders and back ached.

"I'm not a member of the Holy Few, so I'm afraid I lack

access to the necessary materials to burn you to ash," said Margaret as she glanced at the thirteen cairns. "But perhaps a small burning will allow your spirits to pass into the afterlife."

Sergeant Malcolm lit several torches, which he passed to the four of them. They walked through the valley, spreading small tufts of kindling across the cairns, which they lit in silence. Despite her sore muscles, Margaret returned to the valley's edge where she waited.

"Will we wait the full thirteen candlemarks?" Sergeant Malcolm asked, and she shook her head.

"Without the special oils of the Holy Few, the fire's too cold to burn for long. We will remain as long as it burns and honor those fallen."

As she spoke, one of the fires dwindled to a few glowing embers beneath the bones. She could pray, but to whom? The Thirteen who murdered the soldiers in the first place? Margaret pursed her lips together as she watched the fires falter.

When the last one stopped smoking, she returned to her horse and accepted a leg up from one of the guards. She pointed to the cliff overlooking the valley. "If the others are waiting on us to be visible, our honoring the fallen should have been visible enough. But in case it wasn't, that spot is easily viewable from all sides."

"Hard to defend though," said Sergeant Malcolm.

It was, but if she wished the other rulers to meet her under a banner of truce, she would have to show them she trusted them enough to meet at all. "We'll make our new camp atop the cliff," she said. While the three guards followed her lead, they flinched at every bird call or wind gust. Margaret kept her eyes on the cliff ahead. Keeping her focus on the climb helped her ignore the bits of bone, blood, and dust that clung to her armor.

When they reached the top, the whistling sound of an arrow forced her to dismount as she dropped to a crouch, sword drawn. A rustle of pale purple moved in the brush, and a woman stepped out with a bow in her hands. The silver in her hair nearly matched the silver thread on her tunic, and Margaret sheathed her sword. "Queen Catia, I'm honored that you have agreed to meet," she said.

The woman lowered her bow, though she scanned the area thoroughly before doing so. "Cousin," said Queen Catia as she inclined her head. "I apologize for shooting at you, but we weren't sure if you were friend or foe."

"Did you face difficulties in your journey here?" asked Margaret, and the woman nodded. "You're the first one to arrive, I believe—"

"It's her," Queen Catia called out, and tree branches snapped as multiple people stepped forward into the clearing. All of them were well-guarded, but if she counted the colors, eleven kingdoms now circled her. One face in particular, that of King Havin, scowled as the rulers of the Little Dozen Kingdoms drew their weapons.

"Welcome to the meeting, Queen Margaret of Alexander."

ACKNOWLEDGMENTS

The past two years have been a whirlwind of house drama and autoimmune diagnoses, yet throughout it, some very important people propped me up and helped this book come to fruition. Among them are:

Jesikah Sundin and Elise Kreinbring, two of my convention partners in crime, who have encouraged and hugged and *squeed* their way through this adventure with me. You are two of the best friends a writer could have.

Jennifer Brozek, for being a good friend and awesome convention buddy. Thank you for the reminder that there are many different types of families.

Josh Vogt & Megan Thyagarajan for lots of laughs—Wit 'n Word style—via cat videos, freelance disasters, and goofy stories.

Kat Richardson and the rest of the Wayward Writers crew for the support, crazy stories about who has the worst family members, and the reminder of why I love my writing family.

My editor, Mimi, for all the work you put into making my books so much better than they are.

Riley, Malley, & DiNozzo, my super-furry kitties in cheerleader outfits, who belly flop across my keyboard and remind me to smile more.

My readers—you've been so patient in awaiting this book. Thank you. You are much appreciated.

And once again, all the thanks in the world to my husband who continually makes me laugh so hard I cry. You're amazing.

ABOUT THE AUTHOR

 Award-winning and bestselling speculative fiction author Raven Oak is best known for *Amaskan's Blood* (2016 Ozma Fantasy Award Winner and Epic Awards Finalist), *Class-M Exile,* and the collection *Joy to the Worlds: Mysterious Speculative Fiction for the Holidays* (Foreword Reviews 2015 Book of the Year Finalist). She also has several published short stories in anthologies such as *Untethered: A Magic iPhone Anthology* and *Magic Unveiled.* Raven spent most of her K-12 education doodling stories and 500-page monstrosities that are forever locked away in a filing cabinet.

When she's not writing, she's getting her game on with tabletop and video games, indulging in way too many hobbies, or staring at the ocean. She lives in the Seattle area with her husband, and their three kitties who enjoy lounging across the keyboard when writing deadlines approach.

Raven is currently at work on *Amaskan's Honor* and *The Eldest Silence.* When she's not writing, you can find her online at: http://www.ravenoak.net

JOIN THE CONSPIRACY

Stay up to date on future releases from the author by **Joining the Conspiracy**, Raven Oak's official mailing list. Get sneak peeks, exclusives, freebies, & more. Visit **http://www.ravenoak.net** to sign up!

Word of mouth is the number one **best** way to ensure that your favorite authors have continued success—better than any paid advertisement.

If you enjoyed this book (*and others*), please consider leaving a **review** on Amazon, Barnes & Noble, and Goodreads.

Your review is greatly appreciated.